Praise for Anne Emery

Praise for *Cecilian Vespers*

"Anne Emery has already won one Arthur Ellis Award for her first Monty Collins mystery, and this one should get her on the short list for another. *Cecilian Vespers* is slick, smart, and populated with lively characters. It's also a nicely crafted mystery."   — *The Globe and Mail*

"This remarkable mystery is flawlessly composed, intricately plotted, and will have readers hooked to the very last page."
      — *The Chronicle-Herald*

"Emery, winner of Canada's 2006 Arthur Ellis Award for Best First Novel (*Sign of the Cross*), has written a finely plotted crime novel that incorporates some of the key still-unresolved issues confronting the Catholic Church in 1991, when the story takes place. Readers who enjoy ecclesiastical mysteries by William X. Kienzle and Julia Spencer-Fleming may want to try this one."   — *Library Journal*

Praise for *Barrington Street Blues*

"The yin-yang of Monty and Maura, from cruel barbs to tender moments, is rendered in occasionally hilarious but mostly heart-breaking fashion. Emery makes it easy to root for Monty, who solves not only the mystery that pays the bills, but also the one that tugs at his heart."   — *Quill & Quire*

"A solid story of suspense long on mystery and short on excess . . . The writing is lean, linear, and concise . . . it is perhaps Emery's use of character dialogue that gives the book its weight, masterfully chronicling Collins's slow descent into his own personal under-world."   — *Atlantic Books Today*

"This is a wonderful yarn, full of amazingly colourful characters, dialogue that sweeps across the pages like a tsunami, a story that will keep you reading late into the night, and a plot as devious as a lawyer's mind." — *Waterloo Region Record*

Praise for *Obit*

"Emery tops her vivid story of past political intrigue that could destroy the present with a surprising conclusion." — *Publishers Weekly*

"A romping good ride through Halifax and New York . . . the racy writing style and quick repartee makes for a captivating tale." — *Atlantic Books Today*

"There's plenty of intrigue to be found in *Obit* . . . For anyone who loves a good mystery, this one will prove more than satisfying." — *Bookviews*

"Emery has concocted an interesting plot . . . Her depiction of the gregarious Burke clan rings true . . . it is a pleasure to spend time with them." — *Quill & Quire*

Praise for *Sign of the Cross*

"A complex, multilayered mystery that goes far beyond what you'd expect from a first-time novelist." — *Quill & Quire*

"This startlingly good first novel by a Halifax writer well-versed in the Canadian court system is notable for its cast of well-drawn characters and for a plot line that keeps you feverishly reading to the end. Snappy dialogue, a terrific feel for Halifax, characters you really do care about, and a great plot make this one a keeper." — *Waterloo Region Record*

"Anne Emery has produced a stunning first novel that is at once a mystery, a thriller, and a love story. *Sign of the Cross* is well written, exciting, and unforgettable." —*The Chronicle-Herald*

Children in the Morning

A MYSTERY

ANNE EMERY

ECW Press

Published by ECW Press
2120 Queen Street East, Suite 200, Toronto, Ontario, Canada M4E 1E2
416.694.3348 / info@ecwpress.com

This is a work of fiction. Names, characters, places, and incidents either are the product of the author's imagination or
are used fictitiously, and any resemblance to actual persons, living or dead, business establishments, events, or locales is
entirely coincidental.

LIBRARY AND ARCHIVES CANADA CATALOGUING IN PUBLICATION

Emery, Anne
Children in the morning: a mystery / Anne Emery.
Originally published in hardcover in 2010 (978-1-55022-927-1)

ISBN 978-1-77041-045-9
Also issued as
978-1-55490-679-6 (EPUB); 978-1-55490-927-8 (PDF)

I. Title.

PS8609.M47C47 2011   c813'.6   C2011-904411-0

Cover and text design: Tania Craan
Cover image: Nick Daly/Photonica/Getty Images
Author photo: Danny Abriel, Dalhousie University
Typesetting: Mary Bowness
Printing: Friesens   1   2   3   4   5

This book is set in AGaramond

The publication of *Children in the Morning* has been generously supported by the Canada
Council for the Arts which last year invested $20.1 million in writing and publishing throughout Canada,
and by the Ontario Arts Council, an agency of the Government of Ontario. We also acknowledge the financial support of the Government of Canada through the Canada Book Fund for our publishing activities, and the contribution
of the Government of Ontario through the Ontario Book Publishing Tax Credit. The marketing of this book was
made possible with the support of the Ontario Media Development Corporation.

 Canada Council
for the Arts
Conseil des Arts
du Canada
 Canadä
 ONTARIO ARTS COUNCIL
CONSEIL DES ARTS DE L'ONTARIO

PRINTED AND BOUND IN CANADA

ECW PRESS
ecwpress.com

MIX
Paper from
responsible sources
FSC
www.fsc.org   FSC® C016245

Dedicated to the memory of my mum and dad

There are children in the morning.
They are leaning out for love,
And they will lean that way forever.

— Leonard Cohen, "Suzanne"

P

Oh, what did you
Oh, what did you see,
I saw a newborn baby with

— Bob Dylan, "A Hard I

Chapter 1

(Normie)

You should know right from the beginning that I am not bragging. I was brought up better than that, even though I am the child of a broken home. That's another thing you should know. BUT — and it's a big but — (I'm allowed to say "big but" like this but not "big butt" in a mean voice when it might be heard by a person with a big butt, and hurt their feelings) — but, about my broken home, Mummy says people don't say that anymore. Anyway, even if they do, it doesn't bother me. It kinda bothers my brother Tommy Douglas even though he's a boy, and a lot of times boys pretend they're tough. Tommy never says, but I know. We have another brother, Dominic, but he's a little baby so he's too young to know anything. However, the whole thing is not that bad. That's probably because we don't have the kind of dad who took off and didn't care and didn't pay us any alimony. When you've been around school as long as I have — I'm in grade four — you know kids who have fathers like that. But not my dad. We spend a lot of days with him, not just with my mum. And they both love us. They are in their forties but are both still spry and sharp as a tack. It's stupid the way they don't just move back into the same house together but, aside from that, they are great people and I love them very much.

Mum is Maura MacNeil. People say she has a tongue on her that could skin a cat. She is always very good to me and never skins me. But if I do something bad, she doesn't have to stop and think about what to say; she has words ready to go. She teaches at the law school here in Halifax. My dad is Monty Collins. He is really sweet and he has a blues band. I always ask him to sing and play the song "Stray Cat Strut" and he always does. It's my favourite song; I get to do the "meow." He is also a lawyer and he makes faces about his clients. They're bad but he has to pretend they're good when he's in front of the judge so the judge won't send them down the river and throw away the key. Or the paddle, or whatever it is. It means jail.

I forgot to tell you my name. It's Normie. *What?* I can hear you saying. It's really Norma but you won't see that word again in these pages. Well, except once more, right here, because I have to explain that it comes from an opera called *Norma*. Mum and Dad are opera fans and they named me after this one, then realized far too late that it was an old lady's name (even though the N-person in the opera was not old, but never mind). So they started calling me Normie instead.

I am really good in math and English, and I know so many words that my teacher has got me working with the *grade seven* book called *Words Are Important*, which was published way back in 1955 when everybody learned harder words in school than they do these days. And I have musical talent but do not apply myself, according to my music teacher. I am really bad at social studies but that's because I don't care about the tundra up north, or the Family Compact, whoever they are. But it was interesting to hear that we burned down the White House when we had a war with the Americans back in 1812. Tommy says we kicked their butts (he said it, not me). You never think of Canadians acting like that.

Anyway, I must get on with my story. As I said, I'm not bragging and I don't mean about the math and English. I mean I'm not bragging about what I can see and other people can't. Because it's a gift and I did nothing to earn it. And also because it's all there for other people to see, but they are just not awake (yet) to these "experiences" or "visions." I'm not sure what to call them. They say about me: "She has the sight." Or: "She has second sight, just like old Morag." Old Morag is my great-grandmother. Mum's mother's mother. She's from Scotland. And she is really old; it's not just people calling her that. She must be eighty-five or something. But there are no flies on her, everyone says. People find her spooky, but I understand her.

I am looking at my diary, which says *Personal and Private!* on the cover. I hide it in a box under my bed. Nobody crawls under there to spy on my stuff. The diary is where I kept all my notes, day after day, about this story. I am taking the most important parts of it and writing them down on wide-ruled paper, using a Dixon Ticonderoga 2/HB pencil, a dictionary, and a thesaurus. I am asking Mummy about ways to say (write) certain things, but I'm not telling her what I am writing. All the information you will read here is my own.

✝

It all started in the waiting room of my dad's office. He came and got me from school at three thirty on the day I'm talking about, Thursday, February 13, 1992. He still had work to do, so he took me to the office. I sat there with a kids' magazine, which was too young for me really, and the bowl of candies Darlene keeps behind the reception desk. There were two other kids there around the same age as me, a girl and a boy. They looked sad and scared about something, so I tried to cheer them up. They were staring at the candies, and I shared them. They said thanks. Since Daddy was taking such a long time, I decided to work on my poster.

I go to a choir school. It goes from grade four to grade eight. Me and my best friend, Kim, are in grade four so this is our first year at the school. Kim is taller than me and has long blond braids and no glasses. We wear a uniform that's a dark plaid kilt, white shirt, and bright red sweater. The boys don't wear a kilt, but they could, because there are a lot of Scottish people around here and they would think it's normal. But the boys wear dark blue pants.

Anyway, I was making a poster for our new program to give free music lessons to kids in the afternoons when regular classes are finished. One of the teachers came up with the name "Tunes for Tots"

("tots" means little kids), but Father Burke put his foot down and said no. He said that name was too "twee." Another teacher said we should call it "Four-Four Time," and he went along with that. Four-Four Time is a good name because we have it four days a week, Monday to Thursday, and it starts at four o'clock. It goes for an hour and a half. So, four days at four o'clock. "Common time" in music is four beats to a measure and the quarter note has one beat; a whole bunch of songs are written in that time, and it's called four-four time. I didn't go to it that day, but I usually went. Anyway, about the program. The teachers at the choir school take turns staying after school for it, and we, the students at St. Bernadette's, can go as often as we want and help the kids who come from other schools for free music lessons. We also provide healthy snacks. It is really to help poor kids, but nobody would say that to them, because it wouldn't be polite.

I mentioned Father Burke. He runs the school, and he also runs a choir school for grown-ups, including priests and nuns; it's called the Schola Cantorum Sancta Bernadetta. Father Burke's first name is Brennan and he was born in Ireland, which you can tell from the way he talks. People think he is stern, aloof, and haughty. The thesaurus also says "lordly," which would be true if it means he works for the Lord but he doesn't think he's the Lord himself, so I'll leave that one out. But he's not. Or at least, deep down, he's not. He can seem that way to people who don't know him. But I do, and he is very kind, especially to children.

Anyway, I got out my paper and markers, and got down on my hands and knees in Daddy's reception room to work on the poster.

"What's that?" the little girl asked.

"Oh, it's a thing they started at my school. They're giving free music lessons to kids, plus treats, books, stuff like that."

"Can anybody come to it?"

"Yeah! You guys should come!"

"What school is it?"

"St. Bernadette's Choir School, on Byrne Street. Do you want to come?"

"Maybe. It sounds good."

"What's your name?"

"I'm Jenny and that's my brother, Laurence."

Jenny had wavy brown hair down to her shoulders, and she had it pulled over to the side of her forehead with a white barrette shaped like a kitty-cat. Laurence had short, dark brown hair and was bigger than Jenny.

"I'll write your names down on the back of the poster, in pencil, so I can tell Father Burke you're coming." I asked her how to spell their names and I printed "Jenny" and "Laurence" on the paper. "What's your last name?"

"Delaney."

"I know how to spell that," I told them. "I saw that name somewhere."

They looked at each other but didn't say anything. I wrote it down.

Then Daddy came out, and a woman came out with him and took the kids with her.

Later on, I found out why they looked sad and scared. They had a family tragedy!

(Monty)

I was in the courtroom when they came for Beau Delaney. I was early for my own court appearance, and walked in during Delaney's summation on behalf of his client.

"And yet again, My Lord, we witness the spectacle of the state's jack-booted goons trampling the rights of an innocent, law-respecting, own-business-minding citizen of this province. A man to all appearances secure in his home. I'm sure Your Lordship holds dear, as do I, the dictum of the great English jurist, Sir Edward Coke, that a man's home is his castle. That a man should be safe and secure in that castle, however humble an abode it might be. That he should not have to quiver and quake, tremble and twitch lest he hear that most fearsome of sounds, the knock on the door in the dead of night, perpetrated by the rednecks in red serge, poster boys for a nation that has sold its soul for peace, order, and good government, Renfrews of the Mounted, goose-stepping into history over the bodies of those whose rights they are sworn to uphold."

It was vintage Delaney. The mild-looking, bespectacled Mountie who had led the raid on Delaney's client's trailer rolled his eyes as the diatribe went on. He'd heard it all before. Then the Mountie's attention was drawn to something happening at the back of the courtroom. I followed his glance and saw two Halifax police officers coming in the door, looking tense. They sat in the back row, and leaned forward as if ready to spring. Justice MacIntosh made quick work of Delaney's argument that the search of his client's property was illegal, and found the man guilty of cultivating marijuana contrary to Section 6 of the Narcotic Control Act. Sentencing would proceed at a later date. Delaney gave his client a "you win some, you lose some" shrug, stood, and packed up his papers. The two Halifax cops got up and went out the door.

Beau Delaney was the best-known criminal defence lawyer in Nova Scotia. He was probably the only lawyer whose name was a household word across the province. A giant of a man at six feet, five inches in height, with a long mane of wavy salt-and-pepper hair brushed back from his forehead, he wore glasses with heavy black frames, the kind you often saw on Hollywood movie moguls. Delaney was known for his flamboyant manner and courtroom theatrics; he was the object of envy and barroom bullshit. He greeted me after he snapped the locks of his enormous briefcase, and we left the courtroom together.

The minute the courtroom door closed behind us, the cops moved in.

"Beau Delaney?"

"Yes?"

"You are under arrest for the murder of Peggy Laing Delaney." His wife of nearly twenty years.

✝

I heard from Delaney that night. He asked me to represent him on the murder charges, and I arranged to see him at the Halifax County Correctional Centre the following day. So we sat down and faced each other across the table in a lawyer–client meeting room at the Correc. Delaney looked as if he had been there a month.

"What's the story, Beau?"

"I wasn't there."

"You weren't home when Peggy died?"

"No."

"Did you give a statement to the police?"

"I told them I wasn't there. Period."

He shouldn't have said even that much.

"Why do the police think you were home?"

"Because it fits with their theory that I killed her!"

"They must think they have evidence that you were at the house."

"I was out of town, and I came home —"

"— Just after your wife fell down the stairs."

"Save your breath, Montague. I'm a professional so I'm not going to say what Joe Average Client would say: *If you don't believe me, I'm getting another lawyer.* You and I are grown-ups. We're lawyers. Whether you believe me or not, I wasn't there. That's my defence. Take it to trial and get an acquittal. Now I'm tired, having been kept awake by a near riot in this place last night, so let's talk bail."

That could wait.

"Where were you the night she died?"

"I was in Annapolis Royal for a three-day trial. I drove home rather than stay another night when it was over. Didn't bother to call Peg; I just got in the car and headed home."

"Who can we get to say you weren't there?"

"I'm not sure. The kids were all in bed."

"How do you know?"

"Because if they were up, they'd have been looking for their mother and probably would have found her. But they didn't. I did. They were asleep when I got home."

"Where do you park your car? You have a garage, right?"

"Yeah, but we never park in it. It's full of junk."

"So you leave your cars in the driveway."

"Yeah."

"The Crown must have somebody who claims you were there."

"Well, it will be your job to find out, and discredit them."

"Let's hope the Crown doesn't have a pile of will-say statements from your neighbours stating they looked out and saw your car there just before they sat down to watch the evening game shows."

"Won't happen. You'll be interested to hear that the medical examiner did not conclude Peggy was murdered. He said the facts were consistent with an accident or an assault; it was impossible to make a conclusive finding either way. The Crown couldn't hope to prove murder beyond a reasonable doubt with that, so they shopped around for a second opinion. They got lucky with Dr. Heath MacLeod. Ever heard of him?" I shook my head. "He's a new pathologist in town. It's clear he's got a bright future ahead of him as a prosecutor's expert. In his opinion, Peggy was struck on the head with a large rock, and then fell — or more likely was carried by me and placed at the bottom of the stairs."

"A rock? In the house?"

"Yeah, unfortunately, we did have some big rocks in the house. One of our neighbours had a stone retaining wall. He replaced it with a new brick one, and our kids asked if they could have the old stones to build a castle. He said sure. The kids started their building in the backyard. They managed to lay half a dozen stones before a freezing rain storm blew up. End of the season for outdoor construction. They began hauling the rocks inside, with a view to building their castle in the basement. Peggy and I told them to move them out of the way, and wait for spring to do it outdoors. But they never got them all out of there, so some rocks were still on the basement floor when Peggy fell."

"They were piled at the foot of the stairs?"

"No, off to the side a bit. But the way she fell, she hit her head on them."

"And the Crown sees this how?"

"They say I picked up one of the rocks, bashed Peggy's head in with it, then carried her down the stairs. She was found on the basement floor and her injuries were consistent with a fall, so, since the Crown can't get around that fact, they have to say I went down there, picked a rock from the pile, and brought it back to the top of the stairs, where I hit her with it. Then, since the rock was under her head, they say I panicked and arranged her body so her head was lying on the rock that fractured her skull. Panicky but precise is what I'm alleged to have been. I'm sure they'll leave open the alternative theory that I pushed her down with such force that she fractured her skull."

"That's it? That's the Crown's case as you see it?"

"The Crown doesn't have a case."

"What do you say happened?"

"She obviously fell down the stairs."

"Backwards."

"Apparently so."

"How do you suppose that came about?"

"I don't know. I wasn't there."

"You must have given it some thought."

"Of course I have!"

I was silent for a long moment, then said: "Let's talk about the show cause." The bail hearing. We discussed the ins and outs of that, then we dealt with housekeeping matters, that is, fees and payment, and I left to drive back into town.

So. The guy wouldn't say anything beyond "I wasn't there." You'd think Beau Delaney would know better. That may look like the best defence in the world: *My client didn't do it, My Lord; he wasn't even there.* But in fact it's often the worst defence of all, because if it turns out the police can place him there, it's over. With other defences — insanity, self-defence — you have room to manoeuvre. The fact that he was there doesn't kill you on day one. Or day two.

But right now, I had to get him out on bail. I started preparing for that as soon as I got to the office on Barrington Street. I also asked my secretary, Tina, to track down any news stories she could find about Peggy Delaney's death. She had something for me by noon, from the January 17, 1992, edition of the *Chronicle Herald*.

"Selfless Mother" Dies at Home

Margaret Jean ("Peggy") Delaney, 48, prominent children's rights advocate and mother of ten, died in her south-end Halifax home two nights ago. She was the wife of well-known criminal defence lawyer Beau Delaney, and the daughter of Gordon and Margaret Laing. Mr. Delaney said he returned home late on Wednesday night and found his wife at the bottom of the basement stairs. Foul play is not suspected but Mr. Delaney expects that there will be an autopsy because this is an unexplained death. Mr. Delaney said: "Peggy was the love of my life, and the most giving, the most selfless woman and mother I have ever met." The couple had a family of ten: two biological, two adopted, and six foster children. "They are all our children," Mr. Delaney said. "They are devastated. I don't know how to get them through this. We're going on a wing and a prayer at this point." A funeral will be held at St. Mary's Basilica once Mrs. Delaney's remains have been released.

I didn't like our bare-bones defence that Delaney wasn't there. But we had one thing going for us, and it was no small thing: Delaney's character. Loving father of ten children, BCL (big Catholic layman), top-notch lawyer working above and beyond the call of duty for his clients. Part of the Delaney legend was that he had been known to work above and beyond the call even for people who were not his clients, people who had in fact refused his offer of pro bono — free — legal services. This was the Gary's General Store case, which had propelled Beau Delaney to national fame.

Fourteen years ago, in 1978, two men robbed Gary's General Store, a family-owned store in the tiny community of Blockhouse, an hour west of Halifax, shooting the two young employees who were on the night shift. Scott Hubley, the owner's seventeen-year-old son, died on the floor behind the counter. Cathy Tompkins, the other clerk, sixteen years old, was shot in the head and left with permanent mental and physical disabilities. Police arrested two suspects the following day. They went to trial and each pointed the finger at the other, saying the other guy had pulled the trigger. The evidence showed that both men had handled the gun at some point, so it was not clear who had done the shooting. What was clear was that both planned and perpetrated the robbery. Beau Delaney represented one of them; another Halifax lawyer represented the co-accused. Beau gave his client, Adam Gower, a brilliant defence and, to use layman's language, "got him off on a technicality." The co-accused was convicted of the second-degree murder of Scott Hubley and other charges relating to Cathy Tompkins.

Understandably, feelings ran high in the small rural community.

So high that Beau and the other lawyer received threats against their lives and were warned never to set foot in Blockhouse again.

It didn't end there. Delaney's client, Gower, left the province but decided to move back a year or so after the trial. Within days of his return to Nova Scotia, he was found in the woods off Highway 103 in Lunenburg County, beaten to death. Only his dental work identified him as Gower; his injuries were so severe that he was otherwise unrecognizable. Cathy Tompkins's brother, Robby, who had a minor criminal history himself, and who had been heard uttering threats against Gower, was picked up and charged with the murder. Beau Delaney entered the picture again. He contacted Robby Tompkins after his arrest and offered to defend him free of charge. But the Tompkins family, still outraged over Beau's successful defence of Adam Gower, refused his help. Robby Tompkins vehemently denied involvement. He went to trial with another lawyer. The jury took four days but eventually — one can presume reluctantly — found Robby guilty of second-degree murder. He was sentenced to life in prison with no chance of parole for ten years.

Beau worked the case like a cop for two years, trying to find something that would exonerate the young man. His efforts were noticed, and they paid off when he received an anonymous phone call that pointed to a shady character named Edgar Lampman as the real killer of Adam Gower. Lampman was a middle-aged man who had a record of violent offences, and who had been a frequent customer in the convenience store when Cathy was working. She had apparently been uncomfortable in his presence; the suggestion was that he was attracted to her. Since the killing, Lampman had died of natural causes. Beau passed the tip on to the police, who checked it out and found that it was legitimate. The upshot was that Edgar Lampman was posthumously fingered as the killer, and Robby Tompkins was exonerated and set free.

Delaney was lionized after his triumph. There was even a movie about the case, titled *Righteous Defender*, with Jack Hartt starring in the role of Delaney. Known in the tabloids as the Jack of Hearts, the tall, handsome actor was a Canadian raised in a suburb of Toronto. He had gone on to fame and fortune in the United States.

So. I had a hero for a client, and I would make the most of that fact in defending him against the murder charge in 1992. I wished I could play the feature film for the jury. No such luck.

Not surprisingly, Delaney's arrest was front-page news in both of the daily papers, and even earned a spot in the national media. The *Chronicle Herald* showed Delaney in his barrister's gown and tabs, holding forth in the plaza of the Nova Scotia Supreme Court building. Gown and mane of hair lofted by the wind, arm raised to make a point, the lawyer proclaimed a client's innocence to the throng of reporters and cameras. The focus of the piece was a history of Delaney's courtroom triumphs. The *Daily News* showed him waving from the driver's seat of his customized Mercedes twelve-passenger van. Several of his children gave toothy grins from behind the car windows. The story centred on the Delaney family's well-known practice of holding weekend events, such as picnics and sports tournaments, in public spots like the Halifax Commons, Point Pleasant Park, and Dingle Park. Any children who happened by were welcome to join in, pick up a ball glove, have a hot dog or an ice cream cone, take part in a sing-along.

The Delaney kids were now split up, staying with various relatives of Peggy and Beau; they were in a holding pattern until the completion of the trial. None of the relatives was in a position to keep the children indefinitely, and certainly not all ten of them. One of Peggy's sisters broke down and wept — and terminated the interview — when asked if only the Delaneys' "own" children would find a permanent home with relatives. It was clear that if Delaney was convicted, at least some of the kids would go back to government care or foster homes. The family would be ripped apart.

Chapter 2

(Monty)

The news media were out in force on the Wednesday morning Delaney appeared in the Supreme Court of Nova Scotia for his bail hearing. And they weren't disappointed. Or perhaps they were; it was good news, at least for us. Delaney was released, with a number of strict conditions, including a curfew, no unsupervised contact with his children, no alcohol or drugs or firearms. I had never pictured Beau as a gun-totin' boozer or a crackhead, so I didn't think he'd have any trouble on that score. His law firm put up the $100,000 bail money. We had a bit of a public relations coup in that Beau's brother-in-law invited him to stay at his place for the duration. This was not quite as good as it might have been; this was not Peggy's own brother, but the husband of her sister, and the couple had separated. Still, we had a relative on Peggy's side of the family who obviously believed in Beau's innocence and was not afraid to have him in the house.

The release gave Beau the opportunity to grandstand in the plaza in front of the courthouse. He declared his innocence, expressed his faith in our criminal justice system, which he had observed close-up for twenty-five years, and said he was confident that he would be acquitted of the charge of murdering his beloved wife, Peggy.

I drove my client to his new residence in central Halifax. On Brunswick Street there is a row of brick townhouses known locally as the Twelve Apostles. They were built as barracks for British soldiers in the year 1900. Each house has a little gabled roof and front porch with a side-facing door. Delaney's brother-in-law, Angus MacPherson, met us out front. Angus was a piper who played in a local pipe band and also performed at one of the hotels downtown, greeting guests and piping them in. He was in full Scottish regalia, white-and-black Dress-MacPherson tartan kilt, with his *sporran* or purse on the front and the knife called a *sgian dhu* stuck in his right sock. The bagpipes were slung over his shoulder. None of this turned any heads among the locals here in Halifax. Men in kilts were a regular feature in New Scotland.

"If I'd known you were coming right now, I'd have piped you in. Next time!"

"Thanks anyway, Angus, but I'm keeping a low profile. I'll expect a massed pipe band in front of my own house the day I get acquitted."

"You'll have it. I'm off. Make yourself at home. Here's your key. See you later."

"Thanks, Angus."

"*Ciad mile failte!*"

(Normie)

I wasn't scared when I knew Mr. Delaney was coming to the school to see Jenny and Laurence. They really did join Four-Four Time, our after-school music program, when I invited them, and they asked their aunt, who was taking care of them, if they could come. She said okay. The program is for all kids, from any school, and it's free. I planned right from the beginning to go to it myself most days after school and help out. Jenny and Laurence were shy at first, but they were nice. The reason I wasn't scared of Mr. Delaney was that I knew he didn't really kill their mum. He was an innocent man arrested by mistake. Even though that was true, Daddy said there were some rules Mr. Delaney had to follow. One of them was that he was not allowed to see his own kids unless another grown-up was there. They made a plan that, since the kids were coming to Four-Four Time and Father Burke nearly always came in to hear the music, that was the place where Jenny and Laurence could see their dad. I guess their sisters and brothers saw him someplace else. Anyway, when he walked in, the other kids in the music program were whispering and pointing. "Is that him?" they all asked.

"That's him," I told them, because I recognized him from the newspaper and, besides, I had seen him before somewhere. He is really, really big and has a lot of brown and white wavy hair. He has old-fashioned glasses with thick black frames. My own glasses you can hardly see because the frames are thin and metal. Some people don't even notice them. But you noticed his.

Jenny and Laurence ran up to him as soon as he walked in. "Daddy!" they both yelled, and they buried their faces in his jacket. He put one arm around Jenny and one around Laurence, and kissed the tops of their heads.

"I've missed you guys! Don't worry. I'll get this whole mess straightened out, and we'll all be home again. And you guys will be able to play me a song on, what?" He looked around the room and saw the instruments the other kids were playing. "Jenny plays the tuba, and Laurence plays the triangle. Right?"

They laughed and said no, that Jenny was learning to play the piano and Laurence the guitar.

Mr. Delaney noticed there was a priest watching him, and nodded his head at Father Burke. Father came over and said: "Mr. Delaney." It would have been rude if Father did not shake his hand, so he put his hand out and they shook. "I'm Father Burke. Your children have a great deal of musical ability; we're very pleased to have them here."

"Thank you, Father. I appreciate their being here. And I appreciate being here myself."

"You're welcome. Make yourself at home. Is there anything we can get you? Tea? A soft drink? A sweet?"

"No, no, I'm fine."

"Ah, sure you'll have something."

"Well, a cup of tea then."

"Ian!" Father Burke turned to the kid closest to the table, Ian McAllister. "Pour Mr. Delaney a cup of tea, and bring him over that plate of sweets, after you wash . . ." Ian made a grab for a teacup and put his finger right inside it when he picked it up. ". . . after you wash your hands, I was about to say. Then get a fresh cup. Keep your fingers out of it."

"Yes, Father."

Jenny saw me looking at her dad, so she said: "Daddy! This is Normie. She's the one that told us about Four-Four Time."

He looked down at me and smiled, but his eyes behind the big glasses looked sad. "That means you're Miss Collins," he said.

"That's right."

"Your father is a wonderful man and a great lawyer. You know he is helping me."

"I know."

"Well, I think the world of him. And he must have a very fine daughter."

"Thank you."

Then I went over to a little kid I was supposed to be helping with sight-reading. He had dropped his book on the floor and was standing on it and making faces at another boy instead of reading. You have to have a lot of patience with little kids.

I looked back at Jenny and saw that she was clinging to her dad and trying not to cry.

†

You wouldn't believe what happened at our house the night after that. Daddy was out at his place getting a guy to fix his furnace, and Tommy was playing with his band. So Mummy and I decided to order a pizza, just for ourselves. Without pepperoni. Dominic is only a baby and he's too young to eat pizza. Obviously. When the Tomaso's guy came to the door, there were two pizzas; it was a special deal, which Mummy had forgotten about or not paid attention to. So we decided to call Father Burke to share them with us, since he lives only a few blocks away. He said yes and went to the Clyde

Street Liquor Store to get a bottle of wine. He didn't look like a priest when he arrived; he was wearing a regular shirt with a sweater over it. The baby was fussing and crying but when Father Burke arrived, a big grin came on Dominic's face, and he kicked his little fat legs in the air and moved his arms up and down to get Father to pick him up. Dominic was always doing that whenever Father Burke came over. It was really cute, especially because he looks like Father, with black hair and really dark eyes. We put him in his high chair to eat, but he fell asleep.

"Sit your blessed arse down, Father," Mum said. "How may I serve you?"

"Sure I have an awful thirst on me, Mrs. MacNeil, and I'm a bit peckish as well."

So we all sat down. Dinner was really fun. They let me have a tiny bit of wine in a little wee glass. It was a dark red and tasted kind of sharp at first; then, I really liked it.

"This is damn good wine, Father," Mum said. "I hope it didn't cost you a month's pay."

"Well, they took up a special collection for me at the church, Mrs. MacNeil, knowing as they do that I live in the spirit of poverty. Just following in the footsteps of our Lord and His disciples."

"Oh, you're a saint, Father."

"Ah, now, all this talk from yourself and so many others about me being a saint, it embarrasses me. If Holy Mother Church deems it appropriate to canonize me after my passing, so be it. In the meanwhile, I'm here to serve as best I can."

"And serve you do, so generously. Taking your last coin and spending it on a little treat for us."

"And a drop for meself, too, now. I'm not as selfless as I'm portrayed in the local . . ." He said a word like "geography" but with something like "hag" instead of "geo." So I asked what that was.

He said: "Hagiography. A book about the life of a saint."

"Okay."

He looked at me and my wineglass then. "Whoa! Take it easy, little one. Don't be getting too fond of the drink there, Normie!"

"I won't!" If you get too fond of drinking, you become an alcoholic. Which is bad. But I don't have that problem. I can drink or not drink;

either way is fine with me. I didn't ask for seconds when I was done.

"Future sainthood aside, Father, do they ever take you to task over at the rectory for all the high living you do? The worldly pleasures you enjoy? Wine, whiskey, cigars, rich food . . ."

"They do, darlin'. I'm on my knees every night, in contrition. But the bishop usually lets me off the hook when he knows I've eaten here. 'No sumptuous dining tonight, eh, Brennan? Gnawed on a few tough scraps at the MacNeil house again? Offer it up to God, my son.' But you've outdone yourself tonight. By far the best meal I've ever enjoyed here."

"Father?"

"Mmm?"

"Pòg mo thòn."

I didn't get what they were talking about, but I wrote it all down in my personal diary anyway, and looked up the spelling of some words. I think it was just a joke about Mum's cooking. She's not a great cook, even though she's a great mother. But I do know what she said to him at the end: it's Scottish Gaelic for — and it's not me saying this, it's Mum — *kiss my arse!*

So it was funny to listen to them talking, even if some of it didn't make sense to me. A couple of times I saw Father Burke staring at the baby, then he looked away, as if it's rude to stare at someone's baby. But it isn't. Everyone likes people to look at their baby because everybody thinks their own baby is cute. Even if it isn't. But ours is.

Then there was a loud knock on the door.

"Who could that be?" Mum said. It always drives Dad crazy when the phone or the doorbell rings and Mummy asks who it might be. The whole family is like that, Mum's side anyway. Daddy just says: "Answer it. Mystery solved."

Anyway she got up and went to the door.

"Oh!" I heard her say. "What are you doing here?"

"I came to see my son!"

"I don't believe there is a piece of paper filed anywhere in this province that names you as the father of my child!"

"Don't make jokes. I want to see him!"

Anybody would know who that was, because of his Italian accent. He had long curly brown hair and dark eyes, and looked like somebody in a movie. It was Mum's old boyfriend, Giacomo. We had not seen him for ages. Me and Tommy thought they broke up. Now he was at the door. And then he was in the dining room. Gawking at Dominic in his high chair.

"I do not care what your papers say or do not say. Anybody would know, looking at the boy, whose son he is," Giacomo said. Then he caught sight of Father Burke, and glared at him, then looked back at the baby. Father Burke stood up, because it's polite to do that if somebody comes in the room, but he was giving Giacomo a dirty look.

Then Giacomo finally saw me. "Oh! *Mi dispiace*, Normie, *buonasera!*"

"*Buonasera*, Giacomo," I answered, because he had taught us a few words of Italian.

"Giacomo Fornino, this is Brennan Burke. Brennan, Giacomo."

The two of them shook hands, but they did not look happy to be meeting one another.

"Sit down and have something to eat, Giacomo. We'll talk later." He didn't want to eat. He wanted to argue. But he sat down.

Father Burke pulled out a pack of cigarettes and offered them to Giacomo. He took one, and Mum went over and opened up the buffet table, and brought out two old ashtrays. She usually growls if anyone tries to smoke in the house, but that night she didn't bother. Father Burke leaned way over and lit Giacomo's cigarette, glaring through the flame at him the whole time.

Giacomo sucked back on the cigarette and spoke up. "A pleasure to meet you," he said to Father Burke, but he didn't mean it.

"Where are you from, Giacomo?" Father Burke sounded friendly.

"I am from Rome." He talked a bit about Rome, and Father Burke asked him a couple of questions in Italian, which he really speaks, unlike me and Tommy who only know a few words. Giacomo answered sometimes in English and sometimes in Italian.

When he wound down, Father Burke said: "But seriously, now, where are you from?"

"*Roma.*"

"No, you can't be from Rome." Father Burke took a deep drag of his cigarette and blew the smoke away from the table. "I know you're just having us on. So? *Di dov'è?*"

Mummy looked at Father, wondering what was going on.

Giacomo finally said: "I am from a small village originally, of course, but I came to Rome to study and I stayed there until I came to Canada to work for three years."

He was mad and got up and left the room. Went to the bathroom.

Mum gave Father Burke kind of a dirty look. "All right. Give. How the hell did you know he wasn't from Rome?"

"He just said he paid *cinquecentomila lire* for something. Chinkweh-chento, not shinkweh-shento the way the Romans say it. So, a bit of a dissembler you have there, darlin'."

"Hearing the gospel truth was not my main motivation for seeing Giacomo. If I want gospel, I'll get up early on a Sunday morning and go hear you."

"Sounds as if you're more in need of a lawyer right now than a priest."

"I'll send him packing. He's got no proof —"

"But a child's father certainly can claim a right —"

Mum used a big word, and I came up with a sneaky question the next day to find out what it was: "hypothetically." I did that a lot while this was going on. It wasn't really a lie when I told her I was trying to "build up my vocabulary," because that's something they want us to do at school.

Anyway, what Mum said this time was: "If, hypothetically, a child has a father who lives here in the city of Halifax, or even in the province of Nova Scotia, a mother might be more inclined to see those hypothetical rights exercised. But if a child has someone claiming to be the father, and that individual wants to take the child four thousand miles across the ocean, then that individual is never going to succeed in establishing his claim."

Giacomo came back then and said he wanted to get to know his son. Our baby! Then he started going on about his parents in Italy.

That's when Mum interrupted him and said: "Normie, you have lessons to do for tomorrow. Time to go up to your room."

But going to your room in our house is not the end of it, because there's a secret listening post upstairs in the hallway. It's an old thing called a register in the floor, where the heat comes up. It's made of squiggles of black iron. And when the heat's not on, you can hear what people are saying in the kitchen. So I clomped up the stairs and into my bedroom, then tiptoed out to the listening post and sat down.

"My family expect to see their grandson. They expect him to be part of their lives. Which is only right."

Mum said: "You are making an assumption that you are not entitled to make, that you are the father of the child. That's all I am going to say on the matter for now."

Giacomo scraped his chair back. On his way out of the kitchen, he said: "You will be hearing from me, or from my lawyer!"

"Who's your lawyer?"

"You don't know him. He is from home."

"Well, make sure he doesn't reverse the charges when he calls!"

"There will be no need for long-distance telephone charges. He will be here."

"You're bringing a lawyer all the way over here from Italy?!"

"Yes. So you know I am serious. Goodbye. For now."

I heard the front door close. Then Mummy burst out into tears! She kept saying: "This can't be happening. Only over my dead body will that child leave the country!"

I ran downstairs and Father Burke was hugging Mum while she cried. He looked over the top of her head at me and said: "Don't you worry, Normie. Everything will be fine."

"Don't let him take Dominic away!" I didn't mean to yell but I did anyway.

He said: "That's not going to happen, little one. Don't even think about it. Maura, *macushla*, settle yourself down and call the best lawyer you know."

"Ha! I don't think Monty would want to take this on, given that my pregnancy put the kibosh on us getting back together!"

"Well, you have to admit, it did come as a surprise to him!"

"It came as a surprise to me too! I just thought I'd gained a bit of weight! I had no idea . . ."

"All right, let's not get into that again. The point is, you won't be hiring Monty to take the case. Too close to home for him."

"The best family lawyer in town is one of Beau Delaney's partners. Val Tanner. Oh God, I hope Giacomo doesn't twig to the fact that he's going to need someone local here, a member of the Nova Scotia bar, and get to her first! He's probably heard me talk about her. She's relentless. If he gets her, I won't have a hope!"

"Get to her first. Give her a call. Go!" And he kind of pushed her to the phone.

I think he had forgotten that I was there because he looked surprised when his eyes fell on me. "Normie, wouldn't it be better if you went upstairs and did your school work? Your mum will work all this out, never you fear." So up I went again. In a way, I wanted to try to listen some more, but in another way I didn't; I just wanted to remember Father Burke saying Mummy would work it out. So I did my school work.

✝

I didn't find out what they did about Dominic because I went to Daddy's house to spend a few days with him. I do that a lot, and so does Tommy, unless he's with his band, which is called Dads In Suits, or with his girlfriend, Lexie. Daddy's house is right on the water. It's a part of the water that comes in from the ocean and they call it the Northwest Arm. We have a boathouse, but no boat. Yet. But going to Daddy's place always gives me the chance to nag for one. All I wanted was a little rowboat, and I would paint it bright yellow. Daddy used to have a sailboat but then he spent so much time with us and with his blues band, Functus, that he never had time to go sailing, so he sold it. Which was kind of dumb, really. You never know when you're going to want a boat again, so why not keep it? But I would continue to work on him.

I didn't get a chance to nag about the boat on my first night with Daddy because I fell asleep before I could bring it up. Then I had other things on my mind. I had horrible dreams and I woke up in the middle of the night with Daddy standing over me. It took a few minutes to figure out that I was staying at his house and to understand what he was saying: "Normie, sweetheart, wake up. You're having a nightmare. Let yourself wake up, and you'll be fine."

My heart was beating really fast, my head hurt, and I was a sweat ball. My jammies were stuck to me. But Daddy hugged me anyway. Then he sat with me in the bed, and put my head against his chest;

he kept smoothing my hair back.

"Tell me."

"I'm scared."

"It was just a dream, dolly. You're safe here in the house with me. Tell me about the dream; that will make it go away."

"There was a baby. And they were being really mean!"

"Who was?"

"Those guys that were there."

"What were they doing?"

"I don't know. I just know the baby was crying and screaming, and was scared or hungry, and it was those guys' fault!"

"Was the baby a boy or a girl?"

"I don't know that! I don't have dreams about people being bare naked!"

"All right, I understand, sweetheart."

"But I'm pretty sure it was a boy. It just seemed to be a boy."

I wished I could explain it, how scared and sad it made me feel for that baby, but I couldn't. Daddy rocked me and sang to me till I fell back asleep.

(Monty)

The first thing I wanted to arrange with Delaney was a viewing of the scene of the accident, known to police and the Crown as the scene of the crime. I wanted to see where Peggy died, but I did not want to do this in the presence of their children. I left it with him to find a convenient time. It didn't take long. Delaney called me on a mild, sunny day in late February to tell me the children were with an aunt, so I drove to Brunswick Street and picked him up. We left the Twelve Apostles and pulled up a few minutes later in front of the Delaneys' colonial revival house in the city's tony south end. Designed in the 1930s by Halifax architect Andrew Cobb, the white clapboard house had a steeply pitched black roof with dormers on either side of a classical-style entrance. The left side of the residence, which I assumed was the living room side, had a set of three double-hung windows; the right side had a set of two.

We went inside. The entranceway was clogged with kids' boots, skates, hockey sticks, and other debris of family life. There was a sunken living room on the left, and a kitchen and dining room on the right. But it was the basement that interested me. We headed there without comment. The stairs were wooden and surprisingly steep, but I could imagine slipping and sliding down the staircase without suffering much more than a bruising. If you somehow flew or were thrown from top to bottom, that would be another story. And if you fell from that height and landed on a jagged rock, that would be the story we were faced with.

I saw a little memorial the family had set up near the death scene, flowers and cards on a table.

"Where was the pile of rocks, Beau?"

He walked down the steps ahead of me. "They were here." He pointed to an area to the right of the bottom step. "The kids were building their castle over here. They had planned to put up three walls and use the basement wall and window as part of the structure. We couldn't afford to have that much of the basement out of commission so we told them they'd have to revert to their first plan, and build it outdoors. Most of the stones had been carted back outside when this happened. There was just the one pile left. And Peggy landed on it. Along with everything else the kids have to deal with, they are feeling guilty about leaving the rocks there. I told them the result would have been the same if their mother had hit her head on the bare concrete floor. I have no idea of course whether that is the case or not."

"So when you found her, she was lying on her back and her head was on the top rock in the pile."

Beau stared at the place on the floor where his wife had died. "That's right."

I knew the indentation, the fracture, in her skull matched the edge of the rock.

"I haven't seen the rock yet. Can you show me another one of the same type?"

He walked to a corner of the room and pointed to a pile of half a dozen building stones, each of which was about ten by six by four inches in size. I wouldn't have wanted to land on one with the back of my head. I turned back to Beau.

"Did you move her when you found her?"

"No."

"Why not?"

He looked at me and didn't answer. He was not about to say he wanted to preserve the crime scene because, from his point of view, it was not a crime scene. Peggy Delaney had suffered an accidental fall.

"Did you know she was dead?"

"Yes."

I wondered about his story. What would I do, instinctively, if I found someone I loved lying at the foot of the stairs? Would I be calm and collected enough not to touch the person? Or would I shake her to see if I could wake her? Would I cradle her in my arms? Would I be concerned about contaminating a crime scene, if I had no reason to think a crime had been committed?

I didn't pursue that line of questioning, but I knew the Crown prosecutor would. Instead, I asked Beau to tell me what happened next.

"I called for an ambulance. When they saw that she was dead, they called the police and the medical examiner. The police arrived within minutes."

"What was their reaction?"

"If they thought foul play was involved, they didn't let on to me. The medical examiner didn't come down one way or the other on the question, as you know. Then Sergeant Chuck Morash muscled his way into the case. And the rest is history."

"Speaking of history, what's yours with Sergeant Morash?"

"Apparently, Chuck has trouble separating the professional from the personal."

"Meaning?"

"Meaning if I give him a rough time on the stand when he appears as a Crown witness in one or another of my cases, he takes it personally. If I discredit the evidence of a police witness, I'm just doing my job. As you are yourself, when you're defending a case. As Morash is when he's testifying on behalf of the Crown. I have a good rapport with most of the cops here, or many of them anyway, outside the courtroom. Morash can't leave his sensitivities behind when he gets down from the stand. That coloured his approach to the investigation of Peggy's death. Obviously."

"But the Crown accepted his version of events. As did Dr. MacLeod."

"Right. They had to go pathologist-shopping in order to find someone who would declare it a murder."

"We don't know that. MacLeod might have been the first they asked after the medical examiner."

"Well, we're going to find out, aren't we? How many experts they shopped this to, before they found one whose opinion accorded with their own. And we're going to find our own expert, who will take a common-sense view of things and conclude that this was an accident, pure and simple."

(Normie)

We don't just do music at our school. We also have sports, and a new game started up this year. Father Burke used to play a special kind of football when he was little, over in Ireland. It's called Gaelic football. Kind of like soccer, except you're allowed to pick up the ball, and the rules are different. They say it's like rugby, too, but I don't know what that is. Anyway, there are a lot of people on the team. Fifteen players, so your chances of getting picked must be good. I guess that's what Father Burke meant when he said that anybody who could walk upright would probably make the team. He met this other Irish guy, who's a teacher in another school, and they decided to start up Gaelic football teams in that school and ours. So far it's just the boys, but we're going to have a girls' team too. I was watching the first practice with Kim and Jenny and Laurence. It was still winter — February 25, exactly two months after Christmas! — but it was really warm and the snow had melted, so the kids all nagged Father Burke to go outdoors and have a practice. He said it would be too wet, but he must have really been excited about getting out there himself, because he ended up saying yes. We don't have a football field at the school because we're downtown and there's not enough room, so we packed the goalposts and stuff into some parents' cars and went to the Commons. That's the huge big grassy park in the middle of Halifax where they play all kinds of games. We had rain the night before so it was muddy. But that only made it more fun. I wished I was out there.

"Richard! What are you doing?" Oh, no. It was Richard Robertson's mum. She was marching towards the field, and she looked mad. "You're filthy!" she yelled at Richard.

Richard had a big grin on his face. He's in grade six. He has reddish-brown hair and his eyes are almost the same colour; he has freckles across his nose, and people tease him about them, but not in a mean way. "We're playing Gaelic football!" he told his mum. "Father Burke's teaching it to us, and we're even starting a league, and —"

"I don't want to hear it, Richard. Have you forgotten what day it is?"

"Uh . . ." He looked at Father Burke, who saw Mrs. Robertson and came over. You should have seen the face on her when she saw him. Even though he's a priest, he was in shorts and a T-shirt, and had mud on his knees.

"Well! I hardly recognized you, Reverend. This must be casual day."

"Good afternoon, Mrs. Robertson."

"I don't recall signing a consent form to allow my son to participate in games that might be dangerous and that will obviously get him dirty, and give him a chill, and make him late for his other activities." She turned to Richard and said: "You are going to be late for your personal coach."

"His what?" Father Burke asked.

"His personal coach." Father just stared at her. He had no idea what she was talking about.

"A coach who will assist Richard in becoming more goal-oriented, more focused, more successful all round. This is a case in point. The fact that Richard has forgotten and made himself late for his coaching session underscores the need for it. Richard! Get your things and get into the car. This minute."

Me and Jenny and Kim looked at each other. Kim said: "Richard's mum is kind of mean. She makes him do all this extra stuff and gets mad when he doesn't do it. I heard him telling Ian that he wishes he could go to Four-Four Time or Gaelic football every day, so he wouldn't have to see that coach guy, or his French tutor, which his mum says he needs or he'll never be able to get a good job."

"Yeah, that's not like my mum. I mean, before she died," Jenny said. "She used to say kids have to have time for fun, and not always be dragged around to activities their parents put them in."

"I feel really bad about your mum," I told Jenny.

"Yeah."

"Why do you think she died?"

"I think she had a heart attack. Or what's that other thing? They call it a strike. And it made her fall down the stairs."

"They call it a stroke, I think," Kim said. "My grandfather got all upset and then had one, a stroke, and he can't do anything now."

Laurence said: "Maybe she died because she was sad."

"Sad about what?" I asked him.

"Our brother ran away."

"No! Really?"

"Well, he wasn't really our brother, but he lived with us sometimes. Years ago, and again last year. Then he left."

"Where did he go?"

"Nobody knows."

"That's awful!"

"He was mean!" Jenny said.

"Well, yeah, he was sometimes," Laurence said. "But maybe she didn't know that. He always acted good around Mum. She might have been sad about him being gone."

"When did he go?"

"A few months ago," Laurence said.

"Was it a long time before she died?"

"Not very long."

"How old is he?" I asked.

"Fifteen."

"What's his name?"

"Corbett."

"I never heard that name before."

"I suppose. I never thought about it."

"We'll have a family meeting on this, Richard. In the meantime there is no point in arguing." That was Richard's mum again. Richard was walking away from the field, and he didn't seem very happy about it. He didn't look at us or any of the other kids. "Good day, Reverend!"

I don't think Father Burke likes being called Reverend. That's not his proper title. But Mrs. Robertson isn't a Catholic and she doesn't know any better. Father stuck up for Richard, though. "You'll be pleased to hear that Richard is singing so well he's going to be the section leader for the trebles."

"It's about time. Richard? Keep moving. And you'd better not get any mud in that new car. Your father won't be pleased."

They left, and Father Burke made a cross behind her back. I don't mean a sign of the cross that you do when you pray; I mean he crossed his hands in front of himself the way they do in a horror movie when they want to "ward off evil." It was funny. He probably forgot the rest of us kids could see it.

But I think I got him in trouble, even though I didn't mean to. I told Daddy when he picked me up after school. He laughed, but then he said: "No consent form, eh? I'll have to have a word with the good Father about that." Lawyers don't always see the fun in things.

Daddy has to work later than school kids do, so he took me to his office. I like going there except he always tells me to do homework while I wait for him. He had to go to some kind of meeting with the other lawyers so I had his office all to myself. I was good and started doing my lessons, but then I got tired of school work. I could finish it all in twenty minutes at home, so why bother with it now? More fun to go through the stuff in Daddy's office, like the stamp that says "Montague M. Collins, A Barrister of the Supreme Court of Nova Scotia." I made some designs on paper with that. I tried to erase Montague and put Normie, but I made a mess. Then I snuck my Nancy Drew book out of my schoolbag and put it on my lap behind the desk, so nobody could see me reading instead of studying. But it was almost like studying anyway, because this book has all kinds of big words in it, like "creditably" and "supercilious," and I can look them up and sneak them into my school work and get better marks. The book is *The Clue of the Whistling Bagpipes*, where Nancy goes to Scotland and meets all kinds of people like my own ancestors, and solves a mystery. And it made me want to solve a mystery myself. I could call it *The Mystery of the Missing Brother*. Not my brother, but Laurence and Jenny's. Where was Corbett?

Most people go to the police when a person is missing. But the Delaneys would have done that already. So I couldn't start there. Any time I read a book or see a movie about somebody missing, the first thing they ask is "Where was he last seen?" I would ask Jenny and Laurence who saw Corbett before he went away. Other questions would be: Was he happy or sad, or mad at somebody? And: Did he have stuff with him, as if he was going to run away for a long time?

✝

I made up my mind to ask my first question when I saw Jenny the next day at Four-Four Time. Laurence wasn't there, so I used that as an excuse, and said: "Where's your brother? I just mean Laurence, not the other guy. What is his name? I forget."

She looked at me, trying to figure out who I meant, because she has a whole bunch of brothers.

"I wasn't talking about the guy who is missing," I said.

"Oh. Corbett. Yeah, nobody knows where he is."

"Where was he last seen?" There, I got it in.

"The last time anybody saw him was at our house."

"Oh. When was that?"

"I'm not supposed to say."

"Really? How come?"

"Because it was the day Mummy died."

"No! How come you're not supposed to tell?"

Jenny looked around to make sure nobody was listening in. "He wasn't allowed in the house. Daddy said so."

"Did he sneak in?"

"Yeah. Daddy was away for a couple of days on a big case. The trial was in the newspapers. That's when Corbett showed up at the house. Mummy felt sorry for him because he said he didn't have a place to stay ever since he left us."

"So, what happened? Your mum let him in?"

"She said he could sleep there, down in Connor and Derek's room because they were away on their school trip. Corbett could sleep there but he had to go out during the daytime because we would all be at school, and the little kids would be at Aunt Sheila's. And Corbett couldn't stay in the house by himself."

I tried to remember the other questions I should ask to solve the mystery of her missing brother. Was he sad? No, that probably wasn't it.

"Was he mad because he had to leave in the mornings?"

"Probably. He was mean. But I don't know. I didn't talk to him. I just heard him on the back porch with Mum. Then he went to sleep down in the basement room. Derek and Connor's. And he was gone when I got up the next day."

"That was the day your mum died?"

"No, well, the day before that, I guess. Then I think he slept there again the night she died, because I remember hearing somebody moving stuff around in the boys' room. Then it was quiet. The door was closed. But I just went to bed."

"Was he around when your mum fell down the stairs?"

Jenny shrugged her shoulders up. "I don't think so. He would have been asleep. I didn't know about Mum dying until Daddy woke us up that morning. And Corbett wasn't there."

Chapter 3

(Monty)

If Beau Delaney was not home when Peggy died, but arrived late at night afterwards, there was a chance his homecoming was noticed by one or more of his neighbours. Given the circumstances, Beau was able to pinpoint his arrival time with some precision: twelve thirty-five in the morning. His call to the ambulance was logged at twelve forty-three, and the medical examiner arrived just before one thirty. In the M.E.'s estimation, Peggy had been dead for around three hours, which meant the time of death was ten thirty or thereabouts. I had not yet seen the witness statements taken by the police. But I wanted my own answers. I also thought there might be some value in Beau Delaney's own lawyer asking his neighbours for help, or should I say, factual information, so I went on a fact-finding mission to his neighbourhood on Wednesday evening. There seemed little point in asking everyone on his street if they happened to notice his car going by, but his closest neighbours, those on either side and across the street, had a clear view of the Delaneys' driveway and the front of their house. I began knocking on doors, starting with the one adjacent to the driveway. No,

Dr. Harrison and his wife had taken no notice one way or the other. They were very sorry to lose Peggy as a friend, and they had no doubt about Beau's innocence. It was much the same story with Professor Anna Goldberg on the other side of Beau's house, and the Van Bommels directly across the street.

But Harold Gorman had something to say. And unfortunately, it was not what I wanted to hear. Mr. Gorman was in his eighties. He met me at the door in a thin brown housecoat and slippers. He had taken a turn of some kind and could not give me much time. He said he had seen Beau on the night in question, and he had told this to the police when they canvassed the neighbourhood. He just told them what he saw, as any good citizen would do. But that did not mean he thought, even for a moment, that Beau Delaney was guilty of murder or anything else. Anybody who thought Beau would kill Peggy obviously didn't know either of them.

"Peggy probably got startled by something. A trespasser. And lost her balance and fell down the stairs."

What was this? "Why do you say 'trespasser,' Mr. Gorman?"

"It's all in the statement I gave to the police, Mr. Collins."

"Was there somebody on the Delaney property that night?"

"On their property and other people's property and then — poof! — gone."

"Did you hear anything that might have given you an indication what the trespasser was up to?"

But my hopes were dashed. "No, I didn't hear a thing."

"What time was this, Mr. Gorman?"

"I'm not sure, but I don't think Lloyd was on yet, giving the news. I have the TV in my bedroom now, ever since Vera died. I fall asleep watching the news. But that night I got up to watch the snow. I have to go lie down now. You get the police statement; it's all in there."

"Very well, Mr. Gorman. Thanks for your help. Were you awake when the ambulance arrived?"

"Oh yeah. I was still awake then. Or maybe I woke up again. The police came. They must have been in there quite a while. They were still there when I got back into bed."

"Thank you, Mr. Gorman. Bye for now."

I had to get a copy of that statement. What was this about a trespasser? Did we have another suspect? Should we alter our defence accordingly? First thing I did when I returned to the office was call the Crown prosecutor, Gail Kirk, and arrange to get copies of all the witness statements she had.

I got them later that day. I set aside for the time being the pathologist's report and other material about the cause of death, and focused on the neighbourhood witnesses. But the police didn't get any more than I did from the neighbours, with the exception of Harold Gorman. His statement, like the rest of them, was in a question-and-answer format. The investigating officer was Sergeant Chuck Morash. He performed the usual formalities, giving the date and time of the interview, the witness's name, and so on, and then got to the point:

"Mr. Gorman, as you know, we're investigating the death of Mrs. Delaney."

"She was probably startled and fell down."

"Why do you say that?"

"Prowler. She may have heard him, and been frightened. Jumped, or turned suddenly, and wham, down the stairs."

"Did you see a prowler around the Delaney residence that night?"

"Some little punk lurking around people's property. I saw him myself."

"Did you know who he was, recognize him?"

"How would I recognize him? They all wear those hooded sweatshirts now, you can't see their faces."

"What was he doing?"

"Hanging around."

"Where?"

"The place across the street from us, and Delaney's. Then he ran down the street and around the corner."

"Did you get the impression that the Delaney property was his main area of interest?"

"Hard to tell. But I watched him, because I didn't know what he might do. What gives them the right to be skulking around? There ought to be a law against it."

"There is, Mr. Gorman. Next time it happens, call us."

"By the time you fellows show up they'll be long gone. I'll go out and chase them off myself if I have to."

"We wouldn't recommend that, sir."

"No, I suppose you're right. But Beau Delaney isn't afraid of them. I figured he sent that hooligan packing."

"Why do you think that?"

"Well, I don't know for sure. I just thought that's probably why he was out there. But who knows? I never got to ask him, with Peggy dying and all."

"So you saw Mr. Delaney outside his house?"

"Only for a bit."

"What was he doing?"

"Just having a look around, it seemed like."

"What time would this have been, do you remember?"

"Oh, it would have been . . . I was waiting for Lloyd, but he hadn't signed on yet. Then I fell asleep. Guess I missed the news that night. Didn't stay asleep, though, on account of the snow, or it must have been sleet, battering my window. I looked out and saw it was quite a nor'wester. Was glad I paid to have the windows reset. Worth every penny, with the weather we're having these days."

"Did you hear any sounds coming from the Delaney house or grounds that night?"

"No, didn't hear a thing."

"Is there anything you'd like to add?"

"Yes. Beau would never have killed Peggy. It had to have been an accident."

I put down the statement and got Beau on the phone. "I've just read the statement of Harold Gorman."

"He's got his times mixed up."

"That may work for us or against us, depending on which time the jury decides he's mixed up. He says he saw you — not just your car, but you — before Lloyd Robertson's news broadcast. That would make it before eleven o'clock. You tell me you didn't get home before twelve thirty-five."

"I didn't. Harold Gorman dozes, peers out the window, watches television, and dozes again. I've known him for years. He can't sleep, so he frets about things going on outside his house. Nothing is ever going on, but that doesn't stop him."

"He swears you're innocent."

"Good man, Harold, and a sharp-eyed witness! Didn't I just say so?"

"He says he got up to check the weather. It started to snow that night. I'll have to check the time."

"It didn't start till after midnight. I remember."

"Good. We'll get the Environment Canada weather summary into the record. Mr. Gorman had something else to say as well. Said he saw a prowler around your place. Let's hope he's right, and we can create the suggestion that there was somebody else —"

"Forget it."

"What?"

"He's always seeing prowlers."

"The Crown doesn't know that. He never calls the police."

"And he didn't call them this time either."

"Even so, he said he saw a teenager in a hooded sweatshirt."

"That's probably the last image he saw on television before he drifted off to sleep."

"I thought you'd be a little more interested in this trespasser angle, Beau."

"I would be, if there were something in it for me. But there isn't. Nobody broke into our house, for instance. I can't point to a smashed window or a jimmied lock. Or signs of a struggle. It doesn't work."

"All right, all right. Let's just hope we can get Gorman up to twelve thirty in his estimate when we have him on the stand."

(Normie)

"Wow! This is a big house. It's really nice!"

Jenny had invited me to her house after Four-Four Time, and Mum said I could go. She had to think about it for a few minutes, but she said yes. Jenny and I took the bus most of the way, then walked the last part of it. Jenny's was one of those big white houses with a black roof, a door in the middle and windows on both sides. It had shutters on the windows, which I really like. It was huge inside with a big living room that you step down into. Jenny took me to her bedroom, which was painted a pretty colour of green with all the other stuff white or blue. But best of all was the bunk beds.

I said: "I always wanted a bunk bed!"

"Yeah, but you don't have enough kids in your house. You can't fill up the rooms like we can. You have to be in a different room from your big brother."

"I know. But now that we have Dominic maybe he can have a bunk bed with me, when he's big enough to get out of his crib."

"Maybe. Or you should get more kids. Girls."

"I wish."

"So, what do you want to play? Dolls? Or hockey?"

"We can play hockey here?"

"It's a big game that you put on a table. It's down the basement. Laurence is probably playing with it."

"Oh, can I see it?"

"Yeah. Let's go."

So we went to the kitchen and to the top of the basement stairs. Jenny said to be careful. "That's where Mummy fell down and died."

So we didn't run, but they were just ordinary stairs made of wood. There was a little table near the bottom with a jug full of flowers and cards the kids had made, all for their mum, saying how much they loved and missed her. I felt tears coming into my eyes.

"It's really awful when your mum dies," Jenny said. "You wake up crying and wanting her to be there but she never is. Never. And your mum is the only person, except for your dad, that loves you no matter how many dumb or bad things you do. She loves you no matter what, and forever. Nobody else does that, except maybe when you grow up and get married. But even then, it doesn't always work. Your husband may beat you up. So, anyway, that's gone. I hope it doesn't happen to you, Normie. But Daddy says she is still with us, looking over us like a guardian angel. He says dead people aren't way up high in heaven; heaven is down here too, so dead parents and kids and the saints and angels are really all around us. So it makes me feel a bit better knowing she's here even if we can't see her."

"Your dad must be really lonesome for your mum."

"Yeah, he is. Sometimes he talks to her. 'Peg! Will you do something about these kids? They won't listen to me!' And maybe she's working behind the scenes because we usually settle down when he does that. They really loved each other," Jenny said, "and they hardly ever had a fight."

"They never had a fight!" That was Laurence. He came over from wherever he had been in the basement.

"I don't mean a fight, Laurence, hitting each other and all that like they did in my old house."

"Yeah, Jenny's old family where she lived before, they fought all the time, with their fists and their feet. She was really little but she remembers because it was so bad."

"And they used to hit each other with beer bottles!" Jenny added. "But our mum and dad here, Laurence's and mine, never did that. They just argued sometimes. Especially about Corbett. Here's the hockey game."

It was humongous! It was a whole rink with pretend ice. It was white and it was on a big table. There were all these little hockey players that you could move with levers. One team was blue and white with a maple leaf on their uniform, and the other was red and white, with a big C.

Jenny pointed to one of the C sweaters. "Daddy calls that *la sainte flannelle*. It means the holy flannel, because this team, the *Canadiens*, are so holy in Montreal. And the other guys are the Toronto Maple Leafs."

"Wow! This is great. My dad used to play hockey, but he says he wasn't anywhere near the best player on the team. Let's play a game!"

"We can't. It's busted," Laurence said. "I'm trying to fix it."

"Okay. Come on, Normie. We'll do something else." So we left the hockey rink. Jenny said: "The boys always end up breaking it. They're too rough with it! But we can have a tea party. I have a tea set, but it's only a kids' set. We're not supposed to use the real dishes, the old-fashioned ones, because they're from France and they're antiques. A man was here to look at them one time, and he said they are worth a fortune! But it's really only the little kids who might break them. We won't. So we'll sneak them out and play with them, then put them back. They're in an old trunk with some other stuff. There's a huge set of knives and forks and teapots made of silver. And that's out of bounds too because it's really expensive. They're not breakable, though, so we'll get them out."

We went to a separate room in the basement, where a whole bunch of stuff was stored: skis, skateboards, bicycle tires, and old cameras in leather cases that had the shape of the cameras.

"It's in this closet." Jenny got up on her tiptoes and reached up for something by the door. "Oh, this is good! Now I'm big enough to reach . . . the hidden key! I haven't been in here since before last year, and I was too short. The key is for the lock on the trunk."

She fumbled around a bit more till she said: "Got it!" She had a big grin on her face. "I'll be able to play with this stuff any time I want to now!" She yanked the closet door open, and pulled a chain that made a light come on. There was a big blue trunk made of metal. Jenny knelt down and put the key into the brass lock on the trunk. She turned it, and then asked me to help lift the top up. I grabbed one end of it and she got the other, and we yanked it up.

"What?" Jenny screeched. "It's gone! The stuff's all gone! Somebody stole it!"

So we didn't get to play dishes. Or hockey.

(Monty)

I had a long talk with Beau over the phone about his whereabouts the night of Peggy's death. He told me again that he had been in Annapolis Royal for a three-day trial. I had already confirmed his presence at the grand old courthouse. But the proceeding had ended, in an acquittal for Beau's client, at four thirty on the afternoon of January 15. He told me he had been planning to spend a third night because of the impending snowstorm, so he didn't have dinner till mid-evening. Before that, he took his time walking and driving around admiring the town's beautiful eighteenth-century buildings. Where did he stay? At the Bailey House. Where did he eat dinner on the fifteenth? The Garrison. Did he have a receipt for his meal? Of course. He was on his client's expense account. But the client was not made of money, so when the storm still hadn't begun by the time he finished his dinner of poached Atlantic salmon — poached as in method of cooking, not illegally fished, ha ha — he decided to cancel his room reservation and drive back to Halifax. It's about a two-hour trip. The restaurant receipt gave a time of eight-oh-five when he paid for his meal. So this didn't help us. If he had driven straight home, he could have been at the house before ten thirty, well within the medical examiner's estimate of the time of death. But, wait, there was something else. He had stopped for gas on the way into Halifax that night. He would dig out the receipt if he still had it; otherwise, I could check with the service station.

Now, to the matter of expert evidence. Who did he like as a pathologist — not for his or her post-workday bar chat, but for an opinion on an accidental fall? Preferably someone local, so it wouldn't look as if our theory was so off-base we had to search far and wide for someone to back it up. He suggested Ralph Godwin or Andrea Mertens. I would check them out.

In the meantime, we had arranged for Beau to have an escorted visit with his children at the family home.

Bright and early on Friday morning, we pulled up in front of the Delaneys' house. We could see little faces peering out through the panes of the living-room windows. I couldn't imagine what this must have been like for Delaney, coming to his own home with a court-ordered escort, even if the supervisors were me and Brennan Burke, dressed in our most casual clothes. Beau must have felt he was in shackles with all his neighbours looking on. In fact I didn't see anybody around except the kids lined up in the front windows. I saw two hands come out and pull two small children away; there may have been a rule amongst the kids not to line up and stare at their dad, but the little ones couldn't help themselves. Beau saw them and threw his arms open wide for an embrace. With that, the kids scrambled from the window; two seconds later, the front door was flung open and they all poured out. One little fellow tripped and landed on his knees. An older girl picked him up and shushed him before he started to wail. They all rushed at Beau and, depending on their ages, grabbed his legs, hugged him, or begged to be picked up.

I looked over at Brennan just in time to see him blink and turn away. It wasn't hard to read his mind, which was operating on the same track as my own: what would all these children do without their father — where would they end up? — if events should conspire to take him away?

The little huddle of humanity made its way inside the house, and a tall woman with strawberry blond hair came to the door: "Come on inside. I'm Sheila Laing, Peggy's sister."

"I'm Monty Collins, and this is Father Brennan Burke."

"Please," Sheila said, and stood aside so we could enter. We followed her into the living room, which was painted a shade of ochre and had white mouldings. She directed us to a pair of armchairs, and we sat down. The furniture was comfy and well broken in; the only pictures on the walls were the children's brightly coloured artwork. Beau was seated on the chesterfield with a child on each knee and others beside him and at his feet.

"Kids," he said, "stand up and introduce yourselves to our guests."

They got up and stood in a clump, and gave their names. In ascending order of age from about five to seventeen, they were Sammy, Kristin, Danny, Edward, Jenny, Laurence, Ruthie, Connor, Derek, and Sarah. There were redheads, blonds, brunettes, and everything in between, green, blue, and brown eyes, and various body types from rail-thin to comfortably padded.

"Tea, everyone?" Sheila asked.

Everybody said yes except two of the younger boys, who made a face and requested chocolate milk.

Brennan and I simultaneously rose from our chairs and trailed after Sheila when she headed to the kitchen. Supervision didn't mean we had to keep the man in our sights every moment. We sat at the kitchen table. Sheila stood by the sink, facing us.

"If I thought for one minute that he killed my sister, I wouldn't be here. With the children, yes. With him, no," Sheila said to me.

"Of course. I understand."

Brennan nodded in agreement.

"And I would fight tooth and claw to keep him away from the children. Or . . . I think I would. But that might do more damage to them . . . I just don't know. They've already been through so much. Some of them especially, the ones who come from unspeakable backgrounds. They're doing well here in the family, but who knows what this will do to them?"

Sheila cleared her throat, and got busy with the tea things and the chocolate milk. She gave us our tea, then took a tray to the living room. When she returned, she sat at the table with us and said: "You've got a good case in his defence, haven't you, Monty?"

"I think so, yes. So far, so good."

"What do you mean? Things could change?"

"Well, things can always change in the courtroom. But from what the Crown has given me, it looks good for us."

"Jenny and Laurence are very keen on your after-school music program, Father Burke. They love it!"

"And we love having them. They're very talented children, particularly Jenny. She's progressing so fast on the piano that I'm thinking of taking her up to the church organ, and letting her have a go at it."

"Oh, wouldn't she love that!"

"I have to confess I don't play the organ myself, apart from a few chords and the notes for the choir. But I know somebody who does play." He looked at me. My son's girlfriend, Lexie, is who he meant. "Maybe she'd be willing to come in once in a while and help Jenny out."

"She'd be happy to," I told him. And I knew she would. I made a mental note to ask her.

"How are the children doing, Sheila? First their mother's death, then the charges against their father. From what you said earlier, it sounds as if some of them had a lot to deal with even before this."

"Little Danny . . . I don't know if you noticed his right arm?" We shook our heads. "He probably had his sleeve pulled way down. His forearm is crooked. That's from a fracture he suffered at the hands of his mother's boyfriend when he was eighteen months old. The mother was drunk and had a pillow over her head, hollering at Danny to stop that fucking screaming. A neighbour kicked the door in, and took Danny to the hospital. He was in bad, bad shape when he came to live with Peggy and Beau as a foster child. He was really coming around before Peggy's death. Sarah and Jenny try to outdo each other to mother him now! Ruthie came from bad news too; well, several of them did. Laurence and Kristin were adopted as infants; they're fine. Peggy gave birth to Sarah and Connor. They're fine, too. Well, Connor went through a bit of a wild period, but nothing nasty. He eventually settled down. Anyway, about Ruthie. Her mother started writing to some sex offender in a Montreal prison; when he got parole, she ran away to meet him and never came back. After being left alone in her apartment at the age of ten, Ruthie wound up with her grandparents. Her grandfather took a great interest in her, especially when she reached puberty. When it was time for her first bra, the grandfather took her to buy it! He kept picking up all these lacy things, red and black, and making lewd remarks, to the point where the woman in the lingerie department called the store security. I guess nothing every came of that intervention, because Ruthie went home with him. Stayed with the grandparents for another two years. Two years of sexual innuendo, the old goat sticking his tongue in and out whenever she went by, and giving her scanty outfits for birthday presents. She was treated as nothing but a sexual object. The grandfather referred to her as a chick and a babe, and the grandmother called her a slut. You can see Ruthie is overweight. You don't have to be Dr. Freud to know why she deliberately overeats, trying to make herself unattractive. Nothing subtle about it. But she has done wonderfully well since coming here. The children have been thriving. I hope to God they continue to thrive, once Beau has been cleared and comes home for good."

We heard giggles coming from the living room, then shouts of laughter from Beau.

"And they have lots of fun with their dad!" Sheila said.

"If worse comes to worse — and I don't think it will, Sheila — is there anyone who can take in all ten children?"

She shook her head. "Impossible. As much as people would want to, there's nobody in the family who can take them all in. They'd have to be split up. How would any of us decide which children to take, and which ones would be dumped back into the system, into foster care?"

I didn't want to picture the scene: children with bundles of belongings being torn from their home and their brothers and sisters. And their dad. When Beau left with us that day all the kids, with the exception of the two oldest boys who strove to put brave faces on, were in tears. Not just in tears, but weeping inconsolably. The little ones clung to him. All I could do was wave to Sheila, turn away and head for the car.

Chapter 4

(Monty)

Delaney waived his right to a preliminary hearing because he wanted a speedy trial, and we did very well, getting a date in early May of that year. This gave me a little over two months to pull together the evidence and case law I would need to defend my client. I was particularly pleased with the report of our pathologist, Dr. Andrea Mertens. I had consulted her and Dr. Ralph Godwin. I wasn't confident in Godwin because he didn't seem confident in his tentative opinion that Peggy's death was more likely than not an accident. The force of the fatal blow to the back of her head, well, it certainly could have resulted from a fall and it probably did, but he could not rule out a violent shove or a blow to the head administered at the top of the staircase before she ended up below. I could write the Crown prosecutor's script when faced with that kind of dithering in court. Dr. Mertens was much more solid, and she had a very helpful piece of advice for me, which I followed. She recommended an engineer and accident reconstruction expert named Wes Kaulbeck, who, if we were correct in our theory of the incident, would support us with calculations of the magnitude of the forces that would have been required to fracture Peggy Delaney's skull, and the mechanics of a fall that could have produced the fracture. I commissioned him to do an investigation and write a report. If the report didn't help us, it would never see the light of day. As it turned out, it was exactly what we needed, so we added Kaulbeck and Mertens to our line-up of witnesses. I was enormously relieved to have some science in our corner as we looked ahead to the trial.

I had my kids at home on Leap Year Day. Tommy told Normie this would be her only chance in four years to propose marriage to Richard Robertson, given the leap-year tradition of women proposing marriage. She informed him that Richard was just a friend, and she got back at her brother by saying: "I don't hear the phone ringing, I guess Lexie must be proposing to somebody else!" We enjoyed our usual activities: jamming with my guitars, harmonicas, and keyboards; watching old movies on the VCR; walking around Dingle Park and climbing to the top of the Dingle Tower; and not-so-successful fishing expeditions off the edge of my backyard. Normie often went out there with an old fishing rod she had found years before. To my knowledge — and I would know — she had never caught a fish. But that wasn't necessarily a bad thing, from her point of view, because it led in to one of her pet subjects: if I got her a boat, she could go "deep-sea" fishing thirty feet away from the house and provide a trout, a salmon, or a tuna fish for our supper. Tommy had a bee in his bonnet as well. He wanted a car of his own, nothing fancy, just a secondhand vehicle to get him around the city. That wasn't a bad idea, but the rust buckets he saw in the newspaper for a couple of thousand dollars looked to me like nothing but trouble. Nobody in our family was mechanically inclined, so I could picture a car spending a lot of time up on blocks in somebody's shop, and a lot of repair bills coming in. My take on it was that I should just buy him a good used car. But to his mother, Maura, coming from a family of seven kids in the Cape Breton coal town of Glace Bay, giving your child a car of his own was a little too much like spoiling him and making him full of himself. And she worried about him running the roads with a carload of other high-spirited young males. But I figured she would come around eventually.

"Here's one for two thousand," Tom said, pointing to an ad in the classified section. "A Honda. It's ten years old and got rear-ended, but . . ."

"I think we should be looking for something a little newer, Tom. I'll help you find one."

"Yeah, but you know what Mum will say about me getting a car." In a thick Cape Breton accent, he said: "The arse is out of 'er now, b'ys!"

Normie and I enjoyed a laugh over Tom's impersonation of his mother.

But all the talk about cars and repair shops put me in mind of something that was still missing from the Delaney file. Beau was supposed to provide me with a receipt for the night of Peggy's death. He said he had stopped for gas on the way home from Annapolis Royal. The receipt would show he was still on the highway at the time Peggy went down the stairs. I picked up the phone and gave Beau a call.

"Hello?"

"Hi, Beau. How's it going?"

"About as you'd expect under the circumstances."

"Listen, I was just thinking about that gas receipt. Do you have it?"

"No, unfortunately, I can't find it."

"You kept your dinner and hotel receipts to be billed against the file you were working on. Why wouldn't the gas receipt be with the rest of them?"

"I don't know, Monty, but it's not there."

"You paid with a credit card, I assume."

"Uh, yes, of course."

"Maybe we can track it down that way."

"Sure. We'll give it a try."

"All right. Talk to you later."

The one thing we needed, he just didn't happen to have.

(Normie)

Monday was a really nice day, and Mum came to St. Bernadette's after school to listen to us singing and playing music at the Four-Four Time program. She walked over with Dominic in his stroller.

He looked really cute in a little pair of blue jeans and a bright red sweater and sneakers that had pictures of animals on the bottoms of them, and he gave me a lovely smile and reached up for me to hold him. So I picked him up and gave him a big hug. I was so happy, especially when a bunch of the other kids saw him and came over and gawked at him and went "Awwww!" Then I put him back in the stroller, and sat down at the piano and started to play "The Alley Cat Song," and Kim and Jenny sang along with me.

Father Burke came in with a bunch of priests and other people from the grown-ups' choir school, the schola, and he announced to all of us that the grown-ups would love to hear us play and sing a song. Dominic let out a little squeal when he heard Father's voice and recognized him, and Father turned around and saw Dominic with a big grin on his face, and he came over. Dominic was laughing and all excited. Father picked him up and held him high in the air and jiggled him, and he laughed even more. I saw the other priests looking at each other, and one made his eyebrows go up. He must have been thinking the priests are really good with youngsters here. Then Father put Dominic back in the stroller, and I pushed it around the room so Dominic could see all the toys and instruments, and the treats, but he wasn't allowed to eat them because he was too little. I had to leave him because I had to help Richard and Ian organize the kids into a group to sing. We did "Panis Angelicus," and the adults all clapped. When I brought the baby and the stroller back to Mum, she was in a serious conversation with Father Burke. I didn't hear what they said, because they stopped talking. All they did was stare at Dominic.

That's when I looked out the window and saw Jenny, and she had the coolest bike I have ever seen in my whole life. Laurence had his, too, but his was the regular kind. I ran outside. Jenny's bike looked kind of thick and clunky. The crossbar curved up and then down; it wasn't just a bar, it was big and heavy, and made the bike look like a motorcycle. It was bright red. There were silver things around the tires. Jenny called them fenders and said they were made of real chrome. There was only one speed! But I loved it.

"Cool bike," I said.

"Yeah, it's old-fashioned. It was in my dad's family for years. My brothers, Connor and Derek, got it up out of the basement and got the rust off it with steel wool, and put air in the tires. Then Corbett said he wanted it, and he took it over. But he's gone now so I get to drive it sometimes. There are these mean guys that follow us around and they grabbed my bike and said they were going to steal it. Then they said it was an old folks' bike and threw it on the sidewalk."

"That was a rotten thing to say. This is a great bike. Who are the guys you're talking about?"

"Two boys who look like criminals. They hang around watching me and my brothers."

"Aren't you scared?"

"Yeah, but they never do anything but follow us and give us dirty looks. And push my bike down."

"Can I ride it?"

"Sure."

So I grabbed the handlebars and swung my leg up over the seat and pedalled it a little ways. Then I realized I didn't know how to stop because it didn't have any brake lever things on the handles. I didn't want to ask, because I would feel stupid, so I just waited till I was going really slow, then slid off the seat and onto the crossbar and put my feet down to stop. I wheeled it back to Jenny.

"You better bring it inside the school," I told her, "or somebody will steal it."

"No, nobody will. Nobody likes it. But I do."

"They're crazy if they don't steal it! It means they don't know anything about cool, old-fashioned bikes. I don't mean it's right to steal, but if it was, this would be a nice thing to steal. That's all I meant."

"I know."

Anyway, we left it outside and went in to Four-Four Time, and nobody stole it.

†

I dreamed about bikes and strollers that night and so the dreams were good at first, but then I thought I was on the old-fashioned bike and I was going down a hill, faster and faster, and I didn't know how to use the brakes, and I was going to crash at the bottom of the hill and I started to scream, and that woke me up. I was lying in bed thinking how lucky I was to wake up before I hit the bottom, because I would have felt the pain just as if it was really happening. And what would happen if I got killed in a dream? Would I really die? So I didn't want to go back to sleep. But then things came into my mind even though I was awake. I saw a tiny baby lying in a crib and all these people were standing around him wearing long black robes. And I got a really bad feeling that something was going wrong. And I thought there was another little kid in it somewhere, and I felt terrified. Or, I felt the little kid was terrified. Why was I thinking this stuff? I wasn't asleep, but I knew I was safe in my own bed. I wasn't with those people in the robes. I lay there and saw more stuff happening, then I called downstairs for Mummy to come up.

She came up right away, and Daddy was with her. I remembered then that he was coming over, but I had fallen asleep before he arrived. They came in and turned on my light. Daddy was closest to the bed, and I described what I saw. And I told him I was not really asleep when I saw it. He looked like he always does when he hears something weird and wants to pretend it's normal. "What were the people doing, sweetheart?"

I tried to picture it again. "They just stood there. I think they were chanting!"

"Uh-huh. Could you tell whether they were men or women?"

"Both, I think. And then one of them did something to the baby, and the baby cried."

"The one who did something to the baby, was that a man or a woman? Do you know?"

"A man," I said. I knew it was.

"What did he do?"

"He reached in and put his hands all over the baby, on his face and then under his blanket."

"And this happened while the others were around the crib?"

"They just watched while it was going on."

"Then what happened, Normie?"

"I kept seeing the baby lying there, and then he wasn't moving anymore. At all. Something was gone from him. I think he was dead!" My voice went up and I didn't mean it to. But I knew the baby was dead. Maybe they killed him!

I felt really sleepy then. Daddy didn't say anything, just held my hand. Mummy came and kissed and hugged me. I fell asleep, and didn't dream about anything after that.

(Monty)

The weeks leading up to a murder trial can be quite intense, obviously for the client, but also for the lawyer. And, it seemed, for the lawyer's family. It was hard to dismiss the notion that there was a connection between the case, or at least the Delaney family, and the disturbing dreams or visions that Normie was having. This was the topic of discussion as Maura and I and Brennan finished up our combination Greek plates at the Athens restaurant. Brennan was getting ready to leave when the subject came up.

"There haven't been any of those crank news stories about ritual abuse lately, have there?" I asked Maura. To Brennan I said: "Normie's latest nightmare — or vision, given that she claimed to be awake when it occurred — was of people in long robes, and possibly the abuse and death of an infant."

Brennan raised his eyebrows but didn't speak.

Maura answered: "I'm not aware of any news item like that, but then I just tune that stuff out."

"Well, you can be sure Normie wouldn't tune it out if she heard or read anything of that nature. Most likely it would feed into this whole picture that's developing in her mind."

"Why don't you ask *him*?" She gestured towards Brennan.

"Ask me what?"

"Fill us in about satanic cults, devil worship . . . child sacrifices . . ."

The priest rolled his eyes. "As far as I know, these satanic cults, so-called, are few and far between, with the exception of some teenage amateurs. I think most of these tales of ritual abuse are horseshit. We certainly have to suss out what's troubling Normie, but I wouldn't waste time worrying about devil worship or child sacrifices."

"I'm sure you're right," I said. "These visions could have an innocent explanation."

"Since when do you find innocent explanations for things,

Collins?" my wife asked.

"I invent them every day in court, remember?" I reached for my wineglass and said: "It's probably something less exotic, and closer to home, that's working on her mind."

I looked up from my glass and caught a glance passing from Brennan to Maura. "What?" I asked. "Is there something?"

"No, no," Maura insisted.

But I wondered. We were separated and had been heading for a reconciliation when she found out she was pregnant by another man. That certainly derailed the homebound train. (Not that I was blameless myself in our travails.) Now, even though tensions between us had eased somewhat in the months since the child was born, I didn't delude myself that I knew everything that was going on in her life. But maybe, knowing Brennan, he'd been on her case to get to the bottom of Normie's trouble, and there was no more to it than that.

"So," I said, "the dreams began around the time she met Jenny and Laurence Delaney. Is that fair to say?"

"I'd say so," Maura replied. "It would make sense that her connection with them, and no doubt her concern for them and their father and the turmoil in their family, would increase over time. She still sees them regularly at the Four-Four Time program. They've become friends. She's even been over to their house."

Brennan got up then, and gave us a little salute as he left the restaurant. I thought I saw him shoot another look at Maura, but it could have been my imagination. A vision, perhaps! I raised my hand in farewell, then returned to the matter at hand.

"The fact that Delaney is accused of being a murderer could be the key to this. Obviously. Children whose father may be a killer. The stuff of nightmares, for sure. But we've always stressed Delaney's innocence."

"There's another thing now," Maura said, in a quiet voice.

"What?" My reply was far from quiet.

"Over the last few days, she's reported headaches."

"It's causing her physical pain now!"

"The headaches may simply be a result of the loss of sleep caused by waking up from these awful dreams."

"We don't know that. It's like the chicken and the egg."

"What are you saying?"

"I'm saying we don't know whether the emotional turmoil is causing the headaches or the headaches are a symptom of something else entirely, and the whole thing is manifesting itself as emotional disturbance."

My wife's face registered her alarm. "You're not saying it's . . ."

"Something organic. Something physical."

"What?" Her voice was uncharacteristically high-pitched. "You're not saying she has a brain tumour or something!"

"I'm not saying that and I don't think that. But the responsible course of action is to have the doctor look at her, and make a referral if that seems wise. To rule anything out."

"I was going to take her in, but I was convinced — I still am! — that it's something she's upset about. Like, well, the Delaney kids and where they might end up, or . . ." Her voice trailed off. She sat there, staring ahead, her face pale. If there was anything my formidable wife could not face, it was the idea that something might be wrong with her children's health.

Two days later we were on our way to see our family doctor, Lise Gaudet. We got Normie into the car without telling her what it was really about. Lise was quick to reassure us, after examining Normie, talking to her, and sending her out to the waiting room with a kids' magazine.

"You're almost certainly right. She's a sensitive little girl, and all this about the murder of the mother of a large family, the father being charged, his family being split up — all of this is likely the root of it. I don't mean to make light of it, of course. But I wouldn't be concerned about anything physical. I'd give you a referral to neurology, but I have a better idea. I have a patient who's lined up for a CAT scan and, well, he's not going to need it."

"Why not?" Maura asked with trepidation.

The doctor just shook her head. "So, I'm going to do some fancy footwork, and get Normie in for that appointment. I honestly don't believe there's anything sinister going on. But this is the way to rule it out. I'll call you tomorrow morning."

On Tuesday the following week, we were trying to reassure our terrified little daughter that entering this gigantic tube would not hurt, and would not result in any dreadful diagnosis being made. And that she would have something fascinating to tell the other kids about her morning off from school. I thought I was going to have to request sedation for her mother, but she did her best to hide her fears from Normie. Though a bright, cheerful, smiley Maura MacNeil should have been enough to make anyone sit up and pay closer attention to the radar screen. But anyway, the little one allowed herself to be extricated from our embrace and placed on the moving table for the scan. Our son, Tom, showed up at the hospital just after his sister went in for the test.

"This is just procedure, right? There's nothing really wrong with her . . ."

"I'm sure that's right, Tom. They have to rule things out, is all."

He looked around, and his thoughts were there to be read by one and all: there would be no medical school in the future for Tommy Douglas Collins. His namesake, Tommy Douglas, was the father of universal free health care in Canada. Our Tommy would be content to see others deliver the service. And others, presumably, were welcome to receive it. He sat down beside his mother, swallowed, and didn't say another word.

The doctor called with the results later that week.

"Nothing wrong at all, Normie," I assured her. "But we knew that. Doctors have to be extra cautious, and give tests to prove that there's nothing wrong. You're fine."

Her brother chimed in: "You can tell everybody they did a brain scan and they couldn't find anything."

She stared at him blankly for a few seconds, then: "Ha ha, very funny. You're saying I don't have a brain."

"I've been saying it for years, and now we know for sure. Nice hair, though." He ruffled her curls and, try as she might to maintain a pose of righteous anger, she couldn't help but smile.

(Normie)

They put me in that great big machine. They slid me in there on a moving table, and I nearly had a heart attack I was so scared. But it showed there was nothing wrong. That didn't mean people left me alone about it, though. I guess they couldn't, because I made the mistake of telling Daddy about another thing I saw in my mind one day after school.

I told him I was wide awake and still at the school, and I had a bad dream anyway. My mind saw a little kid standing in a room, and suddenly this big shadow came over him and the little kid was crying and screaming. I felt he was scared and sad, and feeling pain. And I thought I heard a kind of echo sound of people laughing. It was laughter, but it sounded mean. I had an awful feeling that something had happened. Or maybe something was going to happen!

After I told Daddy this, he went and called Mummy on the upstairs phone. I heard him whispering something; then he came back down to the living room.

"Mum and I are worried about you, angel. We know there's nothing wrong with you, with your brain or anything, but it still might be good for you to see someone who can help you."

"Who?"

"Well, maybe a different kind of doctor."

"What kind? I don't want to see any more doctors! And I don't want any more tests!"

"This doctor wouldn't do tests; she would just talk to you."

"You mean a mental doctor! You think I'm crazy!"

"No, Normie, you're not crazy. We know that. But these doctors can help. When there's something bothering you, a psychiatrist can help you deal with it."

"Nobody can help me deal with it until we find out what really happened. Or what's going to happen!"

"But, sweetie, we don't know whether anything happened."

"I know it did! Or it's going to! You don't believe me! You think I'm mental!"

"Come here, angel. We won't talk about it anymore now." Daddy pulled me onto his knee and held me, and I felt a bit better. I was still mad, though. Who wouldn't be?

I was even more upset after they took me to a *psychiatrist*! You wouldn't believe what went on in there. Me and Mum and Dad were in the waiting room, and this man with his hair all shaved off went crazy, right there in the room with everybody looking! He started bugging the nurse at the desk about the doctor keeping him waiting. She tried to calm him down, but he picked up her papers and threw them at her. Daddy got up and told him to take it easy, and the guy started screaming in Daddy's face. Then he turned and shoved the desk towards the nurse, and she nearly fell off her chair. Daddy went behind the desk and helped the nurse. I think she pressed some kind of secret buzzer, because she reached under the desk, and then made a little nod at Dad. The guy started screaming even louder, and tried to go behind the desk and grab the nurse, and then Daddy grabbed him, and wrestled him down on the floor and held him there. Mum went over to the nurse. A policeman or a security guy came in then, and the doctor came out of her office, and they all went outside into the hallway, and a few minutes later the doctor came back in by herself. All the time this was going on, a little old lady in one of the seats kept giggling, as if it was funny. Well, it wasn't.

I was shaking by the time it was all over. The man had said all kinds of things that didn't make sense. But one thing I got, loud and clear. He yelled at the doctor that he had been coming to see her for two years, and she never cured him! Two years! So I knew it wasn't going to work for me. When Mum and Dad got up to help the nurse fix up her desk and papers, I made a run for it. I ran out of the office and down the hall, and down a whole bunch of stairs till I was outside the doctor's building on Spring Garden Road. I couldn't remember where we parked the car, so I sat outside on the great big steps the building has. Mum and Dad came flying out the door two minutes later, and tried to talk me into going back in. But I'm not stupid. Either that doctor was no good, or mental patients can't be cured. So there was no point in them dragging me back inside. I made a big, loud fuss, and they looked at each other over my head, and said we'd just go home for now. Sometimes you have to put your foot down, and say no!

Chapter 5

(Monty)

That night at our local, the Midtown Tavern, Brennan lifted his pint, took a long sip, and asked: "How did things go today?"

"A patient freaked out in the waiting room, tried to trash the place and attack the receptionist, and I had to subdue the guy till security came, and the guy revealed he'd been under treatment with this particular shrink for two years, and Normie saw and heard it all, and bolted, and refused to be dragged back inside kicking and screaming, so we took her home. That's how things went today." I picked up my draft, and downed a third of it.

"Ah. A less than successful outing."

"So I don't know where to go from here."

"Well, it just so happens that I called Patrick a couple of nights ago, and filled him in." Patrick was his brother, a psychiatrist in New York.

"Oh! What did he say?"

"Paddy thinks there could be something to it. The visions, I mean, not anything physical. The child is certainly not making it up. Her tests are normal. She's having visions of past or maybe future events. If they're in the future, there's nothing we can do unless they're detailed enough to tip us off. If something has already happened, perhaps we can track it down."

"She's heard so much about Delaney, and his wife dying, and all the children being without their mother. She's become friendly with Beau's kids. It can't be anything Beau has done; they wouldn't keep sending him foster children without being absolutely sure he's above reproach. She's met Beau. She knows he's a lawyer who's handled some disturbing cases."

"As have you."

"True, but surely she's not having nightmares about me! She may be picking up images or emotions from some of the cases Beau's done, those involving children."

"Or it may be something else."

"Like what?"

"Well, who knows?"

"That's not getting us anywhere, is it?"

He looked distinctly uncomfortable.

"What's on your mind, Brennan?"

He just shook his head.

"If you knew what was causing this pain for my daughter, you'd let me know, wouldn't you, Father?"

"I would. Of course. But I don't know what it is."

"Is there something going on at home, do you know?"

"If there is, you'd best ask the MacNeil."

"I will."

"In the meantime, Monty, proceeding on the hypothesis that there may be a Delaney connection, let's look at some of Beau's cases. Do some research."

"I can't say I like this, Brennan. Checking into the past of my own client." I looked into his eyes, and he returned the look without comment. We both remembered all too clearly that I had looked into *his* past when I was defending him against false criminal charges. I fervently hoped that Delaney, like Brennan, would in the end be exonerated. In the meantime, if we could come up with something to show Normie — *see, five years ago Mr. Delaney had to do his job and defend a client who mistreated a child; that must be what you're seeing* — it might be worth the qualms. But I still didn't like it. "I'd rather not do this through my office, Brennan. You know, have a clerk or someone dig up old news clippings about our client."

"I'll do it."

"When are you going to have time for this?"

"I'll make time." He caught the eye of our waiter, and gave him the signal for two more draft.

I looked over at the television, which was showing a basketball game, and thought of another thing we could do. "They made a documentary about Delaney last year. We could check that out."

"Couldn't hurt."

So, the next day, Thursday, I stopped by St. Bernadette's to pick up Brennan, who does not have a television, then headed to Robie Street, drove north to Macara, parked, pulled on the emergency brake, and ran in to the local private television studio, ATV, to pick up the videotape. When I explained that I was Delaney's lawyer, they gave me a copy of my own. We took the tape to my house, shoved it into the vcr, and sat down to watch the show. It occurred to me then that Maura might want to see it. I knew Tom was home and could look after Normie and the baby, so I gave her a call.

"I've got the documentary ATV News did on Beau. Would you like to see it? It's a long shot but there may be something —"

"— in Delaney's life, or his case load, that could explain the visions. I agree with you that it's a long shot, but it's a start — Normie! You're supposed to be cleaning your room, not hanging around down here. Up you go. Monty, see you in ten minutes."

The documentary opened with a shot of Delaney in full court regalia, speaking to reporters after one of his courtroom triumphs. He had just saved his client, a mother on social assistance, from going to jail for breaking the "man in the house" rule. She was accused of welfare fraud for accepting payments and not declaring that her husband, who had previously moved out, had moved back in. Delaney had made an impassioned argument that a poor mother on welfare should not be sent to jail for fraud while rich men — and he produced for the court a long list of recent examples — were not given jail sentences for tax evasion and other white-collar crimes. The judge agreed. That day marked the beginning of the end of "welfare mothers" being dragged away from their families and thrown in jail.

The scene then switched to the Delaney home, where the camera panned around the house, taking in several bedrooms with bunk beds, and Beau and Peggy's own room, where two little kids bounced up and down on the bed and giggled. Peggy's closet was shown; it was a jumble, and she quickly closed the door and laughed. Beau's closet was featured next, and was notable for a rack full of shoes. Someone off camera made a joke about Imelda Marcos and her thousands of shoes, and Beau said when you had feet his size, you had to grab footwear when you could find it.

Then there was a short biography punctuated with career highlights. His father was a surgeon; his mother was trained as a teacher, but stayed home to raise Beau. The only child. He had excelled in school, had gone on to St. Thomas University and Dalhousie Law School, where he won the much-coveted Smith Shield for the moot court competition. After graduation near the top of his class, he was hired by one of the big Halifax firms, then went out on his own doing criminal law. He was made a Queen's Counsel and received various other honours. The focus switched to his large blended family of biological, adopted, and foster children. The family was shown in their customized minibus, on the way to the Commons for one of the sports and picnic days, to which all and sundry were invited. Some of his children spoke on camera; others just performed various hijinks in the grass. Then it was the cottage overlooking Lawrencetown beach; we saw a surfer catch a big wave, and heard squeals of appreciation from the Delaney kids. The next segment dealt with Delaney's efforts to balance his life and work. Beau and Peggy answered reporter Charlene Fay's questions about the stress and even danger that are part of life for a big-time defence lawyer.

"Beau, it's well known that you received death threats following your defence of Adam Gower, the man who committed the Gary's General Store robbery, in which one young clerk, Scott Hubley, was shot to death and the other, Cathy Tompkins, left permanently disabled."

"Yes, I did receive threats. Feelings were running very high in the

Blockhouse area. And I can understand that. Everyone has the right to a legal defence, and I did my job to the best of my ability in that case as in others. That doesn't mean I am insensitive to the pain of the victims or their families. Or their community. It takes its toll even on those of us who work on 'the other side.'"

"You must have been especially concerned in that case, because the perpetrator, your client, was eventually tracked down and killed. Beaten to death."

"Yes, that happened the year after the trial, when Mr. Gower returned from a stint out west and came back to live in Blockhouse."

"He was murdered within days of his return. Pretty scary for you!"

"Yes, I was watching my back for a while there."

The documentary then showed clips of movie star Jack Hartt playing the role of Delaney in *Righteous Defender*, as he stepped in and solved the murder of Adam Gower, thereby exonerating Cathy Tompkins's brother, who had been wrongfully convicted of killing his sister's attacker.

"That wasn't the only time a client met a violent death," the reporter stated.

The scene switched to a Mountie speaking to reporters outside an RCMP detachment. One reporter asked: "Was there a Hells Angels link to the killing?"

The officer didn't answer that, but said: "The victim, Travis Bullard, was shot to death. The weapon was a high-calibre handgun."

"Was he shot more than once?"

"We'll release more details at a future time. Thank you."

Then we were back with Charlene Fay in the Delaneys' living room. "But they never did release more details, did they? Just that the man was shot to death. That happened several months ago. Sources have told us that this case is still unsolved, but that the Mounties have a suspect in mind, someone who has since gone to prison for an unrelated offence. They wouldn't want to jeopardize their case by revealing details about the crime in a situation like that . . ."

"Makes sense," Beau agreed.

"This man, Travis Bullard, had some unsavoury connections . . . links to the Hells Angels, people say."

"He travelled in some rough circles, yes."

"And so he ended up being shot to death one night in Truro."

"That was the longest night of my life!" Peggy Delaney exclaimed. "My God, I thought, if they —"

"It's a scary world out there," Beau interrupted, "but those of us who work in criminal law can't go through life second-guessing every client we take on. We have a job to do."

"That brings us to another point. You have a job to do, defending people accused of terrible crimes. Sometimes it must be very difficult to do that job. Particularly when the crime was committed against a child. You defended a woman who, along with her boyfriend, engaged in prolonged abuse of a child and then killed him. They were convicted despite your best efforts on their behalf."

"Yes, they'll be behind bars for a long time yet."

"A lot of people must wonder: how can you do it? How can you defend someone who has killed or abused a little child?"

Beau leaned forward. "I don't take any of these cases lightly, I'd like to assure everyone of that. These terrible cases mean sleepless nights for defence lawyers, just as I assume is the case for the police, the prosecutors, social workers, and anyone else whose lives are touched by such tragedies."

"It's not all tragedy and violence, though," the reporter assured us. "Tell us about your dog case, Beau."

"I had fun with that. My client was charged with letting his dog run loose in one of the communities outside Halifax, contrary to a village bylaw requiring dogs to be on a leash. The bylaw enforcement officer, the dog catcher, never caught my client, but he claimed to have recognized the dog. It was a German shepherd called Fang. I made an arrangement with the film production company that did my movie to round up a bunch of trained German shepherds, and bring them into the courtroom the day of the trial. The dog catcher was on the stand. I asked him to point out the offending dog. Looking out to the gallery, all he could see was a row of virtually identical German shepherds sitting with their trainers. The dog catcher couldn't identify Fang, and the judge laughingly declared my client not guilty."

The story then returned to Beau's kids, and their hopes and plans for the future. "Any budding lawyers here?" Three hands went up. Everyone laughed when one little girl shook her head and said: "Not me, no way. I'm going to work at the Chickenburger!"

I switched the VCR off and looked at Brennan. He said: "That child abuse case sounds dreadful."

"It was atrocious," Maura said. "Normie may have picked up on that somehow, though I hope not."

"What are we going to do?" I asked. "The last thing we want is for her to learn the details of that incident. Believe me."

"I believe you," Brennan said. "There's also the case in which Delaney's life was threatened because of the feelings running so high about his client. Could Normie have detected something about that?"

"But the client, Adam Gower, got his comeuppance in the end. I think any threat to Delaney would have evaporated after that. The community would have experienced a kind of catharsis once the perpetrator was eliminated. Not that I recommend that form of therapy! But once it was done, I can't see much danger for the man who did his job and defended the guy in court. I think people understand the lawyer's role after they cool off. And Beau redeemed himself completely once he cleared the young girl's brother of murdering Gower. I mean, the story even made it to the big screen, with the Jack of Hearts starring as Beau. Hartt lives in Los Angeles, and he invited Beau and the family down for a weekend a few years ago. They all went to some kind of Hollywood wingding. Cavorting with the stars. Too bad Normie can't have visions of that instead!"

"No such luck," replied Brennan. "So we haven't found the answers we're looking for. No surprise there, I guess. Time for me to embark on phase two of our research."

"What's that?" Maura asked.

"I'm going to spend a couple of hours in one of the libraries and do a CD-Rom search for cases handled by Delaney."

My face must have betrayed my surprise.

"What?" Burke asked.

"I never had you pegged as being in the vanguard of 1990s information technology."

"I do teach the odd course at the university level, Collins. My area of expertise may be twenty centuries old, but word reaches me of the latest research techniques."

"I stand corrected, Reverend Dr. Professor Burke."

"And so you should."

"I'll do some legal research into his criminal cases."

"Depending on what I find, you may not need to. No point in duplicating our efforts."

"True enough. I'll hold off till I see what you come up with."

(Normie)

"What's an 'asylum'?" I asked Mum on the way to school Friday. I said it like "AZ-ee-lum" because I didn't want to say "ASS-ee-lum." But that wasn't the right way to say it anyway.

Mummy answered: "The usual meaning of it is a mental hospital. It can also mean giving shelter to people fleeing evil governments in other countries. But psychiatric hospital would be the most common meaning. You pronounce it 'ah-SIGH-lum.' Why are you asking, sweetheart?"

"No reason, just wondering." Mental people again! I couldn't tell her why I was asking, because they might put *me* in an asylum! So I kept quiet about what I had seen in my mind's eye when I woke up that morning. I drew a picture in my diary of what I saw. It was a really old building and it said "asylum" on it, and there were other words but I forgot them because I was concentrating on remembering "asylum" to ask Mum. I had heard the sound of screaming and crying coming from inside the building, and there was a feeling of sadness there.

I saw Kim waiting for me in front of the school. She had one of her braids in her mouth the way she often did when she thought nobody was looking. "Kim!"

"Normie!"

We went in to school together, and I stopped thinking about the old building.

†

"I heard this really cool song on the radio," Richard Robertson said to Father Burke when we were beginning choir practice that afternoon. "A choir was singing it. And they went 'hoo hoo hoo' and 'yip yip yip' and did all kinds of animal sounds in the middle of it. Can we do a song like that?"

"What you're describing, Richard, is *a choir having fun*. Like a women's choir singing the work songs of a chain gang or something with 'Hey, nonny, nonny' in it. Or, as you say, the hooting and braying of animals. Some of the most excruciating music in the world issues forth from choirs *having fun*. Well, no choir is going to *have fun* on my time. You are going to sing music that cries out to heaven in its beauty and poignancy. Pick up the Palestrina I gave you last week, *Missa Papae Marcelli*. Turn to the *Kyrie*."

Everybody scrabbled around for their music. Except Richard. And Ian. They didn't have it.

"Boys! Where's your music?"

Ian didn't answer. Father Burke glared at him, then at Richard.

Richard said: "I can't find it, Father."

"Fortunately for you, I have a couple of extra copies in my room."

"I'll go get them!"

"No, I'll go," Ian said.

"Neither of you lads will go. You'd be apt to lose them on the way back. Could you take a run up there, Normie? You know where my room is. All the music is piled on my table."

The other kids gawked at me. None of them were ever allowed to go up there. And now they knew I knew where his room was. But that was only because I was up there with Daddy a couple of times. Anyway, I said okay and I went out of the school, across Byrne Street, and into the priests' house. I told Mrs. Kelly, the housekeeper, that I was on an important errand for Father Burke. You have to tell her something like that, or she doesn't know what to do. So I went up to his room and opened the door. The room was really tidy and clean, except for books piled all over the place and doubled up on the bookshelf. Also lots of CDs. There was a cross on the wall and some paintings. One was a picture of the Virgin Mary and the Baby Jesus; He was really cute. Sometimes they have Him looking like a little old man, but not in that picture. It was done by somebody called Botticelli. I wondered if there were any more pictures by him. Angels, maybe. Anyway, I looked on the table, and there were all the music books. I picked them up and looked through them, and there were the Palestrina Mass books. I took two of them.

Then I saw he had something else there, under the music. It was a whole bunch of newspaper stories. One was from 1983, the year I was born! Another one was from 1989. They were all about things that had happened to kids. Crimes, even a murder. And I remembered something Mum said on the phone about my visions and bad cases Mr. Delaney worked on, and I knew then that they believed me about my dreams! Father Burke had all this stuff. He knew I wasn't just making it up about the things I was seeing. He wanted to find out what happened. But I would be the best one to figure it out because I was the one having the dreams. So I grabbed the papers, along with the music. I planned to hide them, then sneak back into his room after I had read them. I would tell Mrs. Kelly I was on another errand. It wouldn't really be a lie, because if Father Burke knew I took the papers he would want me to return them. Some time. So it would be an errand for him. Now I had to figure out how to hide them before I handed him the music sheets. My locker. That would be perfect. I got back to the choir school and snuck along the corridor, opened my locker, shoved the papers inside, and then went to the classroom and handed Father the music. "Thanks, darlin'," was all he said. Whew! We sang the Mass and I tried to do a really good job, so it would seem like nothing else had happened.

But that night, I knew I'd been caught. I was home with Mummy and Tom, and the doorbell rang. Mum answered the door, and it was Father Burke. Uh-oh. I scooted into the dining room.

"Oh, good," Mum said. "Mass for shut-ins. I didn't get out to church today, Father. How kind of you to bring me the sacraments."

"I'll give you a sacrament you won't soon forget, you blasphemous little rip! Now, let me in the door."

I couldn't find "blasphemous" in the dictionary at first because I couldn't spell it, but finally I did. It sounds bad, but they were only joking, not really making fun of the sacraments. He's always telling her she needs to go to confession, but not to him, because then he would need to go to confession himself after hearing all the evil things she said. He pretends to think Mummy's bad, but he knows she isn't.

"Mr. Douglas," he said to Tommy, because my brother's real name is Tommy Douglas.

"Hi, Father. How you doing?"

"Just grand, Tom, grand altogether. Still playing in your band?"

"Oh yeah. I'm heading down to the basement to practise some riffs for a gig on the weekend."

"I'll have to come hear you some time."

"Sure. Just don't show up in your collar!"

"No worries. I won't cramp your style. I'll come in-cog-neat-oh."

I heard Tom go down the basement stairs. Then Father Burke must have made some kind of signal to Mum, because she called to me and told me to go to my room and finish my lessons. I was supposed to be doing math questions. It seemed like a bad time to argue, so I went up to my room. I opened my math book and scribbler on my floor, just in case, then I snuck out again and sat by the hall register to listen.

They yakked about boring stuff for a few minutes, then Mum said something about Giacomo phoning her about Dominic, and bringing his lawyer from Italy. Mum said she would get a lawyer of her own. I don't know why, because she already is a lawyer and so is Dad. Anyway, after that, Father Burke told Mum about the news stories he collected.

"These visions she's having, well, we've gone over this time and again. That they may just be bad dreams that any child would have, or they may be related to more personal concerns. Ahem! But with the Delaney fellow on trial —" Father Burke says it like *fulla* "— and her knowing his children, they could be visions of something that actually happened in the past."

"Or something that is yet to come."

"Let's pray that's not it, given the tenor of the visions. Anyway, I can't help you with the future, but I said I'd do some newspaper research, and I did. I put together a file of old cases involving crimes against children here in the city."

"Oh, God. Does anything match?"

"Couldn't tell ya."

"What do you mean?"

"The file disappeared before I had a chance to read the clippings."

"Disappeared! Who would have —"

Father Burke didn't answer, but I bet he made some kind of face or made his eyes go up, as if to say the guilty person is upstairs in this very house. Because Mum just said: "I see."

"I sent her to my room in the rectory to pick up a piece of music. I forgot about the news articles being on the table. When I went up there after class, I remembered and saw that the papers were gone. Don't be in a lather about it, now. I'll not be pressing charges!" Mum laughed, and then he said: "But we won't want her reading those stories. Terrible things happened in a couple of the cases. So you'll want to retrieve them from her before she reads them and gets upset. I'll leave it with you."

"No, Brennan, hold on. I'll go up and talk to her now."

Oh, no. I heard her feet on the stairs, so I scampered back into my room. I had the papers hidden already, so I grabbed my pencil and sat there looking like I was doing my math homework.

"Hi, sweetie," Mum said when she came in.

I looked up. "Oh, hi, Mum. This math is really easy tonight."

"Good, good. Normie, did you by any chance borrow something from Father Burke's room?"

"Like what?"

"A pile of news stories."

It would only make it worse if I lied. They knew anyway.

"I saw them and I knew he must be trying to help figure out what happened. So I decided to borrow them only for one night, so I can help him investigate."

"You wanted to see if any of the stories matched your dreams?"

"Yes."

"Have you looked through them?"

"Only a couple." That was true. I was going to get into them after everybody else went to sleep, so I only peeked at the first two, and they were nothing like my visions.

"Father Burke and I are afraid those stories will upset you. It's not very often that people do bad things to children, but you know there are some disturbed people in the world, and sometimes things happen."

"I know all that, Mum."

"So why don't you give me the news stories, and I'll look through them. I'll ask you some questions about them later. You've told us what your dreams were like, so if we see something that matches up, we'll ask you."

That's not what I wanted to do. I wanted to read them myself. But now I couldn't. I thought of saying I'd left them in my locker, but she would know if I lied. She can always tell. So I had to give them up. But I didn't want her to know where my hiding place was, so I said I would get them if she would go downstairs.

"No, you just give them to me now, sweetheart. That would be best."

Lawyers always think people are doing something sneaky. She probably thought I was going to steal a couple of the papers and give only some of them back. But I wasn't.

"Okay, but turn around and close your eyes. I don't want you invading my privacy!"

"All right." She turned away, and I went around the room, banging drawers and pulling things off shelves so she wouldn't know about my hiding place under the bed. I have my secret box under there, and when she cleans she just shoves the box around with the vacuum cleaner. I've seen her do it. She probably thinks there are old toys or junk in the box, because I stuck a couple of old things on top.

"Here are the papers, Mum," I said and gave them to her. She said thanks and gave me a kiss, told me not to worry, and went downstairs.

As soon as I heard the squeak of her chair in the kitchen, I went back to my listening post and sat down.

"Ah. Now, let's see what we have," Father Burke said. "Her visions began with the Delaney charges, and they involve harm or danger to a child. So I searched for cases involving children and Delaney's name. Also unsolved cases involving children, but I didn't come up with much there. By the time this class of crime is reported, they seem to know who to arrest for it."

"Yeah, the stepfather," Mum said.

"Right, and there are a couple of cases of foster parents charged with physical or sexual abuse."

"Why doesn't that surprise me?"

"Delaney's a foster parent."

"There's never been a whisper of any problems there. The department keeps bringing children to the Delaney home, for temporary placement. You can be sure it's been checked out over and over again. And from everything I've heard, it's a very happy family."

"Glad to hear it. Jenny and Laurence, the two Delaneys who come to our Four-Four Time program, seem fine. And devoted to their da. Now here's a group of clippings about unsolved murders of young women. Teenaged girls."

"That doesn't seem to fit, but who knows?"

"A child was abused and murdered a few years ago, a little boy, but the killer was convicted and put away for life. No reference to Delaney. Another lawyer handled the defence."

"Not Monty Collins."

"No, not Monty on that one. He did a couple of the other cases, though."

"I remember."

"And here are the ones in which Delaney acted for the defence. There don't seem to be any lingering mysteries about those cases. But that may not be the point. Normie may be seeing the connection between Delaney, the lawyer, and the clients he associated with in his work. It may be nothing more than that."

"Let's hope that's all it is."

"I also looked for unsolved cases and the name Beau Delaney. You'll see them here. I didn't get to them all."

They didn't talk for a few minutes. Then Mum said: "Here's an unsolved murder of a young guy. Suspected drug dealer. The only reference to Beau Delaney is that one of his clients was questioned, and Delaney made a statement to the press that his client had an alibi, and Beau was going to make a formal complaint if the police didn't stop harassing his client."

"And here's the Gary's General Store case, the one where Delaney's life was threatened," Father Burke said.

"The one they made a movie about. *Righteous Defender*. Wouldn't we all love to have that title attached to our name?"

"How did that go again? They discussed it in the documentary, but I'm not sure I have it straight."

"Beau's client, Gower, committed the robbery with another lowlife. Beau got Gower off. A year later, Gower came back to the community and was murdered. The young girl who was left disabled, Cathy, had a brother, and the brother was picked up for the murder. Beau, obviously fuelled by guilt over representing the shooter and seeing the brother charged — Cathy's family victimized again — launched his own investigation, found out the brother was innocent, and fingered the real killer."

"And people think the theology of the Holy Trinity is complicated!"

Chapter 6

(Normie)

We were learning about sins on Monday in catechism class. Mrs. Kavanagh said there used to be more sins and you got in more trouble for them in the old days, but sin is still with us today. Ian put up his hand and asked if it was a sin to disguise your voice in the confession box. Mrs. Kavanagh said it might be like telling a lie but she wasn't sure, so she would ask Father Burke. Ian squawked: "Don't tell him it was me asking!" And the whole class burst out laughing. Then Kim asked what would happen if you committed a sin and went to confession, but then you ran home before saying your Hail Marys or whatever your penance was, and you got run over by a bus and died. Mrs. Kavanagh said she didn't think it would be a problem, at least for our souls, but she gave us a lecture on crossing the street safely.

Ian was teasing Kim afterwards at Four-Four Time, making a noise like a bus and pretending he was going to knock her down. "You're dead! You died in a state of sin! Going to hell. Next. Beep beep." And he went after another kid and pretended the same thing. Jenny Delaney asked what he was doing, so I said it was all about dying with a sin on your soul. Then I told her I remembered something about telling God you're sorry even if you don't get to confession. There's this prayer you can say, the Act of Contrition, and it's supposed to work too.

Jenny looked really worried: "But if you don't have time even to say the prayer, if you sin and then die a second later, does that mean you go to hell?"

"I guess so," I said, "or you have to wait for hundreds of years before you can be with God in heaven. It's an in-between place you go to. I can't remember the name of it. Anyway, people have to say prayers to get you out of there."

"That doesn't sound good!"

"I know, but you don't have to worry about it. Cross at the crosswalk, and look both ways, and you won't get killed. Or just don't commit any sins."

"It's not me." Jenny looked around to make sure nobody was listening. "It's Mum!"

"Your mum wasn't a sinner. They wrote all this good stuff about her in the paper."

"I know. She was always really good. Except just before she died. She committed a sin! Or what might be a sin, I'm not sure."

I was worried then too. "What did she do?" I whispered.

"She swore!"

"No!"

"Yes! My sisters and brothers don't know this because I was the only one awake. And even then, I fell back asleep and didn't get to save her. I don't know how I could have saved her, but maybe I could have done something. Anyway I was so tired I went back to sleep."

"There's probably nothing you could have done. You shouldn't worry, Jenny." Then I couldn't help it, I was curious. "What swear word did she say? Don't say it yourself, just say the first letter."

"Well, I'm not sure if it was swearing, but it sounded like it. She said 'Jesus!' I know it's bad to say that. Then she said 'hell's angels!' in a loud voice. I think that's swearing. That's all I could hear, so whatever else she said must have been in a normal voice and maybe wasn't bad."

Hells Angels! That probably *was* a sin, a sin I had committed myself, and so had my whole family! We have all said those words in our house. I have done my own personal research into angels; I'm trying to figure out if Father Burke is one himself, even though he doesn't look it, because he has spirits around him when he's on the altar in church. You should see the picture I drew of him looking happy all in white with wings in my diary. I added a picture of Dominic peeking around the bottom edge of the robe by Father's feet. Dominic can crawl now, so it's really cute. Anyway, I've seen all kinds of pictures of angels. And I could never figure out how the Hells Angels — who are a motorcycle gang! — are allowed to call themselves that name. Hell is bad, so they must be saying they are bad angels. I figured they looked more like devils. I always secretly hoped I would see one. I only saw them speeding by on their motorcycles, but never up close, standing still. And whenever we drove by their clubhouse, which is near where Tommy's girlfriend lives, we would see all the motorcycles outside but we never saw any of the gang members themselves. Tommy always takes that street to get to Lexie's apartment, even though he doesn't have to. He slows down and stares at all the bikes. And one time our family had a barbecue with the families of a bunch of lawyers, and one of them — Katie Sheehan's dad — said he had actually been to a Hells Angels lobster party!

So all along we've probably been swearing whenever we've mentioned their name. I shouldn't say this, but I got even more curious to see one of these "angels from hell" after Jenny told me about her mum saying their name.

I asked Jenny: "Who was your mum talking to when she said it?"

She looked at me as if I had asked a question she didn't understand, or it didn't make sense to her. Then she said: "She was all alone when she died, so there couldn't have been anybody there for her to talk to."

"So the bad words were the only thing you heard?"

"Yeah. She must have been thinking about something, or remembering something bad, and swore really loud, to herself. How can we find out if 'Hells Angels' is swearing? Is there a list?"

"I don't know. If there's a list, maybe it's a sin to look at it!" We were both quiet then, trying to figure out what to do. I said: "Let's ask Father Burke. I saw him out in the hallway."

So we went over to see him. Jenny was too shy, so I did the talking. "Hi, Father."

"Normie and Jenny. How are the girls today?"

"Fine thank you, Father. Can we ask you something?"

"Sure you can."

"Is it okay if we say something that may be a swear word, but we don't know for sure? 'Cause that's the question we have to ask."

"Ask away."

"Is it swearing if you say 'Hells Angels'? Especially in a loud voice?"

He didn't laugh but his eyes looked like he was going to laugh, if you know what I mean. He said: "It's not swearing, but don't let me catch you girls roaring up here on a motorcycle and coming in with a Hells Angels patch on your jackets! Then I'll think you're up to no good, the pair o' youse."

"What do you mean?" Jenny asked.

"The Hells Angels are a motorcycle gang and some of their activities are, well, not the sort of activities we'd encourage in young Catholic children."

"We won't act like them," I promised him. "Why would your mum say their name, Jenny?"

"Your mum?" Father Burke asked, looking at Jenny.

So Jenny told him: "I was scared Mummy might be in hell because she said 'Hells Angels!' But if it's not a swear word, then it's not a sin, right?"

Father Burke squatted down in front of Jenny and held her hand. He said: "It's not a sin at all. How long have you been worrying about this, Jenny?"

Jenny's eyes flicked over to me and then back to Father Burke. "I wasn't worried all the time. She just said it once, uh, one night."

"Well, you can be sure your mum is right there with God in heaven. Everybody knows what a lovely and kind woman she was. I'll bet she's watching over you right now."

"I hope she's not mad at me, for thinking she might have been a sinner!"

He just shook his head as if to say no, Jenny had no reason to worry.

"I'm sure your dad would reassure you that there's nothing to worry about with respect to your mother's soul! Did you tell him about it?"

She shook her head again.

"How come?"

"Because in our house you're not allowed to say 'hell.' My brother got in trouble one time for telling one of my other brothers to go to hell. We're not allowed to say 'Jesus' in a bad way either, or 'God.' So I didn't want to say it or get Mummy in trouble for saying it. Even though she's dead now."

Father Burke said: "Ah. The perils of a Catholic education." Whatever that meant. "I'm sure you won't be in trouble if you talk it over with your dad. He'll set your mind at ease."

Then he put his arm around Jenny and hugged her because she started to cry. He wiped the tears off her face. "When I say my first Mass tomorrow, I'm going to say it for your mum, and for you and your whole family."

"Okay. That's good. Thank you, Father."

"But in the meantime I think you should have something to lift your spirits a bit. What do you like as a special treat, Jenny? Chocolate? Ice cream?"

"I like both!" she blurted out. Then her face turned red, because she must have thought she was being greedy.

But he just said: "Sure don't we all! A chocolate sundae perhaps?"

"Yeah!" Her eyes were really big.

"What else do you like on it?"

"Sprinkles!"

"How about you, Normie?"

I was glad I was getting one too, but I tried not to let it show. After all, it wasn't me whose mother was dead. But it would be rude not to answer, so I said: "I like marshmallow on mine. Whenever I get one. It doesn't have to be today."

"Tell you what," he said. "Why don't you girls go on with your music and I'll go out and get some stuff for ice cream sundaes, and we'll have kind of a sundae-making party. You two girls will be in charge of making them for the other kids, scooping up the ice cream and putting the toppings on. How does that sound?"

"Great!" Jenny and I both said it at once, and we had big grins on our faces.

So he left to go to Sobeys or wherever priests buy their groceries, and we practised our piano lessons, but we had our minds on the treats to come. When he arrived back at the choir school, he had everything you could imagine. Chocolate, vanilla, and strawberry ice cream, chocolate sauce, butterscotch sauce, marshmallow sauce, coloured sprinkles and cherries, tall plastic sundae dishes, and long see-through sundae spoons in all kinds of colours. He set everything out on a table and called me and Jenny over, and gave us these plastic scoops. Hers was red and mine was blue. The kids freaked out! He told them me and Jenny — Jenny and I — were going to make them whatever kind of sundae they wanted, with as many toppings as we could fit on. He made us wash our hands first, but that was okay. It only took a couple of minutes, and then everybody lined up for their homemade sundaes. Most of the kids wanted every single kind of ice cream and topping we had, but they wanted them in different orders, so then everybody could compare the designs before gobbling them up. Jenny and I had so much fun it didn't even matter that we didn't get to make our own until the end. Then we remembered to make one for Father Burke. He said it was brilliant. Jenny seemed to forget all about the Hells Angels.

☨

I was still stuffed when it came time for dinner that night, which was too bad because we all went out to eat at Ryan Duffy's. I love it there, so I ordered what I always get anyway, fish and chips, even though I could only eat half of it. The whole family was there, including Tom's girlfriend, Lexie, and also Father Burke. The sundaes didn't stop him from eating all his steak. Daddy was with us at first but he had to leave before dessert and write some kind of emergency paper for the Supreme Court, which he was supposed to finish at the office but didn't. He said goodbye to us and left.

Father Burke looked at Dominic in his high chair and then at Mummy and said: "Have you told him yet?" He meant Daddy.

He said it in a really quiet voice, and that made me pay attention. Tom and Lexie were talking in their regular voices, so I knew they weren't talking about anything secret.

"No. Anything to do with the baby puts him all out of gear. He won't want to hear about it."

"He can hardly miss it once things heat up."

"I'll deal with Monty when I have to, not a moment sooner."

"Mother of God," Father Burke muttered. Then he put his hand up, and the waiter came over. "Another Irish here. MacNeil?"

"Nothing for me, thanks."

The waiter brought the Irish, which is a nickname for a kind of booze. They say it's even stronger than beer.

"Do you really need that, Brennan?" Mum said to him.

"Do I *hhwattt?*" That's what it sounded like, as if 'what' had all kinds of extra letters in it. He looked at Mummy as if she had said something crazy.

"Do you need another glass of whiskey? Do you *need* to drink?"

"I enjoy a drink, MacNeil, I don't need it."

"Are you sure you know the difference?"

"What are you on about? You've managed to skate away from the topic of most importance here, custody of little Dominic, which you should be dealing with, and instead you're giving out to me about my drinking!"

They were talking even more quietly now. Tommy and Lexie didn't seem to hear them, but I did.

You would think Father Burke would say to Mum: "It's none of your business!" But he always tells them what to do, like telling Daddy he should sell his house and move back in with us. And they gave up telling him it's none of *his* business because he just laughs, or says he was put on the earth to see that God's will is done. So I guess he figured it was his turn to be told what to do.

She was still going on about it. "I've been concerned about you for a long time, Brennan. You drink too much."

"Amn't I a big strappin' lad who can hold his drink? The amount I sip may be 'too much' for the faint of heart and the delicate of stomach, but it is not too much for me."

"I beg to differ."

"What else is new? At some point in your life you've differed from every other member of the human race and if you had the time, you'd make a point of telling every one of them face to face exactly why they are poor, benighted, misguided eejits, and you and you alone are one hundred percent correct."

"So you don't think your drinking is a problem?"

"Of course it isn't! What's got into you?"

"Prove it. Don't drink it." She looked at his glass.

"Are you daft? Leave a glass of Jameson sitting there, unconsumed? Think of, well, think of all the labour that went into perfecting that glass of whiskey. Distillery workers dedicated to their craft, spending hours . . ."

"Spare me the labour theory of value, Father Marx. Though now that you mention it, I should drink it myself in solidarity with the workers. And of course this way it won't be a temptation in front of you for the rest of the night."

"Jaysus Murphy, now there's a new twist on cadgin' a drink. Tell someone he's a drunk, then take the jar away from him, and down it and get rat-arsed yourself."

"I can hardly get rat-arsed on the wee drop you left in the glass, Brennan. Give it here. Prove to me and to yourself that you don't need the stuff. Go without it for a couple of weeks. See how you do."

"I'll do fine."

"Glad to hear it." And she took his glass, drank the rest of the whiskey, choked, picked up her glass of water and gulped it. Mum can't drink very much. Which is probably a good thing. Then she turned to me and Tom and Lexie and asked if we'd like to see the dessert menu. There's something people say about questions like that, something about the pope and bears pooping in the woods, or being Catholic, I don't know what it is, but it means "duh, that's obvious!"

Father Burke lit up a cigarette and blew the smoke up towards the ceiling. I saw Mum turn around as if she was going to growl at him about that too, but she decided not to.

I had a lot of work to do with the dictionary after that night out, finding "custody" and other words, so I was up really late sneaking the story into my diary. I was very sleepy the next day but I had to act as if I wasn't.

(Monty)

Tuesday was the night I could claim, with justification, to be a choirboy. I was a member of the St. Bernadette's Choir of Men and Boys, directed by Father Burke. We sang magnificent traditional sacred music, then customarily observed another sacred tradition: we went to the Midtown Tavern. Dave arrived with two draft as soon as we sat down.

"Em, none for me, thanks, Dave," Brennan said.

"Sure." Dave laughed and put the glasses on the table.

"Really, I'm not having any tonight."

"Are you okay, Brennan? Are you under doctor's orders or something?"

"No. Well, yes, in a way."

Dave looked at me as if I could explain Brennan's aberrant behaviour. I couldn't. I just shrugged and told Dave to leave both draft for me.

"So, what would you like then, Brennan?"

"Just bring me a . . ." He stopped. Must have drawn a blank. "What else do you have?"

"Pop, juice, water . . ."

"A ginger ale! That would be just the thing."

"Would you like a little umbrella in the glass, and a twist of —"

"You bring me a little umbrella, David, and then you can shove it up your arse so far it'll choke the breath out of ya, and ya won't be able to gasp out your Act of Contrition before dying unforgiven and unmourned."

"Got it. Back in a sec."

After Dave had gone and returned with the ginger ale, ungirlified, I said to Brennan: "What's this all about?"

"Nothing. Why should it be about something?"

"Are you sick?"

"What kind of a world are we living in, when a man orders something different one night of his life, and everyone blathers on and on about it?"

"All right, all right. It just seems unusual, that's all. You here in the Midtown, without —"

"Have you nothing else to converse about, Montague?"

"I'll come up with something."

"Maybe it's time you thought about adoption."

"Whoa! Where did that come from? If you've gone off the sauce to clear your head, it's not working for you! Adoption is for guys who have a wife, but no children. I have children, but no wife. Remember?"

"I'm talking about young Dominic."

"I'm going to pretend I didn't hear you."

"That child needs a father."

I looked at him. There was a whole world of things I could say in response to that, but I wasn't going to give voice to any of them. That did not mean I was unmindful of the little boy growing up — so far — without a father in his life. The truth was that I was seriously concerned about it, about Dominic, but I could not bring myself to get into it with Brennan. Or, God knows, with Maura. All I said was: "Next topic."

We eventually got on to the subject of travel, and reminisced about the road trip we had taken together to Italy. Burke suggested it was time to think about Ireland as our next destination, so we made some half-arsed plans for that. I mused about what the ginger ale would be like over there, and got a damning look in return.

(Normie)

We had concert practice on Wednesday. We were going to be on cable TV because our bit was part of a whole night of concerts to raise money to help the poor. The grown-ups' choir school was going to sing a couple of pieces, too. And Father Burke was doing one himself. He was standing at the front of the room with sheets of music, trying to decide between two songs. One was an Irish song called "Macushla," which I liked. But the other one I liked even better, "La Rondine." It's about a little bird flying away. It has a really nice tune and there are words in it that sound like Mummy and Daddy's name: Monty and Maura. Well, it's actually *monti e mare*, mountains and sea, in the song but it almost sounds like their names. I told him to sing that one. "For you, *mia piccina* — that means 'little one' — I'll sing 'La Rondine.'" Other school choirs were going to be in the show but they weren't as good as us. It's not their fault, though; we are a *choir school* so there would be something wrong, and Father Burke would kill us, if we weren't the best.

We practised "God So Loved the World," by a guy called Stainer, and "O Vos Omnes," by Croce, over and over again. Monsignor O'Flaherty came by to hear us, and said we sounded like the heavenly host of angels. He is so nice! He's the boss of the priests but he's never bossy. He went up to Father Burke after we finished singing.

"Brennan! Could you find it in your heart to say the morning Mass for me tomorrow? Mrs. O'Dell is going into surgery in the morning. Doesn't look good for her at all, God bless her. They found a shadow on her —"

"No need to go into the details, Michael. I'll be happy to say your Mass."

"Thank you, my son. You won't find the wine too rich for your blood, now, will you?"

"Em, no, Mike, I'm pretty well accustomed to it now, after a quarter of a century celebrating the Eucharist."

"Oh, I just thought you might have become a little sensitive to alcoholic beverages! I notice you didn't have your customary nightcap the last couple of evenings when you got in. Not that there's anything —"

"Blessed St. Gobnait! Can a man not change his habits and be left in peace for it?"

Monsignor looked up at him. "Are you feeling all right?"

"I'm feeling no worse than I always do. And no better either!"

"Well, I'll leave you . . ."

"Good!"

See? If Monsignor was bossy he'd boss Father Burke around, but he just laughed and went on his way.

Then the after-school music kids started arriving. There was one little girl who was really cute. Laurie. She had red hair like mine. She looked at me, and I knew she liked me helping her, so I went over to her.

I had just sat down beside Laurie, and started teaching her how to sight-read *do-re-mi*, when I heard somebody bang the door open and come barging in. "We gotta hide in here!" I looked up and saw two of Jenny and Laurence's big brothers talking to Laurence. Their names were Connor and Derek.

Laurence said: "How come you're hiding?"

"They're after us again!" Derek said. "I think they followed us from school."

"They better not come in here!"

"Go look out the window." Derek gave Laurence a little push. "They probably won't recognize your face."

"How do you know?"

"Never mind. We'll just wait. Maybe they'll go away."

"What seems to be the trouble here, lads?" That was Father Burke. He went over to where they were standing.

"Nothing, Father," Connor answered.

"Laurence's brothers, would you be?"

"I'm Connor and this is Derek. We came to see Jenny and Laurence."

"And somebody was bothering you on the way?"

"Just these guys who, well, I don't know. It's okay."

"What is it?"

Father Burke just stood there looking at them. He's used to making kids tell the truth. The two brothers shuffled their feet and looked at each other, then Connor said: "They followed us before."

"Do you know who they are?"

"No. We don't know them at all."

"Have they said anything to you?"

Connor looked at Derek and then back at Father Burke. "No, I don't think so. I don't remember."

You could tell Father didn't believe them, but he didn't say anything. He walked over to the door and went out. By this time Jenny was with the boys, and they all kind of huddled together. Father Burke came back in and said there wasn't anybody out there.

"But it was true, Father! They were there," Connor said.

"I know. How are you planning to get home today?"

They all looked at each other. "We're going to walk. When Laurence and Jenny are finished."

"Well, why don't you treat yourself to some — what's over there today? — banana bread and mango juice, and listen to your brother and sister play a couple of tunes. Then I'll give you a ride home."

"All of us?"

"I'll not be leaving anyone behind."

So they stayed and had something to eat, and heard some music. Then all the parents came and picked up their kids. Daddy came to get me, so we went out with Father Burke and the Delaneys. He told Daddy he was driving them home, and he gave Daddy a kind of look that said: *There's something going on here.* But Daddy didn't ask. Instead he said: "How many shoulder belts do you have in your car, Brennan?"

"Em, four."

"And there are five of you getting in the car."

"Right. I've never had more than four people before . . ."

"And you're not going to now. Who wants to come with me and Normie?"

"I do!" Jenny said.

Daddy knows all the bad things that happen to people, like getting in accidents without seat belts on and getting murdered. And he goes to court for the very people who killed someone or let them in the car without their seat belts. I wouldn't want to do his job.

"So you've got some more family members in the Four-Four Time program, eh, Jenny?" Daddy asked.

"No, those are just my brothers being chased by somebody."

"Who's chasing them?"

"I don't know. Bad guys."

"Kids or grown-ups?"

"Big kids."

"Why are they after your brothers?"

"Nobody knows!"

Chapter 7

(Normie)

Our baby was sick that night, and he was so bad Mum had to rush him to the hospital! He could hardly breathe. She stayed overnight at the IWK — that's the name of the children's hospital, and we're lucky it's not very far from our house. Tom got me up on time for school, and made breakfast for us both. When I got to school, I saw Father Burke with two priests carrying suitcases. They sounded like him with even more of an accent in their voice, so they must have been from Ireland, and all three of them were laughing. I ruined it for them. I couldn't help it. I blurted out that Dominic was in the hospital. Father Burke had a big smile on his face but it disappeared in one second, and he looked shocked. He told the visitors that he would get Michael — that's Monsignor O'Flaherty — to show them around the church and school, because he had to leave. I went into my classroom then, and I figured he took off and went to the hospital. He really cares about the baby, and all of us. I told Mrs. Kavanagh in class about the baby, and she got the whole class to say a prayer for him.

And the praying worked, or maybe Dominic just got better

enough to leave the hospital, because he was home when I got back from school in the afternoon. But he was still really sick, and stuff kept spewing out of his nose. He also had a little cough, which sounded cute, but you knew it was painful and he was upset. I kept wiping his nose, gently, with a Kleenex, and putting a cold face cloth on his forehead. There wasn't much else we could do. So, after supper, Mum told me to go upstairs and write the story I was supposed to have passed in at school the day before. I went to my room and got my scribbler and pencil, and tried to figure out what kind of a story to write. It was supposed to be about a bird, but I didn't feel like doing that, so I just kind of sat there. I'd rather write about a cat, or a little kid. Maybe a cat story with a bird in it, and the bird gets eaten early in the story and then I could write the rest of it about the kitty. I was just getting it figured out when I heard the doorbell, so I went to the front window to see who it was. Father Burke, with a bunch of books under his arm. He was probably on his way to teach a night class. I wanted to go to my listening post, but that made me feel guilty. About listening, and about not getting my story done after I promised Mum I would do it. So I trudged back to my room and got to work.

But then I couldn't help it; I got curious, and crept out to the register to hear if there was anything new. They were talking about little things, and about getting together with Daddy for dinner later on in the week. I was just about to get back to work when I heard the name Giacomo. I didn't understand everything they said but it was like this:

"He wants me to sign this, acknowledging that he's Dominic's father. Then we can work out an arrangement. The arrangement they have in mind is shared custody, six months with me, six months with him and his family in Italy. That can't happen!"

"We won't let it happen."

"You don't know his family."

"Do you?"

"No, but I've certainly had an earful about them from Giacomo. He is their only son. Now they've found out about Dominic, who they believe is their grandson and the only one they have. They are a very powerful family in Panzano, in the Chianti region, and they have a winemaking business that has been passed down along the line of first-born sons for generations. You can be sure they're determined.

They'd be the ones bankrolling the lawyer and his upcoming trip to Nova Scotia. So here's the document they want me to sign, acknowledging that Giacomo is the father. I'd rather get up before the judge and claim that all I can remember about the time of Dominic's conception is that I was entertaining the entire NATO fleet!"

"I wouldn't recommend that."

"Why not?"

"Because you weren't entertaining the fleet or any part of it."

"How do you know?"

"You're not a little tart —" (Little tart? That's what he said!) "— and I wouldn't like to see you stoop to portraying yourself as one."

"All right, all right, Father. Thy will be done."

"That's the spirit. So, have you contacted your lawyer?"

"I've tried. I left a message, but she hasn't returned my call yet."

"Get someone else, then."

"I don't want anyone else. I want Val Tanner."

"Surely there are other lawyers you can call upon."

"Let me tell you a story, Brennan. A father goes into a restaurant with his little boy. He gives the boy three nickels to play with, to keep him occupied. Suddenly, the boy starts choking, turning blue in the face. The dad realizes the kid has swallowed the nickels, and he starts slapping him on the back. The boy coughs up two of the coins, but keeps choking. The father is panicking, calling for help. An attractive woman in a business suit is at a nearby table reading a newspaper and sipping a cup of coffee. She looks up, puts down her coffee, neatly folds her paper and places it on the table, gets up and makes her way, in no hurry, across the restaurant.

"Reaching the boy, she gently pulls down his pants, takes hold of his testicles —" (It was Mum telling this, not me!) "— and starts to squeeze, gently at first and then more firmly. After a few seconds of this, the boy has a violent convulsion and coughs up the last nickel, which the woman deftly catches in her free hand. She releases her grip on the boy, hands the nickel to the father and walks back to her seat without a word.

"The father rushes over, thanks her, and says: 'I've never seen anything like that before. Are you a doctor?'

"'No,' she answers. 'Divorce lawyer.'"

"That story is about . . ."

"Val Tanner."

"I get it. So call her again."

"I will. I don't want to bug her at home."

"Bug her at home. Just get her on the phone long enough to see if she's going to take your case."

I heard Mummy make a phone call, then say she was sorry and hoped the person would be feeling better soon.

"Oh, Val, no! There's no need of that. I'll find somebody. You get some rest. Well, if you're sure, thank you very, very much." Then she hung up.

"Val is off sick. If she says she's sick, that means she's flat on her back. But now she's up worrying about this! Said she's going to call someone else for me. Told me to stand by. Normie!"

Uh-oh. I got up and tiptoed into my room, then stomped out again. "Did you call me, Mum? I couldn't really hear you."

"Yes, sweetheart. How's that story coming along?"

"Good."

"Got it done?"

"Almost. Or kind of."

"Do you have any other homework?"

"Not really."

"Get it done, so you won't be late going to bed!"

"Okay."

So I went into my room and worked on the story. I made up a really sweet striped kitty who lived secretly in our backyard, and a really mean bird with dirty, raggedy feathers, who pecked at other birds and animals. My kitty ate him and spit him out, then went on to have all kinds of adventures. I was nearly done when the phone rang. Out I went to the spy post.

Mum was saying to the person on the phone: "Well! I knew Val was working above and beyond the call of duty, but I didn't expect her to bring in the big, um — big kahuna, right! I'm sure you have enough on your plate without another legal dispute . . . I really appreciate it, as you can imagine. Yes, I have the agreement here. The baby is sick, so I won't bring it over to you tonight, but . . . No! Don't do that! Okay. See you in ten."

She hung up, and said to Father Burke: "You'll never guess who's on his way over here."

"My guess would be another bollocks-squeezing barrister, recommended by Val Tanner."

"Not just a barrister. Val's senior partner. Who is . . . Beau Delaney!"

"What? He's still working?"

"Of course he is. Under the radar. Val called and told him about my panicked call to her, and he's offered to handle it for me himself."

"Well! Is he allowed to do this?"

"I don't know what his arrangements are. You'd have to ask Monty. But don't! Whatever the case, Beau wants to help behind the scenes."

"Never a dull moment in this place."

"I could use a dull moment. Anyway, I told him I couldn't bring the document over to him tonight."

"I could drop it off."

"No need. As I say, he's coming over. You can get going, Brennan. I know you have a class to teach."

"I've got some time yet. I think I'll stick around."

"How come? You think Delaney's going to toss me down the stairs?" She said it like a joke, but Father Burke didn't make a joke back at her.

So Mr. Delaney came over to our house. I went down the stairs and saw him give Mummy a big hug, and she nearly disappeared. She's not a little tiny person but he's a lot bigger.

"Beau, you didn't have to do this. I know there are other things on your mind these days, including, but not limited to, your own ten kids! This isn't a breach of your bail conditions, is it?"

"No, they didn't think to include my lawyer's spouse on the list of forbidden contacts!"

He and Father Burke said hi to each other. Mr. Delaney saw me then and came over and put his hand on my curls, and said: "How are you this evening, Miss Normie?"

"Fine, thank you, Mr. Delaney."

"Good. Jenny and Laurence really like the Four-Four Time program, so thanks for getting them into it."

"You're welcome. Is it true they made a movie about you?"

"It's true, they did, but they wouldn't let me star in it! Guess they figured I'd chew the scenery if I played myself."

"That's not very nice of them. You wouldn't chew up all the scenery!"

"No, that just means I'd ham it up too much. And I would!"

"Still, that's pretty cool."

"Yeah, it was fun. So, where's your baby brother?"

I blurted out: "Do you have to see him?" Then I realized I was rude because Mr. Delaney looked as if I'd said something mean. It was only for a second but I could tell his feelings were hurt. As if I thought he really was a killer. So I said: "He's sick. I wouldn't want you to catch something."

"Oh, well, thank you, Normie. But don't worry. I'll make sure I don't pick up any germs."

"Okay. I'll go get him."

Dominic was asleep and there was crusty stuff around his nose, so I wiped it gently without waking him up. I lifted him from his crib and carried him out to meet Mr. Delaney.

"Isn't he a sweet little fellow!" He reached out and took the baby from me. He held him in one arm and kept looking at him. Dominic seemed even tinier than usual, compared to this great big lawyer. He woke up and stared at Mr. Delaney for a few minutes, then fell back asleep. "All that black hair! And the dark, dark eyes. Definitely got a Mediterranean look going on there."

"Whose side are you on, Beau?"

"Yours, Maura, never fear! I'll have the judge convinced the child is a Swede before I'm finished."

"Oh, God, please don't talk about judges. We can't let it go that far!"

"Don't worry, my love, it won't go that far."

He looked over at Father Burke, then back at Mum, and said: "So, got any black-Irish relations we can trot out in front of the court? Old Grandpa Dominic-*dubh*, black Dominic, they called him back in the old country. That kind of thing?"

"Red- and brown-haired Scots is all I have."

"Great-grandma has black eyes, Mum."

"That's all we need, old Morag involved in this."

"Why do you say that?" he asked her.

"She's my grandmother. She has the sight. Very spooky."

"Hmm. Maybe we'll bring her in to frighten the intruder away."

"We'd better come up with another plan."

"Oh, we will. Trust me."

Mr. Delaney gave Dominic back to me, and said: "All right, let's get to work."

"Can I get you anything, Beau? Drink? Snack?"

"Nothing, thanks, Maura. Let's have a seat and go over our options."

Mummy turned to me and said: "Homework and bed, Normie, in that order. I'll be up to tuck you in. Off you go."

So I gave Dominic to her, said good night to them, and went upstairs. I grabbed my books and sat down at the register to listen. But they must have stayed in the living room because I couldn't hear them. I finished my story instead, and then did a math page I had almost forgotten about, wrote down all the important events of the day in my diary, and then called Mummy to come up and tuck me in.

(Monty)

"Is there a Matthew anywhere in the Delaney files?" That was Maura, who called me at the office Friday morning.

"What do you mean?"

"Was there a client by that name, or a victim of one of his clients?"

"I don't know. It's a popular name. Why?"

"Normie was muttering that name over and over as she was falling asleep last night. She was in the den with me. I was watching the news and trying to get her up off the chesterfield and into her bed. She was bundled up in the quilt, her eyes were closing, and she kept saying: 'Matthew. It's Matthew.' I tried to find out what she meant but she drifted off. I asked her the next morning who Matthew was. Was it the name of a boy at school or the brother of a friend?"

"She said there are a couple of Matthews at school but she hardly knows them. Why was I asking? I told her she had said the name in her sleep. She just gave me a blank look. Didn't remember a thing."

"Well, it doesn't strike a chord with me. Why did you think it had something to do with Delaney?"

My wife didn't answer right away. Eventually, she said: "It's just that she looked upset, fretful, when she was saying the name. She looked the way she does when she has the spells, or the nightmares, whatever they are."

"I'll look through my file. But I hope I don't find anything because I won't want to deal with it! Remember, Normie's experiences may have nothing to do with Delaney. It may be something else altogether bothering Normie. Is there something else, Maura?"

Maura was silent again for a long moment, then said: "Giacomo's been around."

Him again.

"But I can deal with him," she asserted.

"You can't expect her to understand that. Kids take things to heart."

"I realize that, Monty, but she's seeing something else altogether. A child being mistreated. Giacomo may be a nuisance, but he's not somebody who should be taken off the streets because he's a danger to children. So I'll consult those clippings again."

"I hope you're right." She probably was. "And we can forget all about your Italian interlude."

Big mistake. Her silence would be short-lived, and I knew I was in for it.

"Speaking of Italian interludes, Collins, it strikes me that you and Father Burke have been a little evasive on the subject of the road trip you boys took to Italy. Even the most benign questions are met by bland answers that convey very little by way of information, yet speak volumes to those of us who weren't born yesterday. What did you do? Nothing, apparently. Who did you meet? Sister Kitty Curran and Father What's-his-name at the Vatican, and Brother So-and-so at a monastery. Am I to believe you did nothing but consort with known nuns, priests, and monks when you were in the land of wine, women, and song, and thus maintained the decorum of nuns, priests, and monks yourselves? Would you care to answer that, Collins?"

Anything I said would be, well, evasive, so I evaded her questions by claiming the sudden appearance of a penniless widow who was being evicted from her apartment and needed my kind assistance.

"Get up and walk into the office next to yours, and you'll find the guy evicting her." A not entirely undeserved dig at Stratton Sommers, the corporate law firm that employed me. "I'll speak to you later, Collins. Good day."

She did speak to me later. She called and informed me that there was no reference to a Matthew in her news clippings about Delaney. That did not mean he had never had dealings with a Matthew. If his client was seventeen years old or under, his name would not be made public. Similarly if, say, a child was a victim of a sexual crime, the name would not be revealed. And, of course, the news clippings represented only a small sample of Beau Delaney's cases over the years. Most cases never made the news.

As promised, I looked through all the material I had on Delaney. Chances were that, over a long career like Delaney's, he would have had dealings with one or more Matthews but, if so, they were not noted in the papers I had.

So if the name Matthew was a clue to Normie's problems, it was a clue that led us nowhere.

(Normie)

I was allowed to invite Kim over after school on Monday, so we skipped Four-Four Time, which is okay to do, and went to my house instead. When we got home, Father Burke was there in the living room reading a book. Kim gawked at him and didn't know what to say.

"Afternoon, Kim. Normie."

"Hi, Father," I said, and nudged Kim with my elbow.

"Hi," she said then.

"Your mum had to go out and she didn't want to take the baby, so she asked me to stay with him. He's still got a bit of a fever. She'll be getting him some new medicine before she comes home."

"You mean you're babysitting, Father?" Kim said. "How do you know what to do?" Then she thought maybe she shouldn't have said that, and her face turned pink.

"I'm an old hand, Kim. I have five brothers and sisters, you know. Four are younger than I am."

"But not now," she said. "They're probably grown up by now, right?"

"They are. But I remember. I just gave him a cool bath, and he's feeling better."

Me and Kim went out to the kitchen, and I opened the fridge to see if we had any chocolate milk. There was juice. Beer. Cans of ginger ale! We hardly ever had that.

"Father, do you want . . ." Whoops. You're supposed to say "would you like" and you never say "another." These are manners I've been taught. "Would you like a can of ginger ale?"

"Sure, Normie. That would be grand."

"Do I have to . . . would you like me to pour it in a glass, or is the can okay?"

"The can's fine." So I brought it to him. "Thanks, little one."

I went back to the fridge and moved some stuff around, and found the chocolate milk. I poured a glass for me and one for Kim.

Kim still couldn't believe it, about Father Burke. "He looks like someone normal, like somebody's dad. How come he doesn't have his priest uniform on?"

"Because he's not at work, Kim. He always dresses like this when he comes over here. Or a lot of the times anyway."

"He doesn't seem as scary here as he does at school. He comes over here a lot?"

"Sure. He's a friend of the family."

She looked around to make sure he hadn't crept up on us. "Do you think he changed the baby's diaper?!"

"Probably."

"No! Father Burke is always so clean!"

"Well, clean people have to change diapers, too, you know. And he gave Dominic a bath, so he would have washed his hands at the same time."

The doorbell rang then, and I went to answer it. It was Mr. Delaney with a briefcase.

"Hi, Normie. Is your mum home?" I shook my head. "Oh, okay. Could you ask her to call me when she gets in? Are you here alone?"

"No."

"Someone's looking after you?"

"Father Burke's here."

By that time, Father Burke had come to the door too. "Afternoon, Beau."

"Brennan! They've got you on babysitting detail, have they?"

"Just one of the many services I provide." He lowered his voice then, and said: "She wants an adult here with the baby while all this is going on, in case Giacomo turns up. And the little fellow is still sick, so . . ."

"Right. Is he doing any better?"

"He is. Why don't you step in? Herself won't be long, I'm thinking."

"Great. I will."

"There's beer in the fridge."

"It's kind of early in the day for me to be thinking of beer. Are you having one? Oh, you're a ginger ale man, I see."

"Well, not always, Beau. I tend to take a drop of whiskey or a pint of Guinness now and again. But these days, yes, I'm on the ginger ale."

"Problem?"

"Not at all, though I have been wrongfully accused of being a bit of a heavy drinker. So, here's the proof I'm not."

I was back in the kitchen by then, and I found some cookies. They came from a bakery so they were good and not all burnt on the bottom.

"Mr. Delaney comes here too, Normie?" Kim asked.

"Not usually."

"Oh."

Dominic started to cry then. I didn't want to leave the cookies, not that Kim would hog them all, but I wanted to just stay and eat cookies instead of maybe catching germs from a sick baby. Father Burke called out to say he'd get him. Must have read my mind.

I could hear the baby giggling when Father Burke carried him out to the living room.

"Well, you've got a cheerful little guy there, Brennan," Mr. Delaney said. "He's obviously glad to see you!"

"Mmm."

"Handsome little devil. Dark hair, dark eyes. Bit like you, Father!"

Father Burke didn't say anything.

Mr. Delaney asked: "He's how old now?"

"He'll be eight months old next week."

"And where were you, Brennan Burke, on the night in question seventeen months ago?"

Father Burke didn't answer.

"Let the record show that the witness is unresponsive. Father Burke, earlier in these proceedings you admitted that you have been accused — by someone — of heavy drinking, is that correct?"

"Have you no other way to amuse yourself, Mr. Delaney?"

"I'll ask the questions here, Father. Have you ever, on any occasion, consumed so much Irish whiskey that you 'blanked out,' to use a layman's term, and were unable to remember what you did whilst under the influence of said alcohol? Perhaps my question was too general. I'll rephrase it. On a night seventeen months ago, is it possible that you . . ."

Then Mr. Delaney changed from his lawyer voice to a surprised voice. "You *have* thought about this, haven't you, Brennan? You see this little dark-eyed, black-haired baby and you wonder if you got really blitzed one night, and you and Maura . . . I can see it in your face!"

"Will you get off of that?"

"You're the solution to the problem! Tell it to the judge!"

"I think not."

Kim said something and interrupted my listening. But I didn't get what they meant anyway. Was Father Burke drinking whiskey seventeen months ago? He probably was, but so what? He's never drunk; he just drinks, and not all the time. Never at the church or school. Obviously.

Then I heard Father Burke say: "Behave yourself, Delaney. Here she comes now."

"Who?"

"The MacNeil."

"I didn't hear anything."

"It's her car."

"You know the sound of her car?"

"I hear everything, Beau. I'm a musician. Every sound registers. It can be heaven; it can be hell."

Mum came in then, and chased me and Kim outdoors to play.

After Kim's dad came to get her I peeked inside, and Mr. Delaney was gone. Mum and Father Burke were talking in the kitchen. I went into the back porch and stood there for a few minutes.

"I don't like this, Maura. You know that."

"I just don't want the complication of Monty in this, Brennan."

"How would Monty be a complication?"

"His feelings would be complicated, for one thing."

"Oh?"

"He'd want what's best for me and the children, on the one hand —"

"First and foremost, not just on the one hand."

"But on the other hand, and quite understandably, he might —"

"If you're going to suggest that Monty would want to see you lose your child to a man who lives on other side of the Atlantic Ocean, I don't want to hear another word out of you."

"I'm not saying he would consciously wish it, or even admit it to himself . . ."

"Go on out of that. You said his feelings were one thing. What's the next thing?"

"I don't want him getting involved in it, legally or personally. I don't want him in a pissing match with Giacomo."

"All of that seems preferable to deliberately keeping him in the dark about something so fundamental in your life, and in the lives of Normie and Tom."

"Stop worrying about it, Brennan. Monty wouldn't want to know. If I thought otherwise, I'd be the first to tell him. This wouldn't contribute to his peace of mind."

"Why should you make that decision on his behalf? I feel like a double agent helping you mislead him!"

"Look, Brennan. It's not as if we're deceiving him about the facts. He knows there's a baby. He doesn't think it was the Holy Spirit; ergo, there must have been a man. He knows there's a guy called Giacomo."

"I hear you, but that doesn't change things. I don't like it."

I went into the kitchen then, and Father Burke left, and Mum asked me what I wanted for supper. I said spaghetti with pink sauce, so she made that for us. She didn't look very happy. She may have been keeping secrets from Daddy, but she wasn't thinking *Nyah, nyah, nyah, I have a good secret from him!* She really thought he would be upset if he heard all the bad news about Dominic and Giacomo so, really, she was being nice by keeping Daddy in the dark about it.

(Monty)

Beau Delaney laid much of the blame for the murder charge on Sergeant Chuck Morash of the Halifax Police Department. I called and spoke to Morash, and learned that he was a witness in a trial taking place in the Nova Scotia Supreme Court on Tuesday. I arranged to meet him for coffee at Perk's on Lower Water Street in the morning before court got underway. He wasn't there when I arrived, so I stood outside and watched the outline of a navy frigate making its way out of port in a dense, grey Halifax fog. The ship was barely visible, but then, it was almost impossible to see the city of Dartmouth across the harbour.

"Monty?"

I turned, and saw a short, powerfully built dark-haired man approaching me with his hand extended. I realized I had seen him around but we had never met.

"Sergeant Morash?"

"Chuck."

We shook hands and went inside, where we ordered coffee and pastries, and sat down at a table.

"I guess I can figure out what you want to talk to me about," Morash said. "They didn't make me a sergeant for nothing!"

"You're on to me, no question. Chuck, when you arrived at the Delaney house on the night of Peggy's death, what made you think this was a murder and not an accident?"

"She was lying at the foot of the stairs exactly as she landed, in my estimation. Nobody had moved her."

"And this told you what?"

"If I came home and found my wife lying at the bottom of the stairs and she wasn't yet stiff with rigor mortis and I thought it was an accident, I'm pretty sure my first reaction would be to touch her, hold her, shake her, look underneath her . . . something! I'm not speaking as an investigator now, but as a husband. I wouldn't just back off and leave her there, as if I had come upon — or created! —

a crime scene. That's what did it for me."

Yes, I could see that. But I had no intention of saying so.

"You knew who Delaney was, of course."

"Certainly."

"Had you had any dealings with him before this?"

"Just the usual, giving evidence against his clients in court."

"How did that go for you?"

"What do you mean?"

"Did Delaney tend to give you a grilling on the stand?"

"Sometimes, sure. Part of the job. His job to give it, my job to suck it up."

"How did you do at sucking it up?"

"If you're thinking I had it in for your client, Monty, you're wrong. No cop, no witness, likes to have his competence and his credibility attacked in court but, as I say, it comes with the territory. I wouldn't hold a grudge over something like that, and I certainly wouldn't charge a man with murder because he had caused me some embarrassing moments on the witness stand! We can't function like that as police officers."

I took a bite of my cinnamon bun and a sip of coffee, and asked Morash: "What do you think of Delaney?"

His answer surprised me: "Needy."

I had been expecting "good lawyer, too bad he's on the wrong side" or "soft on crime" or "aggressive" or "relentless." Anything but "needy."

"Why do you say that?"

"He does a spectacular job for his clients. Nobody would dispute that. And I don't question his dedication. But hasn't it ever struck you that he needs the fame, the pats on the back, the adulation? That movie, well, that would go to anybody's head. Especially with a title like *Righteous Defender*. I know I'd be cock of the walk if the Jack of Hearts had played me in a film. But I think he thrives on that sort of thing to, well, an inordinate degree."

"Could it be that he attracts all that attention and fame because he is so good at what he does, and that you're looking back and making an assumption that he needs it?"

"What drives him, though, Monty? What motivates him to take on this larger-than-life persona?"

"What's your background, Chuck?" I couldn't help but ask.

He laughed, and said: "I did my B.A. in psychology before joining the department, and I'm plugging away at my Masters at night."

"Yet you didn't use the term 'self-esteem' once in your little personality profile of my client!"

"Don't even go there, on the subject of self-esteem and Beau Delaney!"

"You think he's got it in spades?"

"No, as a matter of fact, I don't."

"Really!"

"I think he needs, and gets, a refill on a regular basis. I can't quite imagine what he'd be like if he didn't. This is a little thing, and you may laugh it off, but I'll tell you anyway. When I went back to the Delaney house with a warrant, after we had laid the murder charge, I was in his bedroom and saw all these shoes in his closet, lined up on a rack. Not so many pairs of shoes that you looked askance at them, but you noticed them for sure. I looked at them, and do you know what I found?"

I shook my head.

"Shoe lifts."

"Shoe lifts! The man is six and a half feet tall! They couldn't have been Delaney's shoes."

"They were. They are. These lifts add maybe an inch, inch and a half, of height."

Odd.

"What's the significance of that?" I asked.

"You tell me," he replied, and I felt as if I was on the analyst's couch.

"I'd rather not speculate," I said to him.

"Fair enough. I would speculate that he very much enjoys being the big man in town, physically and otherwise. I think it's possible that someone like Delaney may feel the need to be the top gun, the expert, in any situation. It's an impression I've formed over the years, seeing him in court or at official functions. I think maybe he's the type who would need to lord it over others, including perhaps his wife, and he might have lashed out if she confronted him or disagreed with him.

"But no, Monty, none of this went into my decision to lay the charge. I based it on what I saw at the scene. A woman who apparently sustained a fatal skull fracture by falling down a set of stairs.

Possible, sure, but how likely? And she fell backwards. If she had tripped, she would have fallen forward. She may have been able to use her arms to break her fall. And then there was Delaney's demeanour at the house. All he told us was that he wasn't there when it happened. He had come home from the Annapolis Valley just after twelve thirty. I found it curious that, well, he wasn't more curious about what happened to Peggy, how she could have fallen like that, how such a fall could have been fatal. He didn't wonder aloud whether somebody else had been with her. To me, Monty, it just didn't add up. And the fact that he lied about what time he came home — Harold Gorman saw him outside the house before eleven o'clock — tipped the scales against him."

To my dismay, I found his analysis compelling, and I did not look forward to trying to discredit him on the witness stand.

"I'll tell you this, Monty. Within the Crown's office, there was some unspoken but obvious *resistance* to taking this on, because it's Delaney . . ."

"No doubt, given the thinness of the case against him."

"But that soon changed to *determination* to take it on because it's Delaney. Equal justice for rich and poor, that kind of thing."

All I said was: "You don't have a motive." Not that he needed one.

Morash drained his coffee and put his cup on the table. "The motive may not have existed until the instant before she was killed."

(Normie)

Wednesday was April Fool's Day, and we had Elvis in our choir. He had thick, shiny black hair puffed up and pushed back, and a white jacket with shiny jewels on it. Father Burke looked at him, blinked, and looked again.

"Good of you to join us, Mr. Presley. You've been missing rehearsals. Where have you been?"

And Elvis answered in a deep voice: "I've been wherever there are true believers."

Father laughed and said: "Would you honour us with something from your repertoire?"

And Elvis did this kind of dance move, and sang something about crying in the chapel, and everybody cracked up, including Father Burke.

Guess who Elvis really was? Richard Robertson! He begged us all not to tell his mother, or she'd kill him.

I drew a picture of Elvis in my diary. But the rest of the day wasn't so funny. Father Burke was at our house when I got home from school, and he stayed with us until Mum got home. He didn't say it, but I knew why he was there. He and Mum were scared that Giacomo might come and steal the baby if it was just me and Tommy babysitting! So Tommy took the bus to Lexie's house, and Father Burke came to babysit. He checked on Dominic, and let him get down on the floor and crawl around, and he played with him for a while. Then he sat at the kitchen table and worked with a bunch of books and papers. Writing sermons maybe, or making notes for the courses he teaches. When Mum came in, she invited him to stay for supper, so he said yes and continued his work. I was at the dining room table, drawing a picture and colouring it. Father Burke looked over at me and smiled, and asked what I was drawing. It was a boat with a big yellow sail, and me steering it and Kim standing in the front with her yellow braids flying back in the wind. I told him I'd show it to him when it was all done.

Then Mr. Delaney arrived, and Mum answered the door.

"Evening, Beau."

"Evening, my dear. I've received the latest missive from Giacomo's counsel. There are some papers here in Italian. I understand you have a translator on hand."

"Yes, I do. He's right here."

So that was another reason Father Burke was there. He knows Italian, so he would tell them what the papers meant.

"Hello, Brennan."

"Beau. How are you?"

"Could be worse. Or so I keep telling myself. Have a look at this lengthy affidavit Giacomo and his lawyer have drawn up."

Father Burke took the papers and started to read them. I could tell by the look on his face that he didn't like what they said. He gave Mum a quick look and went back to the writing. Then he pushed the papers away.

"What's the matter, Brennan?"

"I don't want to be reading this, MacNeil."

"Why not? What is it?"

"Let's just say yer man Giacomo is a true romantic. He seems to remember, presumably with fondness, every time the two of you were together."

I looked at Mum, and I saw her face turn pink. She grabbed the papers off the table, and scrunched them up in her hands and then just stood there as if she didn't know what to do. She looked really upset. Giacomo must have been bragging about taking Mum out for romantic candlelight dinners, and sending her flowers. It ruins things if you do something nice for somebody and then brag about it. She looked around then, and caught me gawking in from the dining room table.

"Up to your room, young lady."

I heard a bit more on my way up the stairs. Father Burke said: "You're forever giving out to me about butting into your lives. Well, here's where I butt out. I'll help in every other way I can, but reading this personal blather by your boyfriend about you — I'm afraid not. Giacomo may not understand the words 'personal' and 'private,' but I do."

"I'm sorry, Brennan. I had no idea the little weasel would stoop to this."

"He's just making his case," Mr. Delaney said. "And it falls to us to unmake it. I'll hire a translator for this bit of —" He said "herodica"? or "airotica"? or something like that.

Whatever they said from then on, I missed, because I went into my room, and didn't dare go out to the listening post. I had to draw the parts of a flower for science class, and Mum knew about it. If I didn't get it done, she would ask what I had been doing instead.

I worked on my flower, and used all kinds of colours in the picture. Then I heard somebody go out the front door. I looked out and saw that it was Mum. So I went downstairs.

"Where did Mum go, Father?"

"She's gone to Lexie's to get Tom."

"Oh. Tom's been bugging Mum to let him buy his own car. He saw one in the paper for eight hundred dollars. And another one for three thousand."

"Well, he'd best hire a mechanic to give it a once-over."

"Yeah, I know. Nobody in our family knows anything about cars if something goes wrong."

"Tell me about it," Mr. Delaney said. "Peggy knew more about cars than I ever did. Now I'm hopeless."

"Tommy promised to learn," I told them.

Then I thought about something else. When Mr. Delaney said Peggy's name, that reminded me of how sad he must have been that she died. And how lonesome Jenny and Laurence and all the other kids were. And I remembered how worried Jenny was about their mum maybe committing a sin by yelling out "Hells Angels" and maybe not going to heaven. Mr. Delaney must have been worried about that, too, if Jenny had told him. I remembered Father Burke saying she wouldn't get in trouble if she talked about it with her dad. I decided to make him feel better. I wouldn't have the nerve to mention it if it was just me, but Father Burke was there and he could explain it.

"Well, I should get back upstairs and finish studying my catechism for school tomorrow." It wasn't really a lie, just because I was working on science. I still had to finish (and start) my catechism.

"Splendid," Mr. Delaney said. "What a dedicated crop of students you have at the choir school, Father Burke!"

"Thank you, Mr. Delaney. We do our best. If only the adult students at my schola were as dedicated."

"Yeah," I said, "I was reading about sins and stuff like that."

"Oh, I don't imagine you have too much to worry about there. Wouldn't you say, Father?"

"I'd like to agree with you, Mr. Delaney, but in fact she's a little divil entirely!"

"Is she? Appearances are deceiving! I would have thought she was one of God's holy angels."

I had to bring it up then or I'd never get it in! So I blurted out: "It's not a sin to say 'Hells Angels,' Mr. Delaney!"

He looked confused. "What do you mean, dear?"

"Jenny told me about Mrs. Delaney yelling 'Hells Angels' . . . one night . . . so we asked Father Burke and he said that wouldn't be a sin!"

Oh my God! Mr. Delaney looked at me as if he was watching a horror movie. As if I really was a devil! But I'm not! I just wanted to help. I was scared of him. Then he looked at Father Burke, and the expression on his face changed to being really mad.

But his voice was so quiet, he almost hissed when he said to Father: "What's this all about, Brennan?"

"Take it easy now, Beau. Your little one apparently overheard something her mother said one night at the house. The children had been learning about sin and redemption in catechism class, and that's how it came up. Jenny mentioned it to Normie, and they asked me. I reassured them. They never brought it up again." Father Burke put his arm around my shoulder and pulled me close to him.

Mr. Delaney said: "Jenny must have been having a nightmare. She has them regularly. I can't imagine my wife saying . . . anything about bikers. But I wouldn't know."

"Don't be troubling yourself about it, Beau. The children had the best intentions in the world. No need to upset Jenny by bringing it up with her now."

But Mr. Delaney didn't say okay. He seemed to be thinking about it, and forgetting we were in the room. He grabbed the papers he'd brought with him, turned around, and left without saying another word.

I started crying, and Father Burke pulled me onto his knee and held me. I could hardly talk, but I tried to say: "I don't want to get Jenny in trouble!" I was glad I didn't tell them the Hells Angels thing happened just before Mrs. Delaney died. That would make it even more serious, and Mr. Delaney might be even more angry.

"Don't you worry about a thing, darlin'," Father Burke said. "You were just trying to help, and Mr. Delaney will understand that once he thinks about it. If Jenny says anything, you come to me, just by yourself, and I'll take care of it for you."

"Really?"

"I promise."

"Are you going to tell Daddy that I got Mr. Delaney mad at me?"

He looked at me for a long time, as if he had to think about it. Then he said: "Don't worry, little one, your sinful secrets are safe with me!"

Then I kind of laughed.

That's when Mummy and Tom came in. "What's wrong, Normie?" She looked at me and then at Father Burke. "Were you down here listening to grown-up talk and getting yourself all upset?"

"I wasn't! I just told . . ." Uh-oh.

But Father Burke rescued me again. "I just explained to Normie that she has nothing to worry about at all, at all. She understands."

Chapter 8

(Normie)

"Daddy, do you know where there's a building that says 'Vince' on it?" I was at Daddy's house after school on Thursday.

"Vince?"

"Yeah. Or, wait . . ." I closed my eyes and tried to bring the picture back into my mind. "Vincent."

He looked at me for a while, then said: "Do you mean Mount St. Vincent, the big university we see up on the hill when we drive out the Bedford Highway?"

"The place where I played piano in the music festival?"

"Right."

"No, that's not it."

"Maybe you're thinking of the building on Windsor Street. St. Vincent's Guest House."

"Is that it?"

"Um, I don't know, sweetheart. Why are you asking about a building?"

"Because I saw one in my, you know, dreams."

"Would you recognize it, do you think, if you saw it?"

"I think so."

"All right. Let's go."

I was scared then. "We're going there?"

"You don't want to?"

"Not with all that scary stuff going on! They might do something to us!"

"Who, dolly?"

"Those people I saw, in the robes."

He was staring at me. "That vision you had, or that dream, about the people in the robes, and the . . . baby dying, did that happen at this Vincent place?"

I nodded my head. "And the other little kid screaming and crying." Daddy looked as if he was mixed up. But he said we were going. "Tell you what. We'll drive by in the car, have a quick look, and keep driving. Would that be all right?"

No, I didn't think so. But I didn't want to say it. Anyway, he took me by the hand and we walked to the car, and went for a drive. We drove around the Armdale Rodeo. That's what we call it, but it's really called the Armdale Rotary, for cars to go around. And then we were on Quinpool Road going towards downtown. We went past some stores and restaurants and the movie theatre. He turned and went up some street and then turned again later. Pretty soon we saw the sign for Windsor Street, and we turned again. He slowed the car down, but I just looked at my hands. I didn't want to see it.

"There's nobody around, Normie. Just look up, over to your right. Is that the building?"

I peeked over and looked at the place. It was a big, wide brick building, not very tall, and it had a round porch or something in front, with a white cross sticking up from it. There's no way it was the same building.

"That's not it! Not even close!"

Daddy looked as if he was glad.

"What is that place?" I asked him.

"It's a nursing home. For old folks."

"Well, it's not the place I dreamed about."

"What did the building look like in your dream?"

"It was made of bricks. But it wasn't a new building like the one we just saw."

"What colour were they, the bricks?"

"They were brick colour, Daddy!"

"Okay. Reddish brown, were they?"

"Duh! That's what colour bricks are."

"Right. How big was the place?"

"Kind of big. And more old-fashioned than this one. It had churchy-type windows."

"Why don't you draw a picture of the windows for me?"

"Okay." I always had a scribbler and a box of coloured pencils in the car, so I drew a picture of the building and shoved the paper at Daddy. He took a quick glance, then kept his eyes on the road. We were on Quinpool again, heading back to his house.

"Gothic windows, those are called."

"Oh."

"Was the place a church?"

"No! How could it be, if it said 'asylum' on it?"

"Asylum!"

Oh no, I thought. I went and blurted out that the sign said "asylum." Now he'd say something about mental patients, and get the idea all over again that I was crazy. I was stupid to mention it.

But he just said: "So this was a red-brick building with Gothic windows like the one you just drew, and it had the word 'asylum' on it?"

I had to admit it now. "Yeah."

"You have a really good memory, Normie."

Hmm. Yes, I do have a good memory. Maybe that means there's nothing wrong with you, if you have a good memory.

"And you said the name 'Vincent' was on it too, right?"

"Right."

"Well, I'll ask around. In the meantime, how about a drive out to Bedford for a chicken burger and a milkshake?"

"Really? Great!"

†

I hoped Daddy would forget all about the old building, the asylum, but he didn't. He and Mummy brought up the subject that night when we went to a movie and came home afterwards. And they went on about doctors and psychiatrists again. They tried not to sound mean but they kept telling me I needed "help" to get over my dreams and visions. Sometimes "help" is a bad word, like "going on the couch." They say that stuff in movies, and it means going to a psychiatrist. I thought I had made them believe I wasn't crazy; now it was happening all over again.

I got really upset and hollered at them: "You guys think I'm nuts! Well, guess what? You guys are nuts for not being able to see the kinds of things I see. It's your fault because you can't see it. All you know is what's in front of your eyes, when they're open, and you don't know anything else. But you make it sound like I'm loony! If you really loved me, you wouldn't think that!"

I ran upstairs to get away from them, and I slammed the door of my room, and shoved my chair up against it so they wouldn't be able to open it. But Daddy opened it anyway, and I yelled at him to go away and leave me alone. Finally, he left and went downstairs. I could just imagine the rotten things they were saying about me down there.

It took me a long time to fall asleep, I was so mad. The next morning, Daddy was there when I went down for breakfast. He must have snuck in early from his own house to catch me being crazy again. I would show him! I didn't even talk to him, or to Mum. They pretended to be really nice and they talked about the concert our school was having that night on TV. I just kept my mouth shut the whole time, till they dumped me off at school. Then I said: "I bet you're glad to get rid of me!"

They didn't even hear me. Or maybe they just didn't care.

I was still upset all through school that day, even though we spent most of the day practising for the concert and skipped all kinds of hard classes because of it, so it should have been one of the best days ever. How would you like it if your own parents thought you were crazy and maybe wanted to put you in a mental hospital? What if they put me in there, and some dangerous mental patient killed me? Mum and Dad would be sorry then! Or if I ran away, and they didn't know where I was. If they really loved me, they would be worried to death. It would serve them right.

We didn't have Four-Four Time after school that day because it was Friday, but Jenny came by anyway. She said she wanted to hang around with me and then go to the concert. Her aunt said it was okay. So we hung out in the music room, and played the pianos. She played the G and D major scales, practising what she had learned the day before. I wasn't in the mood for major scales. So I played the sad ones, the minor ones. When I finished them, Jenny came over. She looked sad too. "Daddy came for a visit last night, but he was mad at me."

"Because of the Hells Angels?" I blurted out, then wished I had shut up instead.

"I don't know why. He didn't say anything, just kept giving me weird looks. Like he wanted to say something but changed his mind."

"Oh, don't worry then."

"Why did you ask about the Hells Angels?"

"No reason," I said.

"You didn't tell anybody, did you?"

"No," I lied. Then I remembered: "But Father Burke knows! We asked him that time."

"Oh, yeah. I hope he didn't tell my dad."

"You never know!"

Then I said: "I'm mad at my parents."

"Why? What did they do?"

"They think I'm crazy. They may try to lock me up."

"No!"

"Yeah."

"Are they coming to your concert tonight?"

"I guess so. It would be too bad for them if I didn't sing in the concert. If I wasn't even there!"

"You mean you're going to hide?"

"Yeah, but more than that."

I thought of something, a plan. Jenny's mother had talked about the Hells Angels. And I always had a secret wish to see what a Hells Angel really looked like, close up and not just speeding by on a motorbike. How could you be good enough to want to call yourself an angel, but bad enough to say you belong in hell? Why would you brag about it by pasting that name on your jacket? Would you look good and evil at the same time? Well, now was my chance to find out!

I said to Jenny: "Let's do something that will make everyone appreciate us for how smart we are."

"Like what?"

"Let's solve the *Mystery of the Hells Angels*!"

"How can we do that?"

"I know where they live. I've been out for drives with Tom and Lexie. She's my brother's girlfriend. On the way to her place there's a big house with all these motorcycles outside it, and Tommy always slows down to gawk at them. And Lexie always teases him by singing this song about motorcycles, 'Born To Be Wild.' That place is the Hells Angels clubhouse, ever since their other place burnt down. Tommy told me. Let's go there, and find out if they had something to do with your mum and how she died!"

"But they won't tell us if they did. They'll kill us!"

"No they won't. Because we'll tell them our parents know where we are and if we don't show up at home, they'll know where to find us."

"They won't believe our parents let us go there!"

"Okay, we won't say that exactly. We'll say our parents let us go for a walk in that neighbourhood because our friend — no, our babysitter! — lives near there. It's not completely a lie because Lexie lives near there, and I would be allowed to go for a walk. And if they think our parents will be driving all around there looking for us, they'll be scared of getting caught if they do anything bad to us."

"I don't know . . . How are we going to ask them about Mum?"

"I'll think of something. Let's sneak out of here and get a taxi."

"A taxi!"

"I have some money. It's supposed to be a donation for the poor at the concert tonight, but I'll give them some later."

So when the teachers weren't looking, me and Jenny snuck out and started walking towards downtown. A couple of taxis came by and we waved at them, but they kept going. Then one circled around and came back.

"You looking for a cab, girls?"

"Yes, sir."

"Do your parents know where you are?"

"Yes, they want us to meet them. That's why we need a taxi. My dad broke his leg and can't drive. So he can't come pick us up."

"Oh yeah?"

"Yeah. Take us to St. Malachy's church."

Jenny looked at me as if I really was crazy, but I wasn't. Lexie was the choir director at her church, St. Malachy's, and she lived really close to it. So finally the driver let us in, and drove us away from downtown, out to where Lexie lives. When we got to St. Malachy's church, there was nobody around, and the taxi driver gave us a weird look.

"It's okay," I said. "Dad will be here."

"How's he going to get here, with that busted leg?"

"My mum is really big. He'll lean on her and they'll both hobble over here. It will take them a while."

"What are your names, girls?"

"I'm Cindy and this is Alicia."

"Uh-huh."

"How much is it?"

"It's thirteen dollars."

Uh-oh. I only had ten. "I don't have that much."

"Have you got ten?"

"Yeah."

"Give me that. And here, take a couple of quarters back in case you need a pay phone."

"Thank you!"

So there we were, in Lexie's and the Hells Angels' neighbourhood. When the taxi disappeared, I told Jenny: "Let's go."

We had to walk around a bit till we found it. But you couldn't miss it once you got the right street. There were a whole lot of motorcycles and there was loud music blaring out of the house.

"I don't think we should go in there, Normie."

"It's okay. Did you ever hear of a biker doing anything bad to a kid? No! They ride around on motorcycles and sell drugs. We won't take any if they try to get us to buy some."

"We don't have any money."

"Right. So they won't give us drugs for free and they won't rob us, because we don't have anything."

Just then a motorcycle rumbled up with a really loud motor noise. A huge guy got off it. I thought Jenny's dad was big, but this guy was a giant. With long straggly black and grey hair and a scary face. He had on a leather jacket that said Hells Angels on the back.

"You steal that bike, girlie, and you're dead meat!" he said to us, then laughed and started to go inside the house.

"Can we come in?" I said, and he turned around and stared.

"Say what?"

"Can we come in?"

"Want to sign up?"

"No! Not really."

"Why not? You got something against motorcycles?"

"No! I think they're cool."

"Good answer. So whaddya want? You selling Girl Guide cookies or somethin'? How 'bout you bring the cookies in, we'll add a special ingredient, and you go out on the street again tonight and sell them for a higher price. That sound good?"

"We don't have any cookies. We'd just like to talk."

"Fuck!" (The only way to tell this story is to use bad language. That's just the way it is.) After the F-word, he said: "I don't believe this. Excuse my French, ladies. Okay, why don't you come in to Big Daddy's house? Never too young to learn the facts of life, eh?" He laughed again.

Jenny and I were scared but we didn't want him to know, so we smiled and went into the house with him.

"Hey, Axe, what the fuck?" This other guy was looking at us. He was sprawled on a couch in front of the television. It was loud. He had all his hair shaved off and had a devilish-looking beard on his chin. "You said you were running a couple new girls, but we didn't think you meant *this* new. Tap into a whole new market with these two! Hey, kids, what's your names? Lemme guess. You're Misty, and this here's" — the guy turned and looked at the television, and there were two girls dancing and they hardly had any clothes on! — "Candy! That's it, Misty and Candy! Just like the two, uh, exotic dancers in this movie! Would you like to dance like that, girls?"

We didn't know what to say. But the guy who brought us in, Axe, told the guy: "Turn that off, asshole. There's kids in the house."

"But I was just getting into it, you know what I mean?"

"I said *turn it off.*"

"I just rented it, and I'm dubbing a copy. If I turn it off, I'll have to . . ."

Then I couldn't believe what happened. Axe walked over to the television and lifted up his foot, and drove it right through the TV screen. The glass smashed and there was a big noise, and that was the end of the TV! "Next time I tell you to turn something off, Pratt, you turn it off. Understand?"

"Okay, Axe, okay, chill out, man!"

Two other guys came in then, with one girl. She was tough-looking. She said: "Hey, Axe, some of your long-lost kids are finally turning up to cash in, eh?"

"Yeah, looks like it."

"So, kiddies, would you like a brownie?" the girl asked.

"Sure!" Jenny said.

But Axe said: "Don't give them any, you dipshit."

"I wasn't going to!"

I wanted to say we'd like to have a brownie, but it's rude to ask for food at other people's houses.

"Smoke a little weed, girls, help you relax?" That was the guy on the couch.

"We don't smoke," I said, "but thanks anyways."

"So what can we do for you, girls?" That was Axe.

I figured I'd better think of a way to ask them about Mrs. Delaney, without really asking whether they killed her or hung around outside their house. So I made something up.

"Somebody lost a wallet with some money in it, outside her house." I pointed at Jenny.

"Oh yeah?"

"It's mine!" one of the guys said. "Hand it over!"

"We don't have it with us."

"Why's that?"

"Because we were scared someone would steal it from us. Someone who didn't really own it."

"You're not saying we're thieves, are you, ladies?" Axe said.

"No! We meant anybody, not you guys!"

"So why did you think one of us lost a wallet?"

"Uh, because it had a picture of a big motorcycle in the photo holder. And because . . ."

"Because my mum said your name before she died!" That was Jenny, obviously. We weren't supposed to sound like we thought they were around when she died, but Jenny blurted it out anyway.

"Let me get this straight. Your mother died, and you're here because you think we had something to do with it?"

"No, no, not really," I said. "It's just that her mum said the words 'Hells Angels' before she died, but we know you weren't there at the time because, well, there was nobody there . . ." I didn't know what else to say.

"Sounds to me like there was somebody there. Sounds to me like maybe her old man should be sat down with a strong light shining in his face and questioned about this death himself, and not bringing our name into it!" Axe again.

"Oh, my dad didn't do it!" Jenny said then.

"If you say so."

"It's true."

"Back to this wallet," another guy said.

I answered: "Yeah, like I was saying, somebody lost a wallet with a bike picture in it, outside the house, so we were just wondering. That's all."

"And this wallet got picked up right around the time of this death, is that it?"

"Yeah."

Axe looked at all the Hells Angels in the clubhouse, and said: "Anybody here lose their wallet when they were killing somebody lately?"

"It wasn't lately; it was a long time ago," I explained.

"Long time ago? Anybody?"

One guy said: "I can't remember all the people I knocked off, but I'd sure as hell remember if I lost my wallet."

They all made jokes like that. Of course it was a dumb idea for me to say the wallet was at Jenny's; they wouldn't confess that they were there, even if there really was a wallet with money in it. It didn't make any sense. But that's all I could think of. I had never tried to do anything like this before. Being a sleuth looked a lot easier in the Nancy Drew books.

Then Axe said to Jenny: "This is bullshit about your mother dying, right, kid?"

"No! She really died."

He looked as if he felt bad for making a joke about it. But he didn't say he was sorry. Then I wondered: Now what?

"So, is anybody coming to pick you girls up? Or should we set two more places for supper?"

I realized we couldn't call Daddy and get him to pick us up at the Hells Angels' house. He'd kill us. And besides, I was still mad at him and Mum, so it served them right if their daughter was hiding out with a biker gang! And we sure couldn't tell Jenny's dad about this. So we didn't know what to do.

"What do you girls want to do? Watch a movie?"

"Yeah, that would be great!" I said.

Pratt twisted around on the couch and gawked at Axe. "You're lettin' them stay here? You got a death wish or somethin'?"

"Nah. Should be fun to see who turns up to get them, after they get bored and call home. It will be worth it to see Daddy's face when he comes to the door. So put a movie on for them, Pratt. How about *Hansel and Gretel*? Or *Easy Rider*. Oh, that's right. We don't have a TV!"

"You had a little accident with the TV, Axe."

"Right. So go get them another one."

"What?"

"Get off your ass and get a TV for them."

"How am I supposed to do that?"

"You're trying out for membership in this club, aren't you, Pratt? So make your bones! Hoist a TV set somewhere, and get back here. I'll give you half an hour."

"What the fuck?"

"Get moving. Now!"

Then Axe got on the phone. "It's me. Bring the kids over. Yeah, I know it's not *my day*. Bring them over on your day, and I'll let you have them on my day. Is that rocket science? Okay, good." And he hung up. He said to us: "I got kids around your age. They're coming over. Now we've got some business to take care of in the back room, some product we gotta move, so make yourselves at home. There's pizza in the fridge. Phone's there if you need it."

"We won't," I said.

"Have it your way."

So they all went into another room and shut the door. Jenny and I sat down, then got up and looked around, but there wasn't much to see. There were some posters on the walls with pictures of motorcycles, and there was a really old leather jacket with the Hells Angels sign, hanging up with some guy's picture underneath it. There was also an old-fashioned picture in the brown colours the cameras used to do. It showed a bunch of men sitting on top of an old airplane with Hells Angels written on it. There were words on the picture that said: "The Original Hells Angels: 303rd Bombardment Group of World War II." I couldn't believe they let the Hells Angels fight in the war. But maybe they were really good at it, so they put them in to fight the Nazis.

That was all I saw. The bad stuff must have been in the other room. They said we could have pizza, so we got it out of the fridge, along with a couple of cans of pop, and we sat down to eat. Pratt came in and, sure enough, he had a TV. The wires were hanging down from it, as if he just yanked it out of a wall some place and brought it to the clubhouse. He hooked it up, and didn't talk to us the whole time. He knocked on the door to the other room, and they let him in.

Then we heard people coming in from outside. A woman shooed two kids into the house, told them to call for a lift later, and left. One was a boy about grade-three age, with short hair and kind of a skinny tail of hair at the back of his neck; the other one was a girl older than us. She had long, wild, curly brown hair. They sat down and had some pizza and didn't talk to us.

Jenny and I went to the couch and clicked through a whole bunch of TV channels. The boy said "Gimme that," and tried to grab the clicker, but his sister whacked him on the side of the head, and he fell over. He got up, went across the room to a table, and opened up a drawer; he pulled out some kind of game that looked like a small computer. He sat in the corner and played it by himself. The girl went to the phone and called her friend. She started talking to her and ignored us.

So we went back to switching TV channels. We saw a choir singing on the cable channel. The concert! Then I felt really bad. Mum and Dad would be at the concert wondering where I was. And I hadn't gone home for supper. They would be really worried. I wanted them to worry, to pay them back for thinking I was crazy. But now I didn't feel so good about it. We watched as the choir finished their song. It was another school and they weren't very good, especially their diction. And they went flat a couple of times. The guy in charge of the show thanked them and asked people to call in with donations for the poor. Then he introduced the next performer: Father Brennan Burke, director of the Schola Cantorum Sancta Bernadetta, and music director of St. Bernadette's Choir School. The man thanked Father Burke for having the show at the choir school; then Father came on to sing. He was in his priest collar and black suit, and he looked nervous. Which he never is. No, he looked as if something was bothering him. Was he worrying about *me*, or mad at me for missing the concert? I would be in so much trouble! Then he was singing *La Rondine*, all about someone who flew away like a little bird, and wouldn't fly over the mountains and the sea to come back.

It seemed like he was talking and looking right at me. He probably wasn't, but it seemed like it. And I started to cry. Jenny started too.

So I got up and hammered at the door to the next room. It took a few minutes, but Axe opened it.

"Can we go home?" I begged.

"We're not keeping you here, girls. I thought you didn't want to go home."

"We do now. Can you call a taxi and we'll pay you back . . . some day? My dad will kill us if he has to . . . come here to get us."

"No shit!" He was laughing. I just waited. What else could I do? "So, you want a taxi, or you want a ride home on a big Harley hog?"

"Is that a motorcycle?"

"Is that a motorcycle, she asks me! Is anything else a motorcycle? Let's roll."

"Really?"

"Up to you."

"Are you fuckin' nuts, Axe?" Pratt called out from the room. "Anybody sees you with these little pieces of jailbait, we'll end up behind bars with a bunch of kiddie diddlers!"

"Watch your mouth, fuckhead! Show some respect!"

"Well, what do you think their old man's gonna do when two of us pull up with these little fender bunnies on the back of our bikes?"

"They won't say anything bad about us, will you, girls?"

"No! Because you didn't do anything bad. Not that you would, I mean . . ."

"Right. You were just here watching TV with my kids. Pratt, get them a couple helmets. Me and Arnason are going to take 'em home in style."

It was unbelievable. It was really fun! They gave us helmets to put on. And I got on the back of Axe's motorcycle, and Jenny got on with the other guy, and we hung on to them, and roared away down the street. We were just flying when we got into the real part of Halifax, and people gawked at us as we went by. I hoped I would be out of trouble with Mum and Dad by the time I got to be sixteen or whatever the age is, when you can get your own motorcycle. Because that's the only thing I wanted in the whole world.

We stopped at a red light, and Axe turned around to ask me what my address was. I realized the concert was still going on, so I said: "St. Bernadette's Choir School," and told him where it was. He said: "Choir school! Whoo-ooo, twilight zone!" And just shook his head, but he drove there.

It was great when we got there, because Father Burke was out on the steps of the choir school with Daddy. They looked like they were arguing, and were going to hit each other. You could tell by the way they were standing, and talking into each other's faces. Then they heard the bike motors and turned around together, and gawked as if they couldn't believe their eyes. Father Burke always has the same expression on his face even if something weird or awful happens. But this time his mouth dropped open and his eyes were huge. And Daddy grabbed the railing and looked as if he was going to faint.

Axe and the other guy turned the bikes around and skidded to a stop. They took the helmets off us, and peeled away on their motorcycles before Daddy and Father Burke could even get down the stairs.

(Monty)

The less said about Normie's disappearance from the school and the concert, and the anguish and recriminations that resulted, the better.

She and Jenny staged a triumphant and never-to-be-forgotten return, and we had to move on from there. The first stop was the Hells Angels clubhouse in Fairview. Burke and I, dressed down for the occasion, headed out there the next day in my quiet little four-wheeled vehicle. Quiet too was Father Burke, who perhaps hadn't quite put behind him the threats and accusations I had launched at him when my daughter went missing from his school.

I broke the silence. "Who knew, Brennan? How, in my wildest dreams, could I ever have imagined that my little girl and her friend would end up in the clubhouse of the Hells Angels? That they went there on their own? I'm just, to borrow a word from you, gob-smacked. She said she would explain later — you got that right, sweetheart — but all she was trying to do was 'help solve the case.' And she was exhausted and needed to sleep. She also made me swear — and here again I'm a sucker for a pretty face — not to tell Beau Delaney that Jenny was there. So it's possible he'll never know she was missing, given that you didn't even call him!"

Burke responded with some acerbity: "I didn't call him because Friday is not a day for the Four-Four Time program. Jenny would not normally be at the school on a Friday. And she was not scheduled to be in the concert. So I didn't know there was anything amiss with Jenny at all."

"All right, all right. I'm sorry."

"The decision to go see the Hells Angels may not have come completely out of the blue, though."

I turned to look at him. *"What?"*

"I didn't attach much significance to this at the time, but —"

"Never mind that. Get on with it."

"A week or two ago, Normie's catechism class was studying the concept of sin. Apparently, the kids were codding each other about it after school, and Jenny heard them. Normie and Jenny came to me and asked me about swearing, specifically whether it was swearing if you said 'Hells Angels.' God love them, the dear little things, I tried not to laugh, and I asked why they were worrying about it. Jenny said her mother had uttered the words 'Hells Angels' one night at the house. In a loud voice, which she thought might have added to the sin! I assured the girls it wasn't swearing, there was no sin, and Peggy

Delaney is with God and the saints and the holy angels in heaven."

"And you didn't tell me this before because . . . what, you couldn't breach the seal of confession?"

"It was not a confession, or I wouldn't be telling you now."

"Well, I should count myself fortunate that I'm hearing it as we approach the precincts of the Hells Angels chapter in Halifax."

"It didn't seem significant at the time. And then, when it came up with Delaney, Normie asked me not to tell you. Being a man who's used to keeping confidences, I kept it."

"What do you mean, it came up with Delaney?"

I looked over, and he gave me a wary look. "The time Beau was at, em, the MacNeil residence."

That made me yank the car right off the street and squeal to a stop at the curb. I turned in my seat and faced Burke head-on. "What are you saying now? Are you telling me Beau Delaney was in my family's house?"

"It had to do with, well . . . Herself needed a bit of legal advice."

"She's a lawyer and so am I!"

"She knows this isn't your favourite subject."

"The baby."

"Right."

"What? The boyfriend wants access?"

"Ex-boyfriend."

"Oh?"

"He's back living in Italy."

"He wants visitation in Italy? She'll never see the child again!"

"That's where Delaney comes in."

"I can't be hearing this, Burke. How does Delaney come into it?"

"Ask him. Ask her. Don't ask me. I'd as lief be talking about the latest outbreak of contagious disease as talking about this."

He did look uncomfortable. He wasn't one to tell tales out of school, and I suspected Maura wanted to keep all this from me to spare me any more aggravation on the subject. But I was aggravated now, for several reasons. My wife's other child, her other man, and, oh yes, my daughter's dalliance with the Hells Angels. And now my client, charged with the murder of his wife, was lolling about in my wife's house.

The hell with Burke's discomfort. "Brennan. How did Delaney get involved in this?"

He sighed. "The MacNeil wanted some advice, or legal services, from one of Delaney's law partners. A woman who deals with, em, domestic disputes."

"Val Tanner! The dispute must be nasty, if she was calling in the big guns."

"Well, it turns out Val Tanner is on sick leave. Delaney got wind of Maura's request, and wanted to do something for the family. Offered his services free of charge. That's why he was there."

"He was planning to appear in court with the murder of his wife still hanging over his head?"

"I think he saw his role as being more of a behind-the-scenes effort."

"What's he doing?"

"He's doing whatever you lawyers do, I imagine." Burke was holding out on me. I didn't like it, but then, I didn't like any of the circumstances surrounding my wife's third child. I didn't like the little bit I thought I knew, and I didn't even want to think of how much I didn't know. I couldn't really blame Burke for his reticence, though. He was caught in the middle. I took a deep breath and let it out slowly. "Very well. Delaney will save the day for Maura. While he waits for me to save the day for *him*."

"I think his heart's in the right place. You're helping him; he's helping, well, herself."

"Okay, okay. Then somehow the Hells Angels came up in conversation. Why do I feel I'm playing a part in some great big cosmic joke?"

"Ah now, the Hells Angels. That's where Normie enters the picture."

"Of course! Little Normie and the HAs. Go on."

"There was the Hells Angels swearing flap at school."

"Yeah. The girls asked you whether it was a sin, or it was swearing, to say the name of the organization. Because Jenny had heard her mother utter the phrase at some point, in a loud voice."

"Right. Well, Normie came downstairs at the house when Delaney was there, and told us she'd been studying her catechism."

"Ha!"

"I know. It must have been a lead-in to what she really wanted to do, namely, reassure Delaney that his wife's outburst didn't set her on the road to eternal damnation."

"And?"

"His reaction was . . . disturbing."

"Jesus Christ! He knows my little girl knows something about his wife and about some concern, or even a possible connection, with a motorcycle gang!" I realized I sounded as if I thought my client was dangerous, and Burke wouldn't miss the inference of guilt, but that was the least of my problems at the moment.

"Delaney stared at Normie in horror. Fear, more like. And then he looked at me, enraged."

"God almighty! I only wish I'd been there. To head it off."

"It came out of left field, Monty. She just blurted it out. I tried to downplay the whole thing, calm Delaney down. But he left in a state."

"Did he say anything?"

"Said little Jenny has nightmares. Must have dreamt it. Couldn't imagine his wife talking about the Hells Angels."

"His reaction suggests otherwise. If there was nothing to it, he would have laughed it off."

"I suppose he would have, yes."

"So Normie and Jenny think there was something to it, and cooked up some hare-brained scheme to investigate on their own. The mind of a nine-year-old! Frightening, isn't it? But maybe the children are ahead of us on this. I wonder if we should be looking at some kind of connection between Peggy — or more likely Beau himself — and the bikers."

"How convenient, then, that we're on our way to their place now, Monty. Was Delaney involved with the bikers? Was he their lawyer?"

"No, I don't recall him ever appearing on their behalf. They have other counsel."

"Maybe he was in trouble with them, crossed them somehow."

"Or represented a client with interests adverse to theirs. And something got Peggy worked up . . ."

"So, get going. We're not learning anything sitting here."

†

"You're the dads, I take it."

"Well, you're half right."

Burke and I were in front of the bikers' clubhouse, speaking to an enormous man wearing Hells Angels colours. When the introductions were made, he said everybody called him Axe.

"Nothin' happened," Axe said. "They must have told you that much."

"Why don't you tell us?"

"Two kids show up at the door in plaid skirts — uniforms — like Catholic schoolgirls or something. 'Dear *Penthouse* . . .' I'm like, where are the hidden cameras? Is this a sting operation? Anyway, they had some story about one of their mothers dying, and she had said something about us. I didn't get it."

"You're not the only one. Then what happened?"

"I called my ex and got her to bring my own kids over. They ate pizza and watched TV. I told them to use the phone whenever they wanted to call their parents. Thought it would be a good laugh to see Hockey Dad and Soccer Mum pulling up to the clubhouse here in their Volvo and coming to the door looking for their kids. The other guys thought I was nuts to let them hang around. So I'm nuts. Not the first time, won't be the last. Sometimes life is too fucking weird, know what I'm saying? And you have to go with it and see how it plays out."

"So then you got them on the motorcycles . . ."

"They wanted to go home, but they wouldn't make the phone call, you know? Guess they couldn't picture the scene either. So I told them to hop on and we flew them home Air Harley. And just when I thought it couldn't get any weirder, the carrot top said to drive her to a choir school! Fuck! Then we pull up and see a priest standing there. I thought all that stuff about acid flashbacks was bullshit, but now I gotta wonder. Hey!" He peered at Brennan. "Was that you?"

"It was."

"What did you say your name was?"

"Brennan."

"You don't look like the kind of guy who's gonna kneel down and kiss the Pope's ring."

"Oh, but I am."

"Well, the Pope's not looking at you now. Wanna smoke a little weed?"

"Thanks, but I had to give it up."

"Oh yeah? Why's that?"

"I was getting way too mellow in the confession box. People would come in and tell me they killed somebody or had impure thoughts, and I'd just say: 'Hey, if it felt good at the time . . .'"

"Everybody's a comedian these days. So, have I answered all your questions?"

"Do you know of any reason Beau Delaney might have been out of favour with your organization?"

"Delaney! The lawyer? What's this got to do with him?"

"It was his —"

"No! Don't tell me that was his kid. And it was his woman they were talking about."

"It was."

"I thought the cops were just trying to fuck Delaney around, and the charges were bogus. That she just died from an accident."

"True. But she seemed to be worried about you guys for some reason."

"You mean like those times when we're looking for somebody to kill and can't make up our minds who, and are saying 'Who should it be? Who should it be?' If it was one of those nights where nobody could make an executive decision, why would it be Beau's old lady? We might need him to defend us. And he wouldn't if we killed his wife. See what I'm saying?"

"Nobody's suggesting you had anything to do with her death. The question was whether Beau had done something to piss off any of the members of your, uh, club. Something like that, which might have got her worried."

"Hey, can't hold us responsible for the things people worry about. They shouldn't read the papers if they're that sensitive. But I never heard anything about Delaney pissing anyone off. Or his wife either."

"Well, all right then."

"Only murder they're trying to connect us to is that one in Truro. They're putting heat on one of our guys, who didn't do it! He's sitting in Dorchester on another bogus charge, and they keep looking at him for this killing. It's bullshit."

"How do you know he didn't do it?"

"I *know*, okay? It wasn't him. The victim was a psycho and got taken out by another psycho. World of freaks out there."

"Right. Well, the victim of that killing was Delaney's client."

"Come again?"

"Delaney represented him at some point."

"For what?"

"Criminal charges. I don't know what they were."

"There you go. Delaney thinks we blew away his client. Next time you see him, tell him we didn't do it. End of story. Too late for the wife, if that's what got her wrapped around the axle. She was worried for nothing."

"All right. Well, thanks for your time, Axe. And thanks for bringing the girls home."

"So, did they get in shit or what?"

"We suggested that they not do it again any time soon."

I turned to leave but Brennan didn't. Axe noticed. "Hey, Brennan. You ever ride one of these?"

"Never."

"But you want to."

"Wouldn't mind."

"Your car a stick shift?"

"Yeah."

"So you know about gears."

"That much I know."

"Okay, look. This is the throttle. Right hand. And that's the front brake. Rear brake is here, right foot. Clutch is this one. Left hand. And you shift with your left foot. Take it for a spin."

There were a couple of false starts but it didn't take long before Brennan got the hang of it, and he was off like a bat out of hell.

"Let's hope nothing goes wrong," I remarked.

Axe laughed. "No sweat off my ass if he dumps it."

"You're not worried about your bike getting wrecked?"

"Do I look like a fuckin' retard? Nobody touches my machine. Nobody."

"Whose bike is it?"

"Belongs to a young up-and-coming guy named Pratt, whose only role in life right now is to make me happy. Good test for his attitude if your buddy fucks up."

We followed Burke's progress by the sound of the engine, as he made his way around the neighbourhood. He was gone for ten minutes and he was a happy man when he returned. He brought the bike to a halt and dismounted, a little smile on his face.

"Had a good time out there, did you?"

"Fellow could get used to that."

"Nothing like it."

"Thanks."

"Any time."

We said our goodbyes, and got into my sedate little vehicle for the drive home.

"So, Brennan, branching out in your ministry? Chaplain to the Hells Angels? You'd have your work cut out for you there."

"It would be worth it, to ride the bike and wear the jacket, pulling up to St. Bernadette's for Sunday Mass. But even if I never get to do that, there is independent evidence of my biker days."

"Oh yeah? What kind of evidence?"

"I didn't know young Lexie lived so close to the clubhouse."

"You saw her?"

"Her and Tom."

"Yeah, I knew he was spending the day there."

"I pulled up beside them and said: 'Hey babe, hop on.' The face on her was priceless. She was rooted to the earth. And Tom, well, he was gobsmacked. I just blasted off and left them in my dust."

"Well done! So, Brennan, what do you make of Axe's plea of innocence?"

His head whipped around to face me. "About the girls, you mean?"

"No, no. Nothing happened there. I mean that killing. The guy in Truro."

"Seemed to me he was telling the truth. I could be wrong."

"Could be, but that was my impression too."

"Now what?"

"Now, I don't know. Our defence is that Peggy simply fell. Beau hasn't made an effort to claim that somebody else came in and killed her. But if at some point she had been concerned about the Hells Angels, well, how can we overlook it? It's a loose end I want to tie off, so we can move on. I'd like to see whether Axe's claim of no Angels involvement in the murder of Beau's old client stands up when presented to someone who's intimately familiar with the bikers and all their works. I know just the guy. I'll let you know what I find out."

(Normie)

I was scared to death about the trouble I'd be in after going to the Hells Angels' house. I wanted to solve the mystery and prove to my mum and dad I was smart and not crazy. Plus, if they thought I was dead or I ran away, they would feel guilty. And it would serve them right!

But afterwards, I found out they were really upset when they learned that Jenny and I ran away from the school, and then didn't come back for the choir concert. It turns out Mummy was crying the whole time, and had to leave the concert. Daddy was worried too and he was ready to kill Father Burke because the school shouldn't have let me and Jenny get away without the teachers seeing us. Except Jenny wasn't even supposed to be there on Friday, but she came early to see the concert. When I saw Father Burke singing on the TV, I knew there was something wrong with him.

Then they all must have got together after Axe brought me back and I was put to bed, and talked about the biker visit and about my dreams and the fact that I said I wouldn't go to any more doctors about them. I know they talked about it because of what they said when Father Burke had dinner with us all the next day. Normally Mum doesn't discuss private family stuff with other people but this was just Father Burke, so it was okay. He knew everything about us anyway.

Daddy said: "I know you're really worried about those dreams and the Delaney kids, Normie, and this is working on your mind. The doctors can help you, sweetheart."

"No, they can't! And I'm not going to that doctor you guys picked out! There were scary people in there. That guy was going to go after the nurse, and you had to push him down on the floor. He said he'd been going to that doctor for two years, and look how he turned out! She can't be a very good doctor if she couldn't cure him. So I'm not going."

"But some people have very serious problems, Normie, and they can't be cured right away. That's not the case with you. You could just talk to her, tell her what's been happening —"

"I'm not going! I'd rather run away and join the Hells Angels, and I just might do that if you guys don't stop bugging me!" I didn't mean to scream, but it ended up that way. Then I started crying.

"Aw, sweetheart," Daddy said, "we didn't mean to upset you." He got up and put his arms around me and gave me a kiss.

"Normie," Father Burke said, "do you remember my brother Patrick in New York? I know you met so many of my family that you might not be able to keep them all straight!"

"I remember him." I tried not to sniffle too much. "He's Deirdre's dad."

"Right. You know he's a doctor."

"Yeah. He's really nice."

"He's a psychiatrist. Did you know that?"

"I think so."

"Would you like to talk to him?"

"But he's not here."

"I could make him appear."

"You can do that?"

"I'm his big brother, and a man of God. My wish is his command."

I could tell he was just kidding. He was always joking about the good old days, saying that in those days priests used to run everybody's life and things were grand. Mum always told him he was "full of it." She didn't say full of what, but I know and I'm not going to say it here. But it was all just a joke, like now.

"We can't very well expect Patrick —" Mum started to say, but Dad interrupted.

"What are the chances he could get away?"

"Only one way to find out. I'll give him a ring tonight."

I thought he would be too busy. Everyone is, in New York. And he was, but only till the next Friday, then he was free. More bad luck for me. A psychiatrist! Coming all the way from New York! He's really friendly, I remembered that. But I kept thinking: what is he going to do to me? Maybe they thought I was more crazy after the Hells Angels visit than I was before, even though I wanted them to think the other way around. What were they going to do? Maybe lock me away in the mental hospital, and leave me there! I saw this movie where a guy was put in a hospital and tied down to his bed, and they give him electric shocks in his head. Then all these really dangerous people kept coming around him. Now it might be me! Or they might yell at me and make me answer questions! I worried all that Friday in school and kept getting answers wrong in every class. So now the teachers thought there was something wrong with me too! I worried all through supper and hardly ate any of my chowder even though it was my favourite with bits of lobster in it.

That night after I went to bed, there was a knock on my door. I could hardly talk out loud, I was so scared, but I said to come in. It was Dr. Burke! He doesn't look all that much like Father Burke. He has light-coloured hair and bright blue eyes.

"Hi, Normie. May I come in for a minute?"

"Okay." I was shaking.

He kind of squatted down a little ways from my bed. "You remember me, don't you, Normie? From the wedding in New York?" He had a softer voice than Father Burke, but it still sounded a little bit Irish too.

"Yes, you're Dr. Burke. Deirdre's dad. I remember how you and Father Burke and your brothers sang for the bride at the wedding party."

"That's right. Did you like our singing at the reception?"

"Yeah! You guys all kneeled down and did those old-fashioned songs, and sang from your hearts! I told Daddy I wanted somebody to sing for me like that at my wedding. When I grow up."

"Why wait? We could give you a song now! Sing you to sleep."

"Really?"

"Sure. Hold on for two minutes."

He went out, and down the stairs. Maybe they weren't going to punish me or lock me up in the mental hospital. He wouldn't trick me, I didn't think. A few minutes later, I heard footsteps on the stairs, a knock on the door, and there were four men in my room. If you include my brother Tom, who's a teenager. So it was Tom, Daddy, and the two Burkes.

"Ready, Normie?" Dr. Burke asked.

"Ready!" I said.

They stood together, put one hand on their hearts and the other hand out to the side, and Father Burke went "one, two, three," and they started to sing a song called "Goodnight, My Love." It was a really sweet song. There was something about having no fear. And there was lots of love in it. Tommy had a cheat sheet with the words; the older guys all knew it. Halfway through, they all got down on their knees and continued to sing. It was so great, I asked them to do it again. I got really sleepy and never heard the end of it. But I woke up safe in my own bed.

Chapter 9

(Monty)

The lawyer who most frequently appeared on behalf of the Hells Angels Motorcycle Club was Barry Sheehan. I knew Barry quite well as a fellow member of the criminal defence bar. I called him in the middle of the week and asked if we could get together for a chat. He couldn't get free of work, so we talked about the weekend. When I mentioned that my blues band, Functus, had a gig that Saturday afternoon at Gus's Pub, Barry said he'd come by and listen and have a beer, then we could talk.

Gus's Pub is located at the corner of North and Agricola streets. There are no frills at Gus's, and that's why people like it. It has square tables, tavern chairs, beer ads, and a large, loyal crowd of regulars. My band and I wailed our way through some blues standards by Muddy Waters and T-Bone Walker, and I wound up with a harp solo on "Trouble No More." We took a break after that, and I joined Barry Sheehan at his table just inside the door.

Barry was big and muscular, and had the striking colouring that graced many people of Irish descent: round blue eyes and black wavy hair. We asked about each other's families and exchanged a bit of lawyerly chitchat, then I got to the point.

"Have to pick your brain about your best-known clients, Barry. Guys who tend to travel in packs, wearing very distinctive clothing."

"The Knights of Columbus?"

"Um, no."

"What do you want to know? You're not representing a co-accused in something I haven't heard about yet, I hope."

"No, nothing like that. And nothing that wouldn't be on the record. It's just that I'm not familiar with the record. But it's got to stay between you and me."

"Okay."

I had to be careful here. In other words, I had to be dishonest. "My client's not opening up to me and I'm worried about him."

"Your client being . . ."

"Beau Delaney."

"I see."

"There's been some suggestion that he may have got himself in trouble with them, or made himself unpopular somehow."

"Oh?"

"Did he ever represent them, do you know?"

"Why don't you ask him?"

"I told you. He's not telling me everything."

"To my recollection he never did much work for them. I think he handled a couple of isolated cases in years past. But nothing regular, or recent. As for pissing them off, I have no idea. I never heard of any animosity, but then I wouldn't necessarily be in the loop. What's going on? Does he think someone's after him?"

"Possibly."

"Or someone's out to smear him? Accuse him of things he didn't do, perhaps?"

"Could be," I equivocated. I tried another approach. "What's been happening with the club lately?"

"Well, we had that extortion trial in the fall. I got the charges thrown out."

"Oh, I remember. Nicely done!"

"Yeah, the case collapsed once I got the wiretap evidence excluded.

And there was that murder last year in Truro. The guy was shot with a handgun. The police have their eye on one of the Hells Angels for that, apparently, but they haven't laid charges yet. No hurry, I guess. The guy got arrested a couple of weeks after that for another incident; he's doing time in Dorchester for aggravated assault. They gave him six years for it. He went to another lawyer, so he has only himself to blame!"

"Oh yeah, I remember hearing something about the killing in Truro. The vic was known to police, as they say."

"That's right. He was no choirboy."

"How come the biker got other counsel for the assault trial?"

"He got it into his head that hiring a local boy to represent him might make him look better in front of a hometown jury. Rather than bringing the big bad bikers' lawyer in from Halifax. Turns out it wasn't such a good idea. Should have called Uncle Barry."

"Do you think you could have got him off?"

"Couldn't have done any worse! At the very least, I could have pleaded it down. Anyway, he's the guy the Mounties think did that shooting in Truro."

"Right. Anything else going on?"

"There was the arson case, of course. Their old clubhouse burned down, with a guy passed out inside. The police tried to say they did it themselves. They're not that stupid. Someone with a grudge, and a lot of balls, did that. The case is still in the unsolved pile. I figure if the guy is identified, he'll turn himself in to the police. Better off in jail than out for some folks. Aside from those incidents, I don't recall anything else."

(Normie)

Monday was the day we were going to surprise Father Burke. He's not always with us at Four-Four Time, so on the days when he was out, we had been teaching the little kids a song he really likes, the *Sanctus* in the green hymn book. It's Gregorian chant. That means it's ancient. Richard Robertson was going to conduct the music. If you knew Richard, you'd never believe he could act like a choir director. But anyway he snuck up to the grown-ups' choir school, the schola cantorum, then came back.

"Burke's wrapping things up in there," he said, sounding almost like a grown-up himself. "He'll probably be down in a minute. So finish gobbling your snacks and get ready." We heard footsteps. "Here he comes!"

Some of the kids tried to stuff whole muffins and doughnuts in their mouths before grabbing their music. But anyway, I helped Richard get them organized in rows with their music. And when Father came in, Richard lifted his arm in the air, and we started: *"Sanctus, sanctus, sanctus, Dominus Deus Sabaoth."* It didn't sound very good. How can you sing with your throat clogged with food? A big wad of crumbs spewed out of Ian McAllister's mouth in the middle of it. But anyway we sang it. Father Burke smiled at us, even though I knew this wasn't the best singing he had ever heard in his life. He thanked us when we were done, and said he appreciated it.

"Can we do it again after I have a drink of juice, Father?" Ian asked, and Father said sure.

But we didn't get to do it because that's when Derek and Connor Delaney burst into the room, scared to death.

"We have to hide in here!" Derek yelled.

Father Burke went over to him. "What's the trouble?"

"Those guys are chasing us again! They've got a baseball bat!"

Father Burke took off from the room, and went outside. We all trailed behind him even though he turned around and told us to stay inside.

There were two guys hiding in the doorway of the church. One was really short and the other was regular size.

"Boys! Come over here!" Father Burke told them.

"Make me!" one of them said.

"I'm hoping that won't be necessary. Come here now and tell me what's going on."

"What's it got to do with you?"

"I don't like people being chased and threatened on the grounds of my church or my school, or anywhere else for that matter."

But they didn't move, so Father Burke went up the stairs of the church and put a hand on the shoulder of each one of them. The guy with the bat lifted it up but he looked more scared than dangerous, and Father Burke grabbed the bat and twisted it out of the guy's hand, and threw it on the ground. Then he took both the boys by the arm and walked down the steps with them to the parking lot. Me and the other kids sneaked a little closer to them.

"All right, lads, what's happening here?"

"We want our money back!" the short guy said.

"What money would this be now?"

"The money they owe us." He pointed to Derek and Connor.

"What's this about money?" Father Burke asked the Delaneys.

"We don't know!" Connor answered.

"You do so!" the other guy argued.

"No, we don't."

"All right, all right, cool it down, fellows. You," Father said, pointing to the short guy, "tell me about the money."

"We paid money to their family so we could meet them and get a ride in the Mercedes. Then maybe even . . ." All of a sudden he sounded like he was going to cry.

Everybody turned around and gawked at Derek and Connor, and at Jenny and Laurence. They all looked shocked.

Father Burke didn't say anything for a long time, just stared at the two boys. Then finally he said in a really quiet voice: "Who did you pay the money to?"

"That other guy, not them." The short boy nodded at the Delaneys. "The other guy gave the money to them. Or he said he did."

"So let me see if I have this right. You paid some money to another fellow, and that fellow said he paid it to one of the Delaneys."

"Yeah."

"Who was this other person?"

The two boys looked at each other; then the taller one said: "Just this guy we met."

Father Burke turned to the Delaney kids and said, not in a mean voice, but a gentle voice: "You didn't know anything about this, did you?"

"No! No, Father!" they all said, and you could tell it was the truth.

Father Burke turned back to the two other guys and stepped towards them. They stepped back and looked scared, but Father Burke said: "It's all right, lads. Nobody's going to hurt you. And you're not going to hurt anybody either, am I correct?" They both nodded their heads. "I want to hear you both say to the boys and girls here that you're not going to chase them or threaten them or do anything to them. Will you do that?"

They shuffled their feet and looked at one another, then the taller one said: "We won't do nothin'."

And the other guy said: "We won't. We thought you guys probably had our money. But I guess you don't."

Father Burke asked them: "How much money did you pay?"

"Three hundred dollars."

And Father looked surprised and said: "How did you come up with that much money?" No answer. "All right, we'd better leave that unexplored. I'll tell you what." He went over and put an arm around each of the two boys. At first they kind of stood really stiffly, but then they relaxed and it was almost as if he was hugging them. "I know you'll keep your word about not bothering these kids anymore. And I'm going to make a promise to you. I'll find out what I can about this money, and I'll make sure — no matter what I find out — that you get all your money back." They stared at him with big, wide-open eyes. "It may take a while. But I'm going to put that money in bank accounts for the pair of you. That way, I hope it won't be spent unwisely. But that will be up to you. So shake hands with Derek and Connor here, and I'll get your names and phone numbers."

"Are you going to call the cops on us?"

"Oh, I think we can settle matters without any need for law enforcement."

They came up and shook hands, and we all went inside except those two and Father Burke. Father stayed outside and talked to them some more. He must have got their names.

(Monty)

I was dictating a pretrial brief for a leaky-condominium case when Brennan arrived at my office. I spoke my last few words into the dictating machine, then turned it off and popped the tape out for my secretary to transcribe.

"What was all that about?" he asked.

"Another condo building has developed leaks. It's three years old."

"Newgrange," he said.

"What?"

"Burial chamber in Ireland, made of turf and stones. It's been watertight for five thousand years. If they could do a proper job of it then, what the hell is wrong with them now?"

"Don't get me started on it."

"I have to talk to you."

"What is it?"

"Did you ever hear anything about young people paying for access to the Delaney family?"

"What?"

"A couple of Beau's young fellows came in to Four-Four Time today. They were being chased by two other boys. I got things calmed down, then spoke to them privately. The long and the short of it is this: the boys say they paid fifty dollars each to get a ride in the Mercedes, and later they each paid another hundred dollars that was supposed to win them a hearing. A chance to plead their case for acceptance into the family as foster children."

I sat there horrified.

Burke went on: "The two young lads have desperate home lives. Well, one of them is in some class of a group home, and the other has a mother who's on crack; she and her boyfriend are pounding each other and their kids from the time they get up to the time they pass out again. Not hard to see why they took the bait. They wouldn't tell me how they came up with the payments, but I think we can conclude they didn't hold a bake sale."

I finally found my voice. "Who did they pay the money to? Please don't tell me it was Beau Delaney. Family is sacred to him. And those amounts of money? Delaney wouldn't take his hand out of his pocket on a frosty day to receive —"

"It wasn't Delaney. The boys couldn't, or wouldn't, tell me who it was. I told the young lads I'd get the money back to them and put it in an account. So whenever you suss out what happened, let me know and I'll contact the pair of them."

"Sure," I answered. But I was barely listening. All I cared about was that it wasn't Beau Delaney. And it was a guy, so I didn't have to waste two seconds on the bizarre notion that it might have been Peggy, and that Delaney found out and confronted her at the top of the stairs. So if it wasn't Beau or Peggy, how could it possibly hurt our case?

Chapter 10

(Monty)

That evening, Brennan and Pat Burke joined me and Normie in my backyard. The property is bounded by the waters of the Northwest Arm, the long, narrow body of water separating the western side of the Halifax peninsula from the mainland. We sat in my Adirondack chairs with our drinks, and enjoyed the mild April weather.

"What a grand spot this is, Monty," said Patrick. "It's therapeutic just sitting here and gazing at the water. I may decide to miss my flight to New York tonight."

"Thanks, Pat. Feel free to send your patients up for a spot of relaxation."

"I may do that. Is it always this balmy in April?"

"Ha!" I responded. "It could be like this, it could be raining or snowing, or both. Or — look out to the ocean — what do you see?"

"A line of clouds, it looks like."

"Fog. A fog bank just sitting out there. If it moves in, that will be the end of all this happy talk about the weather. Even downtown, on the other side of the peninsula, they can probably feel the chill breeze coming off it."

"We'll enjoy the good times while they last, then," he said.

"More seriously, though, Pat, I don't know how to begin to thank you for coming up here and helping us out with Normie. We'll sort things out in terms of compensation, your flight and all that."

He waved me off. "No worries. I was due for a visit anyway. And Bren was overdue for his physical."

"You're his family doctor, are you, in both senses of the word? Quite a distance between doctor and patient."

"Doesn't make much sense, does it? But if I don't insist, he'll never go for a checkup. Have you ever heard of him going to see a doctor here?"

"No, but then he strikes me as the type who wouldn't mention it. Or anything else to do with health or sickness."

"No, of course not. He wouldn't mention it if he had a double lung transplant. 'Brennan, would you like to go over to the Midtown for a pint and a smoke?' 'Ah, no, not today.' That would be all you'd hear on transplant day."

Typically, Brennan ignored the exchange.

"Do you know how to do that stuff?" Normie asked. "Listening to hearts and fixing broken arms and all that? I thought you just knew how to deal with people's heads." She stopped abruptly, and her face reddened. She must have thought she was out of line, but of course she wasn't, and Pat smiled at her.

"Well, now, you wouldn't want me operating on Brennan if he needed that lung transplant — necessitated by his refusal to give up smoking — for instance. Nor would you want me to give you a triple bypass operation. You'd best go to a heart specialist for that! But in fact psychiatrists are medical doctors first. That's how we start out. Then we go on to study psychiatry. So I know the medical stuff, too."

"That makes sense. I get it now. Daddy, what time is it? I said I'd phone Kim after her dance lesson."

"It's just after seven o'clock."

"Okay, I'm going to see if she's home now."

When she left us, I asked Patrick: "So, Pat, where do you come down on the question of psychic phenomena, clairvoyance and all that?"

"I guess I would describe my position as 'cautiously open-minded.' Ask most of my colleagues what accounts for a person hearing voices or having visions, and I think you know what they'll say: psychosis. Quite rightly, most of the time. So they wouldn't welcome me making an address to the American Psychiatric Association on the subject of clairvoyance! There are a lot of charlatans out there, and a lot of wackiness around the whole subject, as is evident from the tabloid press. So we have to tread carefully. I've never had a psychic moment in my life. But it strikes me that some people have insights that can't be explained by coincidence. Sometimes the theories put forward to debunk these stories are just as fanciful and lacking in proof as the wildest of psychic claims. And there is nothing I've ever seen in Normie that would suggest she is lying or psychotic! Even this fellow" — Pat inclined his head towards his brother — "falls short of a finding of psychosis."

"Give it to me straight, Doc."

"And I know he is, shall we say, 'sensitive' to otherworldly phenomena, as left-brained as he otherwise appears to be. I suspect he finds Normie's claims quite credible."

"I do," Brennan replied. "There's a whole lot of codology — foolishness — associated with this stuff, but I believe it's the real thing with Normie. She has the sight, just like the old spook in Cape Breton, her great-grandmother."

"She comes by it naturally, then! I saw something of it myself, when you were all in New York for the wedding. There we were at the table, and she was able to intuit a great deal about our brother, Francis, including the Irish-language pet name our mother used for him when he was a child. I checked with Mam afterwards, and she was adamant that she had never used the phrase in Normie's hearing. She hadn't said it in years. What was it, Bren? It meant 'child of my heart.'"

"Leanbh mo chroí."

"Right. Could she have heard that bit of Irish around the Collins household?"

"Not much chance of that. Monty hasn't had our advantages, *Padraig.* Never mind that he bears the name Montague Michael Collins. His da obviously banjaxed the job of passing on our ancestral history to his poor, benighted son. Or maybe he did, but the lad wasn't listening."

"There you go. She'd never heard it before, and she came out with it, and she spooked the hell out of Francis when she did it. So I'll talk to Normie again, and see what she has to say. Who knows, we may find out she's seeing events that really happened, or that will happen, and I'll be able to present a paper to the American Psychiatric crowd after all!"

(Normie)

I was in my bedroom at Daddy's house. There's a whole wall that he lets me draw and paint on, which was really fun. Except now I had the wall full of pictures, and I wanted to put more on there and didn't know where. I was trying to figure it out when I heard footsteps coming up the stairs, and I knew they weren't Dad's. There was a knock at the door even though it was open. It's nice to know some people are really polite.

"Hi, Dr. Burke."

"Hi, Normie. Would it be all right if I talked with you for a few minutes?"

"Okay."

He sat in my chair. "I'd like to help you, Normie. I know the things you see are upsetting you."

"They think I'm crazy! Like the people in the movies who say they're hearing voices, and everybody looks at each other and makes a face like 'woooo, this guy's loony!'"

"Your mum and dad have talked to me, and so has my brother, and they don't think there's anything crazy about you at all! They believe what you're saying, and so do I."

"Are you sure?"

"Yep. And you know something?"

"What?"

"I work with the kind of people who are sometimes called crazy. Not a very nice way to talk about them, is it? Especially since it's not their fault. They are people who have problems, sometimes mental illnesses. And I can tell that you're not like them in any way."

"Honest?"

"Honest."

"That's good."

"So, Normie, how are you enjoying the choir school? This is your first year, isn't it?"

"Yes, and it's great! I love it! We learn a whole lot of regular stuff like math and history, but then we get to sing, in Latin and Italian and French and German. Me and Kim both switched to the choir school this year."

"So you have your best friend with you?"

"Yeah. She's kinda scared of Father Burke — well, your brother."

"You tell him to stop scaring Kim, or I'll tell our mother on him! She'll get him sorted."

I laughed because he was joking.

"So things are going well at school for you."

"Yep."

"And you have Kim for a friend. Other friends, too?"

"Yeah, some from my old school and some at the new school. And some more at Four-Four Time, the music program we do after school with kids from all over the city."

"Lovely. And you have a big brother who takes good care of you . . ."

"Yeah, Tommy's a really good brother. He teases me sometimes, but in a funny way, not in a mean way. And he has a really nice girl-friend, Lexie."

"Good, good. And you have a baby brother. That must be fun. Are you enjoying being a big sister?"

"Oh, yes! Dominic is so cute. I really love him. I couldn't stand it if . . ."

No! I stopped myself before I started to blurt out anything about Dominic. I figured I'd better not say anything else about him, or all that stuff about Giacomo. Mum didn't want Daddy to know, so I knew it was supposed to be a secret between Mum and Father Burke, because he was trying to help her save the baby. I probably wasn't even supposed to know it myself, but I was there when Giacomo came to the house, so I found out about it that way, and by listening in. And I wasn't supposed to listen in on people, so I really, really didn't think I should mention it to Dr. Burke, even though he would be a good person to talk to about it.

Oh no! I could feel myself starting to cry.

"Are you all right, Normie?" he asked.

"Yes, I was just thinking of . . . a sad song. Talking about the baby, but not just him . . . about Tommy and Lexie, too, and Kim . . . made me think of it."

"Music can certainly bring our feelings out into the open, can't it? Especially if we have something at the back of our minds already. What song were you thinking of, sweetheart?"

Oh, no, now I had to make up something. "It's an old song, about, um, somebody going away for the whole summer and being lonesome for their girlfriend and brother and friends. But it's okay because they all get together again at the end of the summer. So, even though it's a sad song, it has a happy ending!"

"That's nice. Because that's one of the most painful things in life, isn't it? Maybe even the most painful — being separated from the people we love."

"But nobody's going away here! So it's just a song."

He nodded his head and didn't say anything. I wondered if he already knew about Giacomo and the baby. But I couldn't take the chance of being the one to let out the secret if he didn't know.

But he talked about something else. "You've been pretty lucky with your health, I'll bet, Normie. You've never spent a lot of time in the hospital, I'm guessing."

"No, never! Except for that big machine. That was scary."

"I'm sure it was. It's great how it turned out, though, good results right down the line. But I think everybody expected that. Sometimes you have to have tests just so the doctors can check things off and move on."

"Yeah, it turned out good at the end."

"Did you ever have the measles, chicken pox, things like that?"

"I had both of those. Back when I was little."

"Have you ever been troubled by headaches?"

"Sometimes when I'm seeing all those bad things."

"Anything else?"

"No, except for having a cold and being sick to my stomach with the flu. I hate being sick."

"I don't blame you. I do too! Can you tell me this, Normie? We all feel sad sometimes. How about you? Are there many times when you feel sad?"

"Only when I worry about . . . well, the baby was sick, and I was sad and worried about him. And I feel sad when I hear of people getting killed or beat up, especially when it happens to little kids. I don't mean it's okay when it happens to grown-ups!"

"No, I understand. If you were writing a book titled *Normie Collins: A True Life Story*, would you describe yourself as a happy person?"

"Oh, yeah! Almost always! Except when things happen to upset me. Like these bad dreams. The things I see."

"Now, about those dreams or visions. We don't have to wonder whether you're seeing or feeling these things, because we know you are. Are these kind of like movie scenes that appear in your mind, as if you're seeing them with your eyes?"

"Yes, I can see what's going on. Or at least I can see part of it."

"What about sounds? Do you hear things? Voices, or noise of any kind that you think maybe other people can't hear?"

"I can hear voices, but I don't like telling people that. You know why."

"Oh, I know. But, really, if you're seeing something happening, it's probably quite natural that you would hear something too. Would you say so?"

"That's right. I can hear people yelling and sounding mean."

"What about this? Do you ever find that things don't taste the way they should? Or do you notice strange smells? Anything of that nature?"

"No, nothing like that."

"Why don't you describe the things you see and hear, so I can try to picture them."

"But Daddy's going to be mad at me!"

"Why would you think that, sweetheart?"

"Because . . ."

He didn't ask me "because what?" He didn't make a face that said "I wish she would hurry up." He just sat there, as if he didn't have anything else to do for the whole night. It was quiet, and then I felt like talking again. I figured he wasn't going to get me in trouble.

"Because . . . sometimes I think Mr. Delaney is bad!" There, I said it! I hadn't even said it to myself before.

"Maybe he is," Dr. Burke said.

What? I couldn't believe it! He said it as if it was normal! Maybe it was okay to think it: Mr. Delaney could be bad.

"But he can't be! Daddy says he didn't do it. Didn't kill Mrs. Delaney. And besides, he's Jenny and Laurence's dad! They are really good kids and they're my friends. None of my friends' dads are bad!"

"Well, you and I know some people are bad. Just a few of course, in any large group. And some of those bad people have kids. So it could be that you're right, even if you don't want to be right."

"But I must be wrong. Mr. Delaney is always really nice to his kids, and he's nice to me, too. If he was bad, I'd know!"

"Maybe you do know. Maybe that's what your feelings are telling you."

"Do you think he's bad?" I asked Dr. Burke.

"I'm kind of stuck for an answer because I don't know him. I've never met him. But I'll bet you can help me figure him out. When is the last time you saw him?"

"I think it was a couple of weeks ago, at our other house. Our house with Mum."

"How did you feel that day?"

"I was okay when I was with Mum and Father Burke, but after I went up to my room and fell asleep and then woke up again, I had pictures in my head. Like a dream but it seemed more real."

"Was Mr. Delaney in those images?"

"I don't know! I never know. There was a baby. Sometimes it's a baby and sometimes a little kid. And he's scared and sad and sometimes he's hurt really bad. He screams and cries. That night when Mr. Delaney was there I saw a spooky old building that had words on it. One was 'Vincent,' and . . ."

"And?"

"Uh . . ."

"Something else?"

"I forget."

Dr. Burke didn't say anything for a long time, so I thought I'd better tell him more about it, without saying the word *asylum*. "And

144

there's other people in the room. The people in robes."

"Oh, I see, and what kind of robes are they, Normie?"

"Long black ones."

"Many people?"

"A few anyway. Sometimes it seems like more."

"Can you tell if they are women, or men? Or are both men and women there?"

"I always think they're men. But I really can't tell, so maybe there's both."

"Are they doing anything?"

"I can't see it that clearly. I just know it's awful, it's horrible, and . . . and it seems to me as if somebody I know is one of them! And I keep thinking maybe it's Mr. Delaney. I don't see him exactly, but the dreams only started happening after I met him and his kids. Sometimes it's the people in robes in that building, and sometimes it's people in another place, a room, and I hear them talking or yelling in a mean way. But, no matter where it happens, there's always a little kid."

"So let's see if I have it straight. There are two different kinds of dreams, or pictures. One involves the old building and the long robes. The other does not."

"Right."

"When these things are happening, how do you feel yourself?"

"I get upset, as if I'm right there and I'm not doing anything to help!"

"When you reflect on these experiences, Normie, what do you think they mean?"

"I think some grown-ups did something bad to a little kid, and maybe to a baby. Or it might be something that's going to happen later. Way in the future! And that may be even worse because I already know, but I don't know how to stop it!"

"And when you see Mr. Delaney, you feel . . . what? How would you describe it?"

I didn't think I'd better blame Mr. Delaney any more, in case it wasn't really him, so I didn't answer.

Then Dr. Burke said: "Does he make you feel uneasy? As if something's wrong? Or nervous maybe?"

"Yeah, kind of like that."

"Normie, if there's ever anything you want to talk about, you just get hold of me, okay? If you want to do that, I'll be happy to help you. And of course happy just to hear from you any time!"

"Okay."

"This is my card, with my phone numbers at work and home. I'm going to tell your parents that I've given you my card and that I may be speaking to you, but you can call me on your own. Call any time, day or night."

"Thank you."

"You're more than welcome. I'll leave you alone now. You'll be needing your sleep if you're going to sing well at choir school tomorrow and put Father Burke in a good mood!"

I laughed again. He knows what his brother can be like, that some people might find him a little scary, but that's mostly shy people; he doesn't bother me.

So he gave me his card. I decided I would ask for a new wallet just for people's cards. This was the only one I had so far but I would collect others.

(Monty)

"Get your diving gear on."

"What?"

"Strip yourself of your priestly vestments, put on jeans and an old T-shirt, and meet me in your parking lot. We're going to a dive."

"What dive would that be now?"

"The Miller's Tale in Dartmouth. Stand by."

The fog bank had moved in and it was chilly. Burke was in his church parking lot in jeans and a battered leather jacket when I arrived. He raised his left eyebrow at me when he got in the car. I responded: "A client of mine was an associate of the Hells Angels in the not-so-distant past, and he may be able to help us with our inquiries. He recently started work at the Tale as a bartender after being out of the workforce for an extended period of time. He owes me."

"Would he have been a guest of Her Majesty for a couple of years perhaps?"

"Two years less a day in one of her institutions, yes."

"Sounds to me as if he doesn't owe you a thing."

"He should have gone away for ten years, and he's enough of a pro to know it. I worked out a deal for him, he did his time like a man, he's out, and he appreciates it. So I'm going to call in a marker. Try for some information."

"Is he a member of the motoring club?"

"He was an associate. There was a falling out years ago. Somehow he managed to make reparations for whatever offence he committed against them, and there are no hard feelings. I'm sure he's careful not to tread on their turf. As far as I know he's just a regular working stiff now. Like you and me."

The stench of greasy fried chicken assailed our nostrils when we got out of the car at the Miller's Tale. The chicken emporium was two doors down; the club's immediate neighbours were an X-rated video shop and a tattoo parlour. We went into the bar and stood still for a few seconds, letting our eyes get used to the dark. I didn't recognize the bartender. A wasted trip, or the chance for a beer and a game of pool?

"Let's get a drink and I'll see if I can find out when my old friend comes on shift."

We claimed two bar stools and we each ordered a draft. Seeing Burke with a beer glass in his hand reminded me that I hadn't seen him take a drink in weeks.

"Did you fall off the wagon? Were you on it?"

"I took a little break from the stuff for a while."

"How long a while?"

"Would I be counting?"

"How long?"

"Just over three weeks, I believe it is."

"Why'd you do that?"

He shrugged, then said: "Maybe I just wanted to see whether I missed it."

"Did you?"

"I didn't go through the DTs or anything, so . . ."

"Well, did you crave it? Did you have to fight the temptation to get into it?"

"No. I'd reach for a drink out of habit, but I didn't suffer unduly when I reminded myself I was on the wagon."

"So? What did that tell you?"

"That there's no harm in taking it up again!"

"I see. That worked out well for you, then."

"I don't need to drink; therefore, I drink."

"Your Cartesian logic puts me in mind of the Monty Python sketch about the drunken philosophers."

"I love that. It's brilliant. We'll have the choir perform it some day."

Burke was obviously one of those guys who have a considerable capacity for alcohol, but never became an alcoholic. A lot of people thought they were in that category, but were sadly mistaken. He, however, seemed to have it under control.

He drank down a third of his beer, put his glass on the table, said "Ah," and lit up a smoke.

I was just about to make a casual inquiry about Bradley Dwyer when he appeared carrying two large trays of fresh glasses. He was well able to handle the load. Over six feet in height, he was two hundred fifty pounds of pumped-up muscle. Prison tats covered his arms, and his dull brown hair was buzzed on the top, straggly in the back. He saw me right away and looked a bit leery, but recovered quickly and offered me a friendly greeting.

"Monty!" He turned to the other man behind the bar. "Don't take this guy's money, Al. He and his buddy drink free."

"Thanks, Bradley. We won't drink the place dry. This is Brennan Burke. Bradley Dwyer." They nodded to each other.

"How are you doing, Brad?"

"Not too bad."

Two hard-looking women came in, and Bradley served them. They took their drinks to a table, then picked up pool cues and got into a game. When the other barman went out back, I took the opportunity to question my old client.

"Brad, do you remember a guy named Bullard, got killed last spring?"

Warily, he answered: "Yeah, I remember hearing about that." He looked at my companion. "What do you do, Brennan?"

I laughed. "He's not a cop. We're not involved in an investigation of Bullard's death. It may have a connection with something else, or it may not. I heard it was a Hells Angels hit."

"That's bullshit!"

"Bullard was taken to a remote location and shot. And he was known to associate with guys with leather wings."

"He was a hanger-on, a loser! The HAs didn't want to have anything to do with him."

"Why not?"

"He was a fuckin' psycho, that's why."

"How do you know he was a psycho?"

"Because the HAs sent him to do a little intimidation job on a guy who owed them four thousand bucks in a drug deal. All Bullard was supposed to do was scare the guy, threaten to break his legs, just to motivate him, you know? Guy wasn't home, so Bullard goes nuts on the guy's woman. Rapes her, cuts her up. Unfuckinbelievable. And he did it in front of her son. Kid was seven years old. He freaked out, screaming and crying and trying to get Bullard off his mother. Bullard turns on the kid, beats him up."

I looked at Brennan. He was staring at Brad, horrified.

"So," I said, "from the bikers' point of view, eliminating this guy would be damage control."

"No fucking way. Angels didn't go within a mile of this clown after that. Damage control was 'never heard of the guy.' But somebody took him out."

"How about the man whose wife and child were attacked?"

Brad shook his head. "Airtight alibi. Cops had picked him up for selling coke the night before."

We reverted to small talk after that, then finished our drinks, thanked Brad, and left.

"So, where does that leave us?" Brennan asked in the car on the way back to Halifax.

"The Hells Angels apparently weren't after Beau's client. And they wouldn't have been after Beau. That wouldn't make any sense."

"Sounds as if the most dangerous element in this whole thing was Beau's client."

"And he'd already been eliminated before Peggy died, so if she was concerned about the Hells Angels at some point, this guy wasn't the problem."

Chapter 11

(Monty)

My client, Beau Delaney, was the architect, or the beneficiary at least, of a major grandstanding event three days before his trial got underway. Jack Hartt, the actor who played Delaney in the movie about the Gary's General Store case, was well known at the time of the film, but he had enjoyed even greater success in the years since, including two Oscar nominations. He made his home in Los Angeles, and had married his long-time love, Angie Bonner, lead vocalist and guitarist with the all-woman rock band Pink Curlers. The band had been at the top of the charts in the late seventies and early eighties; they still cut the occasional record and played the odd stadium gig. They had a huge following.

Now the Jack and Angie show was coming to Halifax. All in aid of Beau Delaney. Angie had offered to perform on the Commons, rain or shine. This was not the Beau Delaney Legal Defence Fund, but a charity concert to raise money for disadvantaged children. There was no charge for admission, but people were invited to make donations to the charity. When my blues band, Functus, was asked to be the opening act for the concert, I did not jump to the conclusion that our fame had spread to southern California. Or even to the south shore of Nova Scotia. Beau had a hand in that, obviously. But we were delighted to do the gig and add "opened for Angie Bonner" to our résumés, which would probably be done up on beer coasters if anything.

The night was foggy but mild. There were misty halos around the lights, which added a bit of atmosphere — local colour — to the set-up. The stage was at the northeast corner of the Commons, with a great red sandstone castle looming behind it, that is, the Halifax Armouries, which Queen Victoria ordered built at the end of the nineteenth century. There was a huge crowd on hand for the show, and a large media presence. Big, tough-looking guys circulated through the crowd passing the hat for the children's charity. I didn't know who the men were, but I knew nobody would even think of stealing the collection plate. The crowd gave my band a fine hometown welcome when we walked on stage. We did a few blues favourites and closed with Normie's most cherished song, "Stray Cat Strut." I brought her up with me to contribute the "meows." She earned a great round of applause, and loved every minute of it.

The applause went up a few hundred decibels when Angie Bonner and Jack Hartt walked onto the stage, in a blaze of lights from the television cameras and news photographers. Hartt had a mane of light brown hair, not all that different from Delaney's, minus the grey; he was tall and handsome in an athletic way. Angie was smaller than I expected, maybe a couple of inches over five feet and very slim; she had high cheekbones and long blond hair that streamed down over her shoulders. Some in the audience sang the Rolling Stones song "Angie" to welcome her. Others waved large Jack of Hearts cards to honour him. Angie was gracious enough to say a few kind words about Functus. Then Jack took centre stage.

"Hello, Halifax!"

That met with cheers. When they died down, Jack said: "I'd like to say a few words about why Angie and I are in Halifax. I'll start with two words: Beau Delaney. As some of you may know, I played the part of Beau Delaney in a movie shot here a few years back. I played the role, but Beau was the real-life hero, who had taken on a very unpopular case in a town near here and made *himself* very unpopular as a result. In fact he received death threats for acting in the case. But that didn't stop him from going back to that town, investigating a murder on his own time, finding the real killer, and freeing an innocent man who was wrongfully convicted of the killing. And if you want to know more, rent the video! Help pay for my trip!" Everybody laughed at that. "It's called *Righteous Defender*.

"So that was inspiring enough, you'd think. Right?" Cheers from the crowd. "But there's even more to Beau Delaney than that. When I met him, he did not have ten kids the way he has today. But he had a houseful even then. He had a few kids who were permanent parts of the family, of course, but he and his wife Peggy also took in foster children from time to time, on a temporary basis. So the Delaney house was always bursting at the seams with children. And with love!

"I was a Hollywood asshole. I still am, of course." The audience howled with laughter. "But in one way I've tried to be a better person than I was then. I was a single guy, but Angie and I were an item; we'd been together on and off for years. I was so impressed with Beau and Peggy and the life they had made for their children that when I got home, I said to Angie: 'Let's tone down the partying, let's grow up, get married, and start a family. And let's not wait nine months. There are children out there who need love — no child should have to live without love; isn't that the greatest tragedy in the world? — there are children out there who need a home. Angie, let's do something about it.' So we got married that week, and three months later we had two foster children living with us." He was interrupted by heartfelt cheers. "They're still with us, and there are five more now." Cheers again. "Wouldn't trade them for all the Oscars in the world! Beau, from the bottom of my heart, thank you for showing me what life is all about!" He tried to continue but his words were drowned out by the applause.

When it finally subsided, he said: "Angie, over to you."

The crowd roared and whistled, but she signalled for quiet, and the people obeyed. "If Jack was a Hollywood asshole, I was your stereotypical rock singer fuelling my performances with coke and booze. I gave it all up the night before our first appointment with social services to meet our first two foster children. Of course, we dropped the word 'foster' a long time ago. Anyway, I didn't turn into a perfect human being overnight either. I'm not even close. But I sure as hell am trying my very best because Jack and our children mean the whole world to me. And it all started when Jack got home and talked my ear off about Beau Delaney and his wife Peggy and all the adorable children who made up their family. And I always wanted to meet them. Well, that could be arranged. Jack brought them down to L.A., where we all partied — in a good way, a wholesome family-type way, before you start to think anything else — and I got to know Peggy and Beau. Thank God for that, because Peggy's not with us now. I am so blessed to have known her. Anyway, for those of you who don't know the family, I can tell you they're everything they're cracked up to be. So let me join Jack in thanking you, Beau, for being the guiding light in our family life." Roars of approval again. She turned around and picked up her guitar, checked her sound, and said: "Beau, this one's for you!"

She launched into a solo version of the Pink Curlers song "Love of My Life," and rocked for two hours solid after that.

The radio, newspaper, and television coverage the next day was everything a public relations person could hope for. I hadn't planned it. Beau swore he hadn't planned it either, that the idea originated with Angie and Jack. But whatever the case, I pleaded in my mind, *Potential jurors, take note!* Beau stopped by my office to give me a copy of the *Righteous Defender* video, and I watched it the night before the trial. My client's heroics were an inspiration. If only I could play it for the jury and say: "My Lord, I rest my case."

Delaney sat beside me at the defence table as the trial got underway on Thursday, May 7, 1992. He whispered: "All right, counsellor, let's get this show on the road. Or, get this showboat in the water." But he knew enough not to dress like a showboat for the trial. He wore a sedate navy suit with white shirt and soft blue tie. I nodded approvingly at his ensemble.

"Hmmph! I have to say I feel naked here without my robe on, Monty."

"I suppose you do, after all these years."

The prosecutors and I were decked out in our barristers' black gowns and white neck tabs, but Beau was just a civilian for this event.

At the table in front of us were the Crown attorneys, Gail Kirk and Bill MacEwen, facing Justice Kenneth Palmer's bench. The jury box was to our left, farther up the courtroom. The seven-woman, five-man jury had been selected, after much whispering, nudging, and note-passing on the part of Delaney, and it was time for the Crown's line-up of witnesses.

The charge was second-degree murder. There was no way this could be painted as a planned and deliberate killing. The Crown's theory, as presented by the police and the Crown's expert witness, a pathologist, was that Beau killed Peggy by hitting her on the back of the head with a heavy rock, fracturing her skull. The rocks were at the foot of the stairs because the Delaney children had intended to use them to build a fort. After the deadly assault, they said, Beau carried his wife down the stairs, laid her on her back, and arranged the rock under her head so the wound would match the murder weapon. Their backup theory was that Beau pushed her down the stairs, but this was so much like a fall — an accident — that they stressed the clubbing theory at the trial. The Crown dismissed out of hand any idea that Peggy tripped and fell down the stairs. If she had tripped, she would have fallen face first. The Crown, whose formal role is to pursue the truth, could not avoid calling the medical examiner, who candidly admitted in his report and on the stand that his findings were inconclusive: it could have been an accident or a homicide. But the lead Crown attorney, Gail Kirk, got him out of the way quickly, before welcoming her second opinion, Dr. Heath MacLeod, to the stand and spending nearly two hours eliciting his evidence. I got the pathologist to admit, on cross-examination, that it was possible the skull fracture was caused by Mrs. Delaney falling on the rock.

The autopsy showed a bruise on Peggy's left arm, with one mark on the front-facing part of the arm and multiple marks on the back. In other words, this was a mark left by a hand gripping the victim's arm. Dr. MacLeod acknowledged that this appeared to be the result of someone being face to face with Peggy and holding her arm. My point was that this was inconsistent with an attack from behind.

I got the police officers who examined the scene to acknowledge that there was no blood at or near the top of the stairs where the fatal blow was said to have been struck. And no blood on Delaney himself. Or, as the officer said: "Not on the clothing he was wearing when we saw him."

Sergeant Chuck Morash testified about being called to the scene and finding Peggy Delaney's body lying undisturbed on the floor. There were no signs of forced entry into the house. Morash asked Delaney if he had moved her. No. Touched her. No. The sergeant went on to describe how little Delaney said at the scene, apart from stating that he had not been home when his wife died and had arrived from Annapolis Royal around twelve thirty in the morning. Delaney had not asked any questions, rhetorical or otherwise, about what might have happened to his wife. The detective with the degree in psychology left the impression that Beau had been cool and calculating at the death scene. I had nothing to gain, and much to lose, by prolonging his testimony, so I did not cross-examine him.

The Crown's last witness was Harold Gorman, the elderly neighbour who told police he had seen Beau outside his house the night Peggy died. Mr. Gorman was dressed in grey flannel pants, white shirt and tie, and a blue cardigan sweater. He shivered as if from the cold when he took his place in the witness box, was sworn in, and identified himself.

"Mr. Gorman, please tell the court what you saw on the night of January fifteenth."

"Certainly. I looked out the window and saw Mr. Delaney in his driveway."

"And what was he doing?"

"Just having a look around the place, as far as I could tell."

"I see. What time would this have been?"

"I'm not sure. It was pretty late."

"Can you give us an estimate?"

"No, I just can't remember."

"Was it dark?"

"Oh yes, it would have been after midnight. At least I think so, but I'm not sure."

This was good for us, bad for Gail Kirk. Gail exchanged a glance with her fellow attorney.

"Why are you not sure?"

"Well, it was quite a long time ago."

"Mr. Gorman, did you give a statement to the police in connection with this matter?"

"Yes, I did."

"Would you like to read a copy of the statement to refresh your memory?"

"Okay."

Gail handed him the pages.

"Take your time. Read it over."

He read through it, and then looked up.

"Does that help you remember better?"

"I guess so, yes."

"So what time did you see Mr. Delaney that night?"

"Well, according to this, Lloyd wasn't on yet at the time I saw Mr. Delaney. And then I fell asleep and didn't see Lloyd come on."

"Who were you referring to when you said 'Lloyd'?"

"Lloyd Robertson, anchorman for the late-night news on CTV."

"And, to your knowledge, what time does the CTV news come on?"

"Eleven o'clock."

"So your evidence is that you saw Mr. Delaney outside his house before eleven o'clock on the night of January fifteenth?"

"That's what it says here, but when I think of it now, I —"

"Thank you, Mr. Gorman. When did you give that statement, do you recall?"

"Right afterwards."

"Right after Mrs. Delaney was killed?"

"Objection, My Lord," I said dutifully.

"I'll rephrase that, My Lord. Mrs. Delaney died on January fifteenth. And you gave your statement shortly afterwards."

"Must have been the following day."

"Would you agree that your memory of the events of that night would likely be more clear closer to the time of those events than it would be now, four months later?"

"I tend to doze off and wake up a lot, you see, so —"

"Please answer my question, Mr. Gorman. Would you like me to repeat it?"

"No. But let me tell you this. My memory of being in a landing craft on the sixth day of June, 1944, is crystal clear in my mind, much more so than my memory of what time I went out for groceries two days ago!"

The jury laughed at that, not in mockery but in sympathy with Mr. Gorman, *war veteran* Gorman, who had fought for our country in the Second World War. I suspect that squelched any plan Gail might have considered to have Gorman declared a hostile witness, so she could cross-examine him on his prior inconsistent statement. She let him off the hook. The jury had heard that the witness had previously stated that Delaney was home before eleven o'clock. Gail would have to be content with that for the time being.

I, however, had a witness lined up to speak to the Environment Canada weather summary for that day, so I wanted Gorman clearly on the record about the snowfall.

I stood and asked him: "Mr. Gorman, do you recall what the weather was like that night?"

"Snow blew up overnight, I remember that."

"Did you take a look, to see what it was doing outside?"

"Oh yes, I got up and looked out. It was really loud against my window. I had work done on my windows just for that reason, to keep the weather out. They held up just fine."

"That's good. When you looked out to check the weather, did you see anyone around?"

"Well, I saw Beau."

That was as good as it was going to get for us, so I moved on to another thing I wanted the jury to hear.

"Did you see anybody else around that night, Mr. Gorman?"

"Yes, I did. I saw some young fellow skulking around."

"Where exactly was he?"

"He seemed to move around. He was over by Delaney's, then he was at the house next door to Delaney's, then he disappeared."

"How long was he out there, that you could see?"

"A few minutes."

"What was he doing?"

"Just loitering and peering around, at the time I caught sight of him."

"Can you describe him for us?"

"Skinny and wearing a hooded sweatshirt. I couldn't see his face or his hair, or anything, so I wouldn't know him again if I fell over him."

"Those are my questions. Thank you, Mr. Gorman."

After two days of testimony, the Crown rested its case.

†

Court would be sitting for only three days the following week, because Justice Palmer was booked to attend a conference in London. If all went according to plan I would have everybody but my star witness, Beau Delaney, wrapped up in those three days. So I opened the case for the defence on Monday with a silent but fervent prayer that all would go according to plan. No surprises.

The first thing I did was call a meteorologist with Environment Canada, who brought his records for January 15 and 16, 1992. The snow started just after midnight. So if Mr. Gorman saw Beau when he got up to check out the storm, this corroborated Beau's own estimate of the time he arrived home, and not the earlier time asserted by the Crown.

After that, we presented our version of how the fatal head wound was incurred. Our pathology expert, Dr. Andrea Mertens, testified in exacting detail about the shape and depth of the skull fracture, and had no hesitation in concluding that the wound was consistent with Peggy falling and hitting the back of her head on the rock. We went further than that, and had our engineer, Wes Kaulbeck, give us all kinds of impressive evidence on body weight and the velocity of a fall, and the forces in play, and the strength of the materials involved — rock and skull bone. In the engineer's expert opinion, Peggy's fall down the stairs could well have resulted in the skull fracture that caused her death. Gail Kirk and Bill MacEwen spent a couple of hours trying to chip away at our witnesses on cross, but they didn't do us any serious harm.

I went into overdrive the next day with a throng of character witnesses on Beau's behalf. I called his parish priest, the president of the Kiwanis Club, the woman in charge of the food bank where Delaney

158

and his family regularly volunteered. I called the president of the Nova Scotia Barristers' Society. I called Peggy's sister, Sheila, and her brother-in-law, Angus. They both spoke glowingly of Beau, who, along with all his other fine qualities, had never shown any inclination towards violence. I could have called hundreds of witnesses who could speak to Delaney's good character, but we had to be reasonable.

Our next witness was in town as the result of a conversation I had had with my client a couple of weeks before the trial began.

"We're certainly going to build you up, Beau, with all our character witnesses. And I assume the Crown has not been able to find anybody who has ever seen you become violent under any circumstances."

"Exactly."

"And we could call an endless parade of witnesses of our own who can say you've never been violent, but then why would you be violent, unless you were provoked? Which of course is the Crown's theory."

"How about somebody who can say I did not react with violence even when I *was* provoked?"

"Wouldn't that be nice!"

"Did you ever hear about the incident with Wayne Theriault?"

"Who's he?"

"An old client of mine. He ambushed me outside my office one night. Jumped me when I was heading to my car. I got him calmed down. Beau Delaney, cool and non-violent in a potentially explosive situation."

"Any witnesses to this incident?"

"None living."

"*What?* What are you saying?"

"I mean Peggy was in the car."

"Oh. No other witnesses?"

"A baby too young to remember. The only other witness was Theriault himself."

"What are the chances he'd give evidence in your favour, if he was that pissed off at you?"

"Try him and see."

"Where is he?"

"Renous."

"He's sitting in a maximum security prison making crafts for the annual Defence Lawyer Appreciation Day."

"Hey, Wayne and I got along okay. He knew he was going to do time. All we could do was try to keep the parole eligibility date down, and I got him the minimum. And I didn't report him for breach of his bail conditions when he was stalking me at midnight, and threatening my life. Give him a call."

"He'll say anything to get out of there for a day. A point the Crown will be quick to make."

"Give it a try. See what he says."

So on the third day of the defence's case, at my client's insistence, we called a convicted murderer to testify as a character witness for a man accused of murder.

There was extra security in the courtroom, and the jurors were openly curious. Our witness was costumed in an ill-fitting black business suit, but nobody would mistake him for a member of the Chamber of Commerce. He had light brown hair pushed back from his forehead and a nose that looked as if it had been smashed. That might not make him stand out in a line-up of his peers, but the tattoo of a dragon visible on the side of his neck could be considered a distinguishing feature. His knuckles were tattooed as well. Instead of the customary "hate" and "love," his knuckles read "hate" and "tail." He was our man. I plunged in.

"Please state your name for the court."

"Wayne Joseph Theriault."

"Where do you live, Mr. Theriault?"

"I've gone back to my roots, in New Brunswick. Born and raised there; now I'm back. My retirement years, you might say."

That's all I needed, a smartass on the stand. He wasn't this cocky when I went over his testimony with him in the morning, after he arrived with his Corrections Canada escort.

"Where in New Brunswick are you living now?"

"The Atlantic Institution in Renous."

"And that is . . ."

"Maximum security prison."

"How did you end up there?"

"I was convicted of murder."

There was a gasp from a couple of the jurors.

"But I didn't do it. Or, like, I did it, but it wasn't murder."

I saw the two Crown attorneys exchange a glance. The last thing I wanted was any talk of "I did it, but it wasn't really murder" during this trial.

"We're not here to retry your case, Mr. Theriault. Could you tell us how you came to know Mr. Delaney."

"Beau helped me out of a few scrapes during my time here in Halifax."

"Helped you out in what way?"

"Beau's *the man*!"

Now he was affecting ghetto speech. I had to keep him on track.

"Could you be more specific, Mr. Theriault? How did Mr. Delaney help you?"

"He's a great lawyer, man. He got me off on a whole string of theft and robbery-type offences. And it wasn't easy, 'cause I done them! But he's good!"

"So you were a client of Mr. Delaney, and he was successful in defending you on charges you faced before the murder charge."

"Yeah, we ran out of luck on that one. But can't win 'em all, eh? That's the way I look at it."

"Now, do you recall an incident involving Mr. Delaney back in 1986, when you were out on bail awaiting your trial for murder?"

"Yeah, I got a little ticked at Beau that night."

"Why was that?"

"He told me I should plead to the murder because there was no way he could get me off. Said he'd work out a deal with the Crown, get me a good parole date to run by the judge. The usual, you know."

"And you didn't agree with that strategy."

"I didn't want to serve no time. It was self-defence. The guy I wasted, he deserved it. So the night of this incident, I was pounding back the booze and I got hold of some coke and I was all fucked up." Theriault turned to the judge. "Excuse my French, Your Honour. Anyway, I went looking for Beau. I knew he was working late because I cruised by his office and seen the light on. I went to a phone booth and made a call to him, telling him what I wanted him to do. But he told me to go home or I'd get caught for breaching my bail conditions, by being out past curfew and drunk and coked up. I called him again and hollered at him and told him to fuck off and to make sure he got me off the murder rap. He hung up on me. So I went back to his office building and hung around and waited till he came out. I got myself all worked up against him. When he came out the door, I jumped him."

"How tall are you, Mr. Theriault?"

"I'm six foot one."

"And how much do you weigh?"

"Just under two hundred pounds."

"So you're a big man, but not quite as tall and heavy as Mr. Delaney. Would you agree with that?"

"Yeah, he's a big dude, no question."

"What happened when you jumped Mr. Delaney outside his office?"

"He flipped me off him."

"How?"

"I don't know. I just ended up on the ground."

"Then what?"

"I tried to get up and go at him again. But he held me down by putting his foot on my chest."

"Did that hurt?"

"It didn't really hurt; it just kept me from getting up."

"Then what?"

"He tried to talk me down. Get me to chill out. Said we'd talk about the case when I was straight and sober. Told me he'd get a cab and send me home. Said if I got caught breaching my bail, I'd never get bail again."

"And then?"

"When he thought I had cooled off, he eased his foot up. Reached down with his hand to help me stand. I got up, and he turned around and walked over to his car. He put the key in the door, and I ran after him and put my arm around his throat and had my fist ready to slam him in the side of the head."

"What happened at that time?"

"I didn't do nothin'. I backed off."

"How come?"

"Because I seen he had his wife in the car. She was waiting for him. Her and a little kid."

"Witnesses."

"I didn't give a fuck about witnesses! It was the man's wife! And his kid! I wasn't going to beat a man up in front of his family. What kind of an animal would do that?"

"What did Mr. Delaney do at that point?"

"Beau had it all under control. He said: 'Wayne, you don't want to start this. Walk away. We'll talk when you're sober. And if I get a sincere apology and if I think you won't try this again, I'll stay on as your lawyer. If not, I'm cutting you loose. Now back off, or my wife will go for the police.' I looked at the wife and kid. They were staring at me like I was something in a horror movie. I felt like a lowlife piece of shit. I let him go, and I took off."

"Were there any more . . . scuffles . . . between you and Mr. Delaney?"

"No, that was it. I ate crow when I seen him next day, and he stayed on as my lawyer. I swiped a nice bottle of Scotch and gave it to him as a peace offering. He probably still has it. Beau's not much of a drinker. He got me as good a deal as I was going to get on the murder charge. I never seen him again till now."

"Thank you, Mr. Theriault. The Crown attorney may have some questions."

She did indeed. Gail Kirk rose to her feet. "Mr. Theriault, how long have you been in Renous prison?"

"Six years."

"Have you had any other escorted outings or temporary leaves of absence during your time at Renous?"

"Nope."

"So this is your first day away from the prison in six years?"

"Yeah."

"You'd do or say anything to get out of prison for a day, wouldn't you?"

"Yeah, maybe so." I winced when I heard that, but it was a chance we had decided to take.

"Like, I coulda come down to Halifax," Theriault continued, "and told Beau and his lawyer I'd say nice things about Beau, and then I coulda come in here and shit all over Beau's case just for the hell of it, 'cause I got the day out anyway. But I didn't. I came in here and told the truth about Beau because he's a good guy, and a good lawyer, and he gave me a lot of help over the years. And he didn't beat the piss out of me when I went after him all drugged up and tanked up, and he could have killed me, but he didn't."

I could have kissed him, but I didn't. I assumed Gail Kirk had a lot more questions she wanted to ask, but she decided to cut her losses, and said: "No further questions for this witness, My Lord."

"Mr. Collins? Anything arising out of that?"

"No, My Lord."

"Thank you, Mr. Theriault. You may go. With your escort."

Chapter 12

(Monty)

"Beau wants me to call the kids," I said to Brennan at our regular Tuesday night sitting at the Midtown.

"You'd think he'd want to protect them from all this," he said.

"As a father yes, as a defendant maybe, as a showman no. If he had his way, we'd have them all lined up like the Von Trapp family."

"He'd have them burst into song."

"Exactly."

"It's not as if their evidence would add anything to the record. Leave them out of it," Brennan urged me.

"Spoken like a true non-lawyer. It's not about what they say. Of course they're all going to say wonderful things about their dad. That's not the point. The point is to have the jury see them. Ten children who have lost their mother to a tragic *accident*, and who may lose their loving father. A family that will be shattered, the children divided up and dispersed to relatives, foster homes, and government bureaucracy. Ten adorable children who love their father and know he's innocent; that's why they're supporting him. The jury has to see them. To me, that would be sufficient. But he wants them up there, showing no fear, testifying to his good character."

So that's the way it went. I had Peggy's sister Sheila bring all the Delaney kids into the courtroom and seat them before the judge and jury came in. Parading them in after the jury was in place would have been over the top. The kids were scrubbed and dressed in the kind of clothes you'd wear to visit Grandma on a Sunday afternoon. Little Sammy and Kristin, aged five and six, sat on the knees of the two eldest teens, Sarah and Derek. Everyone stood, as protocol demands, when the judge and then the jury entered the room.

"The defence calls Sarah Delaney."

Tall like her dad and blond like her mum, Sarah walked stiffly towards the stand. She wore a tartan skirt, a white blouse and a heathery blue sweater over it; her bangs were pulled to the side with a barrette. I did not detect any makeup, with the possible exception of some colour on her cheekbones.

She was sworn in, and I asked her to give her name.

"Sarah Margaret Delaney."

"How old are you, Sarah?"

"Seventeen."

I smiled at her. "Please tell the court how you are related to Mr. Delaney."

"He's my dad."

"And tell us where you come in the family."

"I'm the oldest of the ten of us."

"What's it like having nine younger sisters and brothers?"

"Sometimes it's fun and sometimes it's frustrating!" The jurors laughed. With her, not at her. "I wouldn't change it, though. There's none of them I'd want to lose!"

"What kind of a dad is Mr. Delaney?"

"He's great! He spends all kinds of time with us, and takes us places, and helps us with our homework and other things. He's sweet, and sometimes he's really funny! Not so much now . . ."

"Once in a while, kids need some direction. Or correction, I might say. Discipline. How does your dad handle that?"

"He tells us to smarten up, or we'll be grounded. And he means it."

"Have you ever been grounded?"

"Well, not me, but . . . the boys. You know."

Everyone laughed again, and I said: "I know! Now I realize children aren't with their parents every minute of the parents' lives, but from what you saw of your parents, did they seem to get along well or not?"

"They were really happy together. He was very, very sad when Mum died. And he still is. He really loved her."

"From what you could see growing up, was there any violence between them?"

"Never! They never hit each other, or, you know, threw things the way you hear of other people doing. He wouldn't have hurt Mum at all, let alone . . ." Sarah looked as if she was going to burst into tears. I wasn't going to promote that.

"I have nothing else to ask you, Sarah. Ms. Kirk may have some questions."

"No questions, My Lord."

Justice Palmer said: "You may step down, Sarah."

Next I called Derek, who was fifteen, tall and thin with short brown hair. He gave pretty well the same evidence. Then it was Connor's turn. He was thirteen and a half. He had dark blond hair, and was considerably shorter than his sister Sarah.

I started off the same way, and then got to the question of whether things ever got physical between Beau and Peggy during an argument.

"No, never! Not even when they got into fights about Corbett!"

I had no idea who Corbett was, and this was not the time to ask questions and get answers I was not prepared for. Instead, I zeroed in on the word "fights."

"Now, Connor, when you say 'fights,' what do you mean?"

"I don't mean hitting people! I just mean when you say something and the other person says something back, and like that."

"Words going back and forth, people arguing? Disagreeing?"

"Yes, arguing! That's what I mean, not fighting. Dad never hit Mum. And Mum sure never hit Dad!"

The jurors laughed a bit at that. I had to decide whether to leave well enough alone, or quash any suspicion that there was a lot of arguing in the Delaney household.

"So arguing happened once in a while in your family?"

"Oh, yeah. Sometimes. It still does!" Laughs again. "But usually, it's us kids arguing with each other. Dad stops it."

I didn't want to leave that dangling, so I took another chance.

"What does your dad do to stop you guys from arguing?"

"He says: 'Stop arguing!'"

Once more, the jurors enjoyed the young kid's testimony.

Encouraged, Connor went on: "He just says to stop yammering or he'll have to bring back the strap." Oh God, no. I could already see the appellant's factum for Beau's appeal. Incompetent counsel — me — would be the first ground of appeal. But Connor hadn't finished. "They used to have a strap that they hit kids with. Not in our house, but in the schools Mum and Dad went to. Dad had a teacher and she was a sister named Little Hitler and she used to hit him and the other students with her strap when they were bad. Dad says that's wrong, and kids should never be strapped or spanked. So that never happened in our house."

Thank you, Sister Little Hitler, wherever you are now, for turning Beau Delaney against corporal punishment. It was time to bring the curtain down.

"Those are all my questions for Connor, My Lord. Connor, you may step down. Unless the Crown lawyer has anything to ask you." And of course, we hope against hope that she hasn't.

But my backside hadn't hit the seat when Gail Kirk was on her feet. "Connor, you said your parents used to argue about Corbett. Could you tell us who Corbett is?"

I could see Delaney tense up beside me. He had been scribbling notes across the page in his large scrawling handwriting. He didn't even leave the margins free; the writing went from edge to edge of the page. But his hand ceased its motion. I hoped nobody else noticed.

"He's our brother," Connor said.

"Oh? So there are eleven children in your family, not ten?"

"No, there's only ten now 'cause Corbett's gone."

"Where has he gone?"

"Nobody knows! One night he just up and disappeared!"

What in the name of God was this? It took every bit of willpower to stop myself from firing that question at my client. I attempted to look as if nothing was wrong. I directed a mild, just-looking-around glance at the jury. They were riveted to the child on the stand.

Gail Kirk asked for more. "And you haven't heard from him?"

I wanted to object that these questions were irrelevant, but I didn't want to draw any more attention to this subject, and I didn't want to show that we were rattled. So I stayed in my seat.

"No. We wanted to look for him, but Dad said we wouldn't be able to find him, so there was no point in trying."

"Have the police been involved?"

I had to object to that. "My Lord, I have been sitting here and not objecting" — I hoped to give the impression that I had not bothered to object till now because the topic was so unimportant — "to all this irrelevant testimony, but now we are going too far astray. None of this is relevant, and we cannot expect young Connor to know what the police may or may not be doing with respect to missing persons." I was flying blind, until I felt a nudge against my leg. I looked down and saw that Delaney had written on his page: "Foster child, didn't work out."

I got my second wind, and improvised. "Mr. and Mrs. Delaney had been foster parents for many years. Sometimes placements work out wonderfully; sometimes they do not, which is very unfortunate, and other arrangements have to be made."

"My Lord!" Kirk exclaimed. "My learned friend is giving evidence. He has not been qualified as an expert in social work. Nor is it time for him to give his summation. I —"

"Thank you, Ms. Kirk," Justice Palmer interjected. "Mr. Collins?"

"My Lord, I just think we are getting way off topic here, and my friend is questioning a child witness about matters that are outside the witness's competence."

"Objection sustained. Move on, Ms. Kirk."

"No other questions for this witness, My Lord."

The judge spoke gently to Delaney's son. "You may step down now, Connor."

"The defence calls Ruth . . ."

I could see Gail Kirk practically squirming with impatience; she would not, however, have wanted to alienate the jury by objecting to the redundancy of the evidence of Delaney's children. But her concentration never flagged. During other trials with Gail, when there were tedious legal motions being argued, I had often noticed her drawing little pictures of leaves and flowers along the edges of her notepad. Not now; she wasn't missing a word of the testimony. In fact, I did not plan to call all ten of the kids. Beau and I had agreed on two girls and two boys. One more to go.

When it came to Ruth, I could see that the young girl was trembling with nerves. She looked miserable with her dark curly hair pulled back from her broad face, and a skirt and sweater that were too small for her heavy build. She did not want to perform in public. So I should have stopped there. But, before I could announce that we would call no more evidence that day, little Jenny was up on her feet and on her way to the stand.

"I'll do it, Ruthie," she said to her older sister. "I know you're feeling sick today."

So Jenny was sworn in, sat in the witness chair, smoothed her flowery skirt, and smiled at me.

"Hello, Jenny."

"Hi, Mr. Collins."

"Thank you for stepping into the breach today."

"You're welcome."

I took her through the same series of questions, and received the same endorsement of Beau Delaney as a wonderful man and loving father.

When I thought she was finished, I thanked her again, and she took the opportunity to express her gratitude to me.

"Thank you too, Mr. Collins, for helping Daddy. He didn't kill Mummy. The Hells Angels didn't come in that night and do it either, so we'll never know what that was about. Nobody killed her." She turned to face the jurors, a few of whom appeared to be amused by the biker reference, but quickly masked their reaction, and smiled at the young witness. "Nobody would have," Jenny said, "because everybody loved her. It was an accident."

If I thought the Hells Angels reference would be dismissed at the Crown's table as a child's idea of how somebody might be killed, I was wrong. Gail Kirk got to her feet and addressed the witness.

"Hello, Jenny. Could you tell us what you meant just now when you referred to the Hells Angels?"

Before I could even get to my feet, I felt the pressure of my client's leg against mine. He scribbled on his notepad: "NO!"

"Objection, My Lord," I said dutifully.

"Grounds, Mr. Collins?"

"Relevance, My Lord. Neither the Crown nor the defence has led any evidence or made any reference to a motorcycle club. The question here is whether Mr. Delaney was involved in his wife's death, or whether it was an accident. We obviously say her death was accidental. We have not raised the spectre of a third party in this."

"My Lord," Gail Kirk argued, "this matter came up on direct. We are entitled to cross-examine the witness on it."

"I'll allow it. Go ahead, Ms. Kirk."

Delaney was deathly still as the prosecutor asked his daughter once more why she mentioned the Hells Angels, and Jenny obliged her with an answer.

"It wasn't anything. They didn't do it. It's just that Mum yelled out 'Hells Angels' the night she died. I heard her, and she sounded upset, and I meant to get up and ask her if she was okay, but I was so tired I fell asleep again! I could have helped her! I might have saved her from falling down the stairs! But I fell asleep, and she died!" The little girl began sobbing uncontrollably.

I was struck dumb at the defence table. Peggy had shouted out the words "Hells Angels" not *some time* or *one night*, but the night she died. I found it hard to believe, and so would the Crown, that she was talking to herself. It sounded to me as if she had been making an accusation, or reacting to a statement; either way, she was not alone when she uttered the exclamation. Not alone, perhaps, at the moment of her death.

Gail Kirk wanted desperately, I knew, to press Jenny about that night, but the child was so distraught that she had to offer a respite first.

"Would you like to take a break, Jenny? Here, please take a tissue."

Jenny wiped her eyes and blew her nose. She took a few minutes to compose herself. I could well imagine the willpower Beau had to summon to keep himself from rushing to the stand to comfort his child. Whatever else was going on in his mind was something I would have to deal with at another time.

When Jenny pulled herself together, Gail asked her gently: "Who was your mum talking to when she said 'Hells Angels,' do you know?"

Jenny shook her head, then said: "I don't know. I just figured . . ." Her eyes went to Beau, and then jerked away. "Nobody, I guess . . . She was by herself, and all us kids were in bed."

"So you didn't hear anyone else? Another voice, or sounds that —"

I got up again. "The witness has already answered the question, My Lord."

The child was shaking her head again.

Gail said: "I'll withdraw the question, My Lord. Jenny, do you remember the Hells Angels being mentioned any other time at your house?"

I was trying to formulate an objection to that one, but Jenny got ahead of me. "No way," she answered. "That was the only time."

"I have no further questions, My Lord."

✝

I certainly had questions. For my client. But rather than have him hauled out of sight for an urgent consultation, I decided to have him leave the courtroom surrounded by his flock of children. I normally didn't play to the press in this way, but I would use anything that would help our case. Never mind that the jurors were not supposed to read, watch, or listen to any news reports about the trial. We would take good publicity whenever we could find it. The television cameras were there, and Delaney performed beautifully, giving all his attention to the kids and none, ostensibly, to the cameras.

But afterwards, in the narrow little kitchen of his place in the Twelve Apostles, I lit into him: "What is this business about the Hells Angels? We've built our entire case on the assertion that you weren't there, Beau! Jenny heard Peggy shout out something about the Hells Angels, and I suspect the jury's impression is the same as my own, and the Crown's, that Peggy wasn't talking to herself. She was reacting to something she had just heard, or she was making an accusation of some sort. My guess — my inference — is that she was talking to you, that you were there when she died. You'd better come up with a damn good explanation!"

"Why the hell did you let her go on about it?"

"Me? Why the hell didn't you warn me that one of your children had information that could blow your case out of the water? I heard something about the Hells Angels, but you can be damn sure I didn't hear that this happened the very night she died! So, were you there or not? Your neighbour thought you were. Gorman."

"You neutralized him with the weatherman and the timing of the snowstorm."

"Of course I did. That doesn't mean the poor old fellow had it all wrong. What happened, Beau?"

But he didn't reply. He just stared at the exposed brick wall of the old house, and tuned me out.

I had no intention of leaving till I got an answer. If he wanted to stew about it for a while, so be it. Then I remembered something else.

"While we're at it, Beau, tell me about Corbett. Funny I never heard his name before."

"Community Services placed him with us last year. He had been with us briefly a few years before that. Despite our best efforts, he never fit in."

"That must happen quite often with foster children."

"True."

"How old is he?"

"Fifteen now."

"So the placement was what? Terminated? How does it work? Is he back in care with the government? That's the impression I got from your note."

"Not exactly."

"Well, what? Where is he?"

"He ran away."

"Just as Connor said on the stand." I glared at him. "Good thing we shut it down when we did." Delaney sat there without speaking. "Beau? What's the story here?"

"The kid was a bad actor. He didn't get along with the other children."

"How did he get along with you?"

"Not great."

"And Peggy?"

"She thought there was hope for him."

"And you didn't."

"He never would have fit in. His presence put a strain on the family."

"Peggy didn't agree?"

"No."

"What did she see in him that you didn't?"

"Or what did I see that she did not? I saw trouble. She saw a boy who could be helped."

"You and Peggy argued about it."

"Inevitably."

"Were you arguing about Corbett the night Peggy died?"

It took him awhile, but he denied it: "No."

I regarded him in silence for a long moment. "Is this a missing person case? Are the police involved? Community Services must be in the loop."

"I did not call the police."

"Why not?"

"Because I informed Community Services, and left it up to them to figure out what to do. Corbett originally came here from the Annapolis Valley, so I expect the department here would have been in touch with their people there. And I would imagine they contacted the police as well."

"I would imagine. You don't just have a child — a ward of the state — wander off the reserve, and nobody wonders where he is."

"We all wonder where he is. The department is handling the situation."

"When did he disappear?"

Another hesitation, then: "Last fall."

I looked Delaney in the eye. "Do you think something happened to Corbett, Beau?"

"What, for instance, Monty?"

"You tell me. Any ideas?"

"I do not know. Period."

"You'd better come up with some lines that will sound better than that on the stand, Beau. And you'd better look a little more compassionate about this young boy when court resumes next week, and the

Crown hammers you on this very point." I waited a few beats, then asked: "Is there some connection between him and the Hells Angels?"

Beau gave a snort of laughter. "Only in his dreams."

"So this thing about the bikers . . ."

"Forget it, Monty. I don't know what that was about. I wasn't there."

"All right. I'll leave you. You've got some thinking to do. You know where to find me."

Chapter 13

(Monty)

I was having an early dinner with the family at the house on Dresden Row that evening. Little Dominic watched us, contentedly, from his high chair. Maura and I worked in the kitchen together, quite companionably, preparing the meal. I decided not to destroy that mood by asking questions, as curious and vexed as I was, about Dominic and the custody dispute with the boy's father.

Maura issued her customary instructions: "Why don't you go up and do some homework before supper, Normie."

"In a minute! I want to watch *Live at Five*. They were out talking to people on Spring Garden Road with TV cameras. It was ATV, and me and Kim walked by, and we may get to see ourselves! I'm going to tape it."

"What were you and Kim doing on Spring Garden Road?"

"We decided to walk that way instead of Morris Street."

"You know you're supposed to come straight home."

"I know." She pounded down to the den. "Here it is!" I heard the program come on, and it was obvious the homework would have to wait. "Aw! They've got something else on first! Oh, it's Mr. Delaney again. There's a picture of him."

My ears perked up at that.

"There has been a new development in the murder case of renowned criminal lawyer Beau Delaney. A surprise witness has come forward in Mr. Delaney's defence. Todd Webber has the story. Todd?"

I didn't want any more surprises. I don't like surprises in the middle of a trial, whether they're billed as good news for the defence or not. That goes double for surprise witnesses. I made a beeline for the downstairs den, with Maura right behind me.

"Steve, I'm at the law courts where the young witness appeared, too late, as it turns out, for today's proceedings, but the following days of the trial should be interesting. The witness, fifteen-year-old Corbett Reeves, says Mr. Delaney did not commit murder, and he, Corbett, can prove it. In other words, Steve, it sounds as if Corbett is an alibi witness for the accused lawyer."

What? The face of a young man filled the screen. He had very light blond hair buzzed short on his skull. He spoke into the camera in a strange, high-pitched voice: "Me and Beau have a history together. And I know there's no way he did any killing. I can tell the judge the truth."

"Why have you just come forward now, Corbett?"

"I was somewhere else, and couldn't be here till now. I'm just glad the trial's still going on and I'm not too late."

The reporter said: "Corbett Reeves lived with the Delaney family for some time, Steve, as a foster child. Mr. Delaney was not available for reaction, and we were unable to reach his lawyer, Monty Collins. Crown prosecutor Gail Kirk said she could not comment on today's surprise turn of events. Steve?"

"Thanks, Todd. Now to Pictou County where our coverage of the Westray mine disaster continues. The families of the twenty-six miners . . ."

At that point Maura shooed Normie up into the kitchen with the assurance that she would call upstairs if Normie and Kim appeared on the screen. Given all the nightmares she'd been having, the last thing the child needed was to hear any more about the twenty-six dads, husbands, sons, and brothers who lost their lives when the Westray mine blew up the Saturday before. Maura, the daughter of a coal miner, was not in the best of shape watching the story; I put my arms around her and held her close. Neither of us spoke.

We heard Normie's footsteps on the stairs again. She was wide-eyed at the sight of her parents in an embrace, but she made no comment.

Maura stepped back, and turned her attention to the lead item on the news. "What's the story on this guy? You didn't know about him?"

"His name came up in court today. Beau told me it was a foster placement that didn't work out, so —"

"Yeah, it's Corbett!" That was Normie.

"You've heard of this . . . Corbett before, Normie?"

"Oh, yeah. He's old news."

"Not to me, he isn't."

"Aw, what have they got on now?" She glared at the television as yet another story came on with no sign of the man-in-the-street interviews on Spring Garden Road.

"Normie, what do you know about Corbett Reeves?"

"He's Jenny and Laurence's brother. Or he was. But then he ran away. But it's okay 'cause he's back now. You guys be quiet, all right? They may have me and Kim on next."

Maura and I left her with her dreams of stardom, and went up to the kitchen.

That's when the phone rang. I grabbed it. "Yes?"

"I don't appreciate this kind of showboating, Monty! Especially with our judge going out of town, and court in recess till next Monday. The jurors will have four days on their own to absorb this little stunt." It was Gail Kirk.

"This isn't my doing, Gail."

"Justice Palmer just called me. He tried your home number. I suggested you might be at Maura's, so expect a call. We're to be in his chambers in half an hour." Click.

I hung up, and the phone jangled in my hand. "Hello."

"Monty, Ken Palmer here."

"Yes, Ken."

"You know why I'm calling."

"Oh, yeah."

"This is outrageous, Monty."

"I know. I didn't —"

"Save it for the conference in my chambers. Half an hour. I assume you'll have your client with you."

"I will. See you there." Click.

I said to Maura: "Ken Palmer is wild, and no wonder. If Delaney engineered this, I'll have his —"

I grabbed the phone and stabbed in Delaney's number. I didn't give him time to say hello. "What is this Reeves kid doing on the suppertime news, Beau? And how the hell am I going to explain this to the judge?"

"I had no idea the kid was going to appear. I thought he was gone for good."

"Are you saying you didn't put him up to this?"

"Of course I didn't!"

"Well, you'd better come up with a good explanation before we see the judge twenty-five minutes from now."

"I'll meet you there."

"No fucking way you're going in there without me. I'll pick you up. Now. Be out there on the sidewalk when I arrive." Click.

When Delaney got into my car, we both started talking at once. I prevailed. "I don't have to tell you how bad this looks for us, sandbagging the prosecution and the court like this. Now what the fuck is going on?"

"I didn't do this. I'm as surprised as you are. More, in fact, which you'd understand if you knew the kid."

"I don't. You do. Tell me."

"All I'll tell you is this: don't put him on the stand."

"Well, he's already been on the news. The judge will be most anxious to know whether any of the jurors heard his testimony over the airwaves —"

"I don't want a fucking mistrial, Monty, I want an acquittal!"

"Well then, Beau, if you believe in a higher power, you should commence prayer! Because I'd say the odds are against twelve jurors *not* hearing something about this. But let's get focused here: why don't you want this Corbett on the stand? If he had gone through proper channels, I mean. Were you with him that night? Is that what he's saying?"

He hesitated, then said: "Whether I was or I wasn't, we don't want him in the trial."

"Why not?"

"Corbett Reeves is bad news."

"Well, he's big news now. What am I supposed to say to the judge and the other side?"

"Say this had nothing to do with us, and the only witness we have left is me."

We were at the law courts, and I pulled in to the parking garage under the building. I parked, wrenched the handbrake up, and got out of the car. I felt sick to my stomach, and wondered in passing how many of these criminal client surprises I could take before an ulcer put an end to my career.

We rode the elevator in silence. The Crown attorneys, Gail and Bill, were waiting outside Justice Palmer's door, and Gail started in on us.

"Save it for the judge, Gail."

Justice Palmer walked in shortly after that, and we followed him into his chambers. He sat, nodded at us all, and said: "Let's hear it, Monty."

"I want to assure you and Ms. Kirk and Mr. MacEwen that neither I nor my client had anything to do with this. I have never met, spoken to, or heard from Corbett Reeves in my life. Mr. Delaney was not aware the boy was even in town. This is not our doing, and we both regret that he went to the media with this claim."

"But now that he is, so conveniently, here at this time," Gail said, "why do I suspect I'm going to get notice of an alibi witness at this late date in the trial and —"

"We're not going to call him."

She was clearly taken aback by this. "There's an alibi witness out there, or so we hear, and you're not going to call him?"

I addressed my remarks to the judge. "We feel we do not need an alibi witness. There is no proof Mr. Delaney was home at or about the time Mrs. Delaney fell. He wasn't there, and he will testify to that fact when he takes the stand."

Gail said: "I have to wonder what's going on, why you *don't* want the court to hear this boy."

"You needn't concern yourself with the conduct of our case, Gail."

Kenneth Palmer took control of the meeting then, and asked again for my assurance that this was not a stunt cooked up by the defence. I gave him that assurance and I knew he believed me. Bizarre human behaviour and grandstanding before the cameras were nothing new to Justice Palmer after fifteen years on the bench.

Gail spoke up again. "Our problem now is to find out whether the jurors saw this or heard about it. No doubt it will be in the papers tomorrow."

"They have been instructed not to consider anything except what they see and hear in my courtroom. And that instruction will be repeated, with particular emphasis, when we resume next week."

†

I didn't get much sleep that night, wondering what accounted for the sudden appearance of Corbett Reeves. In spite of the fact that I'd been hauled into the judge's chambers over it, the emergence of Reeves should have come as a relief. The former foster son alive and well was preferable to the former foster son lying dead at the foot of a set of stairs somewhere, an image that had come to me more than once since I first heard Corbett's name. But why was Delaney reluctant to have him involved in the trial? Was he with Delaney the night of the murder? If so, what was going on that Delaney didn't want told, even at the expense of losing an alibi witness in a murder trial? Where had Corbett been before Peggy's death, and since?

I had my chance to ask him the next day. Brennan and I had a quick lunch and a draft at the Midtown, and we walked back to my office together. When we arrived, I saw the pale figure of Corbett Reeves slouched against the building. He was of medium height and slight build; he looked older than fifteen. He watched us approach. Up close, I saw that his eyes were of a very light shade of greenish grey; I had never seen eyes with so little colour.

I spoke to him. "Corbett Reeves, I presume?"

"Are you Beau's lawyer?" His voice was soft, but somehow strained. It grated on my ears.

"I am," I replied.

181

He put his hand out, and I shook it.

"Did you see me on the news?"

"I did."

"Good news for you guys, eh?"

"Well, we'll talk about that. I assume you were waiting for me."

"The girl said you were out for lunch."

"The girl?"

"The one at the desk."

"The receptionist."

"Yeah, right. Who's this?" He turned his attention to Brennan, who was dressed in a shirt and sports jacket. "Has Beau got a whole team of lawyers?"

"This is Father Burke. Corbett Reeves."

They shook hands. Burke's black eyes bored into the pale eyes of the young man. Reeves tried to pull his hand away but Burke had it in his grasp. They stood there for several seconds. Burke finally released the newcomer, never taking his gaze off him. Without turning to me, Burke said: "Call me if you need me for anything, Monty."

When the priest had gone, Reeves said: "Let's go in your office and get down to business."

"Very well."

He followed me inside, and we went up in the elevator to the offices of Stratton Sommers. Reeves plunked himself down in my client chair, and crossed his legs. He pulled out a pack of cigarettes, lit one up, and said: "Okay if I smoke?"

"No."

He shrugged, wet the thumb and finger of his left hand and used them to extinguish the burning tip of the cigarette. He didn't flinch. He blew the ash on the floor, and put the cigarettes away.

"I'm pretty famous around here today, right?"

"Why don't you tell me what you have to say?"

"What's Beau saying his alibi was that night?" He spoke lazily and his face was set in an expression of nonchalance, but I noticed that his left leg, crossed over the right, was jiggling non-stop.

"Never mind what my client told me. Let me hear your story."

"I can get him off."

I wasn't going to bite on that. "Why wait so long to come forward?"

"I've been out of town."

"Where?"

His face took on a cagey look, and he didn't reply. A state secret, it must have been.

"And you've returned with the idea of testifying for Mr. Delaney?"

"Yeah."

"All right. Go on."

"Me and Beau go way back. Maybe he didn't tell you about it."

"Why do you suppose that is?"

"Maybe it's because he doesn't want to admit he needs me."

"Needs you how?"

The boy leaned forward. The shaking leg banged against my desk. "His life is in my hands!"

"Corbett, either tell me your story, or let me get on with my work."

"You want the facts? I've got the facts. Put me on the stand!"

Corbett obviously had a limited understanding of what a defence lawyer wanted in a trial. Sometimes the facts were not on the wish list at all, or anywhere near it.

"Listen to me, Corbett. I'm not going to call you to testify."

"What? Are you crazy? He needs me! He fucking needs me to get him off!"

"No, he doesn't." The last thing Delaney needed was this kid with his delusions that I would put him on the witness stand without knowing what his testimony would be. I suspected that if I knew what he was going to say, I'd have him kidnapped and bundled out of the country till the trial was over. I didn't know what he was up to, but he wasn't going to play out his drama on my time, in my trial, to the detriment of my client. "It's not going to happen, Corbett."

"Fuck you! I'm going in there!" Reeves erupted out of his seat and stood over me, trembling. His pale face had turned red with anger. "You can't stop me, you fucking asshole!"

"I can, and I will. Now sit down and get yourself under control here. Where are you staying? I'll drop you off —"

He came behind my desk and lunged at me, grabbing me around the throat. I bolted up, gripped his hands, and wrenched them off me. He tried to butt me with his head, and I wrestled him to the floor. I held him down with my hands on his shoulders. He raised his right foot to kick me, and I twisted out of reach.

"You get yourself under control right now, Corbett, or I'll have you arrested. Got that? Now are you going to behave yourself if I let you up?"

"Let me go, for fuck's sake. I want to get out of here! You're some useless lawyer. I wouldn't get you to defend me!"

"Just as well, considering that I'm the victim of your little outburst here. Now get up and get lost. And don't let me see you around here or at the courthouse."

I stepped back, and he stumbled towards the door, then ran away.

Brennan called me later that day to see what Reeves had to say. I filled him in, and said I was glad to see the back of the kid.

"That makes two of us. I looked into that young fellow's eyes, and I didn't like what I saw there. Or what I didn't see."

"What do you mean?"

"There's something missing in him. It gave me a chill just looking at him and touching his hand."

(Normie)

The mystery of the missing brother was solved without me figuring it out. Corbett was back, and he was even on TV. He said he knew Mr. Delaney didn't do the killing because he was with him, Corbett with Mr. Delaney, that night. Wow! That was good news. Daddy was so happy about it, he gave Mummy a big hug. I drew a picture of them in my diary, smooching in front of the TV! And I couldn't wait to see Jenny and Laurence. On the Friday before the holiday week-end, we were all going to the Commons for a Gaelic football game between our school and St. Kevin's. Me and Jenny and Laurence and Kim were going to watch it together. So I would get a chance to ask about Corbett. The *mysterious* Corbett.

Kim and I were the first ones there, so we got to sit on the front bench to watch the game. We kind of spread out and saved room for Jenny and Laurence without looking like we were doing it.

It was really cool seeing our team in their uniforms. They are green and white with a little bit of gold on them, and a picture of a golden harp. So our team is called the Harps because of the picture. Father Burke got them sent over from Ireland, and also got the St. Kevin's uniforms for them. Their colours are white and blue with no picture. They decided on the name "St. Ks." Our team was all lined up on the field, so Monsignor O'Flaherty could take a picture of them. Everybody looked great except Richard Robertson. He had a big, lumpy, ugly brown sweater over his uniform. His mother made him wear it so he wouldn't catch a chill. But it wasn't even cold out. There was his mum gawking at the team and looking mad. Father Burke saw her, and then he went over to Monsignor and talked to him.

Monsignor said: "Good heavens, Father. I think I'm out of film here. I'll be back in a few minutes. Go ahead and get warmed up." So he left and went to his car.

Mrs. Robertson growled at Richard: "Richard. The time is three forty-five. I'll be back here at five o'clock on the dot, and I'll expect you to be ready to leave for Monsieur" — that's his French tutor — "at that time. Be careful. If you fall ill, or if you so much as injure your little finger, as a result of this escapade, we'll have to call a family meeting to rethink our decision to let you play." She turned to leave, and gave Father Burke some kind of a look, which I couldn't see. He just looked back at her, and went over and started talking to the team. As soon as Richard's mum was out of sight, Richard took the sweater off. That's when Monsignor O'Flaherty came back with the camera. He must have put film in it. Or maybe him and Father Burke made up the thing about the film, so Richard could be in the picture and not look like a dork.

The players for both sides had to warm up first, by running around and practising. I kept turning around and looking for Jenny and Laurence, but they weren't there. Other people wanted to squeeze onto the bench with me and Kim and some other kids, so I didn't know how much longer we could save the seats. One little guy sat down beside us. He had dark curly hair and glasses and he was really cute. I thought I recognized him as being the little brother of one of the guys at school, Asher. I'm glad we made room for him. But then I finally saw Jenny and Laurence. And it wasn't just them. Corbett was there too. He looked smaller than he did on TV, but it was him. I waved, and they came over.

"We saved your spots, but there may not be room now," I told them.

"There's room," Corbett said. He had a weird voice, kind of high and painful. Or at least it sounded as if it was painful to talk. He sat down practically on top of Asher's little brother, and ended up knocking him off the bench.

Jenny said we should find places at the back, but Corbett told her not to worry about it, just sit down. The little boy who fell off gave Corbett a dirty look and tried to get back on, but Corbett wouldn't let him. He said: "Get out of my way, Joo-boy." I don't know why he called him that, but it sounded mean. Then Corbett didn't pay any more attention to him, so he went and sat behind us.

"This is Corbett and that's Normie," Jenny said.

"Hi, Corbett."

He kind of made a noise but didn't really say hi.

"Normie's dad is Mr. Collins, Dad's lawyer for the trial."

Then he turned sideways on the bench and looked at me. "Oh, yeah?"

"Yeah."

"Tell him I want to be in the trial."

"Uh, how come? Was it what you said on TV? That you know Mr. Delaney didn't do it?"

"Something like that. I want to get up there and tell the judge where Beau really was that night. He can thank me later."

"Well, that sounds good. Right, Jenny? He should be up there on the witness stand, telling the truth."

"Yeah. That's what I should do," Corbett said and then he gave this creepy laugh that sounded like his voice, painful.

Father Burke's head whipped around, and he looked right at us. Right at Corbett. He glared at him for a good long time, before he turned back to the team, and told them the game was going to start.

The game was really exciting even if this was our first season for Gaelic football and the players were just learning, and dropping the ball a lot. But maybe they were supposed to. There were a bunch of rules saying what you could do with the ball and what you couldn't. You could pick it up with your foot somehow and boot it into your hands, but then you had to do other things with it; you couldn't just keep hold of it and go. There were two referees and they had to run up and down the field after the players. I remember Father Burke saying there was supposed to be a whole bunch of referees and other guys in charge of the game, but he could only find two. It was a great big deal when our guys, the Harps, made a goal. But then the St. Ks tied it up with a goal of their own. All the kids on the benches were cheering and whistling and clapping, except for Corbett. He must have thought the game wasn't very good. It was weird; every once in while, Father Burke would look over at Corbett and fix him with a fierce look in his eyes. He probably thought Corbett was a stranger.

It was really fun having this new team to cheer for. We have basketball and volleyball, and I'm going to play on the volleyball team next year. But this was our only outdoor sport, and it was fun to watch it on a bright, sunny day. Even more fun when the Harps got another goal and won the match. I turned to Corbett to say: "See, we're good!" But he was gone. I never even heard him leave.

Chapter 14

(Monty)

The courtroom was packed with reporters and spectators when Beau Delaney took the stand on Tuesday after the long weekend in May. He had cut his hair shorter, or slightly so, and wore a grey business suit with a soft blue shirt, and a blue and grey striped tie. His demeanour was humble as he stood and swore on the Bible that he would tell the truth, the whole truth, and nothing but the truth.

I hovered over my notes at the defence table for a few seconds before we began, to make sure everything was in place for my carefully worked out direct examination of my client. With only an hour or two of leeway on the night of Peggy's death, I wanted to bring out the evidence very precisely as to Beau's whereabouts, his exact arrival time home, the weather he encountered on the drive, and the length of time between his discovery of Peggy and his call for the ambulance.

Beau had a present for me, just before he got up to testify. He dropped a piece of paper on the defence table. I picked it up and squinted at it. He couldn't miss the surprise on my face. "They don't call me a showboat for nothing!" he said, before he walked to the stand. It was a receipt for a fill-up at a gas station on the highway outside Halifax. It showed that, when the calendar turned over from January 15 to 16, 1992, Beau was still on the road. The time said twelve-fourteen a.m. I clutched it in my hand like a holy relic as I began questioning my client about the night of his wife's death.

I asked him a few warm-up questions to get the jury familiar with him. He was calm and collected, mild and unassuming, as he told the court a little bit about his life with Peggy. He had been living with another woman, but that relationship foundered on the question of children. After going along for years without any desire for children, Beau began to have a change of heart: he wanted kids after all, and wanted them badly. His girlfriend did not. Things had been going downhill for a while anyway. So that was that. As for Peggy, she had been married to someone else. Children were a factor in the failure of that relationship as well, but in a much more tragic way. She and her husband had had a baby boy, Jonathan, who died of sudden infant death syndrome, known as crib death. The marriage could not survive the couple's grief and loss.

"So after ending one relationship with a woman who didn't want kids, I now fell in love with another who felt the same way, although for polar-opposite reasons. Peggy thought that if she had another baby, she would be guilty of trying to replace Jonathan. If she could feel joy with another child, that might mean she had forgotten him, or put him behind her. The thought of that was unbearable to her. Of course that's not what happens. Each and every child is irreplaceable. By giving another child life, and giving a child a home, by giving herself to another child, how could that take anything away from Jonathan, or her love for Jonathan? Anyone who has more than one child knows what I mean: loving the next one doesn't detract from the love of the one before. I should know — I have ten! Anyway, Peggy came around, and we were married, and we had Sarah the next year, and Derek came to us the year after that, and then Peggy gave birth to Connor, and then we got Ruth, and on it goes.

"Peggy and I were made for each other. We loved each other, we loved our children. Life was complicated at times, but life was sweet."

I was vaguely aware of the courtroom door opening behind me, as someone made a noisy entrance and apparently clambered over other spectators to secure a seat. Delaney didn't notice the commotion, so intent was he on telling the jury about his wife.

"Peggy was a social worker by profession and, not surprisingly, she did most of her work with children. By the time we had three kids in our own house, she quit her job to stay home with the family, but she still volunteered with kids, and became an advocate for children in trouble with the law. Understandably, given what had happened in her own life, and what she saw every day in her work, she tended to be a worrier! She knew about the mishaps and misfortunes and tragedies that could befall children at any minute, but she also knew enough to back off and not be overprotective even when she desperately wanted to. She had a finely tuned sense of humour, and could laugh at her own inclinations in this respect."

"He didn't kill, and I can prove it!" The strained, reedy voice of Corbett Reeves had everyone's attention.

I whirled around and looked at him, sitting forward in his seat and peering intently at his sometime foster father on the stand. I turned back to Delaney, who gave me a quick half shake of his head. Get the kid out of here, was the unmistakeable message. We were of one mind on that; I had no idea what the pale, strange young boy intended to say. But if Beau didn't want it said in the courtroom, neither did I.

"My Lord," I said, getting to my feet. "This is not a defence witness, and I respectfully ask either that he be escorted from the courtroom or that the jury be excused while we discuss the matter."

Kenneth Palmer wasn't about to take any chances of the trial tanking at this late stage. He turned to the jury. "Ladies and gentlemen of the jury, I would ask that you retire to the jury room for a few minutes. You'll be called back shortly."

But Corbett did not want to lose his few minutes of fame. He got up and shouted: "You don't want them to —"

The sheriff had reached him by then, and told him not to say another word. The judge had the same instruction, backed up by the threat of contempt of court. That kept him quiet until the jurors were out of earshot.

But then he started again. "I want to be part of this trial. I want to get on the witness stand, and —"

Justice Palmer interrupted him in a booming voice: "I do not intend to hear another word from you! Understand? Now, Mr. Collins, what do you have to say about this?"

"My Lord, this person is not a witness. He is not a part of our case. And I would ask that, rather than risk any more outbursts and disruptions of the trial, he be removed from the courtroom, and in fact removed from the premises altogether."

The judge gave a signal to the sheriff, who quickly hustled Corbett out of the courtroom. His final words were: "Nobody wants to hear the truth!"

Gail Kirk glared daggers at me, as if she thought I would stoop to engineering such a spectacle, or as if she might be able to plant that belief in the judge. But Ken Palmer knew otherwise, which was clear from the sympathetic look he gave me, and that was all that mattered. If I were going to engineer anything, it would have been a lot more clear on the subject of my client's innocence. Corbett's demeanour did not inspire any confidence in me that he was truly on Delaney's side. Beau's reaction said it all: the kid was bad news.

Beau was trying to tell me something else. I stared at him, and he tapped his left wrist with the index finger of his right hand. His eyes darted to the courtroom door. He was directing me to ask for an adjournment. There was a bad moon rising over our case.

"My Lord, I wonder if I could have a few minutes with my client. I respectfully request an adjournment. . . ."

"We'll adjourn for half an hour. Mr. Delaney, I hope there is no need to remind you that you are still under oath, and that you are not to speak to or communicate with anyone other than Mr. Collins."

"Of course not, My Lord. I understand."

Delaney and I fled to a meeting room and shut ourselves inside. I couldn't hold back. "What the hell is wrong, Beau? Why do I have the feeling that a pale stranger by the name of Corbett Reeves has just attached himself to our case like a limpet mine? I thought the case was going to tank after that Hells Angels testimony. Now it's this guy. What do you have to tell me, Beau?"

"I was there."

Of course. He was there when Peggy died. I don't think I ever really believed otherwise.

My client looked as if he was facing his own death now.

"But I didn't kill her! It was an accident."

"What was an accident, Beau?" I realized I was shouting, and I lowered my voice. "You shoving her down the stairs? Accidental because you didn't realize you were going to do it until it happened?"

"I didn't push her down the stairs, Monty! We had an argument, and she fell."

"Can you possibly imagine how this is going to sound to the jury? How it's going to sound on the evening news?"

"Yeah, Monty, I can. I'm a trial lawyer, remember? But I panicked and reacted like a brainless lowlife. I know how lethal this is for me. I made the biggest mistake of my life when I saw her lying there. I must have been in shock. I made the decision to leave the house and come back and 'find' her, and call the ambulance then. Once my story was on tape with emergency services, I was stuck with it."

"That was bad. Changing it makes it exponentially worse."

"I know that," he said between clenched teeth. "Now we have to make the best of it."

Not for the first or last time, I wondered why I did this for a living. I had to undo my entire case, and fly through uncharted territory by the seat of my pants, on a wing and a prayer, with one engine in flames, and a flock of shit-hawks flying in formation just above my head, ready any minute to drop a load. . . . I took a deep breath, and let it out slowly.

"All right, let's go over it."

†

Fifteen minutes later, he was back on the stand. The judge cautioned the jury to disregard the outburst they had heard before they were excused from the room. Does a jury ever really disregard anything it has seen and heard? But I had my client to deal with.

"Now, Mr. Delaney, before we broke, you were telling us about Peggy and her tendency to be a worrier, particularly about her children. Could you tell us what kind of things she worried about?"

"Well, of course, she worried about sickness, given that her first child died in his crib. But she tried not to flutter around the kids all day with a thermometer and a bottle of pills."

"But she had her concerns."

"Things bothered her, no question. Crime and violence were up there at the top of things she worried about." Beau got shakier as he got closer to Peggy's death. Little wonder, given that he was there on the scene when it happened. "The day she died, there was some horror story in the paper, a brutal crime that had been committed against a perfectly innocent bystander. She was going on and on about it, and that's when the argument broke out."

"You and Peggy had an argument . . ."

"Right. She was convinced that the world was getting more violent, more dangerous. People always think that, especially after hearing about a particularly gruesome crime.

"I said to her: 'When has it not been violent and dangerous? Look at the bloodbaths of the twentieth century. World War One, the Russian Civil War, Stalin, World War Two, the Holocaust, China, Cambodia, over a hundred million people killed.'

"She replied: 'That's not what I'm talking about and you know it, so save me your party piece on the warlike impulse in mankind! I'm talking about criminal violence on this continent, in this country, in this city.'

"So I said: 'In the metropolitan area of Halifax, in the run of a year, we get an average of eight homicides. Eight! Compare that to some of the U.S. cities where they have hundreds of murders every year.' This is the way we used to argue, on the few occasions we argued at all. It was never 'You promised you wouldn't do that, and you did!' Or 'You never loved me!' Or 'You seem to be working late a lot these days, ever since you hired that new blond secretary!' It was never stuff like that, because we got along so well on a personal level."

At that point, my client was close to tears and, from my perspective, his distress appeared to be genuine. Obviously, it was out of the question to ask whether he wanted another break; that would have looked contrived even if we hadn't had our time out. So I waited for a bit and then continued.

"So this was the kind of thing you argued about."

"Right. How the world was going. Who was ultimately to blame for the disparity between rich and poor in such and such a country. Crime, of course, was a recurring theme, given what I did for a living.

The point I was making was that this is a comparatively safe area of the world.

"But Peg said: 'People are getting blown away in small-town Nova Scotia! That was your own client, in case you've forgotten.' She was talking about a murder in Truro. The victim was Travis Bullard, who had been my client.

"'That was an execution,' I told her. 'A guy known to police, as the expression goes. Not a random incident. Far from it. The guy was tied to a tree, propped up and shot, no doubt to keep him quiet or to retaliate for offending the Hells Angels or somebody.'

"Then she said: 'The Hells Angels! They're after your clients now. What if they think that guy told you something and they come after you to keep *you* quiet?!'

"I accused her of not listening to reason and said I'd had enough of the argument. I reached out to calm her down, and she yanked her hand out of reach. I grasped her arm, and she pulled back to get away from me, and that's how she fell. Backwards down the stairs."

I could hear the muttering and whispering of voices and the scratching of pens on notebooks behind me, as the news sunk in. The two prosecutors were on the edge of their seats, as if ready to attack. Delaney had been home after all.

He continued his story: "She barely made a sound when she landed on the rocks. She didn't scream or cry out. I just kind of heard the breath go out of her. I stood stock still for a couple of seconds, then leapt down the stairs. She was not breathing. It was obvious that she was dead. That's when . . . that's when I left the house and got into the car and drove away."

I stood there without speaking for a few seconds, then plunged in.

"Mr. Delaney, everyone in this courtroom wants to know why you told the police in your statement that you were not home at the time leading up to Peggy's death. Please clear that up for us."

"It was a lie told for self-preservation. I'm sorry. I wish I could take it back. I wish I had told the whole truth right from the beginning. But I panicked. I knew how bad it would look for me if I said I was there. I was afraid that fact alone — after all, I've been doing criminal law my whole adult life — I was afraid that fact alone would convict me. I'm standing there, a head taller and eighty pounds heavier; she ends up at the bottom of the stairs; there's a pressure mark on her arm."

He turned to face the jury, and spoke to them urgently. "I knew I was innocent, that I hadn't killed Peggy, but I was afraid I looked guilty. I was terrified that I would be sent away for a murder I didn't commit, and that my children would be all split up, some of them in foster homes, in group homes, back with violent and dysfunctional families, after all Peggy and I had done to forge a strong family life for them. For all of us. I couldn't bear the thought of that, so I did what I could to try to avoid it. I have spent my entire career defending people who do illegal, evil, or stupid things and then lie about them. I always thought I would be more honest than that, or at least more clever. But no.

"It was stupid of me," he said, "stupid and unprofessional. Morally and legally wrong. You can perhaps imagine how deeply I regret my actions in that respect. I am truly sorry."

I waited a couple of seconds, then asked him: "What did you do then?"

"I took off in the car, went out driving on the highway, trying to come to grips with what had happened, and what I should do."

"How long were you out driving?"

"An hour and a half, two hours, something like that."

Long enough and far enough to burn off some fuel, and make a credible stop to top up his gas tank. I was thankful that we had not got to the point where I was going to submit the cherished midnight gas receipt as evidence. Nobody else need ever know about it, especially the Crown, the judge, and the jury!

"What time did you get home again?"

"Twelve thirty-five. That is probably when Mr. Gorman saw me. The second time he saw me, I should say. After the snow had started."

"What happened then?"

"I went in and called for the ambulance."

"Thank you, Mr. Delaney."

Now it was time to hand him over for vivisection by the Crown. Gail Kirk rose to her feet. Delaney steeled himself for what was to come.

"Mr. Delaney, you lied to the police, did you not?" Gail wasn't going to waste time on chit-chat.

"Yes, regrettably, I did."

"You now expect us to believe that you are telling the truth today. That you didn't kill your wife, even though you were right there, and the two of you were engaged in a heated argument, and you grabbed her arm. Why should we believe you stopped there? Why should we believe you when we know you lied?"

"I hope I will be believed, because it's the truth. My actions were stupid and cowardly but, despite appearances, they were the actions of an innocent man."

"If you were innocent, Mr. Delaney, why set up an elaborate ruse by leaving the house and staging a second coming? You are well known in this city. You're a long-standing member of the bar. Surely, you would have thought, if you were innocent, people would believe you, or at least give you the benefit of the doubt pending the outcome of the investigation. Don't you agree?"

"We never know how we're going to react when we're tested in a situation of incalculable stress. I failed the test. Miserably."

"You weren't going to tell us the difference, were you, Mr. Delaney?"

Silence.

"You fully intended to maintain that lie, didn't you? You had no intention of coming clean with the court and the jury, until . . . what, Mr. Delaney?"

Silence again.

"Until certain events in this courtroom made it impossible for you to keep up the fiction any longer, starting with your daughter's revelation about the Hells Angels conversation — of course that was a conversation, not a woman talking to herself! And, well, it just became impossible to keep the lie going, didn't it, Mr. Delaney?"

"All I can say, Ms. Kirk, is that I loved Peggy, I didn't kill her, I panicked when she died, and I have lived ever since with the terror of being wrongfully convicted of her death, and being sent away from my children, and seeing my family torn apart and dispersed."

"What did you do when you went down the stairs immediately after Peggy fell?"

No reply.

"Mr. Delaney? Did you bend down, take her in your arms, say something to her?"

He hesitated, then replied: "I knew she was dead."

"You made that decision instantly? She's dead? No cradling her in your arms? No crying out her name? Nothing?"

"Objection, My Lord," I said. "My learned friend is badgering the witness, and not letting him answer the questions."

"Overruled. Carry on, Ms. Kirk."

"Well? Mr. Delaney? What did you do in those first seconds after your wife's fall?"

"I just stood there, in shock."

"Did you touch her?"

Another long hesitation. Then: "No. I panicked and left."

"You tell us you panicked, and yet you were calm enough to refrain from calling out 'Peggy!' or shaking her, or even checking her pulse. You made an apparently calm and collected decision, within seconds of her fall, that she was dead and nothing could be done for her."

Beau said nothing.

"You're a highly trained, very experienced criminal lawyer, aren't you, Mr. Delaney?"

"I am a defence lawyer, yes."

"Were you concerned about contaminating a crime scene, leaving traces of yourself —"

"No. I simply did not know what to do."

It went on like that for two hours. Kirk proceeded to take Delaney through the events of that night, minute by minute, chipping away at his story, leaving no doubt in the jury's mind that she considered his version of events — his Plan B version of events — unworthy of belief.

I got up on redirect, not that I had anything I wanted to do aside from give him another chance to proclaim his innocence to the court. We adjourned in the middle of the afternoon, and would return the next day for our summations and the judge's charge to the jury.

The media were all over us when we left the courtroom, firing questions at Delaney and at me about his dramatic reversal on the stand. I tried to put a good face on it, but I was beyond caring at that point. I had no intention of watching, hearing, or reading any news about the day's events. Beau did a better job. By turns humble and defiant, he pleaded his case as a wrong-headed but innocent man blown completely off course by the sudden death of his beloved wife.

I stayed away from my client that evening. Instead I went to the Midtown Tavern with Father Burke to lift a few pints and confess to the sins of anger and thinking ill of my fellow man. "I say to you that everyone who is angry with his brother shall be liable to judgment, and whoever says 'You fool!' shall be in danger of hellfire." That sort of thing.

†

I gave an impassioned summation on my client's behalf the next morning. I stressed all the glowing references given by our character witnesses. I emphasized that there was no reason Mr. Delaney wanted his wife dead, and every reason for him to want her alive, to be with him and their ten children. True, they had an argument. But that argument had not ended in violence. If it had, there would have been signs of it. Such as blood at the top of the stairs if he had struck her on the back of the head. Significantly, there were no signs of a struggle apart from the pressure wound on Peggy's arm. There was no skin or other material of any kind under her fingernails. And if Mr. Delaney had done this, how, in such a state of rage, did he manage to carry her body down the stairs and arrange it with absolute perfection on the rock at precisely the angle that would have caused the wound as it was measured in the autopsy?

Instead, Mr. Delaney panicked. And what did he do in his panic? Something he himself described as stupid and cowardly. He fled the scene, and then tried to cover up for himself later. He did not, calmly and precisely, arrange his wife's body at the foot of the stairs. The Crown had presented no evidence that Mr. Delaney was, ever, a violent man. In fact, when attacked late at night by a client who was drunk and on drugs, Mr. Delaney defused the situation and did not react with violence, as Mr. Theriault so forthrightly testified. I mentioned the ten children as often as I decently could, to drive home the fact that he would not have wanted Peggy dead, and to remind the jury what was at stake if he were convicted. I did the best I could.

Unfortunately, when the defence calls witnesses, the Crown has the advantage of speaking last. Gail Kirk spoke with considerable eloquence, and barely restrained sarcasm, about the unlikely story Delaney was relying on to avoid conviction for murder. That was followed by Justice Palmer's charge to the jury. The instructions were even-handed and fair; it would not be easy to find in them grounds of appeal. Then it was up to the jury. They retired at three thirty in the afternoon that Wednesday to begin their deliberations.

I was not at all confident of my client's chances. Nor was I confident that I had heard everything I should have heard about him, Peggy, and the unwelcome new boy in town, Corbett Reeves.

(Normie)

"He's going to bleed me of every cent I have! We're going to wind up in the poorhouse! What do you mean, calm myself down? He wants to take my son out of the country, and he obviously hopes to bankrupt me so I'll have to give up the fight. Money is no object in Giacomo's family. The lawyer has come up with all these Charter of Rights challenges. They're bogus, but they'll drag things out and require endless court appearances and filings, and — Brennan, have you heard a word I've been saying?"

The poorhouse? What was that? Was it like an asylum? Were we going to have to live there? I was really scared when I came into the house Thursday after school, and heard Mum on the phone in the kitchen. I usually yell "Hi Mum!" when I get in, but I just tiptoed into the living room and sat down.

"His lawyer is here from Italy, and I met with them. I certainly wasn't going to call Beau Delaney while he's waiting for the jury's verdict! He's probably curled up in the fetal position on his bed. So I left the baby with my friend Fanny, and went by myself. The lawyer, Pacchini, was very cordial in the beginning, and is very knowledgeable about Canadian law." (I had his name down in my diary as "Pakeenee," but the real spelling is "Pacchini." Anyway, Mum was still talking.) "You just have to spend two minutes in this guy's presence and you know he's brilliant. So the pressure is on: settle this now, give us the six months in Italy, or face months — years! — of soul-destroying, family-savings-draining litigation. I've seen this kind of thing, Brennan; it takes over your life, it —"

This was horrible! Mum was really, really upset. Father Burke must have been trying to make her feel better, but how could she? How could any of us ever feel better again? I went out to the porch and made a big noise with the front door, so she'd know I was home.

I heard her say: "Here's Normie. Last thing I want is her hearing this. I have to go." Click. "Hi, sweetie! How are you doing?"

"Fine, thanks, Mum. How about you?"

"Good, dear, good," she said in this funny Cape Breton accent, which usually makes me laugh. "We're going over to Fanny's. She's looking after Dominic today, because I had some errands to run. With any luck, she's made some of her famous chocolate and almond cookies. If she hasn't, we'll plead with her to make them and we'll hang around in the kitchen till she does. Sound like a plan?"

"Yep. Let's go get Dominic and the cookies. Mum?"

"Yes, sweetheart?"

"Do you think he's there?"

"Who?"

"Dominic. At Fanny's."

"Of course he is! He's too young to run away with the circus. Let's go."

(Monty)

We heard nothing from the jury on Thursday. On Friday I got the call at two o'clock in the afternoon. The jury was coming in. The tension while waiting for the verdict in a murder trial is almost unbearable. With any client. Here, we had a highly accomplished, well-respected lawyer with a family of ten motherless children, a family that would be ripped apart if their father was found guilty and sent to prison. I called him. He answered and then dropped the phone. I could hear footsteps pounding away in the opposite direction. I waited. A few minutes later, Beau spoke in a voice I barely recognized. "I'll meet you there."

Beau Delaney was grey and trembling when we met at the law courts. Everyone filed into the courtroom and waited for the jurors.

They came in and took their seats. Had they reached a verdict? Yes, they had. The foreman stood, was asked for the verdict, and gave it: not guilty.

Beau slumped in his seat as if every bone in his body had turned to jelly. His family and supporters behind us loudly expressed their relief. I stood there, stunned. I had hardly dared hope for an acquittal. A wishy-washy manslaughter result, maybe. But, no. My client was a free man. He pulled himself together, rose from his seat, and put out his hand. I shook it. "Monty, thank you for a superb defence. Justice has been done. I'm overcome right now, and I can't begin to express my thanks appropriately. But you can be sure I will, and I'll be forever grateful."

PART II

Yonder stands your orphan with his gun,
Crying like a fire in the sun.
Look out the saints are comin' through
And it's all over now, Baby Blue.

— Bob Dylan, "It's All Over Now, Baby Blue"

Chapter 15

(Normie)

Mr. Delaney didn't do it. They said in court he wasn't guilty. That was great. But now somebody else was guilty. Me! And I didn't want anyone in my family to know about it. Dr. Burke said it's good to talk if something is wrong. And he gave me his card with his address and phone number on it. I dug it out of my drawer, and reminded myself I meant to ask Mum and Dad for a special wallet for cards, but I hadn't done it yet. Anyway, there was the card. There was no picture on it. It just said "Patrick J. Burke, MD," and then some other stuff, and his phone numbers. It was pretty late, so I called his house. But there was no answer, so I tried the office.

"Dr. Burke's office."

"Hi, can I speak to Dr. Burke, please?"

"He's with a patient right now. Would you like to leave your number?" She had the kind of accent they have in New York. Dr. Burke doesn't. He sounds Irish, not like a New Yorker. But anyway, I didn't know what to do. What if he called back and somebody else answered the phone? But it would be rude not to leave my number, so I gave it to her and told her my name. She said she would be sure he got the message.

I went and got my Latin book. We don't have to learn the whole language, but we have to know the words to certain prayers and songs, what they mean and how to pronounce them. I brought the book over to the phone and sat there staring at the words *lacrimosa, malo, morietur*. It wasn't very long before the phone rang, and I grabbed it.

I whispered into the receiver. "Hello."

"Hello, is that you, Normie?"

"Yes, it is."

"This is Dr. Burke." I already knew that, of course.

"Hi."

"It's good to hear from you, Normie. How are you doing?"

"Not too great."

"Oh. I'm sorry to hear that. But let's see if we can sort things out. Can you tell me what it was that started you feeling not so great?"

"Yeah. But I just realized . . ." How was I going to say it?

Oh no! I heard footsteps coming towards the room. The door opened. It was Mum.

"Who's that, sweetie?"

She obviously heard the phone ring. And I knew she would find out who it was. But I would deal with that problem later.

"Mum," I said, "don't be in the room! I'm talking to my psychiatrist!"

She looked really surprised but then she just said: "Oh, I see." And she left and closed the door. I heard her footsteps walking away.

Meanwhile Dr. Burke wasn't saying anything. I thought maybe he had given up, and put down the phone.

"Dr. Burke? Are you still there?"

"Yep, I'm here."

"Sorry we got interrupted. Anyway, well, I'm going to seem really horrible."

"Oh no, I'm sure you won't, Normie."

"It just that Mr. Delaney didn't do it! Didn't kill Mrs. Delaney. The judge found out, and let him go."

"Well! That's a bit of news, then."

"But you remember what I said? I said I thought he was bad! And he isn't. So I was saying mean things about somebody who is good after all."

"I remember our conversation very well, and I didn't think you sounded mean at all."

"Really?"

"Really. You know, I don't recall you saying you thought he killed his wife. You felt something wasn't right, that maybe he was bad in some way. But that could have been anything. People have bad and good in them. You didn't say anything about the death of his wife."

"That's right! My dreams or the things I saw, they weren't about him pushing Mrs. Delaney down the stairs."

"No, and I never got that impression from you. But even if you had thought that, there would be nothing wrong with thinking it, would there? The police believed he had done it, and so did the DA, I mean, the Crown prosecutor. Before people understand what really happened in something like this, some think the person did it, and others think he didn't. That's the way we are; we're all allowed to have different opinions! And when they're more in the nature of feelings, people definitely go their own ways with those! Does that make sense?"

"Yeah. I mean, yes. That's all it was with me. Nothing to do with Mrs. Delaney dying."

"Right. Is there anything else troubling you, Normie?"

"No, that was it."

"I'm really glad you called me. And I hope you'll call again if there's anything I can do to help you."

"I will. Thank you."

"You're welcome, Normie."

"Bye."

"'Night, my love."

†

Mr. Delaney came to our house the Monday after that. Father Burke was there, and even though they thought they were being too smart for me to catch on, I knew Father was there to talk Mum into telling

Dad about Giacomo and the baby. But — ta-*da!* — Mr. Delaney made an announcement.

"Problem solved! Giacomo ain't gonna bother nobody, no more!"

Mum gawked at him and didn't say anything, till she caught on that I was there in the living room, and she told me to go upstairs. I went up, pussyfooted over to the register and sat down, hoping they would go into the kitchen. *Offer him a snack, Mum!* I begged her in my mind. But they stayed in the living room, so I couldn't hear. I almost gave up when I finally heard them go into the kitchen.

Mum was saying: "How did you do this, Beau?" So I knew I hadn't really missed anything. Whatever it was, he hadn't told her.

And he still wasn't going to. "Maura, you don't have to know, and you don't want to know. I handled it. It's over. End of story."

"Well, then, you have my heartfelt thanks. And you'll have my payment of your bill!"

"No bill. Just a favour from my family to yours, a return favour!"

"I don't know what to say, Beau. I'm . . ." Then she sounded as if she was crying. And then it was the baby who was bawling his head off.

"We're on the same crying schedule, I guess," she said.

"You've been listening to the same hurtin' songs. Go take care of him. I'll have a beer with Brennan here. I see he's weaned himself off the ginger ale."

"He couldn't take it. His system went into shock, and they had to pump it out of his stomach. So, have a brew with him. Hold on, Dominic, I'm coming!"

I heard her footsteps leaving the kitchen. The fridge door opened, and there was the popping sound of a can being opened.

Then Father Burke spoke up. "What did you do, Beau?"

"Don't ask, Brennan."

"I'm asking: what did you do?"

"Well, I couldn't help noticing the resemblance between you and the baby and your, well, rapport with him. The little fellow's whole face lights up when you walk in the room. I mean, clearly, he thinks you are his father!"

"Don't be saying that." Father Burke's voice was really quiet.

Mr. Delaney went on: "We had a little joke going when I was here before — or maybe it wasn't entirely a joke — about you being so blitzed one night, maybe you and Maura —"

"Your joke, not mine. I don't really think —"

"Doesn't matter. Nobody else thinks it either, except Giacomo, his lawyer, and one other person, whose lips are sealed."

"What in God's name have you done?"

"Ever hear of DNA testing?"

"Well, I certainly know what DNA is. But what kind of test are you talking about?"

"Paternity testing."

"I thought that was done by blood types."

"This is new, and it leaves the old ABO blood-type testing in the dust. There's a lab in New York. I don't know anyone there, of course, but I know somebody who does. A lab tech here in Halifax. I know her very well, and she owes me for a favour done many years in the past. This is a woman with a great love of children, and a great devotion to motherhood; she would hate to see a good mother lose her child in a custody dispute. She has an equally great devotion to the Catholic Church and its priests and sisters. She understands that a priest is only human and can make mistakes. And that those mistakes can show up in a lab report, and disappear when the report is destroyed. To make a long, very technical story short, she got two DNA test reports from the New York lab, and doctored them to show that Brennan Burke and Dominic MacNeil are a genetic match."

"My God, Beau! The woman could be sacked from her job. Not to mention all the other ethical and legal —"

"The fake papers were shown to Giacomo and his lawyer, Pacchini, and then destroyed. Giacomo and Pacchini are leaving town tomorrow. It's over."

"Christ have mercy on us all, Delaney. If Giacomo *is* the father, you have wrongfully deprived him of his rights as the father. You of all people, a man bringing up ten children, should appreciate that!"

"The best interests of the child are paramount to me. Every single time. And I know whereof I speak. Peggy and I had a little foster daughter, Betsy, years ago, who just didn't thrive in our home. She had problems, maybe a form of" — Mr. Delaney said something like *ott-ism* — "Whatever it was, we couldn't give her the help she needed. There was a treatment centre in Ontario that was working wonders with kids like Betsy. It broke our hearts to let her go, but she was better off there than with us. Peggy and I nearly went nuclear over it. But I know it was the right thing for Betsy. Best interests of the child, not of me or Peggy or you or Giacomo."

"Well . . ."

"Listen, Brennan, this is on my conscience, not yours. My loyalty is to my client. She has what she wants; she doesn't have to know how it was done. And think about this: if Giacomo ever got that child to Italy, and made him part of his family, there's no guarantee Maura would ever get him back!"

"So . . . Maura really has no idea what you did."

"She hasn't a clue. You heard me. I told her I handled it. Period."

I heard someone get up for a minute, then sit down again. Maybe he thought he heard somebody. But I was as quiet as falling snow. Mr. Delaney said then: "Brennan, I know you'd do anything for her. Not publicly maybe, but privately. I *know*. So you and I and a total stranger in a lab have solved this for her. Don't lose any sleep over it. I'm not going to."

I don't really know what goes on with babies and labs and tests, and I didn't learn much from the dictionary when I finally found "genetic," but it sounded as if we wouldn't have to worry about losing our baby. Father Burke would be glad later, even if he sounded upset at first. Because Mr. Delaney was right: Father Burke would do anything for Mum, and for all of us, because that's what good priests do.

(Monty)

Two weeks after the verdict, the Nova Scotia Barristers' Society went ahead with an event it had been planning before news of the Delaney murder charge torpedoed the whole thing: a dinner and award ceremony to honour Beau for his exemplary work as a lawyer, and as a volunteer with various community organizations. This was an annual event, during which several members of the society were recognized for their achievements and service to the community; the Community Justice Award went to the most notable of the group. This year it was Beau, and now that the criminal charges were out of the way and Beau exonerated, the ceremony could go ahead. Maura and I were both attending, so there was no reason not to go together. I drove to her place on Dresden Row, and we walked to the nearby Lord Nelson Hotel for the dinner.

"We should have called Brennan for this," I said to her. "Did you mention it to him?"

"No. I haven't seen him."

"Haven't seen him since when?"

"Quite a while. Couple of weeks maybe."

"Why? What's up?"

She shrugged and made a point of peering ahead of her to the hotel, as if looking for a new subject of conversation. As usual when anything in Maura MacNeil's life changed, I wondered what was going on. But we had social obligations right now, so I let it go.

We entered the banquet room and took our places at one of the long white-draped tables. There were speeches over dinner, and the other honourees gave their little spiels and sat down. When it was Beau's turn, he looked convincingly humble, but it must have been a very moving experience for him to be accorded such respect and appreciation after the soul-destroying ordeal of a very public trial for the murder of his wife. Somebody thought he was enjoying it a bit too much; I heard a lawyer I didn't know whisper to his companion: "He's really lapping this up."

Maura heard the comment too, but disagreed, and said softly: "To me he looks deeply grateful. As if he needs this somehow, this adulation. More than the rest of us maybe."

And there was more of it to come. A large video screen flashed on, showing last year's ATV News documentary. People could watch it or not, as they milled around with drinks in their hands after the meal. I chatted with people, and only gave the show half of my attention, until I heard the now-infamous phrase "Hells Angels." I tuned in as a reporter questioned the RCMP about the death of one of Delaney's clients. She asked whether there was a Hells Angels link to the killing of Travis Bullard, and whether he had been shot more than once. The Mountie played his cards close to his chest, and said more details would be released later on. But the details never were made public. The reporter tried again to establish the biker link, and Beau seemed to confirm it:

"He travelled in some rough circles, yes."

"And so he ended up being shot to death one night in Truro."

"That was the longest night of my life!" Peggy Delaney exclaimed. "My God, I thought, if they —"

"It's a scary world out there," Beau interrupted, "but those of us who work in criminal law can't go through life second-guessing every client we take on. We have a job to do."

The talked turned to the other unsavoury characters a criminal lawyer has to defend, including child abusers, and Beau assured the viewers that defence lawyers lose sleep over these cases just as other people do.

I had the feeling there was something not quite right in what I had heard, and I made a mental note to follow it up. But I would have to wait, because I was being swept along with a bunch of fellow lawyers on their way to the hotel's lounge. I tried to set aside my misgivings as I joined the crowd of revellers in the bar.

Everybody wanted to buy Beau Delaney a drink, to celebrate his award and his acquittal on the murder charge. Beau was not a drinker. I had never seen him have more than two drinks of anything, whether it was a beer or a glass of wine at dinner. Given his size, two drinks would not come close to causing him any impairment, but he limited himself nonetheless. He liked to stay on top of things. Tonight, however, the booze was flowing in his direction, and he must have felt it would be churlish to turn an offering away. There were seven or eight of us at the table, most of whom did their best to keep up. So, almost inevitably, the conversation turned into a dispute between the two sides of the criminal bar, those who try to put the defendants away, and those who try to put them back on the street. The argument was over the value of deterrence in sentencing: should the court mete out a stiff punishment to deter further criminal behaviour on the part of the offender, and send a message to other potential offenders that this is what they would face if they stepped out of line?

Dale Bekkers, a Crown prosecutor, polished off a pint of ale and joined the argument in progress: "I still maintain that deterrence is a legitimate goal in sentencing. It's not only about punishment."

Beau, speaking for the defence, said: "Dale, you speak of deterrence as if the average offender sits back and performs a cost-benefit analysis before slashing buddy with a knife and stealing buddy's sneakers or his car or his stash of drugs. This shouldn't be news to you, ladies and gentlemen of the Crown: most crimes are done on impulse. These people don't think, they don't weigh the options. Never mind how many times they've been hauled to court before, never mind how they just got probation this afternoon and their actions will constitute a violation of their probation order, never mind how the small amount of cash they grab will be gone before the night's out. We're dealing with repetitive, impulsive, irrational behaviour. It's always been that way, it always will be."

The Crown attorney laughed, and responded: "Listening to you, Beau, I get the impression you're ready to cross over to our side of the courtroom. Bid farewell to all those flaming liberals who make up the defence bar, and start prosecuting the evildoers who make your life such a living hell! Come on, cross the floor. In your heart of hearts, you know you want to."

Another prosecutor chimed in: "Dale, you can't believe defence lawyers like Beau, or Monty here, are really liberals, not with what they see every day of their lives."

Beau tipped a glass of whiskey up and drained it in one go, then leaned forward and said: "The liberal world view died on the blood-stained fields of World War One. We just can't bring ourselves to bury the corpse."

One of the other defence lawyers, Jamie McVicar, looked at Delaney in astonishment: "Whoa! That's a little extreme, Beau. I mean, here we still are, trying to —"

Beau made a dismissive gesture with his left hand and interrupted his fellow barrister: "Jamie, the slaughter in the First World War transformed the way the human species sees itself. Rational man? Human progress? Optimism about the future of human society? Forget about it. All blown away in the shit-filled, lice-infested trenches of northern Europe. *Europe*, where the Enlightenment began. Irrationality, violence, conflict, barbarity. It's always there beneath the surface. It can erupt at any time, in any place. Don't take my word for it. Read Hobbes. Read Freud. Before the war, what did Freud think was the primary force driving human existence? The erotic instinct, the life force. The savagery of the war compelled him to rethink his beliefs about human nature. To wonder whether civilization was even possible. He began writing of the death instinct in man. He said the war had 'let the primeval man within us into the light.'"

"Yet you've spent your entire professional life defending that primeval man and trying to ensure he remains free to walk upright amongst us!" Dale Bekkers retorted.

"Hey!" What could have been a smile jolted across Delaney's face. "It pays the bills."

"Come on, Beau. There are other ways for a showboat like you to make money."

"They need me, Dale. Just like they need Monty, and Jamie. Impulsive, irrational, uncivilized creatures need all the help they can get. I'm here to provide it."

Chapter 16

(Monty)

I wasn't going to relax about the Delaney acquittal until the thirty-day deadline for filing an appeal had passed. Two weeks to go. The Crown attorneys could not appeal the jury's verdict just because they didn't like it, but they could appeal if they found any legal errors committed by the judge. If they were successful, Delaney would be tried all over again. I didn't think Ken Palmer made any errors, but then I wasn't looking for any, the way Gail Kirk would be. Until that deadline had safely passed, I would be on guard for anything that might look bad for Delaney if a new trial were ordered.

This was Sunday, however, so I would put those concerns aside for the time being. The choirs at St. Bernadette's took turns singing at the eleven o'clock Mass on Sunday mornings. Sometimes it was my group, the St. Bernadette's Choir of Men and Boys, sometimes it was the girls and boys from the choir school, and occasionally it was the adults from the Schola Cantorum Sancta Bernadetta, which attracted religious and lay people from all over the world. This Sunday, it was a combination of the men and boys and girls, so Normie and I had a gig together. Maura and the baby, Tom and Lexie were in the congregation. We did Palestrina's *Missa Papae Marcelli,* one of my favourite works, and we did justice to it, if I may say so.

Our priest and choirmaster pronounced himself satisfied — even pleased — with our efforts. He stood at the back of the church saying goodbye to people on their way out. Maura, with the baby in her arms, stopped to chat, and I joined them. Dominic smiled and stretched his hands out to the priest. A sentiment that I couldn't read flitted across Burke's face; then he smiled back and took one of the pudgy little hands in his.

"Aren't you a fine Catholic lad, Dominic?"

"Why don't you come over for dinner tonight, Father? We haven't seen you in a while. Have you been slacking off in your parish visits?"

Right. She said he had not been around for a while. I wondered why not. Well, I wasn't about to ask.

"Thank you, Mrs. MacNeil," Burke replied. "You're most kind. But I have other plans for dinner tonight."

Whoa! What was that about?

"You've had a more promising invitation? Something better than my home cooking? Surely I didn't hear you correctly, Father."

"You heard only the preliminaries, madam. I'll be doing the cooking myself."

"Well! I must really have botched things in the kitchen last time."

"Not at all, at all. Mike O'Flaherty and I have the place to ourselves. In the usual course of things, we can't even set foot in the kitchen without inducing heart fibrillations in Mrs. Kelly. But she's out of town visiting her sister. Why don't the crowd of youse join us for dinner?"

"I'll bring a vat of wine," I offered, "as long as I'm not expected to quaff it all myself."

"Oh, you'll be ably assisted there, I'm thinking."

(Normie)

We got invited to the priests' house for dinner. They were going to cook all by themselves! Tom and Lexie couldn't come so it was me and Dominic, Dad and Mum.

I've hardly ever seen Monsignor O'Flaherty without his black suit and collar on, but this time he was wearing light brown pants made of corduroy, like the ones I have, and a bright green sweater. He made a big fuss over the baby in his stroller, and wheeled him into the dining room. He told us Father Burke was busy with his chores in the kitchen but would be out of there soon. Which he was. He had on a pair of jeans and a black sweater with flour spilled down the front of it. He was carrying plates of pasta with delicious-smelling sauce.

Daddy said: "You didn't make the pasta yourself, surely."

"No. Made the sauce though, Monty."

"Just wondering about the flour." Dad pointed at his sweater.

"Ah. I made the dessert. Chocolate cake, with a bit of Baileys in the icing."

I said: "Ooh! I love Baileys!"

They all turned around and gawked at me. "And how do you know what Baileys Irish Cream tastes like, little one?" Daddy asked me. "Being ten years short of drinking age."

"I got into it by accident one day. I didn't know what it was."

"Oh, yeah, the old accident defence again." They all looked at Daddy. "But enough about that. Let's eat."

We settled down to our dinner. The food was good and there was lots of funny talk. "Isn't this great *craic* now?" Monsignor O'Flaherty said. "We should do it more often, I'm thinking."

"We should," Dad and Mum both said at the same time.

That's when we heard a big loud bang. I jumped and spilled my milk. Somebody was hammering on the dining room window. We peeked outside and saw a person staring in. The grown-ups all got out of their chairs, but Father Burke waved at them to sit back down.

"You people enjoy your dinner. I'll deal with this."

Mummy made a joke: "Maybe it's a commando raid by Mrs. Kelly. Rumours reached her that you and Mike were using the stove by yourselves!"

"If that turns out to be the case, I'm sending you out to handle her. I won't be able for it."

But he went to the back door and opened it. He said something, then a woman's voice screeched at him. It sure wasn't Mrs. Kelly, unless she had turned into the type that curses and swears in a loud rude voice!

Daddy excused himself from the table and went to the door. We all scooted out after him to see what was going on. Mummy put her hand up to stop me from going, but I pretended I didn't see her. Out in the parking lot a really tough woman was yelling right into Father Burke's face. She was wearing fake leather boots with high heels, tight white pants showing her belly, and a purple top that showed . . . other things. Her hair looked all dried out and was scraped back from a skinny face.

"Drugs on board," Dad whispered to Mum.

"Why don't you take it easy, now," Father Burke was saying.

(I have to use bad language again. That's her fault, not mine!)

She said: "Fuck you! Are you the preacher here?"

"I am."

"Well, you don't look like it. Where's Cody's money?"

"Cody would be, em . . ."

"Don't you understand English? Give me Cody's money! I need — he needs it now. He's sick and I have to get him medicine. It's an emergency!"

"Calm yourself down now and tell me who you are."

"Who the fuck do you think I am? You told my kid you owe him a hundred and fifty dollars. Well, it was more than that he paid, it was like . . . five hundred dollars, and you're trying to rip him off. I want it all back. Now!" She made a sneaky look behind her shoulder. "I don't got all night."

"Oh, the one hundred fifty dollars. So Cody would be one of the lads who paid for an introduction to —"

Then another rough type of person busted into the scene! This guy was like the guys in the movies who wear really bright clothes and big old-fashioned hats. The woman gave him a scared look, then turned back to Father Burke. "So, like I was saying, I'm not going to do you out here in the parking lot, okay, but if you want to come with me —"

"Ah, now, don't be talking like that. Let us get you some help. We could take you to the clinic —"

"Bitch not goin' to no clinic," the bad guy said. "What was that you was saying to Cody back home about cash? Is this the guy that owes the money?"

The man grabbed her and yanked her around so she was face to face with him. She yelled out in pain, then answered: "Yeah! It's him. Cody told me it was a preacher at this church who said he'd open a bank account and put the money in it. But I told him we need the money now, and it's five hundred!"

"Let go of her!" That was a kid's voice, coming from behind us.

Now we had another person in the parking lot, a short, skinny boy who was maybe ten or eleven years old. I remembered him; he was one of the boys who chased Derek and Connor Delaney at our school! Now he was running towards the woman, but before he could get there, the big man reached out and hit the boy across the face, really, really hard! I couldn't believe my eyes. The boy fell down on the ground, and I saw blood spurting out from his nose.

"Mum!" he cried out. "Mum!"

Then you wouldn't believe it! His mother screamed at him: "Shut your mouth! It serves you right! I told you, Cody, stay home and let me deal with this. Is that the guy who said he'd give you the money?" She jerked her head at Father Burke.

But Cody didn't answer. He just curled up on the ground and began to wail and cry as if the whole world, as bad as it was, was coming to an end.

The bad guy started walking towards him. "Shut up that bawling! What are you, a man or a bitch?"

Father Burke and Daddy went to the bad guy. Father Burke said in a furious voice: "How dare you hurt that child!"

The man whipped around and got a hold of Father Burke, grabbed him by the throat, and slammed him up against the wall of the building. Daddy jumped on the guy's back and tried to drag him off, but all of a sudden the woman glommed onto Daddy and started pulling his hair, and she kicked him in the back of his leg. I was scared to death and started crying. Daddy let go and turned around, to stop her from hitting him. Then I saw Daddy get her arms in front of her, and he held on to her.

But Father Burke was still pinned against the wall, with the bad guy hollering at him: "When I get finished with you, choirboy, you gonna be my bitch!"

By that time, Mum and Monsignor O'Flaherty were in the parking lot, shouting that the police were on their way.

I looked at Father Burke and saw him twist the bad guy's arms away, and he flipped the guy onto the ground, face down. Father held him there and told him off. He said: "Nobody here is anybody's *bitch*. Everybody here, child and woman and man, belongs to God. Not to you. Understand?"

Dad was still holding the woman, and he called out to Mum and Monsignor that there was a little boy lying hurt on the pavement. Mum looked at the boy, Cody, then she disappeared for a second, and came out with a white cloth. She and Monsignor went over to Cody and talked to him. He wouldn't answer them. Mummy sat down on the pavement and gently moved Cody's head till she was cradling him sideways across her knees. She didn't mind about the blood. They looked like that statue by that famous guy, showing Mary holding her Son, except this was a dusty parking lot and it was just my own mum who isn't holy like Mary, and this little guy from a bad part of town. Cody's voice cracked when he talked to Mum and swore at her: "Fuck you! Leave me alone!" But Mummy ignored that and wiped the blood off his face with the cloth and looked at him as if she loved him even though she never saw him before.

That's when we heard loud sirens and saw lights flashing, and two police cars came speeding into the parking lot.

Dad and Mum looked over at me and then at each other, and made signals with their eyes. I could tell they were upset because I saw all the stuff that happened. They never want me to see bad stuff like that. But I did see it, and I will never forget it.

Then the ambulance came. The emergency guys lifted Cody up from my mum and put him on a stretcher. I saw Father Burke take a hold of his hand and talk to him really softly before they loaded him into the ambulance. Father smoothed back his hair and made the sign of the cross on his forehead. Cody's evil mother and that boyfriend of hers were shoved into the police cars. I hoped they'd be thrown in jail for the rest of their lives. The police made us all give "statements," even me, and then they zoomed away in their cars.

After all that, we went back to the dining room. The grown-ups just sat there at the table and didn't say anything. That's what happens in books and movies when people are "in shock." Or maybe they didn't want to talk about it in front of me, because I'm just a kid.

The only lucky one was Dominic. He was fast asleep in his stroller as if nothing had happened. He doesn't know yet about bad people. Bad parents. I wish he could live his whole life and never know. Suddenly I got up and grabbed him out of the stroller and — I couldn't help it, maybe I was in shock too — I kept clinging to him and rocking him, and I said over and over again: "How could they hurt their little boy like that?"

(Monty)

It was a subdued crowd of dinner guests that left the rectory Sunday night.

A wisecrack about supper with the boys without Mrs. Kelly's supervision died on my lips. I had a sleepy girl on my hands. I had taken Normie for a late-evening treat at the Dairy Queen because she was so upset after the scene in the church parking lot, she couldn't eat the Baileys cake. Brennan assured her that he would save it in the fridge for her, and she could sneak over from school on Monday and have a gigantic piece of it with a glass of milk. We decided that she would spend the night at my place. I drove her around the city to calm her down and make her sleepy, and it worked, just as it had when she was a baby. After we got home, she curled up on the chesterfield beside me in the den downstairs, wrapped in a soft blue cotton blanket.

"Normie, it's past your bedtime, dolly."

Her eyes were at half-mast, her voice dreamy. "I'm too tired to move. I'll sleep here."

"No, you'll be more comfortable in your room. I'll carry you up."

"I'm too sleepy . . ."

I wanted to catch a bit of the CBC News, so I switched on the television. My attention was caught by something Peter Mansbridge said about one of the upcoming Democratic primaries in the U.S. I tuned in to a report from Washington and let my daughter off the hook for the time being. When it was over I heard her mumbling: "Matthew. It's Matthew."

I looked at Normie. She was asleep but she was visibly distressed. Her fingers clutched the blanket and pulled it up around her neck. I remembered Maura telling me the name Matthew had come up before. Normie had been mumbling that name in her sleep. I didn't want to wake her, so I said in a quiet, conversational tone: "Could you remind me who Matthew is, sweetheart?"

Her eyes didn't open. She responded: "It's Matthew, not David."

"Right. It's not David because . . ."

"It's Matthew Halton, not David Halton."

Oh! That's all it was. David Halton was a senior correspondent with CBC News. I had just heard his report from Washington. She had obviously heard it too, as she drifted towards sleep. But wait a minute. Matthew was David Halton's father. How did Normie know about him? He had died years ago, long before my daughter was born.

"Can you tell me about Matthew, Normie?"

"This is Matthew Halton of the CBC."

I leaned close to her. "When did you hear Matthew on the CBC, Normie?"

But she was out, fast asleep. I stood there for a minute or so, then tiptoed away and went up to the kitchen to use the phone. I dialled Maura's number.

"Hello?"

"She just mentioned Matthew again."

"Oh!"

"Listen. This is going to sound weird, but bear with me. Do you know if there have been any retrospectives on CBC radio or television about Matthew Halton?"

"David Halton's father? The war correspondent?"

"Exactly." I repeated what Normie had said.

"Well, she must have heard it someplace. On the CBC or maybe at school. Something about World War Two. Tell you what: I'll call my friend Kris at the CBC and you call Brennan."

"Brennan won't know what they've been talking about in class, unless it's music or religion."

"Does he strike you as someone too shy to track down the grade four homeroom teacher and find out?"

"Um, no, he does not. I'll make the call and phone you back in a few minutes."

I called Brennan and he said he'd ask Mrs. Kavanagh. I heard back five minutes later. No, there was some discussion from time to time of the two world wars, but nothing about Matthew Halton or any other journalist. I gave Maura half an hour, in case Kris had to do some checking, then I dialled my wife's number again.

"Nothing," she told me. "Kris said there's been nothing broadcast in recent times about Matthew Halton, but she thanked me for the suggestion!"

"Jesus! Where would Normie have heard it? I'm going to see if I can get her talking again."

"Keep me posted. Never mind what time it is."

"Will do."

I went downstairs and checked on Normie. Still fast asleep. I decided on a bit of subterfuge. Changing my voice to what I hoped was that of a broadcast journalist, I said: "David Halton, CBC News, Washington." No reaction. I waited a few seconds and said it again. I saw her squirm around in her blanket. She licked her lips and started to speak. I couldn't make it out, so I put my ear up against her mouth.

"Matthew Halton. CBC."

"Tell me about Matthew, Normie."

"We've got Jerry on the run now! Jerry on the run!"

Great. Just when we got Matthew identified, we were faced with a Jerry.

"We kicked their ass! What are you blubberin' about? What are you blubberin' . . . Put him in the army, make a man out of him! We're gonna kick a little ass right here if he doesn't stop . . . Shut up! Take that! You little . . . NO! NO! NO!"

I looked at her in horror. Her face was contorted with fear. Tears streamed from her eyes. I couldn't let this go on.

"Normie, sweetheart, wake up. It's Daddy. You're having a nightmare. Everything's all right. Wake up."

"No!" Her eyelids flickered open. She stared at me without recognition. Then her expression softened and she reached up for me with both arms. I held her and told her she was safe.

Once I got her settled in her bed, I called her mother and reported what had happened.

"Jerry? I've never heard of a Jerry. Back to the clippings file."

"Maybe not," I said. "If she's somehow in tune with Matthew Halton's wartime broadcasts for the CBC, she may be hearing talk about the Germans, commonly called Jerry by our boys during the war."

"Oh, *that* Jerry. But would that have been Halton's style?"

"Probably not, any more than he would have been saying 'kicked their ass' or 'make a man out of him.' That must be another voice altogether."

"My God. What's going on? It's not surprising that she'd have a nightmare tonight about someone being hurt, but what's she doing channelling the war?"

✝

I couldn't answer that question, but we had a bit of comic relief the next day, which served to distract Normie from her troubles. She called me at work to tell me about a social engagement we had that evening. This was one of those events the details of which were contained in a note sent from the school and crumpled up and stuffed in the school bag, only to be retrieved the day of the event. Too late to bake the goods, buy the raffle tickets, or register for the bonspiel. But this time we were going to make it.

The choir school was having a party for the students and their parents, to give everyone a bit of relaxation before final exams began the following week. It was originally supposed to be in the gymnasium but one of the families had offered to have it at their house instead, if people didn't mind squeezing in to small quarters. This prompted another set of parents to offer their house in the suburbs. More space, apparently. Normie was on the phone now, taking care of the logistics.

"Mummy is staying home with the baby, which is okay. Dominic's too young to have fun at the party anyway. So it's you and me, Daddy."

"Sounds good. Do you have directions?"

"Yeah, Richard Robertson gave us a map."

"Richard and I are old buddies."

"That's right, you know him, Daddy! He sings in the men and boys' choir."

As young as he was, Richard was quite a character, with a mischievous sense of humour, and he could do a very passable impersonation of our choirmaster behind the master's back. Of course Brennan knew all about it, having caught him at it several times. Didn't faze him in the least; in fact, Richard was one of his favourite students. But — I tried to think — wasn't there something about the mother? I couldn't remember. Anyway, Normie and I hooked a ride with Brennan and headed for the party. I was the navigator, charged with locating 152 The Olde Carriageway, in a subdivision that hadn't existed two weeks ago, west of the city.

It didn't take long before I remembered what it was about the mother. Seeing her severe geometrical haircut and equally severe facial expression brought it all back. I had witnessed more than one encounter between her and Father Burke, during which she expressed her disapproval of whatever it was the choir school was doing or not doing at the moment. Mrs. Robertson met us in front of her monster house on The Olde Carriageway. The place was festooned with numerous ill-proportioned gables and fake-Palladian windows; but the most notable feature of the building was the enormous double garage that was stuck on to the front of the house and nearly blotted out the sight of the front entrance. One of the garage doors was open, displaying a huge collection of, well, stuff. A BMW, a snow blower, several kayaks and canoes, camping gear, electronics. Was it just coincidence that the brand names were all displayed facing forward?

Mrs. Robertson greeted everyone with a tight smile, told us to call her Lois, and urged us to make ourselves at home. We all trooped into the house and dutifully wiped our feet. A couple of dozen guests were already there, perched on fussy-looking chairs and loveseats with teacups in their hands. The furniture looked as if it had all been bought the same day, as if someone had said: "Fill my house with furniture," and that's what was done. There was flowered paper on the walls, a contrasting paper border around the room, and another contrasting pattern above that. Magazines were artfully displayed on gleaming coffee tables. There wasn't a book, or a dirty glass, let alone a toy or an old pair of sneakers, in sight. Something that sounded like elevator music was playing in the room, elevatoresque in content and in the quality of the sound. I realized it was coming from a giant stereo system built into a pricey-looking set of oak cabinets and shelves.

Richard came skidding into the room from outside, in a pair of khaki shorts with grass stains across the butt. His hair was a mess and there were a couple of twigs in it. "Sorry I'm late, but there was this really big —"

"Hey, Richard, your hair's all sproinked out all over your head!" one of the little boys exclaimed. "Where were you?"

"What do you say, Richard?" his mother demanded.

"I saw something crawling under a pipe . . ."

"Richard."

"Uh, oh yeah. Good evening, everyone. Sorry to be late."

"Very well. Now go clean yourself up, change your clothes, and present yourself back in here, fit for company, in five minutes."

"Okay."

I spent a few seconds thinking Richard must have inherited his sense of fun from his father. But I was disabused of that notion when the father arrived. If they had said to the furniture salesman "Fill 'er up," they had said to the purveyor of pricey, trendy casual clothing "Dress me!" The earthy tones of Robertson's ensemble were an uncanny match for those of his wife. The man's face was red, and his eyes were bulging.

"Sorry I'm late! I don't know if anybody has had to do business with the local BMW dealership recently. They're so busy you have to stand in line."

"It's a tough cruel world," Brennan said with just enough volume for me to hear.

"The stresses of a two-Beemer family," I muttered back.

Mrs. Robertson spoke to the assembled group. "This is my husband, Murdoch. I don't know everybody's name, so maybe you could all introduce yourselves." Introductions were made around the room.

One name struck a chord with Murdoch Robertson. "Reverend Burke, you're the director of the school, am I right?"

Burke nodded.

"Great school."

"Thank you."

"At least for music and literature, history, math, science, all that." The man paused. "But it could be more forward-looking. Know what I mean?"

"No."

"You don't teach economics, right?"

Burke looked at him as if he were speaking a foreign tongue.

"Economics," Robertson tried again.

"The dismal science," Burke replied. "No."

"I'm an economist by training," Robertson said.

"Ah."

"I'd be happy to come in and teach a few lessons in the subject. In fact, we could start a 'young entrepreneurs' group at the school. Give the kids early exposure to a business world view."

Burke stared at him blankly.

"So," Robertson said then, "how is my son doing in school?"

It dawned on me then that this was the first time Richard's father had met Burke, despite the fact that Richard had been in the school for at least two years.

"Richard is doing brilliantly. He has the voice of an angel, and his written work is excellent. A sly wit, has Richard, and we all enjoy his sense of humour."

Mrs. Robertson leaned forward in her chair. "Class clown is not the goal we have in mind for our son. Richard has to become more focused. We have a tutor for him in French. A virtual necessity, given the job market in this country. He's not doing very well in that, do you think?"

"He sounds better than I do in French, I can tell you that much!" Burke replied. "I wouldn't be too concerned about Richard getting a job. He's a long way from that, and he'll do fine wherever he winds up."

"I think not. Richard doesn't take things seriously. He has a personal coach, but even there he doesn't seem to meet expectations. We'll have to step up our efforts, obviously."

I sat there wondering what the hell she was on about. A personal coach? What on earth . . .

Richard came bounding in at that point, with his hair slicked down and the arse of his pants wet where he had tried to scrub off the grass stains.

"Richard!" his mother began, but the boy interrupted.

"Psst!" He crooked his finger at my daughter, who was playing a board game with the other kids. "Normie! Where's Kim at?"

"She's supposed to be here! Maybe she couldn't find your house!"

"Okay. Come on downstairs. I got something to show you. Ian, you too. Monty, you come too, and Father Burke."

"Richard! You're not taking people down there! You have guests, and we are hoping for a little recital from you."

"Yeah, okay, after. Please, Mum? Come on, you guys."

Normie and Ian followed him from the room. Burke gave me the eye, and we got up.

"Oh, Reverend! You won't want to go down there . . ."

"Sure it will be fine."

We both made our escape. Whatever Richard wanted to show us downstairs, whether it was a busted pipe or a web full of spiders, would be better than spending one more minute in that stifling living room. Burke and I went through the kitchen, where I noticed an array of appliances and gadgets I could not even begin to identify. We found the basement stairs and saw the kids ahead of us. Richard said to his companions: "I hope Brrrennan O'Burrrke comes to see this. It will freak him right out of his collar!" I recalled Richard's humorously rolled Rs, which had started when Burke took him to task for his failure, despite his Scottish name, to roll them sufficiently when required in singing.

"Brrrennan O'Burrrke is right behind you, laddie," Brennan replied, and Richard turned around and blushed from his neck to his eyebrows.

"Sorry, Father. I was just, you know . . ."

"*Te absolvo*, my son. Go and sin no more."

When we got to the basement, we heard the voice of Neil Young coming from behind a closed door. "That's my uncle's room," Richard explained.

He led us to a wooden crate in the corner of the basement. He pried the lid off carefully.

"Ooh!" Normie squealed. "Can it get out of there?"

"Cool!" Ian exclaimed. "Where did you get it?"

It was a snake of some sort, brown with a pattern on it, about two feet long, writhing around in a makeshift pen.

Burke shuddered at the sight of it, and Richard grinned. "They don't have snakes in Ireland 'cause of St. Patrick, right, Father?"

"Patrick must have done an exemplary job because this is the first time in my long and eventful life I've ever had the misfortune to see a serpent of any kind."

"Hey, man!"

We heard the voice and turned towards it. At the same time, I thought I detected a faint odour of cannabis. The closed door had opened, and standing there was a youngish man with John Lennon glasses and long shaggy curly hair; he wore a pair of cut-off shorts and a T-shirt that showed a heart bleeding all over the white fabric. He looked vaguely familiar.

"How ya doin'?" he said to us all.

"Hey! You guys, this is my uncle, Dad's brother, but I just call him Gordo. And this is Father Burke from school, and Ian and Normie and her dad, Mr. Collins."

"Monty," I said, and we shook hands.

"Gordo's living with us for a while. Until he gets his own place."

"Oh, yeah?" I asked. "How long have you been living here, Gordo?"

"What is it now, Dickie? Five, six years, something like that?"

"I think so. I was just little when you moved in."

"Yeah. Good times, eh?"

"Yeah!"

Gordo looked at me and Burke. "I can't move till I get some legal matters settled. I buy a house, the sheriff moves in, takes it all. You know what I mean."

"Sure," I said.

"Come on in, have a seat."

We entered Gordo's room. My imagination presented me with delightful images of Mrs. Robertson coming in for a gab with her guest. The room could have been a film set, labelled "The Freeloading Brother-in-Law."

He turned down Neil Young, who would no doubt appreciate the fact that he was being played in vinyl on an ancient turntable, and invited us to sit on a saggy chesterfield covered with a worn grey army blanket with a red stripe.

"You promised Ellie you were going to get a new blanket, Gordo. Ellie's his girlfriend," Richard explained.

"Yeah, I asked at the Salvation Army counter the other day; they still don't have anything in. Maybe I'll try Frenchy's," he said to Richard. Then, to us: "I don't buy anything retail."

"Makes sense," I agreed.

His room was decorated with rock band posters and protest signs bearing slogans such as "Resist!" and "Make Brownies Not War." One wall was dedicated to the campaign posters of the Cannabis Garden Party.

That's why he was familiar. "You're the U.S. invasion guy!"

"That's me," he agreed. "Defence critic for the Cannabis Garden Party."

Any time the defence minister or a military spokesman made a public appearance in Halifax, Gordo showed up to needle him on the country's inadequate defence spending. But where other defence critics, on the right, took the government to task for failing to anticipate an attack from rogue leftist states or terrorists, Gordo railed about the dangers of an invasion from the south. Which he considered imminent.

"And never has it been more urgent that I get my message out." He lay back on a pile of Indian-print pillows, and retrieved a home-rolled cigarette that was burning in an ashtray. He took a leisurely drag. His posture bespoke anything but urgency. But then he roused himself to give a stump speech.

"It could happen at any time. People don't realize that. We do anything to really piss the Yanks off, they're over the border in minutes. We're a bunch of unreliable commies, far as they're concerned. The only reason they tolerate us is that we lie down for them and enjoy it. The minute we stop playing that role, the minute, say, the NDP gets in and tries to curb foreign takeovers of our industry, bingo! We're Guatemala, United Fruit Company is pissed, and the democratically elected government of Canada is overthrown. Think Iran 1953, think Guatemala 1954, think Chile 1973, and all the other legitimate governments that were overthrown and replaced with torture states friendly to the U.S. of A. The list goes on and on. But here's the difference: it won't be the usual American practice of engineering a coup and installing a friendly puppet."

Gordo made his hands and feet jerk up and down spasmodically as if on strings, to the delight of his young audience. "Yes, sir, Billy

Bob, we'll mow down those protesters in the name of freedom. No, sir, Bobby Joe, we won't nationalize Kentucky Fried Chicken." Then the puppet collapsed on the bed.

He roused himself again and said: "No, they won't stop at that with us. It will be the tanks rolling in, it will be an invasion, an occupation, and they'll never leave. We'll simply be annexed as part of the U.S.A. Canada will cease to exist as a country. I've got my ticket to the Netherlands for the day they move in. How about you guys?"

The kids were staring at him, wide-eyed.

We heard heels tapping smartly on tile, and looked up to see Mrs. Robertson, who was nearly frantic as she surveyed the party in her brother-in-law's den.

"Gordon! Richard has responsibilities upstairs this evening. Reverend! Mr. Collins! Don't let my husband's . . . sibling detain you here in this . . . this . . . My heavens! We're serving pad Thai upstairs. Please join us. It's the newest thing!"

"Ah, we're grand here, Mrs. Robertson," Burke replied. "No worries. We'll be joining you anon."

"I don't believe this!" she wailed as she turned away.

"Are you enjoying your time here, Gordo?" I asked when she had stalked up the stairs.

"I enjoy my time everywhere, Monty. And I certainly enjoy the company of young Dickie here."

"I hope you stay forever, Gordo!"

"I hope so, too," Brennan muttered just loud enough for me to hear. I concurred.

"Monty Collins!" Gordo exclaimed. "I just realized who you are. You represented Beau Delaney. Good job, congratulations! Beau's my lawyer, has been for years. I was entangled in some nasty legal proceedings; he represented me."

"What was the trouble?"

"I used to own a house, and there was an oil spill. Actually, years of leakage that I didn't know about. And it contaminated the neighbours' properties, and there was a hundred thousand dollars in clean-up costs, and the neighbours sued me, and I sued the oil company and the distributor, and I had to sue my own insurance company. It went on for years. I lost my house, and there were judgments against me. Hence my inability to become a responsible property owner again. None of this was Beau's fault. The cards were stacked against us. He got me out of some other scrapes, no problem. Great guy, great lawyer.

"Except the time he left me stranded. It was after the oil spill litigation, and all the parties were fighting over legal costs. I stood to lose, big time. Again. We were in Beau's office getting ready for the hearing. But he forgot about an appointment he had in Toronto. A conference. He remembered quick enough when his secretary came in. 'Dr. Brayer's office on the line for you, Beau.' Beau looked as if he'd got caught coming out of the shitter with his pants down. He must have thought I knew who this guy was, the doctor. Well-known, I guess, on the subject of psychopaths. Shows up every once in a while apparently as a talking head with Mansbridge on CBC. But I'd never heard of him. So Delaney had to fly out on the next flight, and I had to go to court on my own. He told me to get an adjournment till he came back, but I decided to wing it. Bad idea. I got nailed for contempt of court when I called the judge a tool of the insurance industry and a lackey for big oil. I ended up in jail for two nights. What the hell, it happens. I rag Beau about it whenever I see him, but it's my fault, not his. And he did appeal the costs ruling, so it wasn't as bad as it was going to be.

"But enough about that, eh, Dick? Time to dip into the news files?"

"Yeah!"

"What'll it be today? How about 'Wedding cake icing protruding from buttocks our first clue, police say, after arrest of man in fairy-tale wedding fiasco'? Or 'Granny gulps her dentures'?"

"Granny and the false teeth! Read that one. You guys are going to love this," Richard said to Normie and Ian.

Gordo reached down behind his bed and pulled up a binder. He opened it and displayed a collection of news items. "Here we go: Granny gulps her dentures in whoopee cushion scare. By Crandall McIntosh, the Halifax *Daily News*.

> An eight-year-old prankster's practical joke nearly turned
> into tragedy when he placed a whoopee cushion beneath
> the padding of his great-grandmother's rocking chair,

then watched in stunned horror as the shocked eighty-two-year-old woman swallowed the upper plate of her dentures, nearly choking to death. "We thought it would be a riot to put a whoopee cushion on Granny's chair," says the boy's father, thirty-seven-year-old Jeffrey Berg. "She's pulled many a practical joke on us in her time, so we figured turnabout was fair play. We never dreamed she'd be so startled that she'd swallow her choppers."

It wasn't just the kids who enjoyed a good laugh over the story.

"*Now* I see where Richard gets his sense of the absurd," I said to Gordo.

"What would he do without me?"

Gordo said it lightly, but the eyes behind the rimless glasses radiated a shrewd intelligence. He had his shtick and he knew exactly what he was doing — as a rabble-rouser, and as an uncle.

Burke and I left him to it. We went upstairs and endured the remainder of the party with the other guests. Murdoch Robertson had excused himself shortly after his arrival, saying he had work to do. When it was time to go, Lois decreed that Richard was to stand at the door and shake hands with everyone as they went out.

"Ask yer man to come see me about teaching a class or two at the school," Brennan said to him.

"My dad?"

"Your uncle."

Richard blinked. "Really?"

"Sure. A couple of history classes is what I have in mind."

"But I thought all that stuff was, you know, just Gordo's stories."

"Sadly, no. It's the history of our times. Oh, and tell him not to arrive at the school with a big, fat spliff in his mouth."

"Uh . . ." Richard's face turned pink.

"Can you arrange that for me?"

"Yeah! For sure!" The little boy beamed as his mother, unaware, scowled from the sidelines.

Brennan gave Richard a little salute, I collected Normie, and we took our leave of The Olde Carriageway.

Chapter 17

(Monty)

But it was back to business the next morning. Brennan's story about someone selling access to the Delaney family had gone in one of my ears and out the other the first time I had heard it. With so much else happening, I had just let it go. Then, with Delaney's acquittal, it had faded from my consciousness. But after the squalid scene in the church parking lot, I wanted to know what was going on. The Crown had just under two weeks to appeal, and I would be on edge till the deadline was safely behind us. I couldn't escape the feeling that there was more to the Delaney saga than I had been led to believe, and if there was bad news out there, I wanted to be prepared for it. I called Brennan after I saw a number of clients in my office. He came over, and we directed our minds to the Delaney family access scam.

"Fill me in on this poor little Cody," I said.

"Cody was one of the two boys who followed the Delaney kids to the choir school and demanded their money back. Turned out of course that the Delaney kids knew nothing about the scheme. Anyway, I spoke to the two lads, Cody and Mitchell, and got their contact information. They had each paid one hundred fifty dollars to somebody claiming he represented the Delaney family. Fifty was for a promised ride in the Mercedes van. One hundred was supposed to get them an interview with the aim of, well, becoming part of the family. Whoever cooked up this plan convinced the boys that they had a chance to join the family as foster children. Seeing what young Cody has for a family life, it's little wonder they jumped at it. Mike O'Flaherty was on the phone all morning with social workers. He learned that Cody's mother is a hooker. Well, we gathered that, didn't we? She lives on and off with that individual, that pimp, who wreaked such havoc that night. He beats her, of course, and beats the young fellow. The mother does nothing to stop it, as we saw for ourselves. In fact, she sticks up for the boyfriend. At the expense of the child and anyone who tries to help. We witnessed that first-hand."

"As did Normie."

Burke closed his eyes. He put his hands to his temples and massaged them. He let out a loud, exasperated sigh, then resumed speaking: "Anyway, not surprisingly, Mike learned that Cody has been taken into care."

I nodded. That was inevitable. "And we'll all be called as witnesses when the guy goes to court for assault causing bodily harm."

"Good," he said. "Monty, have you ever heard of psychosocial dwarfism?"

"I have. Also called psychogenic dwarfism. It occurs in children who are so deprived of love and nurturing that they actually fail to thrive and grow."

"Mike was wondering whether that might be the case with Cody. He's thirteen years old. Only looks about ten."

"Could well be."

"I still want to make sure he's reimbursed for the money he paid out."

"It will have to go to the Department of Community Services now that he's a ward of the state."

"Be that as it may, I'd like to arrange it. There's also the other young fellow, Mitchell."

"You know where he lives?"

"I have his phone number."

"Give him a call. I assume he'll remember your voice. How many Irishmen would he have spoken to recently?"

"How many Irishmen have promised him money in the bank?"

"Exactly. Go ahead."

Burke punched in the number. "Hello. Would Mitchell be there, please?" He waited. "All right. I'll try another time. Could you tell him Father Burke called? What's that? Oh." He put his hand over the receiver. "Someone said he's not there. Now, a second later, he is."

"Typical. The first response is always to claim the person's not home."

He took his hand off the mouthpiece and waited. "Ah. Mitchell. It's yourself. Good. This is Father Burke, from the choir school. That's right, and that's why I'm calling you. We could do that today." Burke looked at me and raised his eyebrows. I nodded. "No, I'm not bullshitting you. I promised, didn't I? No police. What? No, I'll be taking care of Cody separately. If you can meet me at the choir school within the hour, we can set up that account today. Fifteen minutes? Even better. See you there."

So Brennan and I made our way to the corner of Morris and Byrne streets to await Mitchell's arrival. When he came, there were two of them. Were we going to be the next victims of a shakedown? Brennan greeted the younger boy. He was bigger than Cody, but he looked to be around the same age, thirteen or so, and hardship was stamped into his face already. The other guy was considerably bigger, and older, probably fifteen or sixteen. He, too, had been down a long, hard road.

"Who would this be now?" Brennan asked.

Mitchell replied: "This here's Kyle. It happened to him, too."

"How many people were victims of this scam?" I asked. I refrained from asking whether they were now running a scam of their own.

They looked at me without speaking. Brennan said to the big guy, Kyle: "This is Mr. Collins. Tell us your story."

"You're the lawyer, right? That did the court case for Delaney?"

I said I was.

"Okay, so Corbo told me he could get the keys to the Mercedes and —"

"Hold it a sec," I said. "Who's Corbo?"

"Corbett."

Of course. The foster son who didn't work out. "Okay, go on."

"He said we could take the Merc for a ride some night when Delaney was asleep."

"I see. Did he make any other kind of offer to you?"

"No, he didn't say nothin' else. Like, he told Mitchell and Cody they could move into Delaney's house with his wife and kids. He didn't try that with me. I woulda known it was bullshit."

Mitchell looked down at his feet.

"Excuse me!" I turned at the sound of a woman's voice. She was coming towards us on Morris Street with a little curly-haired boy in a stroller. When she got past us, she lifted him out and gave him a loud kiss on his cheek. He giggled and she did it again, then placed him gently on the sidewalk. "You come with Mummy to Daddy's office. We'll both push the stroller, and you can walk in and show Daddy that his little boy can walk now. He'll be so excited he won't be able to do his work! Go ahead, darling, keep walking."

The little fellow wore a grin from ear to ear; he looked as if he'd won the Nobel Prize. Proudly, he toddled along the street, one hand on the side of the stroller, savouring every step. His mum beamed as she walked at his side.

Mitchell didn't look up.

I turned my attention to Kyle: "How much money did Corbett demand in return for a joyride in the Mercedes?"

I could almost see the wheels turning in his head. "Seventy-five bucks," he said.

That could have been the truth, if the other boys were charged fifty to ride in the Mercedes minibus with Delaney at the wheel. The joyride with Corbett at the controls would have fetched a higher price. And this guy did not claim he was charged the extra amount for possible admittance to the Delaney household.

"When did this happen?"

Kyle and Mitchell looked at each other. Mitchell said: "After school started, right?"

"Yeah, it was when the leaves were red and starting to come off the trees, 'cause I thought I might be able to earn the money by raking leaves for people. But everybody I asked said no. Anyway, it was last fall."

"Why wait till now to try to get the money back?"

Kyle shrugged, then said: "Corbett was like 'Don't sweat it' when I saw him downtown in the wintertime. He said he'd get hold of the car in the spring."

"I seen him, too," said Mitchell, "and he told me some of the Delaneys' kids would be moving out, so there'd be room for new kids in the house. And then when . . ."

"When what?"

"When the mother got killed, I said to Corbett 'We won't be able to go there now 'cause she died,' and he said 'Don't worry about it. He'll get a new one.'"

"Who would get a new what?"

Mitchell hesitated for a beat before replying: "Delaney would get a new woman." His voice went up in volume when he added: "She was almost, like, Corbett's mother, and he didn't give a shit!"

We were all silent as we thought that over.

Then Burke spoke up: "All right. Mr. Collins and I will take you fellows to the nearest bank, and set up accounts for you."

"You're bullshitting us, right?" Kyle asked.

"No. Let's take a walk. First bank we see, in we go."

So that's what we did. Burke and I split the cost of repaying the boys for Corbett Reeves's fraud, and we put the money in accounts in the names of the two young boys. They said thanks. Burke urged them, for what it was worth, to save the money or at least use it wisely.

"Don't be spendin' it like a pair of drunken gobshites! Oh, and if your mothers see your passbooks and have any questions about all this, get them to call me at St. Bernadette's. I'll assure them it's all legitimate."

I wanted to know a bit more about Corbett Reeves before we let them go. Mitchell said he had met Corbett hanging out on the street somewhere, and the conversations about the Delaney family developed after that. The older guy, Kyle, seemed to know more. They were both anxious to get going, and I told Mitchell he could go. Brennan left with him. But I asked Kyle to stay for a minute and fill me in.

"I met Corbo in Shelburne." The Shelburne Youth Centre in southwestern Nova Scotia. A detention centre for young offenders.

"When was that?"

"A few years ago, I dunno. I was, like, thirteen. Corbo woulda been twelve, I guess, 'cause as soon as he was old enough that they could put him in there, he was in there. Cops had just been waiting for him to come of age. So anyway that's where I met him. This old lady used to come and visit him sometimes, bring him stuff to eat. These meat pies she used to make for him."

"Who was she?"

"Some relative. I think her name was Mrs. Victory. Or Vickery. Something like that. She used to drive all the way to Shelburne from someplace in the Valley, where she lived. Probably took her hours and hours to get there in this old shitbox of a car. He used to joke about what a bad driver she was, because he lived with her sometimes, and she'd take him out in the car, and she'd drive really slow and she was half blind. So Corbo would laugh about her and her meat pies. He wouldn't even eat them, said they tasted like roadkill, and said how funny it would be if the old lady got killed in a car crash when she was bringing him a pie, and she'd be roadkill too, and somebody would make a pie out of her. Sick, eh? Like, she must have really loved him, and all he did was laugh about her behind her back, and he couldn't care less if she died.

"He didn't want to live with her. Because other times he was living with this big, rich family in the south end of Halifax. That was the Delaneys. I thought it was bullshit. But he said it was true, and maybe we could get money off them when we got out. He used to steal stuff from their house and sell it. Like they had all this gold and diamonds, jewels and stuff, that belonged to the grandmother who was dead. It was just lying there in an old suitcase in one of the bed-room closets. The rest of them didn't even catch on that Corbo was taking the stuff out of the house. He figured it served them right for leaving it around. And there was other things he said he'd do."

"Such as?"

"I dunno. I can't remember now."

"Try."

"Well, he said there was a couple of girls in the family. He said he might take pictures of them." Kyle shuffled his feet and looked away. "Like, when they were changing their clothes or taking a bath or something."

I felt sick, but tried not to show it. "Did he ever produce pictures like that?"

"No, no, I never heard nothin' about it after we got out. Guess he never got near them, or he woulda taken the pictures. He's a fuckin' sicko. Delaney woulda killed him if he knew about that."

So would I, I thought.

"Hell, Delaney was gonna kill him about the money he took off me and Cody and Mitchell for the rides that we never got, or the chance to move into the big house. Cody and Mitchell are suckers, if they thought that was gonna happen. But that was Corbo's big scheme when he got out of Shelburne and went back to the Delaneys. Then he disappeared. Corbo did. I figured he was dead."

"Oh? Why did you think that?"

"Because Delaney threatened to kill him."

"Well," I said, "I can believe Mr. Delaney would be a little upset when he learned of the things Corbett was up to."

"You don't get it, man. Delaney wasn't just a little upset. He went ballistic. He took Corbo into the woods at night. Somewhere outside Halifax. He did something to him, some commando move or something that made Corbo scream and cry like a girl. Corbo said he couldn't believe anything could be that painful, and he was scared shitless. Delaney got in his face and told him to get the fuck out of Halifax and told him in all these gory details what he'd do to him if he ever showed his face around here again. He said he'd kill him, and nobody would ever find him. Corbo, who's a psycho himself, didn't have no doubts at all that Delaney would do it. Corbo decided to fuck off that night. He came and woke me up and told me what happened, and bummed some stuff off me, so he could get out of town. I had some cash, and I gave him some. And he went. Like I say, I thought Delaney got him, and he was dead, until he showed up on TV."

I was hardly aware of Kyle. The only thing in my mind was Beau Delaney looming over Corbett Reeves and threatening to kill him. Is this what Reeves had been planning to say on the stand? Had he come back to play out his revenge on Delaney? Was this the alibi he was going to offer Delaney for the night of his wife's death? "I wasn't there, My Lord, I was in the park threatening to kill my foster son. And I was so convincing, the kid blew town that very night."

240

Oh, God. I had to get a grip. I cleared my throat and spoke to Kyle again. "When was this? When did Corbett come to you and say he was running away?"

"It was just before I got arrested again. I gave Corbo some of my cash, so I wanted to go out and get some more. I pulled a knife on a guy on Maitland Street, but I got caught. So they had me in court the next morning. That was at the end of October."

"You're sure of the time?"

"Yeah, 'cause that's when I ended up in a group home in Dartmouth. So I know when it was."

I tried not to show my relief. The night Corbett fled the city after his encounter with Delaney was nearly three months before Peggy's death.

"Do you think Corbett came back to get revenge on Mr. Delaney, by maybe telling this story in court?"

"Corbo's more twisted than that. It's more like he'd mess around with Delaney for the hell of it. Make him nervous. But he'd try to get something out of it too. You know, give fake evidence for Delaney, Delaney gets off because of it, then Corbo squeezes Delaney for money for the rest of his life. He'd have to stay out of reach, though, in case Delaney killed him. You wouldn't want Corbo on the witness stand. No way, man. But you didn't need him anyway. Delaney got found not guilty. Guess you did a good job. But Delaney woulda got off no matter what."

I couldn't help asking: "Why do you say that?"

"Because he didn't do it. No way he killed his wife."

"Again, why do you say that?"

"Because if he lost it with her and freaked out enough to kill her, they'd have had to pick up the pieces. He wouldn't just push her down the stairs and leave it at that."

(Normie)

I went to the Delaneys' house on Tuesday. It was the ninth of June and it was a big day for us at school because we didn't have any. Didn't have any school, I mean, on account of our teachers all going

241

to a meeting. Except Father Burke; he doesn't like meetings. But he let the rest of them go. All the other schools in Halifax had the day off too. It was a hot, sunny day and Jenny Delaney invited me to her house. Mum said it was okay. Even Richard Robertson was allowed, but I kind of wondered if he lied about where he was going. Anyway, he came in this really cool old green car that made a lot of noise. Gordo was driving and he called the car a beetle. Jenny and her sisters and brothers had a big surprise planned for their dad because of him living in the house again and not killing their mum. He'd already moved back in, but they never got the plan together till now.

When we arrived at the house, Jenny and Laurence were in charge because the big kids all went shopping for stuff for the surprise. I asked what kind of stuff, and Jenny said treats and streamers and balloons. Sarah and Ruthie would probably sneak in some shopping for clothes, too, so they would be gone a long time.

The little kids were really cute. There were four of them: three boys and only one girl. Their names were Sammy, Danny, Edward, and Kristin. What they were going to do was draw beautiful pictures all over the driveway with coloured chalk. They were allowed to do whatever pictures they wanted, but Jenny gave them a paper showing how to spell "We love you, Daddy!!!"

I was going to help Jenny bake a big humongous cake and decorate it. She showed me some cookbooks as soon as I got there, and we gawked at all the pictures of amazing cakes that looked like castles or music boxes or even birthday presents with fake ribbons and bows on them. The only cakes we ever had in our own house, unless we bought them, were flat in a square pan. It was going to be hard to decide which kind to make for Mr. Delaney.

Richard was supposed to help Laurence build this big archway to put in front of the door, so Sarah and Ruthie could put flowers and balloons and everything all over it, for their dad to walk under. But when me and Jenny went down to the basement to see what the boys were up to, they weren't doing their job. They were playing with the hockey game, or I should say they were trying to make the Delaneys' two kitty-cats play and chase the players and the puck. But the cats didn't want to play, and kept trying to get away. No wonder the game is always broken!

Richard was talking about his cat, whose name is "Filth." Laurence asked him why he called it that, and he said his mother always called it "that filthy thing" and wouldn't let it come in the house, so him and Gordo built a secret cabin for it outdoors. He said he'd show Laurence how to build a cabin, and even a place for the cats to do number two, and that's when Jenny said: "Ahem! You guys are supposed to be making the archway, remember?" So they said okay and went to look for the wood and the toolbox.

"Boys!" Jenny said, shaking her head, when we were back in the kitchen.

She bent down and looked in the cupboards and got out bowls and a mixer, and she told me where the flour and sugar and food colouring were.

"Do you cook a lot?" I asked her.

"Yeah, I really like it. You?"

"I'm the one in our house that likes to cook. Mum doesn't enjoy it much."

"Ruthie and Derek do most of the cooking here, and Dad."

So we chatted away and gathered all the stuff we needed, and decided not to use any of the designs in the book but to make our own cake, to look like the Delaneys' big white house, with the black roof and shutters. We were going to cut cherries up and make them look like bricks for the chimney, and make some green trees for the front. We didn't even need to keep running out and looking at the front to remember what it looked like, because their house is in a book about beautiful old houses in Nova Scotia, and Jenny had the book open on the counter.

It was fun swirling stuff around in big glass bowls and using the mixer. When we had flour puffing up in our faces and were in a fit of the giggles, Edward and Kristin came in and asked if they could use the paints and brushes, and Jenny said it was okay to play with their paints as long as they didn't use them on the driveway, just chalk. Then we went back to our baking. There was a box of Smarties on the counter and we tried to figure out where to use them in the design, but we couldn't, so we ended up gobbling them all up. We could hear hammering and sawing, and Laurence and Richard making dumb jokes and laughing in the basement. Then we heard them lugging stuff outdoors, and hammering out there. It seemed to take hours to do it all, but not in a boring way. I couldn't wait till we had everything made and could see how happy Mr. Delaney would be when he got home.

Just when we got the cake in the oven we heard somebody burst out crying. The sound was coming from outside the house, so Jenny made a big sigh and ran out. I followed her.

She screamed "Oh my God!" and I knew it must be something bad for her to say that, because she's not allowed to say it.

When I got outside I saw a bunch of big paint cans on the lawn, and thought maybe the little kids had spilled some paint in the grass. Then I saw Sammy all covered with red paint, and crying his eyes out. But that wasn't the worst of it. Jenny was staring at the house like someone in a horror movie. Oh my God is right! You should have seen it. The kids had painted all the parts of the house they could reach. Instead of white, it was now green and black and red and yellow in ugly blobs of colour. It looked horrible! You wouldn't believe it was the same white house that is included in the beautiful Nova Scotia house book.

Jenny turned to the kids. "What did you do? Are you guys crazy?"

They all started to cry. Sammy got mad and threw his brush at Jenny. It made a big red stripe down the front of her blue jumper. Sammy stomped away into the house.

"Why did you do this?" she asked Kristin.

"You said we could play with the paint!"

"I thought you meant your paint-by-number kits, not Daddy's real paint!"

Laurence and Richard came running from the backyard then, and they gawked at the house and their mouths were hanging open.

Jenny started up again at the little kids. "Sarah and Ruthie and Derek and Connor are all going to have a heart attack when they see this! And Daddy's going to kill you. He'll kill us all, if we can't get this paint off before he comes home!"

Richard looked at me and I thought he was going to make a funny joke, but he didn't. He looked worried. Really upset.

"Let's get this off," Laurence said.

"What kind of paint is it?" Richard asked.

"I don't know, just old paint from the garage."

"Because if it's oil paint, you need special chemicals to get it off, and even then it won't really come off." He went over and picked up one of the cans. "Holy shit. It's oil paint, all right. Let's go and look for some paint remover."

But Laurence went to the house, and grabbed a bunch of leaves and tried wiping some of the paint away. All it did was smear around and around without coming off. It looked as if some of the paint was already dry, maybe because of the hot sun.

Richard had left and was gone for a few minutes, then came back. He said there was no chemical to remove the paint.

The little kids were still bawling, and Jenny went over to them. They backed away. "Never mind. You guys didn't know any better. We'll tell Daddy you meant to paint the house as a nice surprise for him."

"We did!" Kristin said. "We thought he'd like the new colours!" She was sniffling and so were Danny and Edward. Jenny gathered them all up in a big hug, and Laurence went over and ruffled their hair.

"We'll get you off. This time!" And he kind of laughed, and they did too, through their tears.

Then we heard the phone ring inside the house, and Jenny ran to answer it. She came back with a scared look on her face. "He's on his way home!"

"Your dad?" I asked.

She nodded her head. Then she gave Laurence a weird sort of look and said: "We'd better check out back."

And they took off around the back of the house. Me and Richard ran after them.

Jenny was standing there as if somebody had put a hand out and stopped her in her tracks. "Where's all the wood?"

Laurence said: "Uh, we used a whole bunch of it for a log cabin. Over behind the maple tree . . ."

"A log cabin! You were supposed to be using those thin, bendy pieces of criss-crossed wood to make an archway. You weren't supposed to get into Daddy's wood pile!"

"I know! We just did, because it was fun."

"Weren't we allowed to use those logs?" Richard asked.

"No, but it's not your fault," Laurence said. "It's just that Dad likes to, well . . ." Then he shut up.

Jenny filled in the rest of it: "When Daddy gets mad, which he hardly ever does, he goes outside and chops at that woodpile with this little axe he has, and he keeps doing it till he's not mad anymore."

Richard's eyes were like great big saucers. Then I couldn't believe it. He started shaking, as if he was cold. Or afraid. Richard!

Jenny said: "He's never mean to us when something gets him upset. He just hits the wood, not us. But now there's hardly any wood."

"What are we going to do?" Laurence asked.

"I don't know! Maybe Sarah will get home before Dad, and she'll tell us what to do."

That's when we smelled something burning. There was smoke coming from the kitchen window.

"No! Our cake!" Jenny took off inside.

I started to follow her. But then I saw Richard going behind one of the trees in the backyard. I didn't know what to do, help Jenny with the cake, or see what Richard was doing. But Laurence went with Jenny, so I walked over to Richard.

"Jesus, Jesus, Jesus," Richard was saying. He's a funny guy, but his jokes don't usually include swearing.

"Don't worry, Richard," I said. "He's not going to go after us with the axe!"

But he didn't calm down. He was curled up in a ball, shivering, and he couldn't seem to stop. There were tears in his eyes. It was as if he didn't know I was there, and when he saw me and caught on, he got mad. In a shaky but angry voice he said: "You think I'm a baby!"

"I don't think that! I just think you're worried. About, uh, the other kids."

"Guys aren't supposed to cry!"

"Who said? I've seen lots of guys cry. What's wrong with it?"

"Well —" he wiped his eyes with his knuckles "— now that I think of it, I've seen tears in Gordo's eyes . . ."

"Sure. Why not?" The things guys worry about! It's sad. "But remember, Jenny said Mr. Delaney never hits the kids."

"Maybe not. But he's going to be really upset. He's not going to approve of what they did."

"Well, not approving . . . that's not so bad."

He looked at me as if I had said something wacky. "I don't know how you've been brought up, Collins, but disapproval is a big deal in our house! Nobody gets hit, but it's almost worse the way they react. You feel like shit when it happens. And you feel it for a long time. It's a big, big deal."

And it must have been, if Richard was shaky and all in a panic.

Then we heard the honking of a horn.

Jenny came running out of the house with oven mitts on and the cake on fire, and stared out at the street. "It's Dad!" she croaked.

Richard said: "Oh God!" And then — it was unbelievable — he threw up in the grass.

I wanted to help him even though it was gross, but I also wanted to help stick up for the Delaney kids, so I ran to the driveway.

There he was. Mr. Delaney, getting out of his car and looking huge and staring at the house. I read somewhere about a person looking "thunderstruck" and that was him. He glared at the house as if it was a house of horrors. Then he turned and looked at all the kids, who were lined up in front of it, including Sammy and Edward who were covered in paint and Jenny with the black, smoking cake. The kids all looked too stunned and scared even to cry.

Then Richard came running towards us. "Don't want you to face the music by yourselves," he whispered to me.

Mr. Delaney saw him and me amongst the crowd of guilty people.

He took his eyes off us and looked down at the driveway. The little kids had written in chalk: "We lave you, Doddy!!!"

Mr. Delaney made this big noise, and everybody jumped. But then they realized it was a big roar of laughter. He started laughing so hard he bent over, and then he leaned against the car and put his arms out, and the kids knew he wanted to hug them, and they all ran into his arms.

Jenny threw the cake on the ground on the way to her father, and Richard picked it up. He grabbed this dirty, paint-covered paper towel from the ground and placed it over his arm the way they do in snobby restaurants. And he had this big grin on his face and he presented the burnt-up cake to the Delaneys' dad. "Welcome home, Mr. Delaney."

(Monty)

When I got back to the office after my conversation with Kyle on Tuesday, I called Beau Delaney at work and then reached him at home, and ordered him to come see me. Now.

When he came in and closed the door, I gestured for him to sit. He kept his eyes on me as he sat down. I didn't waste time.

"I've just received some disturbing information." Delaney blanched, but did not speak. His reaction made me wonder just how many disturbing bits of information might be out there. "It's about Corbett Reeves."

Delaney swallowed and looked down at his hands. He tried to sound bored, but could not quite pull it off: "Yes, what about him?"

"He was selling access to your family!"

"As I said to you during the trial, things didn't work out with Corbett."

"Didn't work out? What if there's another trial? What if the Crown appeals and is successful, and we're in court again, and Corbett Reeves gets another chance to insinuate himself into the proceedings, and into your life? Maybe as a Crown witness. What's he going to say?" I leaned across the desk towards him. "This Corbett took money from disadvantaged children in return for a promise of a ride in your Mercedes bus, and he squeezed them for more money with the promise of a chance to join the family as foster children. Held out the hope that they could have a loving mother and father and a beautiful home and brothers and sisters and a dog and a cat and who knows what else? They could buy into this happy future by paying a few hundred dollars to your foster son at the time, Corbett Reeves! And you can be sure the kids he shook down got the money from criminal activity because there is no other way they could have come up with it. They could have been caught and charged with theft, and had a whole new nightmare forced upon them. I know for a fact one of the kids got into trouble after giving Corbett money to run away. And you tell me 'things didn't work out'? What do you have to say for yourself, Beau? Somehow I suspect you would have reacted quite strongly when you got wind of this. Now, what the fuck happened with this kid Corbett Reeves?"

"There was a blow-up."

"Between you and him."

"Yeah."

"Did it get physical?"

A hesitation, then: "No."

"Why do I find that hard to believe?"

"I don't give a shit what you believe."

"Yes, you do. You want me to believe you were at the top of the stairs with Peggy when she died and yet you had nothing to do with her death! I think there's something going on in the background here. It has me spooked and I think it has you spooked too." He glared at me, fury in his eyes. "And I think the confrontation with Corbett did get physical." I could almost see the effort he made to compose his features into an expression of unconcern.

"If you call pushing the kid to get him out of my way 'physical,' then it was physical. If you heard anything more than that, if Corbett has been spinning tales, all I can say is: consider the source. So get over this stuff about Corbett Reeves. What matters is that I didn't kill my wife, intentionally or accidentally. Got it, Monty? Now stay focused on that fact and on how you're going to counter the Crown's factum if they do appeal. I don't think they have any grounds, but that hasn't stopped them in the past. And if it does happen, I'll expect another superb defence and another acquittal. Now, if you have nothing positive to offer here today, I'll be on my way, so I can have a bit of peace now that I'm back with my family again."

†

I had no intention of getting over Corbett Reeves. And I had a lead to his whereabouts. Kyle had mentioned a Mrs. Victory, or Vickery, a relative who used to visit Corbett in Shelburne. She apparently lived in the Annapolis Valley. It didn't take long to find a few Vickerys, and to narrow the search down to one: Alice Vickery, of Bridgetown. So the day after my confrontation with Beau, as soon as I got away from the office, I was headed west on Highway 101, and it took me an hour and a half to get to Bridgetown. I pulled up at the given address, and saw a big blue Queen Anne–style house with a high corner tower and a wraparound porch.

Mrs. Vickery greeted me on the porch and invited me inside. Her thinning white hair was held together with a number of hairpins. Despite the mild June weather, her trembling hands held a black wool cardigan closed over her wasted body. She led me to the front parlour, where we sat facing each other on Victorian loveseats.

"So. Mr. Collins. How can I help you? Would you like a cup of tea?"

"Sure. Thank you."

She got up, painfully, and went to the kitchen. The tea must already have been on, because she was back in about two minutes with the tray. I took my cup and thanked her.

"Now. You're here about Corbett? Where is he?"

"I'm not sure, Mrs. Vickery. As I explained on the phone, Corbett appeared in the courtroom during Mr. Delaney's trial. I don't know where he is now."

"Oh! Well, now, he lived with the Delaney family for a while last year, spring to fall, and years before that, too. A very wealthy family, Corbett told me. Apparently, they relied on Corbett to help keep things running smoothly in a household full of children. He was indispensable to them. It's a shame he had to leave."

"Right. I was never clear on why he had to leave . . ."

"The jealousy and resentment, from what I hear. Corbett is so gifted, really. Athletic, intelligent, talented. Not everyone has those gifts. It is my understanding that some of the children in the Delaney home had various difficulties, handicaps, unfortunate backgrounds, that sort of thing. It would be quite natural, I suppose, for them to resent a boy like Corbett, with his good looks and his robust health and abilities. The situation just became impossible for Corbett."

"I see."

"But he'll always have a home in this house, as long as I'm here anyway! My husband and I never had any children, so we were over-joyed when Community Services found us all those years ago, and asked us if we could take in this grand-nephew we had never met. We didn't even know our niece had a baby. She hasn't been living in Nova Scotia since she was a child, so we had lost contact with her com-pletely. But we certainly had the space for Corbett when he arrived. He pretty well has the third floor to himself whenever he's here. The whole area up there is one big room, with a magnificent view of the Annapolis River. I haven't been up there in dogs' years, myself. Like the basement, it's out of my range now. I'm not good on stairs. You can go on up, if you wish."

"Maybe I will in a minute, thanks. Tell me a bit more about Corbett. What is he like?"

"He's a sensitive boy, a very trusting child. There are always people who will take advantage of a young person like that. He got in with some ruffians here. I never met them, thank goodness, probably because I go to bed so early and these juvenile delinquents would be a bunch of night crawlers! My daughter came for a visit from Calgary, and she discovered that some of my things were missing. Silver, my husband's cameras, some foreign currency, and other items I had stored in the basement. I can't get down those stairs now, with my hip. So I didn't realize the things were gone. I asked Corbett if he knew anything about it. He said he would look into it. Turned out these companions of his had helped themselves to our family heirlooms! Corbett was mortified. He did his best to track the items down and get them back, but it was too late. He came to me practically in tears. 'I'm sorry, Auntie Alice, I can't get those things back. But I promise you I'll never see those guys again.' And he was as good as his word. He never saw them again."

He never saw them in the first place, because they didn't exist. To Mrs. Vickery, I said: "What else can you tell me about him? How far along is he in school?"

"Well, now, school. You know what the schools are like. Not everybody fits in. So he didn't get the best of grades. But there are different kinds of intelligence, aren't there? Corbett is an extremely bright youngster. He spent a lot of time here, studying on his own. He's very interested in history, which delighted my husband, George, when he was alive. George taught European history at Acadia till he retired, and we came back here. His area of specialty was Germany in the 1930s and 40s — the war and what led up to it. George had been retired for a good many years, so he loved having the young boy around. He had a real student in Corbett! Oh, I miss him. I miss them both. My husband died two years ago. And Corbett, well, he comes and goes. I hope he comes back soon. You go ahead, up to his room. He did some painting up there. I hope he did a good job! Maybe you'll see something that will give me an idea of his plans, or when he might be back."

So I excused myself and headed up the two flights of stairs to Corbett's aerie. If I had expected black walls and heavy metal posters in the teenage boy's room, I had it all wrong. Everything was white. The walls, the painted wood floor, the furniture and linens. And, most emphatically, all the people whose images adorned the walls. Without exception, the pictures he had tacked up were of white folks with blond hair and blue eyes. Some were actors and actresses who looked familiar. Others I did not recognize, with one notable exception: SS Obergruppenführer Reinhard Heydrich. Not only was there a photo of the SS man with a little biography taped underneath it, there were chapters ripped from history books, giving all kinds of details about Heydrich. I flipped through the pages and shook my head.

A small portable television and VCR were shoved in a corner, with a stack of World War Two movies piled precariously on top. Then I found a homemade comic book with a superhero — more like a human killing machine — with an SS uniform and a face and hair-cut that looked a lot like those of Corbett Reeves.

When I returned to the parlour, I told Mrs. Vickery I had not seen anything that would offer a clue to Corbett's intentions, at least not his travel plans. We chatted about him for a few minutes more, then I thanked her and said goodbye.

†

"Corbett Reeves is the blond beast," I reported to Brennan that night at the Midtown.

"The boy reads Nietzsche?" Brennan said.

"Doesn't have to. He has a twentieth-century role model who upheld the ideal of the blond Aryan warrior, and carried it through to its logical conclusion."

"This would be someone from the Third Reich, I presume."

"Reinhard Heydrich. Corbett has a collage of Heydrich memorabilia — photos of him in his SS uniform, excerpts from books about him, how he was taunted and mocked by the other schoolboys for — get this — his high-pitched voice, and whatever other flaws they picked up on, how he rose in the 'racially pure' SS and ran the Gestapo for Himmler, how he helped plan the 'final solution' in which the Jews would be wiped out. A Nazi so feared he made other Nazis tremble at the knee. Did you know Heydrich was the product of a very cultured, musical family?"

"That sounds familiar. He played the violin, didn't he?"

"Right. The father was an opera singer. He sang Wagner — no surprise there. They even gave Heydrich the middle name of Tristan. They had a lovely house, a life of culture. And the son grew up to be a cold and murderous Nazi."

"Well, Germany was one of the most civilized countries in the world when all this happened."

"And the Nazis will always have their admirers. Like our Corbett. I found a comic book he created, with himself as a blond killer in an SS-style uniform."

"What got him on to Heydrich?"

"The great-uncle, dead now, taught German history at Acadia University. When Corbett lived there years ago, the professor used to tell him all about the war, the Third Reich, the Holocaust. He showed him the materials he had collected for his classes on the subject. He didn't expect the child to become a fan!"

"Do we know that? Maybe he did. Maybe the uncle was a fan himself. And Corbett seems to be exactly the type to become fascinated with the Nazis."

"Mrs. Vickery had no insight into the kid at all. You should have heard the poor old soul going on about him. 'Corbett is very bright, you know.' And: 'Corbett does not like the coarser things in life,' she told me when I was leaving. 'He needs comfort, a certain amount of refinement. He always loved this house, the furnishings . . . I cannot bear to think of him living in poverty, in squalor.' He was robbing the old lady blind, and she didn't have a clue! That young fellow, Kyle, told us Corbett used to brag to the inmates in Shelburne about living in a big house in the posh part of Halifax. He obviously thinks that's the style to which he is entitled to become accustomed."

"I'd say the Delaneys were well rid of him."

"And I wish they'd stayed rid of him. I don't like the fact that he's out there, circling around us, with accusations against Beau."

"What sort of accusations?"

I shook my head and raised a "don't ask" hand in his direction.

Then I said: "I want to find Corbett. Either that or receive a message from a higher power, assuring me that Corbett has found true happiness on the other side of the continent, and has no plans to travel east ever again. The latter option is as fantastical as Corbett Reeves's sense of entitlement in this world. So I guess I'm stuck with option one, track him down and try to determine what kind of a threat he might pose to Delaney."

"How do you intend to find him?"

"I'll start with you. Do you still have the phone numbers of those kids, Mitchell and Kyle?"

"I think I know Mitchell's number, but I'll check when I get home to make sure I have it right. I'll give you a call."

✝

Brennan gave me Mitchell's number and, through him, I found Kyle and, after a bit of rigmarole with him, I found out where Corbett Reeves was staying. So, the following morning, Corbett and I were face to face outside his current place of residence, a group home in Dartmouth. He told his story in his high, grating voice.

"Beau took me out to the woods. Somewhere outside the city, off the Bedford Highway. It's got some name like poison. Hemlock Forest or something."

"Hemlock Ravine?"

"Yeah, that's it."

"When was this?"

"I don't know. Well, the leaves were red and yellow, so fall time. He took me along a path and then into the trees. There was nobody around. He told me off for getting money from all those little losers who thought I was going to give them a ride in the Merc, or get them into the family. And some other stuff I did."

"What other stuff?"

"None of your business. So then I badmouthed him back, and he picked me up and practically choked me, then threw me down on the ground. He was going to kill me!"

"And yet, here you are, alive and well."

"Only because he's chickenshit."

"He was afraid of you, is that what you're saying? He's over a foot taller than you, and he weighs twice as much."

His face flushed, and he put his hands on my chest and tried to shove me away. "You fuck off! People who laugh at me don't end up laughing very long."

"All right, all right, settle down and tell me your story."

"Bet you didn't know Delaney wears special shoes!"

What had I heard about that? It sounded familiar, but I didn't let on. "No, I can't say the subject ever came up."

"It wouldn't ever come up! He freaks out if he thinks somebody might find out. They have things in them to make him taller!"

I remembered it then. Sergeant Morash had told me. Well, I wasn't about to get into it with Corbett. "Let's be serious here. Why do you say Delaney was going to kill you?"

"Because he told me!"

The boy was becoming more and more agitated, and in my own way, so was I.

"What did he say to you?"

"He said: 'I know what you are. I'm going to send you to hell.'"

"Corbett, if Delaney was going to kill you, why do you suppose he didn't just flatten you with one big fist? Why all this chat leading up to it?"

"Maybe he was chicken, and he was trying to talk himself into it. Trying to psych himself up."

"What did he mean by saying 'I know what you are'?"

"There are two kinds of people in this world. Did you know that, Monty?"

"What kinds of people, Corbett?"

"Masters and slaves."

"I see."

"Ever hear of the master race?"

"Oh, come on, Corbett."

"I told you, people who make fun of me end up not laughing in the end!"

"Are you saying you have hurt people who have made fun of you?"

255

"Maybe yes, maybe no. It's none of your business."

"Okay, go on."

He studied me for a moment. "What are you? Dutch or something?"

"Irish and English."

"Oh yeah? Well . . . English might not be too bad."

"Glad to hear it."

"That's what Beau meant about me. I'm the blond warrior type, and I could cause a lot of death and destruction if I wanted to."

I wanted to laugh out loud again at this preposterous child, but I kept it in. "Is this what you were going to say if you had taken the stand in Delaney's trial?"

"I don't think so."

"Why not? Didn't you want to take revenge on him?"

"I told the TV and the court that he didn't do it."

"You said he 'didn't kill.' Maybe that meant he didn't kill *you*. But you say he threatened to. Is that what your evidence was going to be?"

"I was going to keep him out of jail."

"How were you going to do that?"

"By telling them he was with me that night."

"Why would you do that, if the man tried to kill you?"

"You're not very smart sometimes, are you, Monty?"

"I guess not."

"I was going to get him off. Then he would be in debt to me for the rest of his life. And he'd pay me money over and over again."

"You were going to blackmail him."

"So what? He would owe me, fair and square."

"But there's a flaw in that reasoning. If he's the killer you say he is, he'd just come get you some night, and bump you off."

"No way." Corbett shook his head. "I would have made sure he knew I left the true story in an envelope in a safe place, with orders for somebody to open it if anything happened to me. Do you think I'm stupid?"

"Do you watch a lot of television, Corbett?"

"I said I'm not stupid, you asshole!" He looked as if he might burst into tears. His fists were clenched and he screamed into my face. "Fuck off! I'm leaving, and you'll never find me! But I know where to find you!"

I grabbed him by the arm and stopped him. "Settle down. And I don't want to hear any more threats out of you."

"Why? What are you going to do about it?"

"It's a criminal offence to utter a threat. Did you know that?"

"Oh yeah? Then maybe Beau Delaney better go to court all over again, because of the way he threatened me."

"Seriously, now, Corbett. You didn't really believe Delaney was going to do anything to you."

"Oh, I believed him all right." The bluster was gone from the young boy's demeanour. "He meant it. He picked me up off the ground and made like he was going to hit me. He looked at me for a long time, like he was thinking. Then he told me to get out of Halifax and not come back. If I went anywhere near his house or his family, or even if I showed up in the city again, he would kill me. He would make me disappear. Then he just dropped me, and walked away. I took off in the other direction, and I got lost. When I finally found my way out, I hopped on a bus to get to my buddy's place downtown. A friend of mine. To get some money and stuff. I got out of town that night, and hitchhiked all the way to the old lady's place in Bridgetown. Because, believe me, I believed him!"

My mind was reeling as I drove to the office after my encounter with Corbett Reeves. In spite of myself, I found the kid credible. Had Delaney really been on the verge of killing his former foster son? "I know what you are." What? A young misfit living in a world of neo-Nazi fantasies? When I got to the office, I saw a couple of clients, did my paperwork, and made some calls. This freed me up for the afternoon, I realized, and I decided to hook off for the rest of the day. As I made preparations to leave, I thought back over what I knew about Beau Delaney. Had I ever heard anything that would suggest he might attempt or threaten to kill a fifteen-year-old boy? I had just defended him on a charge of killing his beloved wife. The jury had found him not guilty. Were they wrong after all?

Chapter 18

(Normie)

I phoned Daddy and caught him just before he left to play hooky from work. I had to tell him about the great day we had at school.

"Hi, Daddy!"

"Hi, Normie. How's my girl?"

"Good! It was so cool today in history class! We had a combined class with the big kids. All the grades were there. And guess who taught the class?"

"Oh, let me see. You?"

"No!"

"Mum?"

"No!"

"I can't guess, then. Who?"

"Gordo!"

"Gordo . . . oh, right. Richard's uncle."

"Yeah!"

"How was it?"

"Great. We learned all this new stuff. Did you ever hear of the CIA?"

"Yep."

"The KGB?"

"Yep."

"Well, he taught us about them and about all these governments that got overthrown, and about death squads that these governments allowed to operate! It was spooky. And the Americans really do have a plan to take over our country. It was made up after the First World War and it was called War Plan Red. And guess what? The first city to be captured was Halifax! And they said they would drop bombs on us if we didn't give in!

"The kids were staring at Gordo they were so amazed, but he had all these papers to prove what he was saying. Father Burke sat in on the class and thanked Gordo, and invited him back! And another day, Monsignor O'Flaherty and Father Burke are going to teach us all about Irish history. And, um, he said something about you."

"Who did?"

"Father Burke. He said you're half Irish and you were never taught the history of your own people, and he expects to see you in the front row with a pen and a notebook when they give the Irish history lesson!"

"Well, I can't very well disobey my priest, can I? So you let me know when it is, and I'll be there."

"He doesn't think you're stupid, though, Daddy. He knows you know all kinds of other history, but he said your dad, my granddad, never told you enough about the old country. It's not your fault."

"Thank you, sweetheart. So, tell me, what did Gordo have on when he taught the class today?"

"He wore his usual clothes, you know, raggedy jeans and a T-shirt. The kids gawked at him when he came in. They didn't think he was the guy who was going to teach the lesson; they thought he got in the school by mistake."

"What did his T-shirt say?"

"It was funny. It showed this old president of the United States asleep at his desk, with a red phone ringing beside him, and the words 'Bedtime for Bonzo!'"

"Love it. So, what else is new, angel?"

I talked with Daddy for a few more minutes, and he told me he'd see me soon and we said goodbye.

On the drive home from work, I pictured Gordo as I had seen him the night of the Robertsons' choir party, and I imagined that he was well able to keep the attention of his students in class. A good story-teller. He had recounted a story about Beau Delaney. Beau was his lawyer in a lawsuit over something, an oil leak, and I suspected there was the occasional drug charge as well. What had he said about Beau? Beau had failed to show for a court hearing, and Gordo ended up in jail. Represented himself. Contempt of court, that was it, for making an insulting remark about the judge. Beau hadn't failed to show up, I remembered then, but was double-booked that day and had to go out of town for a psychiatric conference. That made sense; the question of mental illness arose frequently in the world of criminal law.

This brought Corbett Reeves to mind again. I saw Corbett as a sword of Damocles hanging over Delaney's future, specifically his future in the courtroom if we were forced to go through a new trial. Corbett with his World War Two and Nazi fixation, his grandiose ideas of his place in the world, his attempts to intervene in the murder trial. Kyle described him as twisted, a psycho. Did Corbett have some kind of mental illness? Personality disorder? More than likely, by the sound of things. I remembered another detail from Gordo's anecdote then: the conference was in Toronto, put on by Dr. Brayer. Quinton Brayer, an expert in psychopaths! Were we getting into deep, murky waters here? I wondered about Corbett's background. Even Mrs. Vickery, his great-aunt, didn't seem to know where he had been born or where he had spent his early years. He hadn't started out in Nova Scotia, if I remembered my conversation with her. Community Services had tracked her down. Up until then, Mrs. Vickery hadn't even known the child existed. Did this mean he had no other family? Where had he been before the Vickerys and the Delaneys? My mind lurched then to Normie's talk about an asylum. No, surely he was too young to have been confined to an asylum. Was the word even used anymore?

I had to rein in my imagination. There was no point trying to imagine where Corbett had been, apart from the Vickery and Delaney homes. But I did wonder whether his presence might have been a factor in Delaney's decision to sign up for the conference in Toronto. I knew Corbett had been with the Delaneys several years ago and then again for part of last year. Springtime through fall. When was the conference? Gordo would remember when it was, given that he wound up in jail during Beau's absence.

When I got to the house, I looked up the Robertsons in the phone book and dialled their number. No answer. I could do some research and find out when Gordo's costs hearing took place, but the direct approach would be quicker. I called directory assistance and got the number for the psychiatrist, Quinton Brayer. I would simply ask when the conference had taken place. To save time explaining who I was and why I was asking, I'd use Beau's name. I made the call, and a woman answered.

"Dr. Brayer's office. Marsha speaking."

"Good afternoon, Marsha. This is Beau Delaney. You may recall the time I was up to see Dr. Brayer last year. I'm just wondering if you could give me the dates. I've forgotten and I'd like to . . ."

"Certainly, Mr. Delaney. How are you?"

"Fine, thank you."

"Just hold on for a second. I'll grab those records."

Records? She was gone for a minute or so, then returned. "Sorry to keep you waiting, Mr. Delaney."

"That's all right."

"Let me see. Wednesday, March 8, and then it was Fridays, March 15 and 22, April 5, 12, and 26. Is there anything else I can help you with today?"

"No, no thanks, Marsha. That's all I needed."

"Well, I hope you and your family are well, Mr. Delaney. Call us again any time. Bye-bye!"

What had I done? It wasn't a psychiatric conference. Somebody had been seeing Brayer as a patient. Delaney? A member of his family? Corbett Reeves? I had impersonated Beau and — without intending to — I had been given confidential information that was none of my business.

†

261

I thought again of the asylum in Normie's vision. Where or what was that? I picked up the phone again, and called Debbie Schwartz. She was a clinical psychologist who helped out with clients from time to time. Her receptionist told me she was busy with a patient, but I heard from her a while later.

We exchanged a bit of small talk, then I got down to it. "I won't trouble you with the convoluted reasoning behind my question, Debbie, but here it is: do you know where there is a psychiatric institution that has the word 'asylum' in its name?"

"Not that I can think of. The Nova Scotia Hospital used to be called an asylum, but not in recent times."

"This place would have the word 'asylum' carved into the facade, according to my information. And the name 'Vincent' somewhere as well."

"Vincent?"

"Yeah. It's a long story."

"Okay. Well, I can't think of a place around here, Monty. Though I can't speak for the other provinces. Ontario or wherever. There's an institution in New Brunswick. Moncton? No, it's in Saint John. I've never had occasion to visit, so I don't know what it's called. Or what the building looks like. I could make some inquiries for you."

"No, don't do that. Thanks anyway, Deb. I know somebody from Saint John and if he can't give me any information, maybe I'll call you again."

"Sure."

"Appreciate your help. See you."

"Bye, Monty."

My expert on Saint John, New Brunswick, was Monsignor Michael O'Flaherty. He had grown up there. I got into the car and headed downtown to St. Bernadette's.

Michael was showing a group of Japanese tourists around the church when I arrived. I watched with amusement as they took turns opening the doors of the confession box, sitting in the penitents' seat, and posing for photographs. I could see Michael trying to maintain his usual good cheer in the face of such cavalier behaviour on sacred ground. When he had shepherded them onto their bus and waved goodbye, I walked over to him.

"Not a word out of you, young Collins. I haven't the humour for it today! I had to shoo them off the altar, as politely as I could. So, what brings you here, Monty? "

"Well, Mike, you may find this an odd question."

"It couldn't be any more odd than the questions that came my way over the last half hour. Ask away, my lad."

"All right. There is a mental hospital in Saint John, isn't there, Mike?"

"Indeed there is. We always used to say: 'Go on out of that, or they'll be sending you to Lancaster!' It's not Lancaster anymore. It's all amalgamated into Saint John now. But that's where it is."

"Is the name Vincent connected with it?"

"No. It's never been called that. In fact, its old name was the Provincial Lunatic Asylum! It was built in the nineteenth century."

"They didn't mince words in those days."

"Funny you should say that. At the time it was established, the place was in the forefront of the new, more humane treatment of the mentally ill. It was the first institution of its kind in Canada, the first place for the mentally ill that was separate from a jail. But why are you asking about it, Monty?"

"Somebody mentioned an asylum, but it also had the word 'Vincent' on a sign; I'm not clear on the details." I didn't tell him I was repeating a reference I had heard second-hand, and that even the first-hand account was only a description of a place seen in a dream. Or a psychic vision! The less said the better.

"Well, now, that might be the St. Vincent's Orphan Asylum."

Orphan asylum! "What's that, Mike?"

"The infants' home in Saint John. The orphanage."

I realized I was staring at him. Normie had seen a baby. And a little child. Now I was hearing about an orphanage.

"What does the place look like, do you know?"

"I know it well. It's right around the corner from the cathedral. I lived not far from it myself. The infants' home is a red-brick building, nineteenth century, with Gothic windows and a couple of holy crosses at the top."

That was it. That was the place Normie had described, although she hadn't mentioned the crosses.

"The sisters are still there, although it's not an orphanage anymore. They used to run a school as well."

"Sisters?"

Monsignor O'Flaherty looked at me as if he thought I'd gone a little simple. "The Sisters of Charity, Monty. They have a convent there, and they used to run the orphanage and the school."

"Yes, of course. Sorry, Mike, my mind was off on a bit of a tangent."

"Sure we all have moments like that. Any particular reason you're asking, or have you just taken a sudden interest in my old hometown?"

"There's a reason, but if I tried to explain . . ."

"No need, Monty. But if you ever decide to visit the place, let me know. I'd love to have company on a trip back home."

"You never know, Mike. If it comes to that, I'll give you a call."

†

I didn't play music or read or take a walk when I got home. The Delaney case was the only thing on my mind, so I gave in to that, and put *Righteous Defender* in the VCR. I had watched it before the trial, but it warranted another look. The film opened with a shot of Delaney — Jack Hartt playing Delaney — standing in a courtroom with a flock of other lawyers in their black robes and white throat tabs. The scene switched to the judge saying: "You are free to go." We then saw Delaney's client shake his hand and thank Delaney effusively for his hard work and the perfect result. You know you're in the world of fiction when the client takes the time to thank you. Well, maybe there's something about the drama of a Supreme Court jury trial that induces elaborate protocol even in the clients; looking back on some of my jury trials, I believed I had occasionally been the recipient of a proffered hand and a word of thanks. That never seemed to happen in the lower courts. I recalled one guy I had for trial on a busy day in the ornate nineteenth-century provincial courthouse on Spring Garden Road. By the time our matter was called at eleven thirty, the Crown's main witness had still not shown up. I managed to stave off the Crown's request for an adjournment, prompting the prosecutor to withdraw the charges. I gave my client the good news, in case he hadn't caught on. The trial was not going ahead; he was no longer facing criminal charges; he was free to go. His reaction? "I wasted my whole fucking morning."

But things were going a little better for Delaney on the screen. He returned to his office and took time to gaze at a portrait of his parents on his desk. This led to a flashback to his childhood, shown in black and white. We saw a little boy of about seven, dressed in a checked shirt and a blazer, coming home from school carrying a bookbag. His fair hair was brushed over to the side. The camera followed him as he ditched his schoolbag in the driveway to his house, ran to the back, and climbed up onto a swing. He pumped his legs furiously until he gained the desired height, then sailed off the swing and into a pile of raked leaves. He got up, with leaves sticking to his clothes and hair, and did the same thing again. At that point, his mother came out the back door, called Beau's name, ran over and scooped him up for a big hug. Then we heard a car horn, and saw a big black sedan pull up in the driveway. Dad emerged, wearing a topcoat and fedora. He held his arms out and the young Beau flung himself into them and was hoisted high into the air. The scene switched back to a smiling Beau in his law office.

We went from there to the tiny rural community of Blockhouse in Lunenburg County. We saw the robbery at Gary's General Store. The two terrified young store clerks were shot. Seventeen-year-old Scott Hubley lay dead on the floor. Cathy Tompkins, sixteen, lay grievously wounded, her face a portrait of shock and horror. Then it was Scott's funeral, and his burial, with Cathy at the gravesite in her wheelchair, her hair shaved off and her face disfigured. Beau gave his client, Adam Gower, a brilliant defence, and Adam walked away from the courthouse, cocky and defiant.

Jack Hartt, as Beau, was shown receiving death threats over the phone and by mail. Then we saw Gower back in Blockhouse, strutting by Gary's store and peering inside. Next thing we saw was Gower being beaten to a pulp somewhere out in the country. Then, a midnight knock on the door at the residence of Cathy Tompkins's brother Robby, and the police bundled him into their cruiser, reading him his rights as they booked him for murder.

The next scene in the movie was Beau sitting in his office, tie off, feet up on the desk, reading a legal tome. The phone rang. He answered, answered again, then listened. We heard a voice, which could have been male or female, telling him the brother didn't do it. The police should have looked harder, should have expanded their search to the outskirts of town. Had Beau ever heard of an old creep by the name of Edgar Lampman? No? Well, Beau might be interested in what Lampman had buried in his backyard. Click. The scene faded out with Beau sitting there in silence, telephone receiver in his hand.

After that, we saw Beau at the door of the Royal Canadian Mounted Police detachment in Lunenburg, and then it was Beau's car and an RCMP cruiser pulling into the yard of a small, ratty-looking brown bungalow.

The camera followed the Mounties and Delaney as they entered Edgar Lampman's house and looked around. A shabby brown chesterfield had stuffing and a spring sticking out. Where you might have expected to see a coffee table, there was a television propped up on plastic milk cartons. The cable for the TV came in through a corner of the front window; it served as a makeshift clothesline for a pair of dingy underwear and work socks. In one corner of the room was an old wooden desk, with a model of a World War Two-era battleship and an ancient manual typewriter on it. The police opened the desk drawers. A close-up of one of the cops showed his eyes narrowing in response to something he had found. He drew a pile of news clippings from the drawer, cleared a space on the desktop, and spread them out. They were news stories about Cathy Tompkins and the man who had shot her. One small news item, circled in red, reported a rumour that Adam Gower was coming back to town.

The scene switched to Lampman's backyard, where the Mounties moved towards a small mound of earth and grass. A bit of careful digging produced a manila envelope, which had been sealed with duct tape at both ends. Words were printed on the envelope with red and black marker, in large block letters: "PERSONAL AND PRIVATE!!!! TO ONLY BE OPEN AFTER MY DEATH!!!!" The envelope was photographed, dusted, and otherwise processed, and in a later scene we got to see the contents: a brown leather wallet with darker brown stains, a pewter or silver ring in the design of a skull and crossbones, and a letter, which Lampman had composed for posterity: "Let the world know the truth. And Cathy Herself. I done it for her. I killed that scum with my bare hands! I bided my time. I knew he'd come back to the scene of the crime, so I tricked him to go into the woods and I said 'Scum, now you die!' This here is his skellating ring off his finger. This here is his own blood. I told 'somebody' but nobody believed I had the guts!!!!"

Following that scene, we returned to Beau's office, where two RCMP officers stood by as Beau pulled out his file on the Gary's General Store case. In reality, this would have been several bankers' boxes. full of documents, but in the movie it was a buff folder. He opened it, and sifted through some papers until he came to a yellow legal pad. The camera zoomed in on his handwritten notes. There were drawings and doodles in the margins, including a drawing of a skull and crossbones ring, which had apparently caught Beau's eye while he was interviewing Gower before his trial. Lampman had taken the ring off Gower as a souvenir. Beau and the Mounties stared at the pictures. They had their man.

I was curious about Edgar Lampman, and wanted to see what he had looked like in real life. I ejected the Hollywood version and stuck the local news documentary into the VCR. I pressed fast-forward until I got to Lampman. He was a bizarre individual who affected, with some success, a rakish air. His appearance was distinguished by a white goatee and a supercilious expression on his face. He wore a navy pea jacket; a yachtsman's cap sat at a jaunty angle on his head. He lived on a combination of welfare and long-term disability benefits; I inferred that his disability was of a psychiatric nature. On cheque day, he would go into Gary's General Store and load up on provisions. Cheque day inevitably turned into jail night. He would head to the local tavern, get drunk, tell tall tales of his past exploits, real or imagined, then threaten someone, throw a punch or pull a knife, and be carted off to jail for the night.

Lampman's past exploits, the real ones, included a long and occasionally violent criminal history. He had been in the navy, but had been dishonourably discharged for undisclosed reasons. He had served short sentences in prison for theft, fraud, and common assault. His longest stretch was four years for terrorizing his ex-wife and her new boyfriend; Lampman had kept them tied up in the basement of the woman's house for two nights, feeding them dog food, threatening them, and inflicting minor cuts on their faces and arms with a knife. He walked out and left them there. On the third day of their captivity, their cries attracted the attention of a passerby, and they were freed.

I turned off the video and reflected on what I had seen. I thought about Lampman and about Cathy Tompkins's brother, Robby. I thought about Beau Delaney's dedication to the defence of the innocent, and the guilty.

Edgar Lampman wrote that he had tricked Gower into entering the woods along the 103 Highway. The beating of Adam Gower, to the point where he was unrecognizable, did not speak to me of trickery. To me it was an act of uncontrollable rage, the anger of someone who cared very deeply about Cathy Tompkins. Would Lampman have felt that strongly about a young girl he knew only from his occasional visits to the general store? The documentary had showed an arch sort of individual, who seemed to enjoy the eccentric image he cultivated. He was a violent man, to be sure. He had served several years in prison for the forcible confinement and wounding of his ex-wife and her boyfriend. If ever there was a crime of passion, it was a jilted lover's lashing out at an ex-wife or girlfriend who had moved on to another man. Yet, Lampman's actions in that case were those of a torturer, who toyed with the couple either for revenge or for his own gratification. He inflicted frightening but minor wounds, kept this going for two nights, then walked away. What was missing from that crime was the element of rage. The kind of wrath that was let loose on Adam Gower.

The man who did that was a man whose emotions were laid bare, someone who couldn't stop himself from what he was doing. Someone like the brother of a young girl whose life had been destroyed by the man who shot her. Had Cathy's brother committed the crime after all? The jury had thought so. Was the Lampman angle a set-up? Delaney had received the information from an anonymous caller. Was that caller Robby Tompkins, or someone acting on his behalf?

There was something else that bothered me about the Delaney movie and documentary: the skull ring that was found in Lampman's stash of souvenirs from the murder of Adam Gower. Had anyone ever come forward and said Gower had worn such a ring? Not that I could recall. How then had the police connected the ring with him? Through Delaney's sketch of it. Lawyers, like so many other people, occasionally doodle on paper while they're waiting for something to happen. I remembered noticing the little cartoons drawn by Gail Kirk, the Crown attorney prosecuting the Peggy Delaney murder case. She tended to do this when her co-counsel was handling a procedural motion, or when we were waiting for the judge to come in. She did not do it when she was listening to a witness on the stand. The only time I heard Beau Delaney's pen scratching paper was when he was scribbling a note to tell me what to do in court, in case I forgot. Beau didn't draw pictures in the courtroom. And I was willing to bet he didn't do it when he was sitting across from a client in his office, taking down information and wanting to move him out so the next client could move in.

All of this painted a picture for me. It told me Delaney knew perfectly well that Cathy's brother Robby wasn't innocent. And Delaney didn't care. The way I saw things now, Delaney acquiesced in the Lampman frame-up, even helped it along with the fiction of the skull ring, redoing or inventing notes and adding drawings of the ring. Delaney was determined to save Robby Tompkins, whom he viewed as another victim of the Gary's General Store shooting, someone who did not deserve to sit in jail for a murder he committed in a fit of grief and fury.

✝

"I know about Robby Tompkins. I want to hear the full story."

Delaney went perfectly still as he faced me across the desk in my office on Friday morning. He didn't speak.

"If the Crown is determined to appeal your acquittal and if they dig into your background, the tangled protective web you wove around Robby Tompkins could unravel, and you could be hit with all kinds of charges arising from that."

He finally found his voice. "Let it be, Monty. Leave it alone. Edgar Lampman is six feet under, and the Tompkins family has suffered enough. This stays buried. Period. Now if that's all you have to say, I have work to do. You may have called this meeting, but I'm adjourning it. Good day."

He got up and walked out. I wasn't about to chase him down Barrington Street, so I let him go. I tried not to dwell on the ramifications for Delaney, for me, and for the Tompkins family, if the true story got out.

(Normie)

I always thought of Father Burke as being really big, but not after I saw him standing in front of Mr. Delaney, with Mr. Delaney looming right over him and talking down into his face. Father didn't look so big anymore and I was scared for him. Because it looked as if Mr. Delaney was yelling. Except he wasn't. He was talking so low that I couldn't hear what he said, but you could tell he really wanted Father Burke to pay attention and do whatever Mr. Delaney wanted.

This was at school on Friday, and the grade fours were going from math to gym class. I was straggling behind because I knew Richard Robertson was going to be standing up in front of the grade six class reading a funny story and making faces to go along with it, so I wanted to peek into his classroom to see him doing it. But the door was closed, and I couldn't very well go up and peer inside and everybody would look up and see this face pressed up against the window gawking in, and they'd laugh at me. So I didn't. But that's when I heard great big loud footsteps down the corridor behind me, and I turned around. Mr. Delaney had caught up with Father Burke, who had just come into the corridor carrying a prayer book, the kind with the coloured ribbons to mark your place.

Even if I hadn't been able to see the expression on Mr. Delaney's face, I would have known there was something going on, because I could sense strong feelings around him and coming out of him. I can't explain it, but it was like being in a big, dark storm with lots of wind.

Father Burke put his hand on Mr. Delaney's arm, and I could tell he was trying to calm him down. I wondered if Father had done something that got Mr. Delaney all upset, or made him mad. Anyway, they started walking away, out of the school, with Father Burke in front and Mr. Delaney behind him. That's when I got even more scared. Was he going to clobber our priest on the back of the head? Or take him somewhere and beat him up? That's not the kind of thing I would normally think about people, but the storm of feelings around Mr. Delaney made me think something scary might happen. I even wondered if I should call the cops, or tell one of the teachers. But if it turned out to be nothing, I would be in trouble for being a tattletale and not minding my own business. So I went to gym class and was almost late for the first lap around the room. After that, I asked if I could use the school phone, and I called Daddy to tell him about what I saw. But all I could do was leave a message because he wasn't there.

(Monty)

I had no intention of letting Delaney off the hook. I didn't want to stir things up, or do anything to draw attention to the elaborate criminal justice coup he had orchestrated all those years ago. But I wanted to know the story, so there would not be any surprises out there if the court ordered a new trial for the murder of Peggy Delaney.

First, though, I had to focus on an emergency injunction hearing in Supreme Court — the last thing anyone needs on a Friday afternoon. My firm's client wanted to tear down a row of Victorian townhouses and put up a parking garage; the local heritage group wanted an injunction to stop the demolition. I did my best, but wasn't the least bit sorry when we lost, and the buildings were given a reprieve. When I got back to the office, I took my stack of phone messages and returned the calls. One was from Normie during school hours. I tried the choir school, but she had already left, so I called Maura's number. Normie answered on the first ring.

"Daddy! Maybe nothing happened to Father Burke, but you should check!"

"What, sweetheart?" I tried to keep the alarm out of my voice. "What do you mean?"

"Mr. Delaney came to the school, and I could tell there were bad feelings whirling around him, and he was standing over Father Burke and made him leave the school and go somewhere!"

"When was this?"

"At gym class time."

"When's gym again, dolly, remind me?"

"Just before lunch."

"So the two of them left the school together at that time?"

"Yes!"

"Well, I'll check on Father Burke and make sure he's all right. I'll let you go now. Don't worry. It's probably not as bad as it looked."

"Okay, okay, Daddy, get going!" Slam.

I made a call to Brennan's direct number at the rectory. No answer. That didn't mean anything one way or the other. I would go and see if someone knew where he was. Two minutes later I was in the car and on my way to St. Bernadette's. When I squealed to a stop in the parking lot and got out of the car, I met Michael O'Flaherty emerging from the rectory. I made an effort not to look rattled.

"Afternoon, Monsignor. How's it going?"

"Ah. Monty. Just grand, and yourself?"

"Can't complain. I just popped over to see your curate. I tried to reach him on the phone."

"No, you wouldn't be able to get him on his line."

"Is everything all right?"

"Oh yes, you'll find him in my room, watching a movie on my TV."

Relief coursed through me. All I said to Michael was: "Now there's something you don't see every day: Burke in front of a television. What movie is it, *The Bells of St. Mary's*?"

"No, it's something a little closer to home. The Hollywood movie about Beau Delaney. *Righteous Defender.* Brennan rented the video. He said they had several copies at Video Difference."

"Is that right?"

"Yes, and I suffered through the viewing."

"You didn't like it?"

"Oh, it wasn't that. It's a fascinating story about a fascinating man. But watching it with Brennan was aggravating beyond words. He kept pressing the rewind button over and over."

"Oh?"

"He must be intrigued by the new technologies. We'll bring him into the 1990s yet."

"I never think of him as a techie sort of guy. But he has surprised me on occasion."

"True enough. Anyway, on this particular occasion, he kept replaying certain parts of the movie."

"Which parts did he like?"

"I didn't keep track of the interruptions, Monty. I just know that's not the way I prefer to watch a show. He's on to the news documentary about Delaney now. He got it from the TV station. I didn't stick around for that."

"I'll go up and watch it with him."

"Sure thing. Go right up, Monty. I'll see you later."

"See you, Mike."

Never mind that I had already seen both shows. I had new reasons for wanting to view them now, or rather, I had reason to be curious about what parts Brennan found so important. Add that to my curiosity over the scene Normie had witnessed earlier in the day.

I went into the rectory and headed up the stairs to the room I knew belonged to Monsignor O'Flaherty. The door was ajar, and I saw the back of Brennan's head. The VCR was on pause, and I peered in to see what he was looking at. But I couldn't make it out. Then he resumed playing the video. There was Peggy, talking about the murder of Beau's client, allegedly done in by a member of the Hells Angels. Peggy said: "That was the longest night of my life." Brennan pressed rewind and watched it again. Then he sensed my presence and turned around. He gave a little start when he saw it was me. But he did not look as if he had been in any kind of scuffle with Beau Delaney. He nodded, turned back to the VCR, and switched it off.

"What?" I said, entering O'Flaherty's room. "I'm not going to see the show?"

"You've seen it."

"So have you. Why are you watching it again?"

"I don't have *The Exorcist* so I'm watching this."

"You kind of remind me of the younger priest in that, come to think of it. The kind of dark, brooding, haunted . . . but I guess he was Greek."

"The character was Greek. The actor was an American Irishman, Jason Miller."

"Well! Who knew you'd be such a fount of movie trivia?"

"There's nothing trivial, Collins, about the battle for supremacy between the forces of good and evil."

"I stand corrected, Father."

"It's about time. So, what's up?"

I didn't want to spring Normie's story on him right away, so I came up with something more benign.

"Dinner and drinks at O'Carroll's? I was going to give MacNeil a call about it."

"Sounds good."

I thought of something else that I had been meaning to do, and reached for my chequebook. I grabbed a pen from O'Flaherty's desk and wrote out a cheque.

"This is for Patrick, to reimburse him for his mercy flight to Halifax on Normie's behalf. Make sure he gets it."

"He doesn't want it."

"Make him want it. Do whatever you have to do."

"My brother and I had a grand time together. He was due for a visit."

So I took the cheque, scratched out the name Patrick Burke, wrote in St. Bernadette's Church, initialled it, and slapped it down on the desk.

"Ready?"

"I will be in five minutes. I'll get cleaned up."

When had the fastidious priest ever been dirty? But I followed him to his own room, gave Maura a call about dinner, then sat at Brennan's table by the window and waited while he performed his ablutions in the bathroom. When he emerged, we headed out together.

"How are things?" I asked him.

"Good."

"Anything new?"

"Nothing."

I would try another tack.

"What were you looking for in that documentary?"

"Nothing in particular."

"Well, then, why were you rewinding and playing parts of it again?"

"The sound wasn't very good. I couldn't hear it."

This was a man who could hear when a note sung by one section of a four-part choir was off by a quarter of a tone. Well, I could hear too. And what I was hearing was that it was none of my business what he had been looking for. I knew that something about the program had struck a false note for me when I watched it, too, but I would figure it out later.

Brennan and I arrived at O'Carroll's and made ourselves at home at the bar. I ordered a pint of Guinness and he got a double Jameson. He had downed it by the time I'd had two sips of my pint. It didn't make him garrulous, by any means. He ordered a second drink and stared into it, as if he had forgotten there was anyone else around.

"Is everything all right with you, Brennan?"

"Sure, yes, I'm grand."

He made an obvious effort to rally. If there was something on his mind, he put it aside, and told me a long, funny story about the Gaelic football team he played on as a young boy in Ireland, and the mishaps they endured on their trip to play a team in Mayo-God-Help-Us. Maura joined us half an hour later.

"You look as if you were born and raised, schooled and ordained, right there on that bar stool, Burke," said Maura. "You, too, Collins."

"Ah, just like the oul country itself, so it is," Burke replied in a stagy brogue.

"Well, if you can detach yourself from it without doing internal damage, I'd prefer to have dinner at a table."

"No worries, no damage."

So we got ourselves settled at a table, ordered drinks, and procured menus. Conversation resumed.

"Speaking of the old country, now, Mr. *Collins*." Brennan raised his glass to his lips, and his left eyebrow to me. "Your father's people were from Cork, you've told me, and came over here around the turn of the century." He took a sip of his whiskey. "Your mother's family, on the other hand, was long established in Halifax by that time."

"Right. They'd been here almost since the city was founded in 1749. Originally from England. Catholics, though, Brennan, as you know."

"Bless them and save them," he said with mock piety.

"The Earls of Halifax were Montagues, you know, back in the day," Maura put in, affecting a snooty British accent. She pointed at me. "He's schizo, Brennan. Lord Halifax by day, Irish rabble-rouser by night."

"An Irish rabble-rouser is exactly what he should be if my speculations are correct. His crowd was still in County Cork when *Michael* Collins was toddling around in his nappies. No doubt if he made even the most elementary inquiries, he'd uncover a connection with that illustrious branch of the family. *Have* you made any efforts in that regard, Montague Michael Collins?"

"Well, no, I haven't."

"No sense of history. Did your father never tell you tales of your Irish ancestors when you were a boy?"

"Oh, he did, but you know what kids are like. They don't listen. Then they grow up and want to know, and they find out they've left it too late. I hear there's going to be an Irish history lecture at St. Bernadette's Choir School, Brennan."

"There is, and you'll be expected to attend. A command performance, let us say."

"I wouldn't miss it, Father."

"There's hope for you yet, then."

"Monty's father helped *make* history, Brennan," Maura said. "Did you know that? He did very secret intelligence work, code-breaking, during the war."

"Right. Didn't someone tell me he was at Bletchley Park in England?"

"Yep," I said, "my dad had left Halifax to do his Ph.D. in math at Cambridge University. Bletchley Park recruited him from Cambridge and got him working on the codes. They couldn't have broken the German ciphers without him, I'm convinced. My mother boarded a ship here and sailed over to be with him. Brave soul, to sail the Atlantic during the war years."

"Montague didn't make his appearance till they moved back here, though, a couple of years later," Maura said.

"Hey, I could wait! Putting Hitler away was more important than getting me started."

"I've never heard you so humble, Collins," she said. "But what about you, Brennan? You were a wartime baby. What year did you come into the world," Maura asked him, "bringing joy and laughter to those around you?"

"The people walked in darkness until 1940. Then they saw a great light."

"Yeah, it was called the Blitz."

"No blitzkrieg where I came from, in Dublin."

"That's right. You guys were neutral during the war."

"During *the emergency*. That's what we called it in Ireland."

"Do you remember anything from those times?" she asked him. "Did young boys play at fighting Hitler, or did you sit around being quiet and doing nothing and pretending you were Swiss?"

"I know you're takin' the piss out of me, MacNeil, but I won't reply in kind. I do recall listening to news on the wireless about the war. It was a long time ago so I couldn't tell you exactly what the broadcasts said, but . . ."

I tuned them out. I went through the motions as we ate our meal and gabbed, but I was distracted all the while. Because I had just caught on to something that was so obvious I had simply overlooked it before.

Chapter 19

(Monty)

"Michael," I said into the phone when I got home from O'Carroll's and dialled the number of the rectory. "I apologize for the very short notice here. But you'll recall our conversation about the orphanage in Saint John."

"Of course I do."

"It's important that I go there and speak to the people in charge."

"Really! The sisters, you mean."

"Yes. And you mentioned a trip home if ever I went. But, under the circumstances, I don't want to wait. I'm sorry about the rush."

"No worries. When are you leaving?"

"I'd like to go first thing in the morning. I don't know what Saturdays are like for you. But I can't go during the week."

"I'll palm my Saturday Mass off on Brennan — God forgive me for putting it like that; I'm only joking — and I'll be ready whenever you are."

"Great, Mike. See you at eight?"

"Eight it is."

So we took off for Saint John, New Brunswick, first thing in the morning. Michael kept me entertained during the four-and-a-half-hour drive with stories of his childhood in the old port city, where the orange and the green played out their ancient roles over and over again in the New World. We stopped for a quick bite to eat when we arrived, then headed along Waterloo Street past the Cathedral of the Immaculate Conception and around the corner to Cliff Street.

St. Vincent's Convent, as it was now called, was a three-storey red-brick building, with dormers giving it a partial fourth storey. Crosses topped two of the dormers, and the building had rows of Gothic windows. A stone set high up in the facade displayed the words: "St. Vincent's Orphan Asylum, A.D. 1865."

Michael accompanied me inside and introduced me to Sister Theodora. She looked to be in her early seventies, with short steel-grey hair and glasses. She was dressed in a dark navy skirt and white blouse, with a large silver crucifix on a chain around her neck. I explained the purpose of our visit.

"I am eighty years old," she said, "and I will never forget my first sight of Burton Delaney. Burton McGrath, he was then. We always called him Beau. One of our sisters — Soeur Marie-France — said 'Qu'il est beau!' when she first saw him. And it stuck. It would have been when? Forty-five years ago? No, more than that. We were called to see about an abandoned child in a flat on Paddock Street. The boy's father was a bitter and ferocious man. He had been given a dishonourable discharge from the army early in the war, and never got over it. He and his cronies used to sit around the house and get drunk and rant about the war, and berate little Beau, and humiliate him and beat him. At other times, the child was neglected completely. The mother was cowed into submission. Oh, it was a dreadful situation.

"He was just a wee little boy. Four years old, I think he was. The morning we arrived, he was standing inside the doorway, skinny and filthy, his shorts soiled from, well, lack of proper hygiene. There were tear tracks in the grime of his face. He was holding a fireplace poker in his hands, ready to defend himself, it seemed. I took a step towards him, and he pointed it at me as if it were a gun or a bayonet. I said: 'You could hurt somebody. You don't want to do that.' 'I do! I'm going to!' he cried out, and he raised it up and started to bring it down on my head. But I got the poker out of his hands. He began to scream, and scream, and scream. Rage, fear, God only knows what else. I knelt down and took him in my arms. He went absolutely rigid.

"It took a long, long time to bring him around, to get him to the point where he could accept love and affection. I remember sitting in the parlour after we had fed the children. It was around Christmastime and someone had brought us a box of Florida oranges. The children went crazy; you'd think they'd each been given a brand new bicycle. But Beau refused his. Wouldn't even look at it. Anyway, I was sitting by myself, peeling my orange, and he wandered in. I ate a section of the orange and offered him one. He hesitated, then took it. Tasted it. His eyes grew wide, and he gave me a great big smile. I leaned over and hugged him. He hugged me back. He began to sob and soon he was positively howling. With grief and desolation. Only now was he getting the love and attention he should have had all his life. He clung to me and wouldn't let go. He was like that for the next little while. Always around, holding one or another of us by the hand, or by the leg. He suffered a setback when we had a little baby die here. Beau came into the room when Father McDevitt was giving the baby extreme unction. We were standing around the crib, me and some of the other sisters, while he gave the last rites."

Was this what Normie had seen? People in black robes standing around a dying baby? And another child in the room, crying.

"Sister, what goes on during the last rites? What does the priest do?" I turned to Monsignor O'Flaherty. He gestured towards Sister Theodora to reply.

"This time, when the baby died — his name was Timmy — the ritual of extreme unction was burned into my mind because we all loved that poor little baby. The priest anointed his eyes, his ears, mouth, hands, and feet, and then we said goodbye and pulled his blanket up over his face."

The man touching the baby under his blanket in Normie's vision. Not abuse, but the last rites of death.

"Beau wandered in and saw this, and began crying and screaming. It took a long time for him to come around again. But eventually he did.

"He began to be a regular little helper about the place. Couldn't do enough for us. He was adopted shortly after that, by the Delaneys. A match made in heaven. How they doted on him! He blossomed under their care. He was a tiny, undersized little boy when he came to us. You wouldn't know it, he's such a big man now. Children don't thrive when they're neglected, when they're not given love and affection. But we loved him when he came here! Then of course he was all set once he went with the Delaneys. And he grew to the size his genetic makeup intended for him! There are studies showing the same phenomenon over and over again. Anyway, Beau never gave the Delaneys a moment's grief, at least not that I ever heard. They moved to Halifax just before he started school. Well, you know the rest. He buckled right down, became an A student, the perfect son. He went on to university and law school. Once in a while, his courtroom exploits make the news up here, and we love to read about him, especially when he's defending the less fortunate, those who never get a break. It's not surprising that Beau would have an affinity for the underdog. So there you have it. A life well lived, after a disastrous beginning."

Chapter 20

(Monty)

"You and I are going to talk about Robby Tompkins," I told Beau on Monday when I had seated myself in his luxurious office overlooking Halifax Harbour. I could see him making a conscious effort not to react, but his eyes went to the door. Yes, it was firmly closed. He turned and gazed out the window at the magnificent view of the water. Then he took a deep breath and faced me.

"The whole time I was representing Adam Gower, I was barely able to stomach it. I couldn't look the Hubley or Tompkins families in the eye. Gower just didn't give a damn. Anything would have been better than that. 'The other guy made me do it.' 'I didn't mean to aim at her head.' 'I was drunk.' Anything but 'yeah, I did it, so what are you going to do for me?' All those months of that insufferable little shit, leading up to the trial. Then sitting in court hearing about what became of the victims. Scott Hubley, of course, lost his life at the age of seventeen. Cathy Tompkins was a top student in high school. Her dream was to be a nurse at the IWK Children's Hospital. But she knew she'd have to earn some money before going for her nursing degree, because the family couldn't afford it. So she was working every hour she could while attending school. After the shooting, she was in a coma for several days. Suffered paralysis and irreversible brain damage. Confined to a wheelchair. Pretty face twisted, like that of an old woman with a stroke. Her moods would swing from weeping depression to screaming rage. Life over. And everybody in the community hated my guts because I was helping the guy who did this to her. Well, you know what that's like. It never used to bother me. I was on a crusade, I was the champion of the despised, I defended people other decent human beings wouldn't be in the same room with. But it got to me this time. Anyway, as you know, I got him off. He went out west to look for work. And I couldn't show my face in Blockhouse, Lunenburg County, again.

"Then, in November of the following year, I got a call from Gower. He'd had enough of working construction in Fort McMurray; he was coming home. And he'd got himself into some kind of scrape out there in the oil patch, so he left in a hurry. Could I help him again? He was here in Halifax, calling from a pay phone at the bus station on Almon Street. I didn't want him in the office, didn't want word to get out that he was back in the province. There were rumours that he might be returning, but that was nothing new; there had been rumours before. I didn't know what to do about him but I said I'd pick him up, maybe drop him off at a youth hostel or something. I left the office and didn't mention Gower's name to anyone, just said I had to go out. So I pulled up outside the bus station and waited. He got into the car, said he wanted to go back to Blockhouse. I reminded him there were death threats against him — and against me, for that matter — and I pleaded with him not to go there. Not that I really cared whether somebody shot him in the head. What I couldn't stand was the thought of how painful it would be for Cathy and her family, and the family of Scott Hubley. But I started driving out of town anyway. I knew Gower had an aunt in Hebbville, farther out Highway 103, so maybe he could go there till he came to his senses. He just babbled on, as if he was a normal guy who hadn't destroyed all these people's lives.

"We were driving along and I was thinking how much I hated this guy. We were out on the 103, coming into Lunenburg County, and do you know what he said to me? 'Wait till word gets around that Adam's back in town. I'll be front-page news!' He was sitting there laughing about it! I turned and gave him a look of disgust and he said: 'Fuck 'em if they can't take a joke!' I could barely speak but I managed to ask him: 'What the hell are you going to say to Cathy Tompkins if you see her in her wheelchair?' This is what he said: 'I don't know. Maybe, like, *sucks to be you, babe!*' And he pulled the left side of his face down. Making fun of Cathy's facial deformity!"

As I listened to Beau telling the story of what happened back in 1980, I realized this was not the story of Robby Tompkins taking revenge on the man who had destroyed his little sister's life. As I struggled to grasp what I was hearing, Beau continued:

"I fucking lost it, Monty. I yanked the steering wheel to the right and screeched to a stop on the shoulder of the highway. Then I looked ahead and saw a turnoff to a dirt road, an old logging road or something. I gunned it and made a turn into that road. I nearly flipped the car over. I got it under control and parked. Adam started to freak out. I told him to get the fuck out of the car, and he fumbled with the door handle. He practically fell out onto the ground. I started to get out; then I thought of something. I grabbed a pair of old leather gloves from the glove compartment, pulled them on, got out, went around to the other side, and grabbed him. He was nearly shitting himself. With good reason. I shoved him in behind some trees. I went at him in a rage. I beat the crap out of him, and when he was down I kicked him, and kicked him, and kicked him. In the face, in the head, everywhere. I don't think there was a bone in his body that wasn't broken. I left him there and went back to the car."

I stared at Delaney, but he was barely aware of my presence. He was back on the 103 Highway in November of 1980.

"I started to drive away, then figured I'd better take his wallet. Believe me, there was no other way to identify him. Like everything else, his wallet was soaked with blood. I had a plastic grocery bag in the trunk, so I placed the wallet in that. There wasn't much blood on me, except on the front of my jacket and on the gloves.

"I was terrified that I'd be spotted, but I drove back in the direction of Halifax, then took the long way around to the eastern shore. Went all the way to our cottage at Lawrencetown Beach. Of course at that time of the year there was nobody around. I went inside and got myself cleaned up, wrapped the gloves for later disposal, called Peg to tell her where I was, and gave her some bogus reason why I was there. I pretended I got interrupted and asked her to call me back, so we'd have double phone records to show I was really there, if the need ever arose. But it never did. Anyway, once I got rid of all the traces of blood, and got over the shakes, I drove back to Halifax, approaching the city from the opposite direction from where the murder had taken place. But, as I say, I never needed to produce any evidence of my innocence. The body wasn't found for several days, and nobody connected me with it. Ever. They arrested Robby Tompkins for it. I knew I had to do something to get him off the hook. When Edgar Lampman died, it all fell into place. I set up the Edgar Lampman story and planted the evidence in his yard. Then invited the Mounties along to find it. Murder solved, deceased habitual criminal framed, innocent brother set free."

I was shell-shocked. I had no idea how to react.

Beau seemed to shake himself back to the present. "I'm going to give Father Burke the benefit of the doubt here, and assume he didn't tell you anything about my confession."

"Your confession!?"

"He didn't tell you I went to see him on Friday?"

"No! Brennan Burke wouldn't break the confessional seal if they had his feet to the flames."

That's what Normie had witnessed at the school: Delaney urging Burke to hear his confession. This was after I confronted Beau at my office, after I told him I "knew about Robby Tompkins." I knew a hell of a lot more now than I did then. And I understood why Burke had been paying such close attention to the movie that had made Beau Delaney a household name all across Canada as a crusader for justice.

Then there was the documentary. Something had struck me a while back, something about the documentary that didn't make sense when I had seen it the second time, on the night of the awards dinner. Now I had it. And maybe Brennan did too. Beau's client Travis Bullard had been killed last spring. The RCMP gave a press conference outside the detachment in Truro. A reporter asked whether there was a Hells Angels link to the killing. The officer sidestepped the question and said only that Bullard had been shot with a hand-gun. More details would be released later. But they never were, presumably because the police weren't yet able to make a case against their prime suspect, a member of the Hells Angels. Beau and the reporter talked about Bullard being a Hells Angels associate. Then Peggy chimed in and said that was the longest night of her life. And Beau cut her off.

That was the line that had bothered me when I heard it. And that was the line Brennan had been zeroing in on when I found him in Michael O'Flaherty's room. Why would Peggy have described that as the longest night of her life? She would not have known about the killing that night. It happened in Truro, a town an hour north of Halifax. She would have heard about it the next day, perhaps, or the day after that. Unless Beau got a call about it at home. But then why was that a long night for her? Or maybe Beau was not home, and she was waiting for him to return.

I looked across the desk at Beau. He was a man lost in his own thoughts.

There was something else, too, I remembered: testimony at Beau's trial. But I had not understood its significance at the time. Beau testified about his argument with Peggy at the top of the stairs. She said something about people being blown away in small town Nova Scotia, and that one of the victims was his own client. She was worried that the killers might come after Beau himself. And he had reassured her by saying that the killing had been an execution. The guy, Bullard, had been tied to a tree and shot.

Now I asked him: "How did you know Travis Bullard was tied up when he was shot, Beau?"

He looked right through me, and didn't respond.

I spoke again: "You know, I spent a few seconds here consoling myself with the idea that one of the Mounties might have leaked the information to you, given the fact that the victim had been a client of yours in the past. But I had to dismiss that notion. Defence lawyers, and famous ones in particular, are not all that popular with the police. You're the last person in the world the Mounties would leak sensitive case information to. Yet you testified on the stand that Bullard had been tied to a tree and propped up while he was shot.

How did you know that?"

Delaney leaned over and spoke intently.

"Travis Bullard was your quintessential lowlife with an antisocial personality disorder. A skinny little runt with tiny eyes; I don't even know what colour they were. He had patchy facial hair and a front tooth missing and he always had a hood pulled up over his head even when it was the middle of July. I first represented him as a young offender on a rape charge, two or three years before he was killed. The victim was twelve. Travis had drifted to Halifax from Bible Hill, in Colchester County, after dropping out of school in grade ten. He found trouble as soon as he got here, stealing from corner stores, getting into fights with other lowlifes, grabbing girls and terrifying them. Then he got ambitious, started doing favours for some of the bikers here in town. That fostered in Travis delusions of grandeur. He saw himself driving a Harley and wearing a Hells Angels patch on his back. Never going to happen, of course. But these guys don't perceive reality the way you and I do. That is to say, they're not in touch with reality at all.

"Anyway, Steve Crossman, who as you probably know is a member of the local chapter of the Hells Angels, had a beef against a guy named Ronny Brown, who was from Bible Hill or somewhere around Truro. This guy had absconded with some property rightly belonging to the Angels. A quantity of blow he was supposed to sell on their behalf. Crossman knew Travis Bullard was from Bible Hill, so he engaged Travis for a little intimidation job. 'Go find Ronny Brown and threaten to break his legs off at the knees unless he comes up with four thousand dollars by two weeks from today. Motivate him, then leave him to go and scrape up the cash. Got that?'

"Travis got it. Or so he said. But he didn't get it. He thought that, when Ronny Brown wasn't home and couldn't be located, he, Travis, could then do a nut job on Brown's common-law wife. Rape, a beating that amounted to torture, while her little boy, Nicky, looked on in terror. A seven-year-old boy whose life, and personality, from that day on, would never be normal. Because of Travis the psycho. Travis, who then turned on Nicky, who was screaming and, however ineffectually, trying to save his mother . . . Travis turned on him and started beating him." Delaney's voice had risen, his face was red, and there was a look of intensity in his eyes as he recounted the horrors that were inflicted on the mother and her child.

"Well, she had no trouble identifying my old client Travis Bullard as the savage who did this to her and little Nicky. They arrested him and he called me, whining that they had him in jail and were going to keep him there the whole weekend before he could get bail. Imagine that. But I'm dedicated to my clients, as you are yourself. We were scheduled for a bail hearing in Truro before hangin' judge William Chamberlain. I wasn't about to take a chance on him. He'd never let my guy see the light of day. So I did some fancy footwork and put it off until we could get Diane MacKinnon, who lives by the dictum that there's no such thing as a bad boy. You and I know better. Anyway, I gave the judge a sob story about Travis Bullard's hard life, which was true enough, and racked up enough bail conditions that if he got out he'd barely be allowed to take a leak without reporting it or being supervised, let alone get near a woman or child anywhere in the province. However improbably, the judge fell for it, and I got Travis released. I told him to keep his nose clean and stay out of trouble if he wanted to remain free on bail. No more attacks on women and children. He just laughed and made an obscene gesture and a crass remark about the victim. Something to the effect that maybe Nicky would take his, Travis's, place with Nicky's mother, since he'd been shown what to do.

"Right then and there, I decided I had had enough of Travis Bullard. This time, Monty, it was premeditated. I had a gun. Hard to believe, eh? Well, I suppose nothing is hard for you to believe at this point. I got the gun a few years ago — I stole it actually — from the 'estate' of a deceased client. Never really thought I'd use it. I kept it hidden under the floor of our cottage in Lawrencetown. Anyway, to make a long story short, I drove to the cottage, retrieved the gun, made sure it was loaded, and also took a length of rope from the shed. I set Travis up with a hare-brained scheme that required him to meet somebody in a remote wooded area outside Truro. This was the sixth of March last year.

"The moon was rising, and the trees were bare and spooky against it. I had the gun and the rope in my jacket pocket. There was Travis, right where he was supposed to be, for the first and last time in his life. I didn't waste any time. I took aim and shot him in the leg. He screamed and went down. I ran over and grabbed him, shoved him up against a tree, and bound his wrists together behind the tree trunk with my rope. He was in extreme pain but he couldn't fall. He stared at me in sheer terror. And he had reason. I stood in front of him and told him in precise detail what I was going to do and why."

Listening to Delaney, I felt a chill all over me in spite of the warmth of the room.

"I reminded Bullard of what he had done to that mother and her little son. I told him that could not have happened unless he was a fucking psycho, and that I was not going to allow him to do that to any woman or child or anyone else ever again. He was going to die so the world could be a better place. He was pleading and crying, but I was beyond caring. I got down on my knees in front of him. To pray for the repose of his soul? No. I knelt down so the entry wounds on his body would not reveal that the shooter was six and a half feet tall.

"I shot him in the stomach. He screamed in agony. I wanted to prolong it, to punish him for what he had done. But I couldn't. I didn't have it in me. I shot him in the heart to end it. Then I got up and ran away from the scene and was sick. I threw up in the stream there. I don't know how much time passed. I went back, unfastened his arms, and let him slump to the ground. He may have been still alive, but barely. That's when I shot him in the back of the head, behind his ear, to make the point that this was an execution. I picked up the rope, returned to the stream, got sick again, and then got into my car and drove away.

"It was late, and Peggy would be wondering where I was, so I had to boot it home and hope for the best. When I got to the house, she was all in a lather worrying about me. Turns out Bullard's girlfriend — yes, despite his history of rape and violence, there was a devoted girlfriend — had made a call to my home number. She wanted to ask if I knew where Bullard had gone after the bail hearing, because he was supposed to go to her place and he never showed up. She called around everywhere. No Travis. Luckily, Peggy never tells people where I am, just says — used to say — I can't come to the phone. I told Peggy the last I saw of Travis was outside the Truro courthouse at four o'clock that afternoon, and I decided to go to our cottage afterwards to check things out there. I apologized for not calling and letting her know. As for Travis, I said, 'Let's hope nothing happened to him. He was known to be in trouble with the Hells Angels.' That's what she believed, and that's what the police believe."

I sat there looking at Delaney, unable to speak. Peggy had said that was the longest night of her life. Now I knew what she meant. And why Beau had cut her off in mid-sentence.

"This was the cause of the blow-up with Peggy at the top of the stairs. We were talking about crime, and my work, and one thing led to another and I ended up confessing to her that I had killed the guy. Of course she was horror-struck. She said: 'You told me it was the Hells Angels! How could you?' Well, you can imagine. I grabbed her arm, she shoved me away from her and the recoil from that propelled her down the stairs. I didn't kill Peggy! Please understand that, Monty. No matter what else I have ever done, I did not kill my wife. I loved her. It really was an accident. But I panicked and made all the stupid moves you know about. And I knew that little wacko Corbett was around somewhere. Peg told me she had let him in. I started to look for him, but then I had to take off, get out to the highway and get a gas receipt to show I wasn't home from the trial in Annapolis Royal yet. And then I had to make a noisy return to the house at twelve thirty! I believe Corbett was hanging around outside. I know he was in the house after I left. He saw Peg lying there, and just walked around her dead body, over and over again, as he carted stuff out of the house to sell!"

By this time I was sitting with my head in both hands as I tried to come to grips with what I had just heard. Beau Delaney was an executioner. He had not killed his wife in an uncontrolled moment at the top of the stairs, but he had killed Adam Gower in a fit of uncontrollable rage. And his second killing was a premeditated execution of a person he believed — he knew — to be a brutal abuser of women and children.

I would have to digest all this later. But while I had him there in front of me, I wanted all the information I could get. "Corbett Reeves says you threatened to kill him. Says in fact you started to kill him, and changed your mind!"

"He's a psychopath."

"You're not trying to tell me he's like this Bullard guy, who attacked the woman and her son."

"He's worse. Or he will be. They don't label them psychopaths when they're that young . . ."

"Conduct disorder," I said.

"Right, but that's what it is. He's a grandiose, self-involved, deluded little shit. Your classic kid without empathy, without a conscience. Brennan Burke told me he saw what Corbett was the first time he looked into his eyes." Delaney paused for a bit, then continued: "The kid had a consistent pattern of very bad and disruptive behaviour, aggressive behaviour, when he was with us, and he hurt the other children. By that I mean he was deliberately, physically cruel to some of them. That's why I got rid of him, before he did something worse. Which he will, somewhere, some time."

"What's his background? He lived with your family a couple of times. Where was he the rest of the time?"

"Foster homes, group homes, an elderly relative in the Valley."

"Who are the natural parents, does anybody know?"

"Well, the mother is the niece of the woman in the Valley. The girl was a cocktail waitress in Toronto. The father is a rich American. I don't know his name, but I did learn this much: he was some kind of management consultant in the U.S., the guy you'd bring in to 'downsize' your company and throw your workers out into the street without a job. He was in Toronto for a convention. He got the young waitress pregnant, and was back in the States, of course, before he found out about it. She tried to chase him for money, but he told her to drop dead. I also heard he rose to the level of chief financial officer of a major American corporation and ended up in prison for swindling his shareholders out of millions of dollars. A role model for Corbett, if only he knew."

"What about the mother, the waitress? What else do you know about her?"

"Not a thing. As far as I know, she's had no contact with Corbett since he was a baby."

"Did you threaten to kill Corbett?"

"Yes."

"Did you intend to carry out the threat?"

"I just wanted to frighten him off."

"He says you were ready to do it when you took him to Hemlock Ravine."

Delaney gave me a long look. "I backed off. I don't think I would have done it. I really don't think so," he repeated.

Who was he trying to convince? Me, or himself?

"You can understand, Monty, why I will never let these stories get out. I'm the man who cleared Robby Tompkins of his wrongful conviction for murder. I'm the man they made a movie about, with the Jack of Hearts in the leading role. Righteous defender! Exemplary father of ten children. I will not let anyone, or anything, sully that reputation, or come between me and my children again."

"Are you threatening me, Beau?"

He looked at me with an expression of astonishment. "Of course not! You're not going to reveal this. You're my lawyer. Our conversation is covered by solicitor-client privilege. Have you any idea how many unsolved murders and other crimes I have the solution to, having learned the truth from my clients? I've never said a word, and I never will. It's the same for you, in your own practice. And I know Brennan Burke's not going to reveal anything I told him either — seal of the confessional."

I sat in silence, wondering what on earth I could possibly say.

"Monty, you've spent twenty years doing criminal law. You know the score. Most of the people we represent are no-hopers, lowlifes, screw-ups, people who never had a chance. Most of them are bad, impulsive, not too bright. But they're not evil. You've probably heard these stories, you know, the guy who broke into a family's house and ended up shovelling piles of their belongings into a kit bag. Then it was revealed in the news that among the items taken were the only photos the family had of their baby who had died. The burglar heard the story, packed the photos up and left them in a safe place, then made an anonymous call to announce where they could be found. Or the guy who was being chased by a lone Mountie way out in the country, and the Mountie had a heart attack, and the fugitive went back and called on the police radio and waited till the other Mounties came to get their comrade. Saved his life. These are people who misbehave, but they are not evil. They have a conscience.

"The ones who are truly evil, with a staggering sense of entitlement for themselves and not a shred of sympathy for other people — they are rare, but they're out there. You've probably come across them yourself."

"A few. Not many, thank God."

"Exactly."

Delaney was silent for a few seconds, then said: "Of course all this led me to wonder whether I myself was a sociopath. I feel no remorse over these killings. No, let me rephrase that. I do feel remorse — contrition — over my actions, the fact that I took a life, twice, with such brutality. But do I wish that Bullard and Gower were still walking the earth? No, I do not. Yet I don't feel I am devoid of a conscience. I know I'm not. After all, I did it because of what they did to other people. And, unquestionably, I feel regret over the fact that I am capable of such violent, unlawful acts. Naturally, I live with the fear that I might do it again some day. I stopped myself with Corbett. I hope I'll always be able to stop myself.

"After the second killing, of Bullard last year, I made a panicked call to Quinton Brayer in Toronto. You may have heard of him. He's an expert in psychopathology. I rushed up to Toronto after I killed Bullard. I had several sessions with him.

"Monty, I think you know this. I love my family with all my heart. I feel truly guilty about putting my kids' future in jeopardy; I am distressed about this to the point where I still get the shakes at the thought of ending up in prison, and the family breaking up. And I still worry about poverty and illness and illiteracy here and abroad. I continue to support the charities I always supported. I don't believe I am a sociopath, but I obviously need intensive psychotherapy."

It was difficult for me to find the words to respond. I would not walk away from this encounter with a clean conscience. I knew of two murders, I knew my client was a killer, and I knew I was going to keep it to myself. I was not seriously concerned that Beau was going to go out and do it again. Certainly, I had no fear that he would hurt any of his children. His execution of Travis Bullard — as cold-blooded as it was — had been done to avenge a vicious attack on a mother and her child. Still, it was first-degree murder, a premeditated killing. I took some small comfort in the fact that he had got sick in the middle of the episode with Bullard, and had not been able to prolong it. He had not enjoyed his role as executioner. But, no matter what I had learned, I would not be sharing my knowledge with the police. I had no intention of breaking the bonds of solicitor-client confidentiality, any more than Brennan would break the seal of the confessional. Brennan and I could not even discuss between ourselves what we both knew about Beau Delaney.

Finally, I said: "What do you think accounts for this in you, Beau, this . . . ability, we'll call it, to go through with these killings?"

"We're all capable of murder, Monty. In my own case, the first few years of my life were pretty rough. I won't get into it. Things were so good from then on, though, it seemed I wouldn't have any problems. And yet . . . this happened. If children are in danger, or are neglected or mistreated, or unloved, they have to be rescued early, in infancy. The more time that goes by, the greater the damage, and the greater the risk that the damage can't be reversed."

"How much did Peggy know of this?"

"She knew that I could get very, very upset — enraged, I guess I'd have to call it — when I heard of certain kinds of things happening to people, especially to kids, and most especially to our own ten kids. At those times, she knew I had to be by myself and work off the anger. I never gave her any cause to worry that I would take it out on her or the children. Peg didn't know until the last minute of her life that I had killed someone."

He stopped speaking, and then resumed in a voice I could barely hear: "And it killed her. In a way, although God knows I didn't mean to, I did kill her, didn't I?"

Chapter 21

(Normie)

I was right! I do have the sight, and everybody knows it now. So I thought it would only be fair to tell my psychiatrist that I wouldn't be needing any more help. Until next time, maybe. Who knows what else I might see? But anyway, I called New York, and Dr. Burke came to the phone.

"Hi," I said.

"Hi, Normie. How are you doing, my love?"

"Great! You were right. I'm not crazy and I'm not sick, and I don't have headaches anymore. All those things I saw were true. Daddy and Father Burke sat me down and told me that what I was seeing was Mr. Delaney, when he was a baby and when he was a little boy. There really was a St. Vincent's Orphan Asylum. That's the orphanage where Mr. Delaney was kept after he got rescued from the horrible people who were being mean and hurting him. That was his own father and his father's friends who were making fun of Mr. Delaney and hitting him, way back in the years when those World War Two radio programs were on! He was just a little boy!" My voice had a crack in it, and I realized I was sad all over again, because I thought of Mr. Delaney being beaten up as a little kid, like that boy Cody in the church parking lot, when the man hit him and his mother didn't care . . . But the reason for my call was to show Dr. Burke that my imagination wasn't playing tricks on me when I had my visions, so I knew I'd better just tell him that. I didn't want him to worry that there was something else wrong with me.

"Oh yeah, and my little brother Dominic isn't going away anywhere. You figured out I was scared about that, right, Doctor?"

"Well, I did think that might be taking a toll on you. I'm glad, for everyone's sake, that it's been resolved."

"And there was another baby, who died in the orphanage, and Mr. Delaney was there when it happened, but he didn't do it. He was a little kid at the time. And the baby was just sick. So Daddy said I didn't have to worry if I ever thought Mr. Delaney had done something to a child. And he, Mr. Delaney, phoned and apologized to me for getting upset about the Hells Angels."

"Hells Angels?"

"Yeah, but that's all over now."

"Oh. Good. Well, then, do you feel better about Mr. Delaney?"

"The honest truth?"

"Yes, the honest truth."

"I saw him the other day. And I saw a storm of darkness coming from him, or felt it. I don't know how to say it. But . . . I think he did something. Not to Mrs. Delaney or to a little kid. But . . . something."

(Monty)

Brennan was hearing confessions at St. Bernadette's on Monday evening. I sat in the church and gazed at the stained-glass windows with the evening sun coming through them, creating beams of light in red and yellow and green and blue and amethyst. Beautiful. When Brennan emerged from the confessional in his clerical black and his purple stole, he sat beside me in the pew.

"What's on your mind, Montague?"

"We each know something, or some things, about Beau Delaney."

"If we do, we can't discuss it, you being his lawyer, me being his confessor."

"That's right. By the way, I heard through the legal grapevine today that the Crown is not going to appeal Delaney's acquittal in Peggy's death."

"Ah. Well, that's that."

We sat in the silence of the church for a while. Then Brennan said: "Now I'm wondering, Monty . . ."

"Yes?"

"Will you be telling herself what you know?"

"Maura?"

"Are you going to tell her? I can't reveal anything from a confession. But lawyers don't get excommunicated for whispering to their wives about something that happened at work."

"I have no intention of telling her. The fewer people who know this, the better."

"But . . ."

"It's only the two of us who know. There's an old saying, Brennan: *Secret de deux, secret de Dieu. Secret de trois, secret de tous.*"

"Meaning?"

"A secret between two is a secret of God. A secret among three is everybody's secret. Sounds much better in French."

"Maura's not exactly the six o'clock news. But, I suppose, why burden her with it? It will be tough enough for us to live with."

"Exactly."

"But, are we leaving people in danger, Monty?"

"I honestly don't think so."

"Are we in danger ourselves?"

I looked at him. "Do you think we are?"

"I'm thinking no. You?"

"I'm like you, Brennan. I think not. We're betting our lives on it, though, aren't we?"

Acknowledgements

I would like to thank the following people for their kind assistance: Laurel Bauchman, Dr. John Doucet, Joe A. Cameron, Joan Butcher, Rhea McGarva and, as always, PJEC.

All characters and plots in the story are fictional, as are some of the locations. Other places are real. Any liberties taken in the interests of fiction, or any errors committed, are mine alone.

I am grateful for permission to reprint lyrics from the following:

SUZANNE, written by LEONARD COHEN. © 1967 Sony/ATV Music Publishing LLC. All rights administered by Sony/ATV Music Publishing LLC, 8 Music Square West, Nashville, TN 37203. All rights reserved. Used by permission.

A HARD RAIN'S A-GONNA FALL by BOB DYLAN Copyright © 1963; renewed 1991 Special Rider Music. All rights reserved. International copyright secured. Reprinted by permission.

IT'S ALL OVER NOW, BABY BLUE by BOB DYLAN Copyright © 1965; renewed 1993 Special Rider Music. All rights reserved. International copyright secured. Reprinted by permission.

*Here's a sneak peek at Anne Emery's
next Collins-Burke mystery*

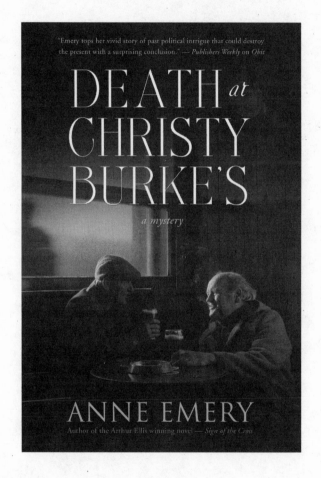

"Emery tops her vivid story of past political intrigue that could destroy
the present with a surprising conclusion." — *Publishers Weekly on Obit*

DEATH *at*
CHRISTY
BURKE'S
a mystery

ANNE EMERY
Author of the Arthur Ellis winning novel — *Sign of the Cross*

Prologue

July 3, 1992

Kevin McDonough was early arriving at the pub. Eight-fifteen in the morning. The sooner he got the place scrubbed to a shine, the sooner he could get to rehearsal with his band. Tonight would be their third paid gig, and this time it was at the Tivoli. At this rate, they'd soon be opening for U2! These odd little jobs had been tiding him over till he could earn his living as a musician. He didn't mind cleaning the floors, washing the windows, and polishing the bar at Christy Burke's pub twice a week. It was no worse than his other jobs, and there were articles of interest to him inside the place.

Oh, would you look at that. Finn Burke was going to be wild. Finn had just repainted the front wall after the last incident of vandalism, and now some gobshite with a can of paint had hit the pub again. Kevin noticed a glass of whiskey on the ground, tipped against the wall. The fellow must have been lifting a jar while doing his handi-work. More than one maybe, by the looks of the paint job this time round. Or perhaps it was the heavy rain last night that threw him off. The message was "Come all ye to Christy's, killers own loc . . ."

Must have meant "local"; the words ended in a smear. If the message was meant to slag Finn Burke about his Republican activities, Kevin suspected Finn would be more vexed about the look of it than the meaning; no doubt he'd faced worse in his time. Well, Kevin wasn't about to call Finn at this hour of the morning. Finn would be seeing it with his own eyes soon enough.

Kevin picked up the glass, singing to himself, "There's whiskey in the jar-o." It was the rock version by Thin Lizzy that Kevin liked, and he tried to draw the words out the way Phil Lynott did, "I first produced my pistol and then produced my rapier." There was a bit of a mess in the garden beside the front door. "Garden" was too grand a word for it really. A few years back, the city had torn up the pavement to repair some water lines. And before they replaced the pavement, one of the patrons of Christy's had talked Finn into letting him plant some flowers. The man didn't keep it up, so now it was just a little square of patchy grass in the midst of all the city concrete. But still, Finn was none too pleased when the rubbish collectors drove their lorry right onto the grass and tore it up with the spinning of their tires. They'd obviously been at it again; a big clump of grass had been gouged out and overturned. Early, though, for refuse collection; they usually didn't get to Christy's till at least half-nine. Ah. Sure enough. Kevin checked the bins and they hadn't been emptied.

He went to work inside. Washed the glasses, polished the bar, filled a bucket with water and suds for the old stone floor. But his mind was on music, not mopping up the pub. He decided to take "Highway to Hell" off the set list and replace it with "Whiskey in the Jar." Maybe the band should dust off some other old standards. Could they work up a heavy-metal arrangement of "The Rose of Tralee," he wondered. Ha, wouldn't his old gran be turning in her grave over that! Just as he was heading to the loo for his last and least favourite chore, he heard a lorry roar up outside. He glanced out the window and saw the rubbish collectors, out in the roadway where they were supposed to be. No worries there.

When his work was done, Kevin grabbed an electric torch and treated himself to a trip downstairs. He loved the once secret tunnel that had been dug beneath Christy Burke's back in the day when the pub was a hideout for the old IRA. Somebody said Christy had dug the tunnel in 1919, and Michael Collins himself had hidden in it, when Ireland was fighting its War of Independence against the Brits. Nobody was supposed to go in there, but Kevin did. And he knew some of the regulars had made excursions down there as well, when Finn Burke was away. The fellows who drank at Christy's day after day knew everything there was to know about the pub, including where Finn kept the tunnel key, under one of the floorboards behind the bar. More than once Kevin had tried to prime Finn for information about the old days, hoping he would let his hair down and regale Kevin with some war stories from his time fighting for the Republican cause. Kevin's da was a bookkeeper and stayed away from politics and controversy; a great father, no question about that, but Kevin thought of him as a man without a history. Not like Finn. But Finn kept his gob shut about his service to the cause. So what could Kevin do but poke around on his own? He inserted the key in the padlock, opened the heavy trap door, and eased himself down into the tunnel. You could only get into the first part of it, which was around twenty feet in length; the rest of it was blocked off, and Kevin didn't know of any key that would get you in there.

But that was all right. There was lots to see right here. The place was a museum. There were old photos, hand-drawn maps, packets of faded letters, uniforms, caps, and, best of all, guns. Kevin had no desire to point a gun at anybody, let alone fire one, but he was fascinated by the weaponry stashed beneath the pub. A Thompson submachine gun, some rifles, and two big pistols. But there was one weapon Kevin particularly liked, a handgun, wrapped in rags and squirrelled away from everything else behind a couple of loose bricks. He had noticed the bricks out of alignment one morning, and took a peek. He'd handled it a few times since then. The gun was all black and had a star engraved on the butt of it — deadly! He thought it might create a sensation at a party some night. He knew it was loaded, but he'd take the bullets out first, if he ever got up the nerve to "borrow" it. Where was it? Not in its usual spot. Not anywhere. Kevin looked all over, but the gun was gone.

Maybe Finn took it himself. But Kevin doubted that. If Finn needed a weapon, he'd likely have one closer to home, and it would be something a little more up-to-date. Well, Kevin certainly wasn't going to mention it. He wasn't supposed to be here in the first place. He was supposed to do his job, cleaning up the pub. And, whatever had become of the gun, he knew this much: there were no dead bodies on the premises to clear away. So his job was done. He locked up and left the building. When he got outside, he kicked the overturned sod back into place. Didn't look too bad.

Chapter 1

July 11, 1992

Michael

Nobody loved Ireland like Michael O'Flaherty. Well, no, that wasn't quite the truth. How could he presume to make such a claim over the bodies of those who had been hanged or shot by firing squad in the struggle for Irish independence? Or those who had lived in the country all their lives, in good times and in bad, staving off the temptation to emigrate from their native soil? Nobody loved Ireland *more* than Michael did. He was on fairly safe ground there. He was a student of history, and his story led him straight back to Ireland. A four-cornered Irishman, he had four grandparents who emigrated from the old country to that most Irish of Canadian cities, Saint John, New Brunswick. His mother was fourteen when her parents brought her over on the boat in 1915, and Michael had inherited her soft lilting speech.

He was in the old country yet again. How many times had he been here? He had lost count. Monsignor Michael O'Flaherty cut quite a figure in the tourist industry. The Catholic tourist industry,

5

to be more precise. Every year he shepherded a flock of Canadian pilgrims around the holy sites of Ireland: Knock, Croagh Patrick, Glendalough. And he showed them something of secular Ireland as well — all too secular it was now, in his view, but never mind. He conducted tours of Dublin, Cork, Galway; it varied from year to year. All this in addition to his duties as pastor of St. Bernadette's Church in Halifax, Nova Scotia. He had moved to Halifax as a young priest, after spending several years in the parishes of Saint John. Why not pack his few belongings in a suitcase and cross the ocean once and for all, making Ireland his home? Well, the truth was, he was attached to Nova Scotia, to his church, and to the people there. He had made friends, especially in the last couple of years. And two of those friends were in Dublin right now. He was on his way to meet them, having seen his latest group of tourists off at the airport for their journey home to Canada.

He looked at his watch. It was half-noon. Brennan Burke had given him elaborate directions but there was no need. Michael knew the map of Dublin as well as he knew the Roman Missal, and he was only five minutes away from his destination at the corner of Mountjoy Street and St. Mary's Place. His destination was Christy Burke's pub.

Michael, decked out as always in his black clerical suit and Roman collar, kept up a brisk pace along Dominick Street Upper until he reached Mountjoy and turned right. A short walk up the street and there it was. This was an inner-city area of Dublin and it had fallen on hard times. But the pub had a fresh coat of cream-coloured paint. There was a narrow horizontal band of black around the building above the door and windows. Set off against the black was the name "Christy Burke" in gold letters. Lovely! He pushed the door open and stepped inside. It took a moment for his eyes to adjust to the smoke and the darkness after the bright July sunshine.

"Michael!"

"Brennan, my lad! All settled in, I see. Good day to you, Monty!"

Michael joined his friends at their table, where a pint of Guinness sat waiting for him. Brennan Burke was a fellow priest, Michael's curate technically. But it was hard to think of Burke, with his doctorate in theology and his musical brilliance, as anybody's curate. He had lived here in Dublin as a child, then immigrated to New York before he joined Michael at St. Bernadette's in Halifax. It was a long story. Christy Burke was Brennan's grandfather, long deceased by now, of course. Brennan himself was fifty or a little over. Young enough to be Michael's son, if Michael had been tomcatting around in his seminary days, which he most certainly had not! In any case, they looked nothing alike. Brennan was tall with greying black hair and black eyes. Michael was short and slight, with white hair and eyes of blue. Monty Collins, though, could be mistaken for Michael's son. Same colour eyes and fair hair. A few years younger than Brennan and deceptively boyish in appearance, Monty was their lawyer and confidant.

Michael greatly enjoyed their company. So it was grand that they were able to arrange this time together in Dublin. Brennan had signed on to teach at the seminary in Maynooth for six weeks. Michael was on an extended vacation, with the blessings of his bishop. It was the first time he had been away for more than two weeks, ever. And why not? In any other job, he'd be retired by now! They had left the home parish in the capable hands of another priest they both knew. Monty, too, was on vacation. Told his office he was taking a month off. Made whatever arrangements he had to make for his law practice, and boarded the plane. So here they were.

Brennan

Brennan Burke was a man of firm opinions. He knew where he stood, and those who were acquainted with him were left in little doubt about who was standing and where. But that sense of certainty deserted him each and every time he came home to the land of his birth. He was glad to be in Ireland, to be sure, but he was afflicted with sorrow, anger, and frustration over the violence that was tearing apart the North of Ireland. Catholics and Protestants, Nationalists and Loyalists, Republicans and Unionists — however you labeled them — had been blasting one another to bits for the past two decades. This was the nation that had sent monks into continental Europe to evangelize and educate the barbarians after the fall of Rome, monks who had helped keep the light of European civilization glowing through the Dark Ages. St. Thomas Aquinas had been taught by an Irishman in thirteenth-century Naples, for the love of Christ. And look at us now.

Brennan's own family had been steeped in the events of Irish history, certainly in the first half of the century. History had stalked his father, Declan Burke, all the way to New York City. Declan had fled Ireland at the point of a gun when Brennan was ten years old; he remembered as if it were yesterday his loneliness and terror as the ship slipped out of Cobh Harbour in the dark of night and began the long, heaving voyage across the Atlantic. Brennan's father had not laid shoe leather on the soil of Ireland since that hasty departure in 1950. But that wasn't the end of it. History caught up with Declan as recently as a year ago in the form of a bullet in the chest, at a family wedding in New York. The wound was not fatal, but nearly so.

Well, his son was a frequent visitor to the old country even if Declan was not. And here he was again. The Burkes of Dublin were spoken of as a "well-known Republican family." Were they in the thick of things still?

But there was pleasure to be had today, so why not just bask in it for a while and banish dark thoughts to the outermost chambers of his mind? He picked up his glass of whiskey, inhaled the alcoholic fumes, and took a sip. Ah! Tingling on the lips, honey on the tongue. Cigarette? No, wait. As usual. Enjoy a pure hit of the Jameson first. The warmth spread through him as the whiskey went down. And there was more to come.